HOUSE OF NIGHT
THE BEGINNING

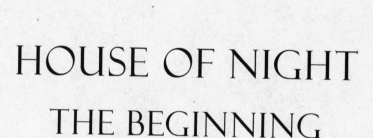

HOUSE OF NIGHT
THE BEGINNING

MARKED and BETRAYED

P. C. CAST and KRISTIN CAST

ST. MARTIN'S GRIFFIN
NEW YORK

HOUSE OF NIGHT: THE BEGINNING. MARKED Copyright © 2007 by P. C. Cast and Kristin Cast and BETRAYED Copyright © 2007 by P. C. Cast and Kristin Cast. All rights reserved. Printed in the United States of America. For information, address St. Martin's Press, 175 Fifth Avenue, New York, N.Y. 10010.

www.stmartins.com

ISBN 978-1-250-03723-7 (trade paperback)

St. Martin's Griffin books may be purchased for educational, business, or promotional use. For information on bulk purchases, please contact Macmillan Corporate and Premium Sales Department at 1-800-221-7945 extension 5442 or write specialmarkets@macmillan.com.

First Edition: May 2013

10 9 8 7 6 5 4 3 2 1

MARKED

For our wonderful agent, Meredith Bernstein, who said the three magic words: vampyre finishing school. We heart you!

ACKNOWLEDGMENTS

I would like to thank a wonderful student of mine, John Maslin, for research help and for reading and giving feedback on many early versions of the book. His input was invaluable.

A big THANKS GUYS goes out to my Creative Writing classes in the school year 2005–2006. Your brainstorming was lots of help (and quite amusing).

I also want to thank my fabulous daughter, Kristin, for making sure we sound like teenagers. I couldn't have done it without you. (She made me write that.)   —PC

I want to thank my lovely "mam," better known as PC, for being such an unbelievably talented author and so easy to work with. (Okay, she made me write that.)   —Kristin

PC and Kristin would both like to thank their dad/grandpa, Dick Cast, for the biological hypothesis he helped create as the basis for the House of Night's vampyres. We love you Dad/G-pa!

From Hesiod's poem to Nyx, the Greek personification of night:

"There also stands the gloomy house of Night;
ghastly clouds shroud it in darkness.
Before it Atlas stands erect and on his head
and unwearying arms firmly supports the broad sky,
where Night and Day cross a bronze threshold
and then come close and greet each other."
(Hesiod, *Theogony*, 744 ff.)

CHAPTER ONE

—

Just when I thought my day couldn't get any worse I saw the dead guy standing next to my locker. Kayla was talking nonstop in her usual K-babble, and she didn't even notice him. At first. Actually, now that I think about it, no one else noticed him until he spoke, which is, tragically, more evidence of my freakish inability to fit in.

"No, but Zoey, I *swear to God* Heath didn't get *that* drunk after the game. You really shouldn't be so hard on him."

"Yeah," I said absently. "Sure." Then I coughed. Again. I felt like crap. I must be coming down with what Mr. Wise, my more-than-slightly-insane AP biology teacher, called the Teenage Plague.

If I died, would it get me out of my geometry test tomorrow? One could only hope.

"Zoey, please. Are you even listening? I think he only had like four—I dunno—maybe six beers, and maybe like three shots. But that's totally beside the point. He probably wouldn't even have had hardly any if your stupid parents hadn't made you go home right after the game."

We shared a long-suffering look, in total agreement about the latest injustice committed against me by my mom and the Step-Loser she'd married three really long years ago. Then, after barely half a breath break, K was back with the babbling.

"Plus, he was celebrating. I mean we beat Union!" K shook my shoulder and put her face close to mine. "Hello! Your boyfriend—"

"My almost-boyfriend," I corrected her, trying my best not to cough on her.

"Whatever. Heath is our quarterback so of course he's going to celebrate. It's been like a million years since Broken Arrow beat Union."

"Sixteen." I'm crappy at math, but K's math impairment makes me look like a genius.

"Again, *whatever*. The point is, he was happy. You should give the boy a break."

"The point is that he was wasted for like the fifth time this week. I'm sorry, but I don't want to go out with a guy whose main focus in life has changed from trying to play college football to trying to chug a six-pack without puking. Not to mention the fact that he's going to get fat from all that beer." I had to pause to cough. I was feeling a little dizzy and forced myself to take slow, deep breaths when the coughing fit was over. Not that K-babble noticed.

"Eww! Heath, *fat!* Not a visual I want."

I managed to ignore another urge to cough. "And kissing him is like sucking on alcohol-soaked feet."

K scrunched up her face. "Okay, sick. Too bad he's so hot."

I rolled my eyes, not bothering to try to hide my annoyance at her typical shallowness.

"You're so grumpy when you're sick. Anyway, you have no idea how lost-puppy-like Heath looked after you ignored him at lunch. He couldn't even . . ."

Then I saw him. The dead guy. Okay, I realized pretty quick that he wasn't technically "dead." He was undead. Or un-human. Whatever. Scientists said one thing, people said another, but the end result was the same. There was no mistaking what he was and even if I hadn't felt the power and darkness that radiated from him, there was no frickin' way I could miss his Mark, the sapphire-blue crescent moon on his forehead and the additional tattooing of entwining knot work that framed his equally blue eyes. He was a vampyre, and worse. He was a Tracker.

Well, crap! He was standing by my locker.

"Zoey, you're *so* not listening to me!"

Then the vampyre spoke and his ceremonial words slicked across the space between us, dangerous and seductive, like blood mixed with melted chocolate.

"Zoey Montgomery! Night has chosen thee; thy death will be thy birth. Night calls to thee; hearken to Her sweet voice. Your destiny awaits you at the House of Night!"

He lifted one long, white finger and pointed at me. As my forehead exploded in pain Kayla opened her mouth and screamed.

When the bright splotches finally cleared from my eyes I looked up to see K's colorless face staring down at me.

As usual, I said the first ridiculous thing that came to mind. "K, your eyes are popping out of your head like a fish."

"He Marked you. Oh, Zoey! You have the outline of that thing on your forehead!" Then she pressed a shaking hand against her white lips, unsuccessfully trying to hold back a sob.

I sat up and coughed. I had a killer headache, and I rubbed at the spot right between my eyebrows. It stung as if a wasp had bit me and radiated pain down around my eyes, all the way across my cheekbones. I felt like I might puke.

"Zoey!" K was really crying now and had to speak between wet little hiccups. "Oh. My. God. That guy was a Tracker—a vampyre Tracker!"

"K." I blinked hard, trying to clear the pain from my head.

"Stop crying. You know I hate it when you cry." I reached out to attempt a comforting pat on her shoulders.

And she automatically cringed, and moved away from me.

I couldn't believe it. She actually cringed, like she was afraid of me. She must have seen the hurt in my eyes because she instantly started a string of breathless K-babble.

"Oh, *God,* Zoey! What are you going to do? You can't go to that place. You can't be one of those things. This can't be happening! Who am I supposed to go to all of our football games with?"

I noticed that all during her tirade she didn't once move any closer to me. I clamped down on the sick, hurt feeling inside that threatened to make me burst into tears. My eyes dried instantly. I was good at hiding tears. I should be; I'd had three years to get good at it.

"It's okay. I'll figure this out. It's probably some . . . some bizarre mistake," I lied.

I wasn't really talking; I was just making words come out of my mouth. Still grimacing at the pain in my head, I stood up. Looking around I felt a small measure of relief that K and I were the only ones in the math hall, and then I had to choke back what I knew was hysterical laughter. Had I not been totally psycho about the geometry test from hell scheduled for tomorrow, and had run back to my locker to get my book so I could attempt to obsessively (and pointlessly) study tonight, the Tracker would have found me standing outside in front of the school with the majority of the 1,300 kids who went to Broken Arrow's South Intermediate High School waiting for what my stupid Barbie-clone sister liked to smugly call "the big yellow limos." I have a car, but standing around with the less fortunate who have to ride the buses is a time-honored tradition, not to mention an excellent way to check out who's hitting on who. As it was, there was only one other kid in the math hall—a tall thin dork with messed-up teeth, which I could, unfortunately, see too much of because he was standing there with his mouth flapping open staring at me like I'd just given birth to a litter of flying pigs.

I coughed again, this time a really wet, disgusting cough. The dork made a squeaky little sound and scuttled down the hall to Mrs. Day's room clutching a flat board to his bony chest. Guess the chess club had changed its meeting time to Mondays after school.

Do vampyres play chess? Were there vampyre dorks? How about Barbie-like vampyre cheerleaders? Did any vampyres play in the band? Were there vampyre Emos with their guy-wearing-girl's-pants weirdness and those awful bangs that cover half their faces? Or were they all those freaky Goth kids who didn't like to bathe much? Was I going to turn into a Goth kid? Or worse, an Emo? I didn't particularly like wearing black, at least not exclusively, and I wasn't feeling a sudden and unfortunate aversion to soap and water, nor did I have an obsessive desire to change my hairstyle and wear too much eyeliner.

All this whirled through my mind while I felt another little hysterical bubble of laughter try to escape from my throat, and was almost thankful when it came out as a cough instead.

"Zoey? Are you okay?" Kayla's voice sounded too high, like someone was pinching her, and she'd taken another step away from me.

I sighed and felt my first sliver of anger. It wasn't like I'd asked for this. K and I had been best friends since third grade, and now she was looking at me like I had turned into a monster.

"Kayla, it's just me. The same me I was two seconds ago and two hours ago and two days ago." I made a frustrated gesture toward my throbbing head. "This doesn't change who I am!"

K's eyes teared up again, but, thankfully, her cell phone started singing Madonna's "Material Girl." Automatically, she glanced at the caller ID. I could tell by her rabbit-in-the-headlights expression that it was her boyfriend, Jared.

"Go on," I said in a flat, tired voice. "Ride home with him."

Her look of relief was like a slap in my face.

"Call me later?" she threw over her shoulder as she beat a hasty retreat out the side door.

I watched her rush across the east lawn to the parking lot. I could see that she had her cell phone smashed to her ear and was talking in animated little bursts to Jared. I'm sure she was already telling him I was turning into a monster.

The problem, of course, was that turning into a monster was the brighter of my two choices. Choice Number 1: I turn into a vampyre, which equals a monster in just about any human's mind. Choice Number 2: My body rejects the Change and I die. Forever.

So the good news is that I wouldn't have to take the geometry test tomorrow.

The bad news was that I'd have to move into the House of Night, a private boarding school in Tulsa's Midtown, known by all my friends as the Vampyre Finishing School, where I would spend the next four years going through bizarre and unnameable physical changes, as well as a total and permanent life shake-up. And that's only if the whole process didn't kill me.

Great. I didn't want to do either. I just wanted to attempt to be normal, despite the burden of my mega-conservative parents, my troll-like younger brother, and my oh-so-perfect older sister. I wanted to pass geometry. I wanted to keep my grades up so that I could get accepted into the veterinary college at OSU and get out of Broken Arrow, Oklahoma. But most of all, I wanted to fit in—at least at school. Home had become hopeless, so all I was left with were my friends and my life away from my family.

Now that was being taken away from me, too.

I rubbed my forehead and then messed with my hair until it

semi-covered my eyes, and, with any luck, the mark that had appeared above them. Keeping my head ducked down, like I was fascinated with the goo that had somehow formed in my purse, I hurried toward the door that led to the student parking lot.

But I stopped short of going outside. Through the side-by-side windows in the institutional-looking doors I could see Heath. Girls flocked around him, posing and flipping their hair, while guys revved ridiculously big pickup trucks and tried (but mostly failed) to look cool. Doesn't it figure that I would choose *that* to be attracted to? No, to be fair to myself I should remember that Heath used to be incredibly sweet, and even now he had his moments. Mostly when he bothered to be sober.

High-pitched girl giggles flitted to me from the parking lot. Great. Kathy Richter, the biggest ho in school, was pretending to smack Heath. Even from where I was standing it was obvious she thought hitting him was some kind of mating ritual. As usual, clueless Heath was just standing there grinning. Well, hell, my day just wasn't going to get any better. And there sat my robin's egg–blue 1966 VW Bug right in the middle of them. No. I couldn't go out there. I couldn't walk into the middle of all of them with this thing on my forehead. I'd never be able to be part of them again. I already knew too well what they'd do. I remembered the last kid a Tracker had Chosen at SIHS.

It happened at the beginning of the school year last year. The Tracker had come before school started and had targeted the kid as he was walking to his first hour. I didn't see the Tracker, but I did see the kid afterward, for just a second, after he dropped his books and ran out of the building, his new Mark glowing on his pale forehead and tears washing down his too white cheeks. I never forgot how crowded the halls had been that morning, and how everyone had backed away from him like he had the plague as he rushed to escape out the front doors of the school. I had been one of those kids who had backed out of his way and stared, even though I'd felt really sorry for him. I just hadn't wanted to be labeled as that-one-girl-who's-friends-with-those-freaks. Sort of ironic now, isn't it?

Instead of going to my car I headed for the nearest restroom, which was, thankfully, empty. There were three stalls—yes, I double-checked each for feet. On one wall were two sinks, over which hung two medium-sized mirrors. Across from the sinks the opposite wall was covered with a huge mirror that had a ledge below it for holding brushes and makeup and whatnot. I put my purse and my geometry book on the ledge, took a deep breath, and in one motion lifted my head and brushed back my hair.

It was like staring into the face of a familiar stranger. You know, that person you see in a crowd and swear you know, but you really don't? Now she was me—the familiar stranger.

She had my eyes. They were the same hazel color that could never decide whether it wanted to be green or brown, but my eyes had never been that big and round. Or had they? She had my hair—long and straight and almost as dark as my grandma's had been before hers had begun to turn silver. The stranger had my high cheekbones, long, strong nose, and wide mouth—more features from my grandma and her Cherokee ancestors. But my face had never been that pale. I'd always been olive-ish, much darker skinned than anyone else in my family. But maybe it wasn't that my skin was suddenly so white . . . maybe it just looked pale in comparison to the dark blue outline of the crescent moon that was perfectly positioned in the middle of my forehead. Or maybe it was the horrid fluorescent lighting. I hoped it was the lighting.

I stared at the exotic-looking tattoo. Mixed with my strong Cherokee features it seemed to brand me with a mark of wildness . . . as if I belonged to ancient times when the world was bigger . . . more barbaric.

From this day on my life would never be the same. And for a moment—just an instant—I forgot about the horror of not belonging and felt a shocking burst of pleasure, while deep inside of me the blood of my grandmother's people rejoiced.

CHAPTER TWO

—

When I figured that enough time had passed for everyone to have left school, I flopped my hair back over my forehead and left the bathroom, hurrying to the doors that led to the student parking lot. Everything seemed all clear—there was just some random kid wearing those seriously unattractive gang wanna-be baggy pants cutting across the far end of the lot. Keeping his pants from falling down as he walked was taking all his concentration; he wouldn't even notice me. I gritted my teeth against the throbbing pain in my head and bolted out the door, heading straight for my little Bug.

The moment I stepped outside the sun began to batter me. I mean, it wasn't a particularly sunny day; there were plenty of those big, puffy clouds that looked so pretty in pictures floating around the sky, semi-blocking the sun. But that didn't matter. I had to squint my eyes painfully and hold my hand up as a make-believe sun block against even that intermittent light. I guess it was because I was focusing so hard on the pain the ordinary sun-light was causing me that I didn't notice the truck until it squealed to a stop in front of me.

"Hey Zo! Didn't you get my message?"

Oh crap crap crap! It was Heath. I glanced up, looking at him from between my fingers like I was watching one of those stupid slasher movies. He was sitting on the open tailgate of his friend Dustin's pickup truck. Over his shoulder I could see into the cab of the truck where Dustin and his brother, Drew, were doing what they were usually doing—wrestling around and arguing over God only knows what stupid boy thing. Thankfully, they were ignoring me. I glanced back at Heath and sighed. He had a beer in his hand and a goofy grin on his face. Momentarily forgetting that I'd just been Marked and was destined to become an outcast blood-sucking monster, I scowled at Heath.

"You're drinking at school! Are you crazy?"

His little boy grin got bigger. "Yes I am crazy, 'bout you, baby!"

I shook my head while I turned my back to him, opening the creaky door to my Bug and shoving my books and backpack into the passenger's seat.

"Why aren't you guys at football practice?" I said, still keeping my face angled away from him.

"Didn't you hear? We got the day off 'cause of the ass-kicking we gave Union on Friday!"

Dustin and Drew, who must have been kinda paying attention to Heath and me after all, did a couple of very Okie "Whoo-hoo!" and "Yeah!" yells from inside the truck.

"Oh. Uh. No. I musta missed the announcement. I've been busy today. You know, big geometry test tomorrow." I tried to sound normal and nonchalant. Then I coughed and added, "Plus, I'm getting a crappy cold."

"Zo, really. Are you pissed or somethin'? Like, did Kayla say some shit about the party? You know I didn't really cheat on you."

Huh? Kayla had not said one solitary word about Heath *cheating* on me. Like a moron, I forgot (okay, temporarily) about my new Mark. My head snapped around so I could glare at him.

"What did you do, Heath?"

"Zo, me? You know I wouldn't . . ." but his innocent act and his excuses faded into an unattractive open-mouthed look of shock when he caught sight of my Mark. "What the—" he started to say, but I cut him off.

"Shh!" I jerked my head in the direction of the still clueless Dustin and Drew, who were now singing at the top of their totally tonedeaf lungs to the latest Toby Keith CD.

Heath's eyes were still wide and shocked, but he lowered his voice. "Is that some kinda makeup thing you're doing for drama class?"

"No," I whispered. "It's not."

"But you can't be Marked. We're going out."

"We are not going out!" And just like that my semi-reprieve from coughing ended. I practically doubled over, hacking a seriously nasty, phlegmy cough.

"Hey, Zo!" Dustin called from the cab. "You gotta lay off those cigarettes."

"Yeah, you sound like you're gonna cough up a lung or somethin'," Drew said.

"Dude! Leave her alone. You know she don't smoke. She's a vampyre."

Great. Wonderful. Heath, with his usual total and complete lack of anything resembling good sense, thought he was actually standing up for me as he yelled at his friends, who instantly stuck their heads out of the open windows and gawked at me like I was a science experiment.

"Well, shit. Zoey's a fucking freak!" Drew said.

Drew's insensitive words made the anger that had been simmering somewhere inside my chest ever since Kayla had cringed from me bubble up and boil over. Ignoring the pain the sun caused me, I stared straight at Drew, meeting his eyes.

"Shut the hell up! I've had a really bad day and I do not need this crap from you." I paused to look from the now wide-eyed and silent Drew to Dustin and added, "Or you." And as I kept eye contact with Dustin I realized something—something that shocked and weirdly excited me: Dustin looked scared. Really scared. I glared back at Drew. He looked scared, too. Then I felt it. A tingling sensation that crawled over my skin and made my new Mark burn.

Power. I felt power.

"Zo? What the fuck?" Heath's voice broke my attention and pulled my gaze from the brothers.

"We're outta here!" Dustin said, throwing the truck into gear and stepping on the gas. The pickup lurched forward, causing Heath to lose his balance and slide, with a windmill of arms and flying beer, onto the blacktop of the parking lot.

Automatically, I rushed forward. "Are you okay?" Heath was on his hands and knees, and I bent down to help pull him to his feet.

Then I smelled it. Something smelled amazing—hot and sweet and delicious.

Was Heath wearing new cologne? One of those weird pheromone things that are supposed to attract women like a big genetically engineered bug zapper? I didn't realize how close I was to him until he stood up straight and our bodies were almost pressed together. He looked down at me, a question in his eyes.

I didn't back away from him. I should have. I would have before . . . but not now. Not today.

"Zo?" he said softly, his voice deep and husky.

"You smell really good," I couldn't stop myself from saying. My heart was pounding so loud that I could hear its echo in my throbbing temples.

"Zoey, I've really missed you. We need to get back together. You know I really love you." He reached up to touch my face and both of us noticed the blood that smeared the palm of his hand. "Ah, shit. I guess I—" his voice closed off when he glanced at my face. I could only imagine what I must look like, with my face all white, my new Mark blazingly outlined in sapphire blue, and my eyes staring at the blood on his hand. I couldn't move; I couldn't look away.

"I want . . ." I whispered. "I want . . ." What did I want? I couldn't put it into words. No, that wasn't it. I *wouldn't* put it into words. Wouldn't say aloud the overwhelming surge of white-hot desire that was trying to drown me. And it wasn't because Heath was standing so near. He'd been close to me before. Hell, we'd been making out for a year, but he'd never made me feel like this—nothing ever like this. I bit my lip and moaned.

The pickup truck squealed to a halt, fishtailing beside us. Drew jumped out and grabbed Heath around the waist, and jerked him backward into the cab of the truck.

"Knock it off! I'm talking to Zoey!"

Heath tried to struggle against Drew, but the kid was Broken Arrow's senior linebacker, and truly ginormous. Dustin reached around them and slammed the door to the truck.

"Leave him alone, you freak!" Drew yelled at me as Dustin floored the truck and this time they really did speed off.

I got into my Bug. My hands were shaking so hard I had to try three times before I got the engine started.

"Just get home. Just get home." I said the words over and over between wrenching coughs as I drove. I wouldn't think about what had just happened. I couldn't think about what had just happened.

The drive home took fifteen minutes, but it seemed to pass in the blink of an eye. Too soon I was sitting in the driveway, trying to get ready for the scene I knew, sure as lightning follows thunder, was waiting inside for me.

Why had I been so eager to get here? I suppose I hadn't technically been all that eager. I suppose I'd just been escaping from what had happened in the parking lot with Heath.

No! I wasn't going to think about that now. And, anyway, there was probably some kind of rational explanation for everything, a rational and simple explanation. Dustin and Drew were retards—totally immature beer-brains. I hadn't used a creepy new power to intimidate them. They'd just been freaked that I'd been Marked. That was it. I mean, people were scared of vampyres.

"But I'm *not* a vampyre!" I said. Then I coughed while I remember how hypnotically beautiful Heath's blood had been, and the rush of desire I'd felt for *it*. Not Heath, but Heath's blood.

No! No! No! Blood was not beautiful or desirable. I must be in shock. That's it. That had to be it. I was in shock and not thinking clearly. Okay . . . okay . . . absently, I touched my forehead. It had stopped burning, but it still felt different. I coughed for the zillionth time. Fine. I wouldn't think about Heath, but I couldn't deny it any more. *I* felt different. My skin was ultrasensitive. My chest hurt, and even though I had my cool Maui Jim sunglasses on, my eyes kept tearing up painfully.

"I'm dying . . ." I moaned, and then promptly clamped my lips shut. I might actually be dying. I glanced up at the big brick house that, after three years, still didn't seem like home. "Get it over with. Just get it over with." At least my sister wouldn't be home yet—cheerleading practice. Hopefully, the troll would be totally hypnotized by his new Delta Force: Black Hawk Down video game (um . . . ew). I might have Mom to myself. Maybe she would understand . . . maybe she would know what to do. . . .

Ah, hell! I was sixteen years old, but I suddenly realized that I wanted nothing as much as I wanted my mom.

"Please let her understand," I whispered a simple prayer to whatever god or goddess might be listening to me.

As usual, I went in through the garage. I walked down the hall to my room and dumped my geometry book, purse, and backpack on my bed. Then I took a deep breath and headed, a little shakily, to find my mom.

She was in the family room, curled up on the edge of the couch, sipping a cup of coffee and reading *Chicken Soup for a Woman's Soul.* She looked so normal, so much like she used to look. Except that she used to read exotic romances and actually wear makeup. Both were things her new husband didn't allow (what a turd).

"Mom?"

"Hum?" She didn't look up at me.

I swallowed hard. "Mama." I used the name I used to call her, back in the days before she married John. "I need your help."

I don't know whether it was the unexpected use of "Mama" or if something in my voice touched an old piece of mom-intuition she still had somewhere inside her, but the eyes she lifted immediately from the book were soft and filled with concern.

"What is it, baby—" she began, and then her words seemed to freeze on her lips as her eyes found the Mark on my forehead.

"Oh, God! What have you done now?"

My heart started to hurt again. "Mom, I didn't *do* anything. This is something that happened *to* me, not because of me. It's not my fault."

"Oh, please, no!" she wailed as if I hadn't said a word. "What is your father going to say?"

I wanted to scream *how the hell would any of us know what my father was going to say, we haven't seen or heard from him for fourteen years!* But I knew it wouldn't do any good, and it always just made her mad when I reminded her that John was not my "real" father. So I tried a different tactic—one I'd given up on three years ago.

"Mama, please. Can't you just not tell him? At least for a day or two? Just keep it between the two of us until we . . . I don't know . . . get used to it or something." I held my breath.

"But what would I say? You can't even cover that thing up with makeup." Her lips curled weirdly as she gave the crescent moon a nervous glance.

"Mom, I didn't mean that I'd stay here while we got used to it. I have to go; you know that." I had to pause while a huge cough made my shoulders shake. "The Tracker Marked me. I have to move to the House of Night or I'm just going to get sicker and sicker." *And then die,* I tried to tell her with my eyes. I couldn't actually say the words. "I just want a couple of days before I have to deal with . . ." I broke off so I didn't have to say his name, this time purposefully making myself cough, which wasn't hard.

"What would I tell your father?"

I felt a rush of fear at the panic in her voice. Wasn't she the mom? Wasn't she supposed to have the answers instead of the questions?

"Just . . . just tell him that I'm spending the next couple days at Kayla's house because we have a big biology project due."

I watched my mom's eyes change. The concern faded from them and was replaced by a hardness that I recognized all too well.

"So what you're saying is that you want me to lie to him."

"No, Mom. What I'm saying is that I want you, for once, to put what I need before what he wants. I want you to be my mama. To help me pack and to drive with me to this new school because I'm scared and sick and I don't know if I can do it all by myself!" I finished in a rush, breathing hard and coughing into my hand.

"I wasn't aware that I had stopped being your mom," she said coldly.

She made me feel even more tired than Kayla had. I sighed. "I think that's the problem, Mom. You don't care enough to be aware of it. You haven't cared about anything but John since you married him."

Her eyes narrowed at me. "I don't know how you can be so selfish. Don't you realize all that he's done for us? Because of him I quit that awful job at Dillards. Because of him we don't have to worry about money and we have this big, beautiful house. Because of him we have security and a bright future."

I'd heard these words so often I could have recited them with her. It was at this point in our non-conversations that I usually apologized and went back to my room. But today I couldn't apologize. Today I was different. Everything was different.

"No, Mother. The truth is that because of him you haven't paid any attention to your kids for three years. Did you know that your oldest daughter has turned into a sneaky, spoiled slut who's screwed half of the football team? Do you know what nasty, bloody video games Kevin keeps hidden from you? No, of course you don't! The two of them *act* happy and *pretend* to like John and the whole damn make-believe family thing, so you smile at them and pray for them and let them do whatever. And me? You think I'm the bad one because I don't pretend—because I'm honest. You know what? I'm so sick of my life that I'm glad the Tracker Marked me! They call that vampyre school the House of Night, but it can't be any darker than this *perfect* home!" Before I could cry or scream I whirled around and stalked back to my bedroom, slamming the door behind me.

I hope they all drown.

Through the too thin walls I could hear her making a hysterical call to John. There was no doubt that he'd rush home to deal with me. The Problem. Instead of sitting on the bed and crying like I was tempted to, I emptied the school crap out of my backpack. Like I'd need it where I was going? They probably don't even have normal classes. They probably have classes like Ripping Peoples

Throats Out 101 and . . . and . . . Intro to How to See in the Dark. Whatever.

No matter what my mom did or didn't do, I couldn't stay here. I had to leave.

So what did I need to take with me?

My two favorite pairs of jeans, besides what I had on. A couple of black T-shirts. I mean, what else do vampyres wear? Plus, they are slimming. I almost passed on my cute aqua-colored sparkly cami, but all that black was bound to make me more depressed . . . so I included it. Then I stuffed tons of bras and thongs and hair and makeup things into the side pouch. I almost left my stuffed animal, Otis the Shish (couldn't say fish when I was two), on my pillow, but . . . well . . . vampyre or not I didn't think I could sleep very well without him. So I tucked him gently into the damn backpack.

Then I heard the knock on my door, and *its* voice called me out of my room.

"What?" I yelled, and then I convulsed in a bout of nasty coughing.

"Zoey. Your mother and I need to speak with you."

Great. Clearly they didn't drown.

I patted Otis the Shish. "Otis, this sucks." I squared my shoulders, coughed again, and went out to face the enemy.

CHAPTER THREE

—

At first glance my step-loser, John Heffer, appears to be an okay guy, even normal. (Yes, that's really his last name—and, sadly, it is also now my mom's last name. She's Mrs. Heffer. Can you believe it?) When he and my mom started dating I actually overheard some of my mom's friends calling him "handsome" and "charming." At first. Of course now Mom has a whole new group of friends, ones Mr. Handsome and Charming thinks are more appropriate than the group of fun single women she used to hang with.

I never liked him. Really. I'm not just saying that because I can't stand him now. From the first day I met him I saw only one thing—a fake. He fakes being a nice guy. He fakes being a good husband. He even fakes being a good father.

He looks like every other dad-age guy. He has dark hair, skinny chicken legs, and is getting a gut. His eyes are like his soul, a washed-out, cold, brownish color.

I walked into the family room to find him standing by the couch. My mother was crumpled near the end of it, clutching his hand. Her eyes were already red and watery. Great. She was going to play Hurt Hysterical Mother. It's an act she does well.

John had begun to attempt to skewer me with his eyes, but my Mark distracted him. His face twisted in disgust.

"Get thee behind me, Satan!" he quoted in what I like to think of as his sermon voice.

I sighed. "It's not Satan. It's just me."

"Now is not the time for sarcasm, Zoey," Mom said.

"I'll handle this, hon," the step-loser said, patting her shoulder absently before he turned his attention back to me. "I told you that your bad behavior and your attitude problem would catch up with you. I'm not even surprised it happened this soon."

I shook my head. I expected this. I really expected this, and still it was a shock. The entire world knew that there was nothing anyone could do to bring on the Change. The whole "if you get bit by a vampyre you'll die and become one" thing is strictly fiction. Scientists have been trying to figure out what causes the sequence of physical events that lead to vampyrism for years, hoping that if they figure it out they could cure it, or at the very least invent a vaccine to fight against it. So far, no such luck. But now John Heffer, my step-loser, had suddenly discovered that bad teenage behavior—specifically my bad behavior, which mostly consisted of an occasional lie, some pissed off thoughts and smart-ass comments directed primarily against my parents, and maybe some semi-harmless lust for Ashton Kutcher (sad to say he likes older women)—actually brought about this physical reaction in my body. Well, hell! Who knew?

"This wasn't something I caused," I finally managed to say. "This wasn't done *because* of me. It was done *to* me. Every scientist on the planet agrees with that."

"Scientists are not all-knowing. They are not men of God."

I just stared at him. He was an Elder of the People of Faith, a position he was oh, so proud of. It was one of the reasons Mom had been attracted to him, and on a strictly logical level I could understand why. Being an Elder meant that a man was successful. He had the right job. A nice house. The perfect family. He was supposed to do the right things and believe the right way. On paper he should have been a great choice for her new husband and our father. Too bad the paper wouldn't have shown the full story. And now, predictably, he was going to play the Elder card and throw God in my face. I would bet my cool new Steve Madden flats that it irritated God as much as it annoyed me.

I tried again. "We studied this in AP biology. It's a physiological reaction that takes place in some teenagers' bodies as their hormone levels rise." I paused, thinking really hard and totally proud of myself for remembering something I learned last semester. "In certain people the hormones trigger something-or-other in a . . . a . . ." I thought harder and remembered: "a Junk DNA strand, which starts the whole Change." I smiled, not really at John, but because I was thrilled by my ability to recall stuff from a unit we'd been done with for months. I knew the smile was a mistake when I saw the familiar clenching of his jaw.

"God's knowledge surpasses science, and it's blasphemous for you to say otherwise, young lady."

"I never said scientists are smarter than God!" I threw my hands up and tried to stifle a cough. "I'm just trying to explain this thing to you."

"I don't need to have anything explained to me by a sixteen-year-old."

Well, he was wearing those really bad pants and that awful shirt. Clearly he did need some things explained to him by a teenager, but I didn't think it was the right time to mention his unfortunate and obvious fashion impairment.

"But John, honey, what are we going to do about her? What will the neighbors say?" Her face paled even more and she stifled a little sob. "What will people say at Meeting on Sunday?"

He narrowed his eyes when I opened my mouth to answer, and interrupted before I could speak.

"We are going to do what any good family should do. We are going to give this to God."

They were sending me to a convent? Unfortunately, I had to deal with another round of coughing, so he kept right on talking.

"We are also going to call Dr. Asher. He'll know what to do to calm this situation."

Wonderful. Fabulous. He's calling in our family shrink, the Incredibly Expressionless Man. Perfect.

"Linda, call Dr. Asher's emergency number, and then I think it would be wise to activate the prayer phone tree. Make sure the other Elders know that they are to gather here."

My mom nodded and started to get up, but the words that burst from my mouth made her flop back down on the couch.

"What! Your answer is to call a shrink who is totally clueless about teenagers and get all those uptight Elders over here? Like they would even begin to try and understand? No! Don't you get it? I have to leave. Tonight." I coughed, a really gut-wrenching sound that hurt my chest. "See! This will just get worse if I don't get around the . . ." I hesitated. Why was it so hard to say "vampyres"? Because it sounded so foreign—so final—and, part of me admitted, so fantastic. "I have to get to the House of Night."

Mom jumped up, and for a second I thought she was actually going to save me. Then John put his arm around her shoulder possessively. She looked up at him and when she looked back at me her eyes seemed almost sorry, but her words, typically, reflected only what John would want her to say.

"Zoey, surely it wouldn't hurt anything if you spent just tonight at home?"

"Of course it wouldn't," John said to her. "I'm sure Dr. Asher will see the need for a house visit. With him here she'll be perfectly fine." He patted her shoulder, pretended to be caring, but instead of sweet he sounded slimy.

I looked from him to my mom. They weren't going to let me leave. Not tonight, and maybe not ever, or at least not until I had to be hauled out by the paramedics. I suddenly understood that it wasn't just about this Mark and the fact that my life had been totally changed. It was about control. If they let me go, somehow they lose. In Mom's case, I liked to think that she was afraid of losing me. I knew what John didn't want to lose. He didn't want to lose his precious authority and the illusion that we were the perfect little family. As Mom had already said, *What would the neighbors think—what will people think at Meeting on Sunday?* John had to preserve the illusion, and if that meant allowing me to get really, really sick, well then, that was a price he was willing to pay.

I wasn't willing to pay it, though.

I guess it was time I took things into my own hands (after all, they are well manicured).

"Fine," I said. "Call Dr. Asher. Start the prayer phone tree. But do you mind if I go lay down until everyone gets here?" I coughed again for good measure.

"Of course not, honey," Mom said, looking obviously relieved. "A little rest will probably make you feel better." Then she moved away from John's possessive arm. She smiled and then hugged me. "Would you like me to get you some NyQuil?"

"No, I'll be fine," I said, clinging to her for just a second, wishing so damn hard that it was three years ago and she was still mine—still on my side. Then I took a deep breath and stepped back. "I'll be fine," I repeated.

She looked at me and nodded, telling me she was sorry the only way she could, with her eyes.

I turned away from her and started to retreat to my bedroom. To my back the step-loser said, "And why don't you do us all a favor and see if you can find some powder or something to cover up that thing on your forehead?"

I didn't even pause. I just kept walking. And I wouldn't cry.

I'm going to remember this, I told myself sternly. *I'm going to remember how awful they made me feel today. So when I'm scared and alone and whatever else is going to happen to me starts to happen, I'm going to remember that nothing could be as bad as being stuck here. Nothing.*

CHAPTER FOUR

—

So I sat on my bed and coughed while I listened to my mom making a frantic call to our shrink's emergency line, followed quickly by another equally hysterical call that would activate the dreaded People of Faith prayer tree. Within thirty minutes our house would begin to fill up with fat women and their beady-eyed pedophile husbands. They'd call me out to the family room. My Mark would be considered a Really Big and Embarrassing Problem, so they'd probably anoint me with some crap that was sure to clog my pores and give me a Cyclops-sized zit before laying their hands on me and praying. They'd ask God to help me stop being such an awful teenager and a problem to my parents. Oh, and the little matter of my Mark needed to be cleared up, too.

If only it were that simple. I'd gladly make a deal with God to be a good kid versus changing school and species. I'd even take the geometry test. Well, okay. Maybe not the geometry test—but, still, it's not like I'd asked to become a freak. This whole thing meant that I was going to have to leave. To start my life over somewhere I'd be the new kid. Somewhere I didn't have any friends. I blinked hard, forcing myself not to cry. School was the only place I really felt at home anymore; my friends were my only family. I balled up my fists and squidged my face up to keep from crying. One step at a time—I'd just take this one step at a time.

No way was I going deal with clones of the step-loser on top of everything else. And, as if the People of Faith weren't bad enough, the horrid prayer session would be followed by an equally annoying session with Dr. Asher. He'd ask me a lot of questions about how this and that made me feel. Then he'd babble on and on about teenage anger and angst being normal but that only I could choose how it would have an impact on my life . . . blah . . . blah . . . and since this was an "emergency" he'd probably want me to draw something that represented my inner child or whatever.

I definitely had to get out of there.

Good thing I've always been "the bad kid" and was well prepared for a situation like this. Okay, I wasn't exactly thinking about escaping from my house so I could run off and join the vampyres when I put a spare key to my car under the flowerpot outside my window. I was just considering that I might want to sneak out and go to Kayla's house. Or, if I *really* wanted to be bad I might meet Heath at the park and make out. But then Heath started drinking and I started to change into a vampyre. Sometimes life doesn't make any sense.

I grabbed my backpack, opened my window, and with an ease that said more about my sinful nature than the step-loser's boring lectures, I popped out my window screen. I put on my sunglasses and peeked out. It was only four thirty or so, and not dark yet, so I was really glad that our privacy fence hid me from our totally nosy neighbors. On this side of the house the only other windows were to my sister's room, and she should still be at cheerleading practice. (Hell must truly be freezing over because for once I was sincerely glad my sister's world revolved around what she called "the sport of cheer.") I dropped my backpack out first and then slowly followed it out the window, being careful not to make even a small *oof* noise when I landed on the grass. I paused there for way too many minutes, burying my face in my arms to muffle my horrible cough. Then I bent over and lifted up the edge of the pot that held the lavender plant Grandma Redbird had given me, and let my fingers find the hard metal of the key where it nestled against the smushed grass.

The gate didn't even squeak when I cracked it open and inched out like one of Charlie's Angels. My cute Bug was sitting there where she always sat—right in front of the third door to our three car garage. The step-loser wouldn't let me park her inside because he said the lawnmower was more important. (More important than a vintage VW? How? That didn't even make sense. Jeesh, I just sounded like a guy. Since when did I care about the vintage-ness of my Bug? I must really be Changing.) I looked both ways. Nothing. I sprinted for my Bug, jumped in, put it in neutral, and was truly thankful that our driveway was ridiculously steep when my wonderful car rolled smoothly and silently into the street. From there it was east to start it and zip out of the neighborhood of Big Expensive Houses.

I didn't even glance in the rearview mirror.

I did reach over and turn off my cell phone. I didn't want to talk to anyone.

No, that wasn't exactly true. There was one person I really wanted to talk to. She was the one person in the world who I was positive wouldn't look at my Mark and think I was a monster or a freak or a really awful person.

Like my Bug could read my mind it seemed to turn all by itself onto the highway that led to the Muskogee Turnpike and, eventually, to the most wonderful place in this world—my Grandma Redbird's lavender farm.

Unlike the drive from school to home, the hour-and-a-half trip to Grandma Redbird's farm seemed to take forever. By the time

I pulled off the two-lane highway onto the hard-packed dirt road that led to Grandma's place, my body ached even worse than it did that time they hired that crazy new gym teacher who thought we should do insane weight circuits while she cracked her whip at us and cackled. Okay, so maybe she didn't have a whip, but still. My muscles hurt like hell. It was almost six o'clock and the sun was finally starting to set, but my eyes still stung. Actually, even the fading sunlight made my skin feel tingly and weird. It made me glad that it was the end of October and it had finally turned cool enough for me to wear my Borg Invasion 4D hoodie (sure, it is a *Star Trek: The Next Generation* ride in Vegas and, sadly, I am on occasion a total *Star Trek* nerd) which, thankfully, covered most of my skin. Before I got out of my Bug I dug around in the backseat until I found my old OSU trucker's hat and pulled it down on my head so that my face was out of the sun.

My grandma's house sat between two lavender fields and was shaded by huge old oaks. It was built in 1942 of raw Oklahoma stone, with a comfortable porch and unusually big windows. I loved this house. Just climbing the little wooden stairs that led to the porch made me feel better . . . safe. Then I saw the note taped on the outside of the door. It was easy to recognize Grandma Redbird's pretty handwriting: *I'm on the bluffs collecting wildflowers.*

I touched the soft lavender-scented paper. She always knew when I was coming for a visit. When I was a kid I used to think it was weird, but as I got older I appreciated the extra sense she had. All my life I've known that, no matter what, I could count on Grandma Redbird. During those awful first months after Mom married John I think I would have shriveled up and died if I hadn't been able to escape every weekend to Grandma's house.

For a second I considered going inside (Grandma never locked her doors) and waiting for her, but I needed to see her, to have her hug me and tell me what I had wanted Mom to say.

Don't be scared . . . it'll be okay . . . we'll make it be okay. So instead of going inside I found the little deer path at the edge of the northern-most lavender field that would lead to the bluffs and I followed it, letting my fingertips trail over the top of the closest plants so that as I walked they released their sweet, silvery scent into the air around me like they were welcoming me home.

It felt like years since I'd been here, even though I knew it had been only four weeks. John didn't like Grandma. He thought she was weird. I'd even overheard him tell Mom that Grandma was "a witch and going to hell." He's such an ass.

Then an amazing thought hit me and I came to a complete stop. My parents no longer controlled what I did. I wasn't going to live with them ever again. John couldn't tell me what to do anymore.

Whoa! How awesome!

So awesome that it sent me into a spasm of coughing that made me wrap my arms around myself, like I was trying to hold my chest together. I needed to find Grandma Redbird, and I needed to find her now.

CHAPTER FIVE

—

The path up the side of the bluffs had always been steep, but I'd climbed it about a gazillion times, with and without my grandma, and I'd never felt like this. It wasn't just the coughing anymore. And it wasn't just the sore muscles. I was dizzy and my stomach had started to gurgle so badly that I was reminding myself of Meg Ryan in the movie *French Kiss* after she ate all that cheese and had a lactose-intolerance fit. (Kevin Kline is really cute in that movie—well, for an old guy.)

And I was snotting. I don't mean just sniffling a little. I mean I was wiping my nose on the sleeve of my hoodie (gross). I couldn't breathe without opening my mouth, which made me cough more, and I couldn't believe how badly my chest hurt! I tried to remember what it was that officially killed the kids who didn't complete the Change into vampyres. Did they have heart attacks? Or was it possible that they coughed and snotted themselves to death?

Stop thinking about it!

I needed to find Grandma Redbird. If Grandma didn't have the answers, she'd figure them out. Grandma Redbird understood people. She said it was because she hadn't lost touch with her Cherokee heritage and the tribal knowledge of the ancestral Wise Women she carried in her blood. Even now it made me smile to think about the frown that came over Grandma's face whenever the subject of the step-loser came up (she's the only adult who knows I call him that). Grandma Redbird said that it was obvious that the Redbird Wise Woman blood had skipped over her daughter, but that was only because it had been saving up to give an extra dose of ancient Cherokee magic to me.

As a little girl I'd climbed this path holding Grandma's hand more times than I could count. In the meadow of tall grasses and wildflowers we'd lay out a brightly colored blanket and eat a picnic lunch while Grandma told me stories of the Cherokee people and taught me the mysterious-sounding words of their language. As I struggled up the winding path those ancient stories seemed to swirl around and around inside my head, like smoke from a cere-monial fire . . . including the sad story of how the stars were formed when a dog was discovered stealing cornmeal and the tribe whipped him. As the dog ran howling to his home in the north, the meal scattered across the sky and the magic in it made the Milky Way. Or how the Great Buzzard made the mountains and valleys with his wings. And my favorite, the story about young woman sun who lived in the east, and her brother, the moon, who lived in the west, and the Redbird who was the daughter of the sun.

"Isn't that weird? I'm a Redbird and the daughter of the sun, but I'm turning into a monster of the night." I heard myself talk-ing out loud and was surprised that my voice sounded so weak, especially when my words seemed to echo around me, as if I were talking into a vibrating drum.

Drum . . .

Thinking the word reminded me of powwows Grandma had taken me to when I was a little girl, and then, my thoughts some-how breathing life into the memory, I actually heard the rhythmic beating of ceremonial drums. I looked around, squinting against even the weak light of the dying day. My eyes stung and my vision was all screwed up. There was no wind, but the shadows of the rocks and trees seemed to be moving . . . stretching . . . reaching out toward me.

"Grandma I'm scared . . ." I cried between wracking coughs.

The spirits of the land are nothing to be frightened of, Zoeybird.

"Grandma?" Did I hear her voice calling me by my nickname, or was it only more weirdness and echoes, this time coming from my memory? "Grandma!" I called again, and then stood still listening for an answer.

Nothing. Nothing except the wind.

U-no-le . . . the Cherokee word for wind drifted through my mind like a half-forgotten dream.

Wind? No, wait! There hadn't been any wind just a second ago, but now I had to hold my hat down with one hand and brush away the hair that was whipping wildly across my face with the other. Then in the wind I heard them—the sounds of many Cherokee voices chanting in time with the beating of the ceremonial drums. Through a veil of hair and tears I saw smoke. The nutty sweet scent of piñon wood filled my open mouth and I tasted the campfires of my ancestors. I gasped, fighting to catch my breath.

That's when I felt them. They were all around me, almost-visible shapes shimmering like heat waves lifting from a blacktop road in summer. I could feel them press against me as they twirled and moved with graceful, intricate steps around and around the shadowy image of a Cherokee campfire.

Join us, u-we-tsi-a-ge-ya . . . Join us, daughter . . .

Cherokee ghosts . . . drowning in my own lungs . . . the fight with my parents . . . my old life gone . . .

It was all just too much. I ran.

I guess what they teach us in biology about adrenaline taking over during the whole fight-or-flight thing is true because even though my chest felt like it was going to explode and it seemed as if I was trying to breathe underwater, I ran up the last and steepest part of the trail like they'd opened up all the stores at the mall and they were giving away free shoes.

Gasping for breath I stumbled up the path—higher and higher—fighting to get away from the frightening spirits that hovered around me like fog, but instead of leaving them behind it seemed I was running farther into their world of smoke and shadows. Was I dying? Was this what happens? Was that why I could see ghosts? Where's the white light? Completely panicked, I rushed forward, throwing my arms out wildly as if I could hold off the terror that was chasing me.

I didn't see the root that broke through the hard ground of the path. Completely disoriented I tried to catch myself, but all of my reflexes were off. I fell hard. The pain in my head was sharp, but it lasted only an instant before blackness swallowed me.

Waking up was weird. I expected my body to hurt, especially my head and my chest, but instead of pain I felt . . . well . . . I felt fine. Actually, I felt better than fine. I wasn't coughing. My arms and legs were amazingly light, tingly, and warm, like I had just slipped into a bubbly hot tub on a cold night.

Huh?

Surprise made me open my eyes. I was staring up at a light, which miraculously didn't hurt my eyes. Instead of the glaring light of the sun, this was more like a soft rain of candlelight filtering down from above. I sat up, and realized I was wrong. The light wasn't coming down. I was moving up toward it!

I'm going to heaven. Well, that'll shock some people.

I glanced down to see *my body!* I or it or . . . or . . . whatever was lying scarily close to the edge of the bluff. My body was very still. My forehead had been cut and it was bleeding badly. The blood dripped steadily into a gash in the rocky ground, making a trail of red tears that fell into the heart of the bluff.

It was incredibly weird to look down on myself. I wasn't scared. But I should be, shouldn't I? Didn't this mean I was dead? Maybe I'd be able to see the Cherokee ghosts better now. Even that thought didn't scare me. Actually, instead of being afraid it was more like I was an observer, as if none of this could really touch me. (Kinda like those girls who have sex with everyone and think that they're not going to get pregnant or a really nasty STD that eats your brains and stuff. Well, we'll see in ten years, won't we?)

I enjoyed the way the world looked, sparkling and new, but it was my body that kept drawing my attention. I floated closer to it. I was breathing in short, shallow pants. Well, my *body* was breathing like that, not the I that was me. (Talk about confusing pronoun usage.) And I/she didn't look good. I/she was all pale and her lips were blue. Hey! White face, blue lips, and red blood! Am I patriotic or what?

I laughed, and it was amazing! I swear I could see my laughter floating around me like the puffy things you blow off a dandelion, only instead of being white it was birthday-cake-frosting-blue. Wow! Who knew hitting my head and passing out would be so much fun? I wondered if this was what it was like to be high.

The dandelion icing laughter faded and I could hear the shining crystal sound of running water. I moved closer to my body, able to see that what I had at first thought was a gash in the ground was really a narrow crevasse. The living water sound was coming from deep inside it. Curious, I peered down, and the sparkling silver outline of words drifted up from within the rock. I strained to hear, and was rewarded by a faint, whispering of silver sound.

Zoey Redbird . . . come to me . . .

"Grandma!" I yelled into the slash in the rock. My words were bright purple and they filled the air around me. "Is that you, Grandma?"

Come to me . . .

The silver mixed with the purple of my visible voice, turning the words the glistening color of lavender blossoms. It was an omen! A sign! Somehow, like the spirit guides the Cherokee people have believed in for centuries, Grandma Redbird was telling me I had to go down into the rock.

Without any more hesitation, I flung my spirit forward and down into the crevasse, following the trail of my blood and the silver memory of my grandma's whisper until I came to the smooth floor of a cave-like room. In the middle of the room a small stream of water bubbled, giving off tinkling shards of visible sound, bright and glass-colored. Mixed with the scarlet drops of my blood it lit up the cave with a flickering light that was the color of dried leaves. I wanted to sit next to the bubbling water and let my fingers touch the air around it and play in the texture of its music, but the voice called to me again.

Zoey Redbird . . . follow me to your destiny . . .

So I followed the stream and the woman's call. The cave narrowed until it was a rounded tunnel. It curved and curled around and around, in a gentle spiral, ending abruptly at a wall that was covered with carved symbols that looked familiar and alien at the same time. Confused, I watched the stream pour down into a crack in the wall and disappear. What now? Was I supposed to follow it?

I looked back down the tunnel. Nothing there except dancing light. I turned to the wall and felt a jolt of electric shock. Whoa! There was a woman sitting cross-legged in front of the wall! She was wearing a white fringed dress that was beaded with the same symbols that were on the wall behind her. She was fantastically beautiful, with long straight hair so black it looked as if it had blue and purple highlights, like a raven's wing. Her full lips curved up as she spoke, filling the air between us with the silver power of her voice.

Tsi-lu-gi U-we-tsi a-ge-hu-tsa. Welcome, Daughter. You have done well.

She spoke in Cherokee, but even though I hadn't practiced the language much in the last couple years I understood the words.

"You're not my grandma!" I blurted, feeling awkward and out of place as my purple words joined with hers, making incredible patterns of sparkling lavender in the air around us.

Her smile was like the rising sun.

No, Daughter, I am not, but I know Sylvia Redbird very well.

I took a deep breath. "Am I dead?"

I was afraid she would laugh at me, but she didn't. Instead her dark eyes were soft and concerned.

No, u-we-tsi-a-ge-ya. You are far from dead, though your spirit has been temporarily freed to wander the realm of the Nunne 'hi.

"The spirit people!" I glanced around the tunnel, trying to see faces and forms within the shadows.

Your grandmother has taught you well, u-s-ti Do-tsu-wa . . . little Redbird. You are a unique mixture of the Old Ways and the New World—of ancient tribal blood and the heartbeat of outsiders.

Her words made me feel hot and cold at the same time. "Who are you?" I asked.

I am known by many names . . . Changing Woman, Gaea, A'akuluujjusi, Kuan Yin, Grandmother Spider, and even Dawn . . .

As she spoke each name her face was transformed so that I was dizzied by her power. She must have understood, because she paused and flashed her beautiful smile at me again, and her face settled back into the woman I had first seen.

But you, Zoeybird, my Daughter, may call me by the name by which your world knows me today, Nyx.

"Nyx," my voice was barely above a whisper. "The vampyre Goddess?"

In truth, it was the ancient Greeks touched by the Change who first worshiped me as the mother they searched for within their endless Night. I have been pleased to call their descendents my children for many ages. And, yes, in your world those children are called vampyre. Accept the name, u-we-tsi-a-ge-ya; in it you will find your destiny.

I could feel my Mark burning on my forehead, and all of a sudden I wanted to cry. "I—I don't understand. Find my destiny? I just want to find a way to deal with my new life—to make this all okay. Goddess, I just want to fit in someplace. I don't think I'm up to finding my destiny."

The Goddess's face softened again, and when she spoke her voice was like my mother's, only more—as though she had somehow sprinkled the love of every mother in the world into her words.

Believe in yourself, Zoey Redbird. I have Marked you as my own. You will be my first true u-we-tsi-a-ge-ya v-hna-i Sv-no-yi . . . Daughter of Night . . . in this age. You are special. Accept that about yourself, and you will begin to understand there is true power in your uniqueness. Within you is combined the magic blood of ancient Wise Women and Elders, as well as insight into and understanding of the modern world.

The Goddess stood up and walked gracefully toward me, her voice painting silver symbols of power in the air around us. When she reached me she wiped the tears from my cheeks before taking my face in her hands.

Zoey Redbird, Daughter of Night, I name you my eyes and ears in the world today, a world where good and evil are struggling to find balance.

"But I'm sixteen! I can't even parallel-park! How am I supposed to know how to be your eyes and ears?"

She just smiled serenely. *You are old beyond your years, Zoeybird. Believe in yourself and you will find a way. But remember, darkness does not always equate to evil, just as light does not always bring good.*

Then the Goddess Nyx, the ancient personification of Night, leaned forward and kissed me on my forehead. And for the third time that day I passed out.

CHAPTER SIX

—

Beautiful, see the cloud, the cloud appear.
Beautiful, see the rain, the rain draw near . . .

The words of the ancient song floated through my mind. I must be dreaming about Grandma Redbird again. It made me feel warm and safe and happy, which was especially nice, since I'd felt so crappy lately . . . except I couldn't remember exactly why. Huh. Odd.

Who spoke?
The little corn ear,
High on top of the stalk . . .

My grandma's song continued and I curled up on my side, sighing as I rubbed my cheek against the soft pillow. Unfortunately, moving my head caused an ugly pain to shoot through my temples, and like a bullet through a pane of glass, it shattered my happy feeling as the memory of the last day overwhelmed me.

I was turning into a vampyre.

I had run away from home.

I'd had an accident and then some kind of weird near-death experience.

I was turning into a vampyre. Oh my God.

Man, my head hurt.

"Zoeybird! Are you awake, baby?"

I blinked my blurry eyes clear to see Grandma Redbird sitting on a little chair close beside my bed.

"Grandma!" I croaked and reached for her hand. My voice sounded as terrible as my head felt. "What happened? Where am I?"

"You're safe, Little Bird. You're safe."

"My head hurts." I reached up and felt the place on my head that was tight and sore, and my fingers found the prick of stitches.

"It should. You scared ten years of my life from me." Grandma rubbed the back of my hand gently. "All that blood . . ." She shuddered, and then shook her head and smiled at me. "How about you promise not to do that again?"

"Promise," I said. "So, you found me . . ."

"Bloody and unconscious, Little Bird." Grandma brushed the hair back from my forehead, her fingers lingering lightly on my Mark. "And so pale that your dark crescent seemed to glow against your skin. I knew you needed to be taken back to the House of Night, which is exactly what I did." She chuckled and the mischievous sparkle in her eyes made her look like a little girl. "I called your mother to tell her that I was returning you to the House of Night, and I had to pretend that my cell phone cut out so I could hang up on her. I'm afraid she's not happy with either of us."

I grinned back at Grandma Redbird. Hee hee, Mom was mad at her, too.

"But, Zoey, whatever were you doing out during the daylight? And why didn't you tell me earlier that you had been Marked?"

I struggled to sit up, grunting at the pain in my head. But, thankfully, it seemed I'd stopped coughing. *Must be because I'm finally really here—at the House of Night . . .* But the thought disappeared as my mind processed all of what Grandma had said.

"Wait, I couldn't have told you any earlier. The Tracker came to school today and Marked me. I went home first. I really hoped Mom would understand and take my side." I paused, remembering again the awful scene with my parents. In total understanding, Grandma squeezed my hand. "She and John basically locked me in my room while they called our shrink and started the prayer tree."

Grandma grimaced.

"So I crawled out my window and came straight to you," I concluded.

"I'm glad you did, Zoeybird, but it just doesn't make any sense."

"I know," I sighed. "I can't believe I got Marked, either. Why me?"

"That's not what I mean, baby. I'm not surprised you were Tracked and Marked. The Redbird blood has always held strong magic; it was only a matter of time before one of us was Chosen. What I mean is that it makes no sense that you were *just* Marked. The crescent isn't an outline. It's completely filled in."

"That's impossible!"

"Look for yourself, u-we-tsi-a-ge-ya." She used the Cherokee word for daughter, suddenly reminding me very much of a mysterious, ancient goddess.

Grandma searched through her purse for the antique silver compact she always carried. Without saying anything else, she handed it to me. I pushed the little clasp. It popped open to show me my reflection . . . the familiar stranger . . . the me who wasn't quite *me.* Her eyes were huge and her skin was too white, but I barely noticed that. It was the Mark that I couldn't quit staring at, the Mark that was now a completed crescent moon, filled in perfectly with the distinctive sapphire blue of the vampyre tattoo. Feeling like I was still moving through a dream, I reached up and let my fingers trace the exotic-looking Mark and I seemed to feel the Goddess's lips against my skin again.

"What does it mean?" I said, unable to look away from the Mark.

"We were hoping you would have an answer to that question, Zoey Redbird."

Her voice was amazing. Even before I looked up from my reflection I knew she would be unique and incredible. I was right. She was movie-star beautiful, Barbie beautiful. I'd never seen anyone up close who was so perfect. She had huge, almond-shaped eyes that were a deep, mossy green. Her face was an almost perfect heart and her skin was that kind of flawless creaminess that you see on TV. Her hair was deep red—not that horrid carrot-top orange-red or the washed-out blond-red, but a dark, glossy auburn that fell in heavy waves well past her shoulders. Her body was, well, perfect. She wasn't thin like the freak girls who puked and starved themselves into what they thought was Paris Hilton chic. ("That's Hott." Yeah, okay, whatever, Paris.) This woman's body was perfect because she was strong, but curvy. And she had great boobs. (I wish I had great boobs.)

"Huh?" I said. Speaking of boobs—I was totally sounding like one. (Boob . . . hee hee).

The woman smiled at me and showed amazingly straight, white teeth—without fangs. Oh, I guess I forgot to mention that in addition to her perfection she had a sapphire crescent moon neatly tattooed in the middle of her forehead, and from it, swirls of lines that reminded me of ocean waves framed her brows, extending down around her high cheekbones.

She was a vampyre.

"I said, we were hoping you would have some explanation about why a fledgling vampyre that hasn't Changed has the Mark of a mature being on her forehead."

Without her smile and the gentle concern in her voice her words would have seemed harsh. Instead, what she said came off as worried and a little confused.

"So I'm not a vampyre?" I blurted.

Her laughter was like music. "Not yet, Zoey, but I would say that already having your Mark complete is an excellent omen."

"Oh . . . I . . . well, good. That's good," I babbled.

Thankfully, Grandma saved me from total humiliation.

"Zoey, this is the High Priestess of the House of Night, Neferet. She's been taking good care of you while you've been"—Grandma paused, obviously not wanting to say the word unconscious—"while you've been asleep."

"Welcome to the House of Night, Zoey Redbird," Neferet said warmly.

I glanced at Grandma and then back at Neferet. Feeling more than a little lost I stuttered, "That's—that's not really my name. My last name is Montgomery."

"Is it?" Neferet said, raising her amber-tinted brows. "One benefit of beginning a new life is that you have the opportunity to start over—to make choices you weren't given before. If you could choose, what would your true name be?"

I didn't hesitate. "Zoey Redbird."

"Then from this moment on, you shall be Zoey Redbird. Welcome to your new life." She reached out like she wanted to shake my hand, and I automatically offered mine. But instead of taking my hand, she grasped my forearm, which was weird but somehow felt right.

Her touch was warm and firm. Her smile blazed with welcome. She was amazing and awe-inspiring. Actually, she was what all vampyres are, *more* than human—stronger, smarter, more talented. She looked like someone had turned on a blazing inner light within her, which I realize is definitely an ironic description considering the vampyre stereotypes (some of which I already knew were totally true): They avoid sunlight, they're most powerful at night, they need to drink blood to survive (eesh!), and they worship a goddess who is known as Night personified.

"Th-thank you. It's nice to meet you," I said, trying really hard to sound at least semi-intelligent and normal.

"As I was telling your grandmother earlier, we have never had a fledgling come to us in such an unusual manner before—unconscious and with a completed Mark. Can you remember what happened to you, Zoey?"

I opened my mouth to tell her that I totally remembered it—falling and hitting my head . . . seeing myself like I was a floating spirit . . . following the weirdly visible words into the cave . . . and finally meeting the Goddess Nyx. But right before I said the words I got a weird feeling, like someone had just hit me in my stomach. It was clear and it was specific, and it was telling me to shut up.

"I—I really don't remember much—" I broke off and my hand found the sore spot where my stitches poked out. "At least not after I hit my head. I mean, up until then I remember everything. The Tracker Marked me; I told my parents and got into a ginormic fight with them; then I ran away to my grandma's place. I was feeling really sick, so when I climbed the path up to the bluffs . . ." I remembered the rest of it—*all* of the rest of it—the spirits of the Cherokee people, the dancing and the campfire. *Shut up!* the feeling screamed at me. "I—I guess I slipped because I was coughing so much, and hit my head. The next thing I remember is Grandma Redbird singing and then I woke up here." I finished in a rush. I wanted to look away from the sharpness of her green-eyed gaze, but the same feeling that was ordering me to be quiet was also clearly telling me that I had to keep eye contact with her, that I had to try really hard to look like I wasn't hiding anything, even though I didn't really have a clue why I was hiding anything.

"It's normal to experience memory loss with a head wound." Grandma said matter-of-factly, breaking the silence.

I could have kissed her.

"Yes, of course it is," Neferet said quickly, her face losing its sharpness. "Do not fear for your granddaughter's health, Sylvia Redbird. All will be well with her."

She spoke to Grandma respectfully, and some of the tension that had been building inside me loosened. If she liked Grandma Redbird, she had to be an okay person, or vampyre or whatever. Right?

"As I'm sure you already know, vampyres"—Neferet paused and smiled at me—"even fledgling vampyres, have unusual powers of recovery. Her healing is proceeding so well that it is perfectly safe for her to leave the infirmary." She looked from Grandma to me. "Zoey, would you like to meet your new roommate?"

No. I swallowed hard and nodded. "Yes."

"Excellent!" Neferet said. Thankfully she ignored the fact that I was standing there like a smiling stupid garden gnome.

"Are you sure you shouldn't keep her here another day for observation?" Grandma asked.

"I understand your concern, but I assure you Zoey's physical wounds are already healing at a pace you would find extraordinary."

She smiled at me again and even though I was scared and nervous and just plain freaked out I smiled back at her. It seemed like she was genuinely happy that I was there. And, truthfully, she made me think turning into a vampyre might not be such a bad thing.

"Grandma, I'm fine. Really. My head just hurts a little, and the rest of me feels way better." I realized as I said it that it was true. I'd completely stopped coughing. My muscles didn't ache anymore. I felt perfectly normal except for a little headache.

Then Neferet did something that not only surprised me, but made me instantly like her—and begin to trust her. She walked over to Grandma and spoke slowly and carefully.

"Sylvia Redbird, I give you my solemn oath that your granddaughter is safe here. Each fledgling is paired with an adult mentor.

To ensure my oath to you I will be Zoey's mentor. And now you must entrust her to my care."

Neferet placed her fist over her heart and bowed formally to Grandma. My grandma hesitated for only a moment before answering her.

"I will hold you to your oath, Neferet, High Priestess of Nyx." Then she mimicked Neferet's actions by putting her own fist over her heart and bowing to her before turning to me and hugging me hard. "Call me if you need me, Zoeybird. I love you."

"I will, Grandma. I love you, too. And thank you for bringing me here," I whispered, breathing in her familiar lavender scent and trying not to cry.

She kissed me gently on my cheek and then with her quick, confident steps she walked out of the room, leaving me alone for the first time in my life with a vampyre.

"Well, Zoey, are you ready to begin your new life?"

I looked up at her and thought again how amazing she was. If I actually Changed into a vampyre, would I have her confidence and power, or was that something only a High Priestess got? For an instant it flashed though my mind how awesome it would be to be a High Priestess—and then my sanity returned. I was just a kid. A confused kid at that, and definitely not High Priestess material. I just want to figure out how to fit in here, but Neferet had certainly made what was happening to me seem easier to bear.

"Yes, I am." I was glad I sounded more confident than I felt.

CHAPTER SEVEN

―

"What time is it?"

We were walking down a narrow hall that curved gently. The walls were made of an odd mixture of dark stone and jutting brick. Every so often flickering gaslights that hung from old-fashioned-looking black iron sconces stuck out of the wall, giving off a soft yellow glow that was, thankfully, really easy on my eyes. There were no windows in the hall, and we didn't meet anyone else (even though I kept peeking nervously around, imagining my first glimpse of vampyre kids).

"It is nearly four A.M., which means classes have been out for almost an hour." Neferet said, and then she smiled slightly at what I'm sure was my totally shocked expression.

"Classes begin at eight P.M., and end at three A.M.," she explained. "Teachers are available until three thirty A.M. to give students extra help. The gym is open until dawn, the exact time of which you will always know as soon as you have completed the Change. Until then dawn time is clearly posted in all the classrooms, common rooms, and gathering areas, including the dining hall, library, and gym. Nyx's Temple is, of course, open at all hours, but formal rituals are held twice a week right after school. The next ritual will be tomorrow." Neferet glanced at me and her slight smile warmed. "It seems overwhelming now, but you'll catch on quickly. And your roommate will help you, as will I."

I was just getting ready to open my mouth to ask her another question when an orange ball of fur ran into the hall and without a sound, hurled itself into Neferet's arms. I jumped and made a stupid little *squee* sound—then I felt like a total retard when I saw that the orange ball of fur was not a flying boogieman or whatever, but a massively big cat.

Neferet laughed and scratched the fur ball's ears. "Zoey, meet Skylar. He's usually prowling around here waiting to launch himself at me."

"That's the biggest cat I've ever seen," I said, reaching my hand out to let him sniff me.

"Careful, he's a known biter."

Before I could jerk my hand out of the way, Skylar started rubbing his face on my fingers. I held my breath.

Neferet tilted her head to the side, as if she was listening to words in the wind. "He likes you, which is definitely unusual. He doesn't like anyone except me. He even keeps the other cats away from this end of campus. He's really a terrible bully," she said fondly.

I carefully scratched Skylar's ears like Neferet had been doing. "I like cats," I said softly. "I used to have one, but when my mom got remarried I had to give it to Street Cats to be adopted. John, her new husband, doesn't like cats."

"I've found that the way a person feels about cats—and the way they feel about him or her in return—is usually an excellent gauge by which to measure a person's character."

I looked up from the cat to meet her green eyes and saw that she understood a lot more about freaky family issues than she was saying. It made me feel connected to her, and automatically my stress level relaxed a little. "Are there a lot of cats here?"

"Yes, there are. Cats have always been closely allied with vampyres."

Okay, actually I already knew that. In World History with Mr. Shaddox (better known as Puff Shaddy, but don't tell him) we learned that in the past cats had been slaughtered because it was thought that they somehow turned people into vampyres. *Yeah, okay, talk about ridiculous. More evidence of the stupidity of humans . . .* the thought popped into my mind, shocking me by how easily I'd already started thinking of "normal" people as "humans," and therefore something different than me.

"Do you think I could have a cat?" I asked.

"If one chooses you, you will belong to him or her."

"Chooses me?"

Neferet smiled and stroked Skylar, who closed his eyes and purred loudly. "Cats choose us; we don't own them." As if to demonstrate what she said was true, Skylar jumped out of her arms and, with a stuck-up flick of his tail, disappeared down the hall.

Neferet laughed. "He's really awful, but I do adore him. I think I would, even were it not part of my gift from Nyx."

"Gift? Skylar is a gift from the Goddess?"

"Yes, in a way. Every High Priestess is given an affinity—what you would probably think of as special powers—by the Goddess. It's part of the way we identify our High Priestesses. The affinities can be unusual cognitive skills, like reading minds or having visions and being able to predict the future. Or the affinity can be for something in the physical realm, like a special connection to one of the four elements, or to animals. I have two Goddess gifts. My main affinity is for cats; I have a connection with them that is unusual, even for a vampyre. Nyx has also given me unusual powers of healing." She smiled. "Which is why I know you're healing well—my gift told me."

"Wow, that's amazing," was all I could think to say. My head was already reeling from the events of the past day.

"Come on. Let's get you to your room. I'm sure you're hungry and tired. Dinner will start in"—Neferet cocked her head to the side as if someone was weirdly whispering the time to her—"an hour." She gave me a knowing smile. "Vampyres always know what time it is."

"That's cool, too."

"That, my dear fledgling, is just the tip of the 'cool' iceberg."

I hoped her analogy didn't have anything to do with Titanic-sized disasters. As we continued walking down the hall I thought about time and stuff, and remembered the question I had started to ask when Skylar had interrupted my easily derailed train of thought.

"So, wait. You said that classes start at eight? At night?" Okay, I'm usually not this slow, but some of this was like she was speaking a foreign language to me. I was having a hard time getting it.

"Once you take a moment to think about it you'll understand that having classes at night is only logical. Of course you must know that vampyres, adult or fledgling, don't explode, or any other such fictional nonsense, if subjected to direct sunlight, but it is uncomfortable for us. Wasn't the sunlight already difficult for you to bear today?"

I nodded. "My Maui Jims didn't even help much." Then I added quickly, feeling moronic again, "Uh, Maui Jims are sunglasses."

"Yes, Zoey," Neferet said patiently. "I know sunglasses. Very well, actually."

"Oh, God, I'm sorry I—" I broke off, wondering whether it was okay for me to say "God." Would it offend Neferet, a High Priestess who wore her Goddess Mark so proudly? Hell, would it offend Nyx? Oh, God. What about saying "hell"? It was my favorite cuss word ever. (Okay, it was really the only cuss word I used regularly.) Could I still say it? The People of Faith preached that vampyres worshiped a false goddess and that they were mostly selfish, dark creatures who cared about nothing except money and luxury and drinking blood and they were all certainly going straight to hell, so wouldn't that mean that I should watch how and where I used . . .

"Zoey."

I looked up to find Neferet studying me with a concerned expression and realized that she had probably been trying to get my attention while I had been babbling inside my head.

"I'm sorry," I repeated.

Neferet stopped. She put her hands on my shoulders and turned me so that I had to face her.

"Zoey, quit apologizing. And remember, everyone here has been where you are. This was new to all of us once. We know what it feels like—the fear of the Change—the shock at your life being turned into something foreign."

"And not being able to control any of it," I added quietly.

"That, too. It won't always be this bad. When you're a mature vampyre your life will seem your own again. You'll make your own choices; go your own way; follow the path down which your heart and soul and talents lead you."

"*If* I become a mature vampyre."

"You will, Zoey."

"How can you be so sure?"

Neferet's eyes found the darkened Mark on my forehead. "Nyx has chosen you. For what, we do not know. But her Mark has been clearly placed upon you. She would not have touched you only to see you fail."

I remembered the Goddess's words, *Zoey Redbird, Daughter of Night, I name you my eyes and ears in the world today, a world where good and evil are struggling to find balance,* and looked quickly away from Neferet's sharp gaze, wishing desperately that I knew why my gut was still telling me to keep my mouth shut about my meeting with the Goddess.

"It's—it's just a lot to happen all in one day."

"It certainly is, especially on an empty stomach."

We had started walking again when the sound of a ringing cell phone made me jump. Neferet sighed and smiled apologetically at me, then she fished a small phone out of her pocket.

"Neferet," she said. She listened for a little while and I saw her forehead wrinkle, and her eyes narrow. "No, you were right to call me. I'll come back and check on her." And she flipped the phone shut. "I'm sorry, Zoey. One of the fledglings broke her leg earlier today. It seems she's having trouble resting, and I should go back and be sure all is well with her. Why don't you follow this hallway around to the left until you come to the main door? You can't miss it—it's large and made of very old wood. Right outside is a stone bench. You can wait there for me. I won't be long."

"Okay, no problem." But before I'd finished speaking Neferet had already disappeared back down the winding hallway. I sighed. I didn't like the idea of being by myself in a place that was full of vampyres and vampyre kids. And now that Neferet was gone the little flickering lights didn't seem so welcoming. They seemed weird, throwing ghostly shadows against the old stone hall.

Determined not to freak myself out, I started slowly down the hall in the direction we had been heading. Pretty soon I almost wished I'd run into some other people (even if they were vampyres). It was too quiet. And creepy. A couple of times the hall branched off to the right, but like Neferet had told me, I kept to the left. Actually, I also kept my eyes to the left because those other halls had hardly any lights in them.

Unfortunately at the next right-hand turn off the hall I *didn't* avert my eyes. Okay, so the reason made sense. I heard something.

To be more specific, I heard a laugh. It was a soft, girly laugh that for some reason made the hair on the back of my neck stand up. It also made me stop walking. I peeked down the hall and thought I saw movement in the shadows.

Zoey . . . My name was whispered from the shadows.

I blinked in surprise. Had I really heard my name or was I imagining things? The voice was almost familiar. Could it be Nyx again? Was the Goddess calling my name? Almost as afraid as I was intrigued, I held my breath and took a few steps into the side hallway.

As I walked around the gentle bend I saw something ahead of me that made me stop and automatically move closer to the wall. In a little alcove not far from me were two people. At first I couldn't make my mind process what I was seeing; then in a rush I understood.

I should have gotten out of there then. I should have backed silently away and tried not to think about what I'd seen. But I didn't do any of those things. It was like my feet were suddenly so heavy I couldn't pick them up. All I could do was watch.

The man—and then with a little jolt of additional shock I realized that he wasn't a man, he was a teenager—not more than a year or so older than me. He was standing with his back pressed against the stone of the alcove. His head was tilted back and he was breathing hard. His face was in the shadows, but even though he was only partially visible I could see that he was handsome. Then another breathy little laugh drew my eyes downward.

She was on her knees in front of him. All I could see of her was her blond hair. There was so much of it that it looked like she was wearing it as some kind of ancient veil. Then her hands moved up, running along the guy's thighs.

Go! my mind screamed at me. *Get out of there!* I started to take a step back, and then his voice made me freeze.

"Stop!"

My eyes got huge because for a second I thought he was talking to me.

"You don't really want me to."

I felt almost dizzy with relief when she spoke. He was talking to her, not me. They didn't even know I was there.

"Yes, I do." It sounded as if he was grinding his words from between his teeth. "Get off your knees."

"You like it—you know you like it. Just like you know you still want me."

Her voice was all husky and trying to be sexy, but I could also hear the whine in it. She sounded almost desperate. I watched her fingers move, and my eyes widened in amazement when she drew the nail of her index finger down his thigh. Unbelievably, her fingernail slashed through his jeans, just like it was a knife, and a line of fresh blood appeared, startling in its liquid redness.

I didn't want it to, and it grossed me out, but at the sight of the blood my mouth started watering.

"No!" He snapped, putting his hands on her shoulders and trying to push her away from him.

"Oh, quit pretending," she laughed again, a mean, sarcastic sound. "You know we'll always be together." She reached up with her tongue and licked along the line of blood.

I shuddered; against my will I was completely mesmerized.

"Cut it out!" He was still pushing at her shoulders. "I don't want to hurt you, but you're really starting to piss me off. Why can't you understand? We're not doing this anymore. I don't want you."

"You want me! You'll always want me!" She unzipped his pants.

I shouldn't be there. I shouldn't be seeing this. I tore my eyes from his bloody thigh and took one step back.

The guy's eyes lifted. He saw me.

And then something truly bizarre happened. I could feel his

touch through our eyes. I couldn't look away from him. The girl in front of him seemed to disappear, and all there was in the hallway was him and me and the sweet, beautiful smell of his blood.

"You don't want me? That's not how it looks now," she said with a nasty purr in her voice.

I felt my head begin to shake back and forth, back and forth. At the same moment he cried "No!" and tried to push her out of the way so that he could move toward me.

I ripped my eyes away from his and stumbled back.

"No!" he said again. This time I knew he was speaking to me and not her. She must have realized it, too, because with a cry that sounded uncomfortably like the snarl of a wild animal, she started to whirl around. My body unfroze. At the same instant I turned and ran back down the hall.

I expected them to come after me, so I kept running until I reached the huge old doors Neferet had described. Then I stood there, leaning against their cold wood, trying to get my breathing under control so I could listen for the sounds of running feet.

What would I do if they did chase me down? My head was pounding painfully again, and I felt weak and totally scared. And completely, utterly grossed out.

Yes, I was aware of the whole oral sex thing. I doubt if there's a teenager alive in America today who isn't aware that most of the adult public think we're giving guys blow jobs like they used to give guys gum (or maybe more appropriately suckers). Okay, that's just bullshit, and it's always made me mad. Of course there are girls who think it's "cool" to give guys head. Uh, they're wrong. Those of us with functioning brains know that it is not cool to be used like that.

Okay, so I *knew* about the whole blow job issue. I'd definitely never seen one. So, what I had just seen had definitely freaked me out. But what had freaked me out more than the fact that the blonde was doing the nasty to him was the way I'd responded to seeing the guy's blood.

I'd wanted to lick it, too.

And that's just not normal.

Then there's the whole issue about me sharing that weird look with him. What had that been all about?

"Zoey, are you all right?"

"Hell!" I gasped and jumped. Neferet was standing behind me looking at me with total confusion.

"Are you feeling ill?"

"I—I . . ." My mind flailed about. No way could I tell her what I'd just seen. "My head just really hurts," I finally managed to say. And it was true. I had a killer headache.

Her frown was full of concern. "Let me help you." Neferet placed her hand lightly over the line of stitches on my forehead. She closed her eyes and I could hear her whispering something in a language I could not understand. Then her hand started to feel warm and it was as if the warmth became liquid and my skin absorbed it. I closed my eyes and sighed in relief as the pain in my head began to fade.

"Better?"

"Yes," I barely whispered.

She took her hand away and I opened my eyes. "That should keep the pain away. I don't know why it suddenly came back with such force."

"Me, neither, but it's gone now," I said quickly.

She studied me silently for a little while more while I held my breath. Then she said, "Anything upset you?"

I swallowed. "I'm a little scared about meeting my new roommate." Which technically wasn't a lie. It wasn't what had upset me, but I was scared about it.

Neferet's smile was kind. "All will be well, Zoey. Now let me introduce you to your new life."

Neferet opened the thick wooden door and we walked out into a large courtyard that fronted the school. She stepped aside and let me gawk. Teenagers wearing uniforms that somehow looked cool and unique while still being similar walked in small groups across the courtyard and along the sidewalk. I could hear the deceptively normal sound of their voices as they laughed and talked. I kept staring from them to the school, not sure which to gawk at first. I chose the school. It was the less intimidating of the two (and I was scared I'd see *him*). The place was like something out of a creepy dream. It was the middle of the night, and it should have been deeply dark, but there was a brilliant moon shining above the huge old oaks that shaded everything. Freestanding gaslights housed in tarnished copper fixtures followed the sidewalk that ran parallel to the huge red brick and black rock building. It was three stories tall and had a weirdly high roof that pointed up and then flattened off at the top. I could see that heavy drapes had been opened and soft yellow lights made shadows dance up and down the rooms, giving the entire structure an alive and welcoming look. A round tower was attached to the front of the main building, furthering the illusion that the place was much more castle-like than school-like. I swear, a moat would have looked more like it belonged there than a sidewalk ringed by thick azalea bushes and a neat lawn.

Across from the main building was a smaller one that looked older and church-like. Behind it and the old oaks that shaded the schoolyard I could see the shadow of the enormous stone wall that surrounded the entire school. In front of the church building was a marble statue of a woman who was wearing long, flowing robes.

"Nyx!" I blurted.

Neferet lifted one eyebrow in surprise. "Yes, Zoey. That is a statue of the Goddess, and the building behind it is her temple." She motioned for me to walk with her down the sidewalk and gestured expansively at the impressive campus that stretched before us. "What is known today as the House of Night was built in the neo-French-Norman style, with stones imported from Europe. It originated in the mid-1920s as an Augustine monastery for the People of Faith. Eventually it was converted into Cascia Hall, a private preparatory school for affluent human teenagers. When we decided that we must open a school of our own in this part of the country, we bought it from Cascia Hall five years ago."

I only vaguely recalled the days when it had been a stuck-up private school—actually the only reason I'd ever thought about it at all was that I remembered hearing the news that a whole herd of kids who went to Cascia Hall had been busted for drugs, and how shocked the adults had been. Whatever. No one else had been shocked that those rich kids were majorly into drugs.

"I'm surprised they sold it to you guys," I said absently.

Her laugh was low and a little dangerous. "They didn't want to, but we made their arrogant headmaster an offer even he couldn't refuse."

I wanted to ask her what she meant, but her laugh gave me a skin-crawly feeling. And, plus, I was busy. I couldn't stop staring. Okay the first thing I noticed was that everyone who had a solid vampyre tattoo was incredibly good-looking. I mean, it was totally insane. Yes, I knew that vampyres were attractive. Everyone knew that. The most successful actors and actresses in the world were vampyres. They were also dancers and musicians, authors and singers. Vampyres dominated the arts, which is one reason they had so much money—and also one reason (of many) that the People of Faith considered them selfish and immoral. *But really, they're just jealous that they're not as good-looking.* The People of Faith would go see their movies, plays, concerts, buy their books and their art, but at the same time they'd talk about them and look down at them, and God knows they'd never, ever mix with them. Hello—can you say hypocrites?

Anyway, being surrounded by so many totally gorgeous people made me want to crawl under a bench, even though many of them greeted Neferet and then smiled and said hello to me, too. Between hesitantly returning their hellos I snuck looks at the kids who walked by us. Each of them nodded respectfully to Neferet. Several of them bowed formally to her and crossed their fists over their hearts, which made Neferet smile and bow slightly in response. Okay, the kids weren't as gorgeous as the adults. Sure, they were nice-looking—interesting actually, with their crescent moon outlines, and their uniforms that looked more like runway designs than school clothes—but they didn't have the glossy, inhumanly attractive light that radiated from inside each of the adult vampyres. Uh, I did notice that, as I had suspected, their uniforms had a lot of basic black in them (you'd think that a group of people so up on the arts would recognize a cliché when one goes walking by in boring Goth black. I'm just saying . . .). But I suppose if I was going to be honest I'd have to admit it looked good on them—the black mixed with tiny plaid lines of deep purple, dark blue, and emerald green. Each uniform had an ornate design embroidered in gold or silver on either its jacket breast pocket or blouse pocket. I could tell that some of the designs were the same, but I couldn't see exactly what they were. Also, there was a weirdly large amount of kids with long hair. Seriously, the girls had long hair, the guys had long hair, the teachers had long hair, even the cats that wandered across the sidewalk from time to time were long-haired balls of fur. Odd. Good thing I'd talked myself out of getting my hair cut in that short duck butt style Kayla had cut hers off in last week.

I also noticed that the adults and the kids had one other thing in common—their eyes all lingered with obvious curiosity on my Mark. Great. So I was beginning my new life as an anomaly, which figured about as much as it sucked.

CHAPTER EIGHT

—

The part of the House of Night that held the dorms was way across campus, so we had a fairly long walk, and Neferet seemed to be walking slowly on purpose, giving me plenty of time to ask questions and gawk. Not that I minded. Walking the length of the sprawling castle-like cluster of buildings, with Neferet pointing out little details about what was what, gave me a sense of the place. It was weird, but in a good way. Plus, walking felt normal. Actually, as odd as it sounds, I felt like myself again. I wasn't coughing. My body didn't ache. My head even had stopped hurting. I was absolutely, totally not thinking about the disturbing scene I'd accidentally witnessed. I was forgetting it—on purpose. The last thing I needed was to have more to deal with than a new life and a weird Mark. So, blow job—forgotten.

Deeply in denial I told myself that if I hadn't been walking through a school campus at an ungodly hour of the night beside a vampyre I almost could pretend that I was the same today as I had been yesterday. Almost.

Well, okay. Maybe not even *almost,* but my head did feel better, and I was just about ready to face my roommate when Neferet finally opened the door to the girl's dorm.

Inside was a surprise. I'm not sure what I expected—maybe everything to be all black and creepy. But it was nice, decorated in soft blue and antique yellow, with comfy couches and clumps of puffy pillows big enough to sit on dotting the room like giant pastel M&Ms. The soft gaslight coming from several antique crystal chandeliers made the place look like a princess's castle. On the cream-colored walls there were large oil paintings, all of them of ancient women who looked exotic and powerful. Fresh-cut flowers, mostly roses, sat in crystal vases on end tables that were cluttered with books and purses and fairly normal-looking teenage girl stuff. I saw several flat screen TVs, and recognized the sounds of MTV's *Real World* coming from one of them. I took in all of this fast, while I tried to smile and appear friendly to the girls who had shut up the instant I walked in the room and were now staring at me. Well, scratch that. They weren't exactly staring at *me*. They were staring at the Mark on my forehead.

"Ladies, this is Zoey Redbird. Greet her and welcome her to the House of Night."

For a second I didn't think anyone was going to say anything, and I wanted to die of new-kid mortification. Then a girl stood up from among the middle of a group that was clustered around one of the TVs. She was a tiny blonde and darn near perfect. Actually, she reminded me of a young version of Sarah Jessica Parker (who I don't like, by the by—she's just so . . . so . . . annoying and unnaturally perky).

"Hi Zoey. Welcome to your new home." The SJP look-alike's smile was warm and genuine, and she was clearly making an effort to make eye contact instead of gawk at my darkened-in Mark. Instantly I felt bad for making a negative comparison about her. "I'm Aphrodite," she said.

Aphrodite? Okay, maybe I *hadn't* been too hasty in my comparison. How could anyone normal choose Aphrodite as her name? Please. Talk about delusions of grandeur. I plastered a smile on my face, though, and said a bright, "Hi Aphrodite!"

"Neferet, would you like me to show Zoey to her room?"

Neferet hesitated, which felt really odd. Instead of answering right away she just stood there and locked eyes with Aphrodite. Then, just as quickly as the silent stare-down had started, Neferet's face broke into a wide smile.

"Thank you, Aphrodite, that would be lovely. I am Zoey's mentor, but I'm sure she would feel much more welcomed if someone her own age showed her the way to her room."

Was that anger I saw flash through Aphrodite's eyes? No, I must have imagined it—or at least I would have believed I'd imagined it if that weird new gut feeling of mine hadn't told me otherwise. And I didn't need my new intuition to clue me in that something was wrong, because Aphrodite laughed—*and I recognized the sound of it.*

Feeling like someone had punched me in the gut I realized that this girl—Aphrodite—had been the one I'd just watched with the guy in the hall!

Aphrodite's laugh, followed by her perky, "Of course I'd be happy to show her around! You know I'm always glad to help you, Neferet," was as fake and cold as Pamela Anderson's humongously huge boobs, but Neferet just nodded in response and then turned to face me.

"I'll leave you now, Zoey," Neferet said, squeezing my shoulder. "Aphrodite will take you to your room, and your new roommate can help you get ready for dinner. I'll see you in the dining room." She smiled her warm, mom-smile at me, and I had the ridiculously childish urge to hug her and beg her not to leave me alone with Aphrodite. "You'll be fine," she said, as if she could read my mind. "You'll see, Zoeybird. All will be well," she whispered, sounding so much like my grandma that I had to blink hard not to cry. Then she nodded a quick good-bye to Aphrodite and the other girls, and left the dorm.

The door closed with a muffled, dead sound. Oh, hell . . . I just wanted to go home!

"Come on, Zoey. The rooms are this way," Aphrodite said. She motioned for me to come with her up the wide stairs that curved to our right. As we walked upstairs I tried to ignore the buzz of voices that instantly erupted behind us.

Neither of us spoke, and I felt so uncomfortable that I wanted to scream. Had she seen me back there in the hall? Well, I sure as hell wasn't going to mention it. Ever. As far as I was concerned it never happened.

I cleared my throat and said, "The dorm seems nice. I mean, it's really pretty."

She cut her eyes sideways at me. "It's better than nice or really pretty here; it's amazing."

"Oh. Well. That's good to hear."

She laughed. The sound was totally unpleasant—almost a sneer—and it crawled up the back of my neck like it had when I'd first heard it.

"It's amazing here mostly because of me."

I glanced at her, thinking that she must be kidding, and met her cold blue eyes.

"Yeah, you heard me right. This place is cool because I'm cool."

Oh. My. God. What a bizarre thing for her to say. I didn't have a clue how to respond to that very stuck-up piece of info. I mean, like I needed the stress of a fight with slutty Ms. Thinking-She's-All-That added on top of a life/species/school change? And I still couldn't tell whether she knew it had been me watching her in the hall.

Okay. I just wanted to find a way to fit in. I wanted to be able to call this new school home. So I decided to take the safest road and keep my mouth shut.

Neither of us said anything more. The stairs led to a large

hallway lined with doors. I held my breath when Aphrodite stopped before one that was painted a pretty light purple, but instead of knocking, she turned to face me. Her perfect face suddenly looked hateful and cold and definitely not so pretty.

"Okay, here's the deal, Zoey. You have this weird Mark, so everyone's talking about you and wondering what the fuck is up with you." She rolled her eyes and clutched her pearls dramatically, changing her voice so that she sounded really silly and gushing. "Oooh! The new girl has a colored-in Mark! Whatever could that mean? Is she special? Does she have fabulous powers? Oh my—oh my!" She dropped her hand from her throat and narrowed her eyes at me. Her voice went as flat and mean as her gaze. "Here's what's what. I'm *it* here. Things go my way. You want to get along here, then you'd best remember that. If you don't, you'll be in for a world of shit."

Okay, she was starting to piss me off. "Look," I said, "I just got here. I'm not looking for trouble, and I have no control over what people are saying about my Mark."

Her eyes narrowed. Ah, crap. Was I going to have to actually fight this girl? I'd never been in a fight in my life! My stomach knotted up and I got ready to duck or run or whatever would not get me beat up.

Then, just as quickly as she'd gone all scary and hateful, her face relaxed into a smile and she turned back into sweet little blonde again. (Not that I was fooled.)

"Good. Just so we understand each other."

Huh? I understood she'd forgotten to take her meds, but that was all I understood.

Aphrodite didn't give me time to say anything. With one last, weirdly warm smile, she knocked on the door.

"Come on in!" called a perky voice with an Okie accent.

Aphrodite opened the door.

"Hi y'all! Ohmygosh, come on in." With a huge grin, my new roomie, also a blonde, rushed up like a little countrified tornado. But the instant she saw Aphrodite, her grin slid from her face and she stopped hurrying toward us.

"I brought your new roommate to you." There was nothing technically wrong with Aphrodite's words, but her tone was hateful and she was putting on a terrible, fake Oklahoma accent. "Stevie Rae Johnson, this is Zoey Redbird. Zoey Redbird, this is Stevie Rae Johnson. There, now ain't we all nice and cozy like three little corns on a cob?"

I glanced at Stevie Rae. She looked like a terrified little rabbit.

"Thanks for showing me up here, Aphrodite." I talked quickly, moving toward Aphrodite, who automatically stepped back, which put her out in the hall again. "See you around." I closed the door on her as her look of surprise was just beginning to change to anger. Then I turned to Stevie Rae, who was still pale.

"What's with her?" I asked.

"She's . . . she's . . . ,"

Even though I didn't know her at all, I could tell that Stevie Rae was struggling with how much she should or shouldn't say. So I decided to help her. I mean, we were going to be roommates. "She's a bitch!" I said.

Stevie Rae's eyes went round, and then she giggled. "She's not very nice, that's for sure."

"She needs pharmaceutical help, *that's* for sure," I added, making her laugh some more.

"I think we're gonna get along just fine, Zoey Redbird," she said, still smiling. "Welcome to your new home!" She stepped aside and made a sweeping arm gesture at the little room, like she was ushering me into a palace.

I looked around and blinked. Several times. The first thing I saw was the life-sized Kenny Chesney poster that hung over one of the two beds and the cowboy (cowgirl?) hat that rested on one of the bedside tables—the one that also had the old-fashioned-looking gas lamp with the base shaped like a cowboy boot. Oh, nu uh. Stevie Rae was a total Okie!

Then she shocked me with a big hello hug, reminding me of a cute puppy with her short, curly hair and her smiling round face. "Zoey, I'm so glad you're feelin' better! I was so worried when I heard you'd hurt yourself. I'm really glad you're finally here."

"Thanks," I said, still staring around what was now my room, too, feeling totally overwhelmed and weirdly on the edge of tears again.

"It's kinda scary, isn't it?" Stevie Rae was watching me with big, serious blue eyes that were filled with sympathetic tears. I nodded, not trusting my voice.

"I know. I cried the whole first night."

I swallowed back my own tears and asked, "How long have you been here?"

"Three months. And, man, I was glad when they told me I was getting a roommate!"

"You knew I was coming?"

She nodded vigorously. "Oh, yeah! Neferet told me day before yesterday that the Tracker had sensed you and was going to Mark you. I thought you'd be here yesterday, but then I heard that you'd had an accident and been brought to the clinic. What happened?"

I shrugged and said, "I was looking for my grandma and I fell and hit my head." I wasn't getting the weird feeling that told me to keep my mouth shut, but I wasn't sure how much I should say to Stevie Rae yet, and I was relieved when she nodded as though she understood and didn't ask any more questions about the accident—or mention my weird colored-in Mark.

"Your parents freaked when you got Marked?"

"Totally. Didn't yours?"

"Actually, my mama was okay with it. She said anything that got me out of Henrietta was a good thing."

"Henrietta, Oklahoma?" I asked, glad to move to a subject that was not all about me.

"Sadly, yes."

Stevie Rae flopped down on the bed in front of the Kenny Chesney poster and motioned for me to sit on the one across the room from her. I did, and then felt a little jolt of surprise when I realized that I was sitting on my cool hot-pink and green Ralph Lauren comforter from home. I looked at the little oak end table and blinked. There was my annoying, ugly alarm clock, nerdy glasses for when I'm sick of wearing my contacts, and the picture of Grandma and me from last summer. And in the bookshelves behind the computer on my side of the room I saw my Gossip Girls and Bubbles series books (along with some of my other favorites, including Bram Stoker's *Dracula*—which was more than a little ironic), some CDs, my laptop, and—*oh my dear sweet lord*—my *Monsters Inc.* figurines. *How incredibly embarrassing.* My backpack was sitting on the floor next to my bed.

"Your grandma brought your stuff up here. She's really nice," Stevie Rae said.

"She's more than nice. She's brave as hell to have faced my mom and her stupid husband to get this stuff for me. I can only imagine the overly dramatic scene my mom caused." I sighed and then shook my head.

"Yeah, I guess I'm lucky. At least my mama was cool about all of this," Stevie Rae pointed to the outline of the crescent moon on her forehead. "Even if my daddy lost every bit of his mind, me being his only 'baby girl' and all." She shrugged and then giggled. "My three brothers thought it was awesome and wanted to know if I could help them get vampyre chicks." She rolled her eyes. "Stupid boys."

"Stupid boys," I echoed and smiled at her. If she thought boys were stupid she and I would get along fine.

"Mostly now I'm okay with all of this. I mean, the classes are weird but I like them—especially the Tae Kwan Do class. I kinda like to kick butt." She grinned mischievously, like a little blonde elf. "I like the uniforms, which totally shocked me at first. I mean, would anyone expect to *like* school uniforms? But we can add stuff to them and make them unique, so they don't look like typical stuck-up, boring school uniforms. And there are some seriously hot guys here—even if boys are stupid." Her eyes sparkled. "Mostly I'm just so darn glad to be out of Henrietta that I don't mind all the other stuff, even if Tulsa is kinda scary because it's so big."

"Tulsa isn't scary," I said automatically. Unlike too many kids from our suburb of Broken Arrow, I actually knew my way around Tulsa, thanks to what Grandma liked to call "field-tripping" with her. "You just have to know where to go. There's a great bead gallery where you can make your own jewelry downtown on Brady Street, and next door to that is Lola's at the Bowery—she has the best desserts in town. Cherry Street is cool, too. We're not far from there now. Actually, we're right by the awesome Philbrook Museum and Utica Square. There's some excellent shopping there and—"

I suddenly realized what I was saying. Did vampyre kids get to mingle with regular kids? I searched my memory. No. I'd never seen kids with crescent moon outlines hanging around the Philbrook or Utica's Gap or Banana Republic or Starbucks. I'd never seen them at the movies. Hell! I'd never even *seen* a vampyre kid before today. So would they keep us locked up here for four years? Feeling a little short of breath and claustrophobic I asked, "Do we ever get out of here?"

"Yeah, but there are all sorts of rules you have to follow."

"Rules? Like what?"

"Well, you can't wear any part of the school uniform—" She broke off suddenly. "Shoot! That reminds me. We have to hurry. Dinner is in a few minutes and you need to change." She jumped up and started to rummage through the closet that was on my side of the room, chattering at me from over her shoulder the whole time. "Neferet had some clothes delivered here last night. Don't worry about the sizes not being right. Somehow they always know what size we'll be before they actually see us—it's kinda freaky how the adult vamps know way more than they should. Anyway, don't be scared. I was serious before when I said the uniforms aren't as awful as you'd think they'd be. You really can add your own stuff to them—like me."

I looked at her. I mean, really looked at her. She was wearing a pair of honest-to-God Roper jeans. You know, the kind those ag-kids wear that are way too tight and have no back pockets. How anyone could think no back pockets and tightness was cute, I'd honestly never understand. Stevie Rae was totally skinny, and the jeans even made her butt look wide. I knew before I looked at the girl's feet what she'd be wearing—cowboy boots. I glanced down and sighed. Yep. Brown leather, flat-heeled, pointy-tipped cowboy boots. Tucked into her countrified jeans was a black, long-sleeved cotton blouse that had the expensive look of something you'd find at Saks or Neiman Marcus, versus the cheaper see-through shirts that overpriced Abercrombie tries to make us believe aren't slutty. When she glanced over at me I saw that she had double-pierced ears with little silver hoops in them. She turned and held out in one hand a black blouse like the one she had on, and a pullover sweater in another, and I decided that even though the country look wasn't for me she was kinda cute with her mixture of hayseed and chic.

"Here ya go! Just throw these on over your jeans and we'll be ready."

The flickering light from the cowboy-boot lamp caught on a streak of silver embroidery that was on the breast of the sweater she was holding out. I got up and took the two shirts, holding the sweater up so I could see the front of it better. The silver embroidery was in the shape of a spiral that glittered around and around in a delicate circle that would rest over my heart.

"It's our sign," Stevie Rae said.

"Our sign?"

"Yeah, each class—here they call them third formers, fourth formers, fifth formers, and sixth formers—has their own sign. We're third formers, so our sign is the silver labyrinth of the Goddess Nyx."

"What does it mean?" I asked, more to myself than to her as I traced my finger around the sliver circles.

"It stands for our new beginning as we start walking the Path of Night and learn the ways of the Goddess and the possibilities of our new life."

I looked up at her, surprised that she suddenly sounded so serious. She grinned a little shyly at me and shrugged her shoulders. "It one of the first things you learn in Vampyre Sociology 101. That's the class Neferet teaches, and it sure beats the heck outta the boring classes I was taking at Henrietta High, home of the fighting hens. Ugh. Fighting hens! What kind of a mascot is that?" She shook her head and rolled her eyes while I laughed. "Anyway, I heard Neferet is your mentor, which is really lucky. She hardly takes on any new kids, and besides being High Priestess, she's way the coolest teacher here."

What she didn't say was that I'm not just lucky, I'm "special" with my weird colored-in Mark. Which reminded me . . .

"Stevie Rae, why haven't you asked me about my Mark? I

mean, I appreciate you not bombarding me with a hundred questions, but all the way up here everyone who saw me stared at my Mark. Aphrodite mentioned it almost the second we were alone. You haven't even really looked at it. Why?"

Then she did finally look at my forehead before she shrugged and met my eyes again. "You're my roommate. I figured you'd tell me what was up with it when you were ready. One thing growing up in a small town like Henrietta taught me is that it's best to mind your own business if you want someone to stay your friend. Well, we're gonna be rooming together for four years . . ." She paused and in the gap between words sat the big, ugly unsaid truth that we'd be roommates for four years only if both of us survived the Change. Stevie Rae swallowed hard and finished in a rush, "I guess what I'm trying to say is that I want us to be friends."

I smiled at her. She looked so young and hopeful—so nice and normal and not at all what I imagined a vampyre kid would be. I felt a little stirring of hope. Maybe I could find a way to fit in here. "I want to be friends, too."

"Yea for that!" I swear she looked like a wriggly puppy again. "But come on! Hurry—we don't want to be late."

She gave me a shove toward a door that sat between the two closets before she hurried over to a makeup mirror on her computer desk and started brushing at her short hair. I ducked inside to find a tiny bathroom, and quickly pulled off my BA Tigers T-shirt and put on the cotton blouse and over it the silk knit sweater that was a deep, pretty shade of purple with little black plaid lines going through it. I was just getting ready to go back into the room to grab my backpack so I could try to fix my face and hair with the makeup and stuff I'd brought, when I glanced in the mirror over the sink. My face was still white, but it had lost the scary, unhealthy paleness it had earlier. My hair looked insane, all wild and uncombed, and I could faintly see the slim line of dark stitches just above my left temple. But it was the sapphire-colored Mark that caught my eyes. While I stared at it, entranced by its exotic beauty, the bathroom light caught the silver labyrinth embroidered over my heart. I decided that the two symbols somehow matched, even though they were different shapes . . . different colors . . .

But did I match them? And did I match this strange new world?

I squeezed my eyes shut tightly and hoped desperately that whatever we were eating for dinner (oh, please let there not be any blood-drinking involved) wouldn't disagree with my already screwed-up, nervous stomach.

"Oh, no . . ." I whispered to myself, "it would be just my luck to get a raging case of diarrhea."

CHAPTER NINE

—

Okay, the cafeteria was cool—oops, I mean "dining hall," as the silver plaque outside the entrance proclaimed. It was nothing at all like SIHS's freezing cold monstrous cafeteria where the acoustics were so bad that even though I sat right next to Kayla I couldn't hear what she was babbling at me half the time. This room was warm and friendly. The walls were made of the same weird mixture of jutting bricks and black rock as the exterior of the building and the room was filled with heavy wooden picnic tables that had matching benches with padded seats and backs. Each table sat about six kids and radiated out from a large, unoccupied table situated at the center of the room that was practically overflowing with fruit and cheese and meat, and a crystal goblet that was filled with something that looked suspiciously like red wine. (Huh? Wine at school? What?) The ceiling was low and the rear wall was made up of windows with a glass door in the center. Heavy burgundy velvet drapes were pulled open so that I could see outside to a beautiful little courtyard with stone benches, winding paths, and ornamental bushes and flowers. In the middle of the courtyard was a marble fountain with water spouting from the top of something that looked an awful lot like a pineapple. It was very pretty, especially lit up by the moonlight and the occasional antique gaslight.

Most of the tables were already filled with eating, talking kids who glanced up with obvious curiosity when Stevie Rae and I entered the room. I took a deep breath and held my head high. Might as well give them a clear view of the Mark they all seemed so obsessed with. Stevie Rae led me to the side of the room that had the typical cafeteria servers handing out food from behind buffet-style glass thingies.

"What's the table in the middle of the room for?" I asked as we walked.

"It's the symbolic offering to the Goddess Nyx. There's always a place set at that table for her. It seems kinda weird at first, but pretty soon it won't seem so weird and it'll feel right to you."

Actually, it didn't seem that weird to me. In a way, it made sense. The Goddess was so alive here. Her Mark was everywhere. Her statue stood proudly in front of her Temple. I was also starting to notice all over the school little pictures and figurines that represented her. Her High Priestess was my mentor and, I had to admit to myself, I already felt connected to Nyx. With an effort, I stopped myself from touching the Mark on my forehead. Instead I grabbed a tray and moved behind Stevie Rae in line.

"Don't worry," she whispered to me. "The food's real good. They don't make you drink blood or eat raw meat or anything like that."

Relieved, I unclenched my jaws. Most of the kids were already eating, so the line was short, and as Stevie Rae and I got up to the food I felt my mouth start to water. Spaghetti! I sniffed deeply: *with garlic!*

"That whole vampyres can't stand garlic thing is total bullshit—pardon my French," Stevie Rae was saying under her breath to me as we loaded up our plates.

"Okay, what about that whole vampyres have to drink blood thing?" I whispered back.

"Not," she said softly.

"Not?"

"Not bullshit."

Great. Wonderful. Fantastic. Just exactly what I wanted to hear—*not*.

Trying not to think about blood and whatnot I got a glass of tea with Stevie Rae, and then followed her to a table where two other kids were already talking animatedly while they ate. Of course the conversation totally stopped when I joined them, which didn't seem to faze Stevie Rae at all. As I slid into the booth opposite her she made introductions in her Okie twang.

"Hey, y'all. Meet my new roommate, Zoey Redbird. Zoey, this is Erin Bates," she pointed to the ridiculously pretty blonde sitting on my side of the table. (Well, hell—how many pretty blondes could one school have? Isn't there some kind of limit?) Still in her matter-of-fact Okie voice, she went on, making little air quotes for emphasis. "Erin is 'the pretty one.' She's also funny and smart and has more shoes than anyone I've ever known."

Erin pulled her blue eyes away from staring at my Mark long enough to say a quick "Hi."

"And this is the token guy in our group, Damien Maslin. But he's gay, so I don't really think he counts as a guy."

Instead of getting pissed at Stevie Rae, Damien looked serene and unruffled. "Actually, since I'm gay I think I should count for two guys instead of just one. I mean, in me you get the male point of view *and* you don't have to worry about me wanting to touch your boobies."

He had a smooth face that was totally zit free, and dark brown hair and eyes that reminded me of a baby deer. Actually, he was cute. Not in the overly girly way so many teenage guys are when they decide to come out and tell everyone what everyone already knew (well, everyone except their typically clueless and/or in-denial parents). Damien wasn't a swishy girly-guy; he was just a cute kid with a likable smile. He was also noticeably trying not to stare at my Mark, which I appreciated.

"Well, maybe you're right. I hadn't really thought about it like that," Stevie Rae said through a big bite of garlic bread.

"Just ignore her, Zoey. The rest of us are almost normal," Damien said. "And we're desperately glad you finally got here. Stevie Ray's been driving everyone crazy wondering what you'd be like, when you'd get here—"

"If you'd be one of those freaky kids who smell bad and think being a vampyre means seeing who can be the biggest loser," Erin interrupted.

"Or wondering if you'd be one of *them*," Damien said, cutting his eyes at a table to our left.

I followed his gaze and felt a zap of nerves when I recognized who he was talking about. "You mean Aphrodite?"

"Yeah," Damien said. "And her stuck-up flock of sycophants."

Huh? I blinked at him.

Stevie Rae sighed. "You'll get used to Damien's vocabulary obsession. Thankfully, this isn't a new word so some of us actually know what he's talking about without having to beg him for a translation. Again. Sycophant—a servile flatterer," she twanged proudly like she was giving an answer in English class.

"Whatever. They make me want to retch," Erin said without looking up from her spaghetti.

"They?" I asked.

"The Dark Daughters," Stevie Rae said, and I noticed she automatically lowered her voice.

"Think of them like a sorority," Damien said.

"Of hags from hell," Erin said.

"Hey, y'all, I don't think we should prejudice Zoey against them. She might get along okay with them."

"Fuck that. They're hags from hell," Erin said.

"Watch that mouth, Er Bear. You have to eat out of it," Damien said a little primly.

Incredibly relieved that none of them liked Aphrodite, I was just getting ready to ask for more of an explanation when a girl rushed up and, with a big huff, slid herself and her tray into the booth beside Stevie Rae. She was the color of cappuccino (the kind you get from real coffee shops and not the nasty, too-sweet stuff you get from Quick Trip) and all curvy with pouty lips and high cheekbones that made her look like an African princess. She also had some seriously good hair. It was thick and fell in dark, glossy waves around her shoulders. Her eyes were so black they looked like they didn't have any pupils.

"Okay, please! Just please. Did *nobody*," she stared pointedly at Erin, "think to bother to wake me the hell up and tell me that we were going to dinner?"

"I do believe I'm your roommate, not your mamma," Erin said lazily.

"Do *not* make me cut that Jessica Simpson look-alike blond hair of yours off in the middle of the night," the African princess said.

"Actually, the consuetudinary way to phrase that would be 'Do not make me cut that Jessica Simpson look-alike blond hair of yours off in the middle of the day.' Technically day is night for us and so night would be day. Time is reversed here."

The black girl narrowed her eyes at him. "Damien, you are getting on my damn last nerve what that vocab shit."

"Shaunee," Stevie Rae broke in hastily. "My roommate finally got here. This is Zoey Redbird. Zoey, this is Erin's roommate, Shaunee Cole."

"Hi," I said through a mouthful of spaghetti when Shaunee turned from glaring at Erin to me.

"So, Zoey, what's up with your Mark being colored in? You're still a fledgling, aren't you?" Everyone at the table was shocked silent by Shaunee's question. She looked around. "What? Do not pretend that every last one of you isn't wondering the same thing."

"We might be, but we also might be polite enough not to ask," Stevie Rae said firmly.

"Oh, please. Whatever." She shrugged off Stevie Rae's protest. "This is too important for that. Everyone wants to know about her Mark. There's no time to play games when good gossip is involved." Shaunee turned back to me. "So, what's up with the weird Mark?"

Might as well face this now. I took a quick drink of tea to clear my throat. All four of them were staring at me, waiting impatiently for my answer.

"Well, I'm still a fledgling. I don't think I'm any different than the rest of you." Then I blurted something that I'd been considering while everyone else had been talking. I mean, I knew that I was going to have to answer this question eventually. I'm not stupid—confused, maybe, but not stupid—and my gut told me I needed to say something besides the real story about my out-of-body experience with Nyx. "I don't actually know for sure why my Mark is filled in. It wasn't that way when the Tracker first Marked me. But later that day I had an accident. I fell and hit my head. When I woke up the Mark was like it is now. I've been thinking about it, and all I can come up with is that it must have happened as some kind of reaction to my accident. I was unconscious and I lost a lot of blood. Maybe that did something to speed up the darkening-in process. That's my guess, anyway."

"Huh," Shaunee huffed. "I was hoping it'd be somethin' more interesting. Something good and gossipy."

"Sorry . . . ," I muttered.

"Careful, Twin," Erin said to Shaunee, jerking her head at the

Dark Daughters. "You're starting to sound like you should sit over at that table."

Shaunee's face twisted. "I wouldn't be caught undead with those bitches."

"You're confusing the crap outta Zoey," Stevie Rae said.

Damien gave a long-suffering sigh. "I'll explain, proving once again how valuable I am to this group, penis or no penis."

"I really wish you wouldn't use the P-word," Stevie Rae said. "Especially when I'm trying to eat."

"I like it," Erin chimed in. "If everyone called things what they are we'd all be a lot less confused. For instance, you know when I have to go to the bathroom I state the obvious—I have urine that needs to come out of my urethra. Simple. Easy. Clear."

"Disgusting. Gross. Crude," Stevie Rae said.

"I'm with you, Twin," Shaunee said. "I mean, if we talked plainly about things like urination and menstruation and such, life would be much simpler."

"Okay. Enough with the menstruation talk while we're eating spaghetti." Damien held up a hand like he could physically stop the conversation. "I may be gay, but there's only so much even I can handle." He leaned toward me and launched into his explanation. "First, Shaunee and Erin call each other Twin because even though they are *clearly* not related—Erin being an extremely white girl from Tulsa, and Shaunee being of Jamaican descent and a lovely mocha color from Connecticut—"

"Thank you for appreciating my blackness," Shaunee said.

"Don't mention it," Damien said, and then continued smoothly with his explanation. "Even though they aren't related by blood they are freakishly alike."

"It's like they were separated at birth or something," Stevie Rae said.

At the same moment Erin and Shaunee grinned at each other and shrugged. It was then that I noticed they were wearing the same outfit—dark jeans jackets with beautiful golden wings embroidered on the breast pockets, black T-shirts, and low-riding black slacks. They even had on the same earrings—huge gold hoops.

"We have the same shoe size," Erin said, sticking out her foot so we could see that she was wearing pointy-toed black leather stiletto boots.

"And what's a little melanin difference when a truly soul-deep love of shoes is involved?" Lifting up her foot Shaunee showed off another great pair of boots—only these were smooth black leather with sharp silver buckles across the ankles.

"Next!" Damien cut in, rolling his eyes. "The Dark Daughters. The short version is that they're a group made up of mostly up-perclassmen who say that they are in charge of school spirit and such."

"No, the short version is that they're hags from hell," Shaunee said.

"That's exactly what I said, Twin," Erin laughed.

"You two aren't helping," Damien told them. "Now, where was I?"

"School spirit and such," I prompted.

"That's right. Yeah, they're supposed to be this great, pro-school, pro-vamp organization. Also, it is assumed that their leader is being groomed to be a High Priestess, so she's supposed to be the heart, mind, and spirit of the school—as well as a future leader in vamp society, et cetera, et cetera, blah, blah. Think National Merit Scholar in charge of the Honor Society mixed with cheerleaders and band fags."

"Hey, isn't it disrespectful to your gayness to call them band fags?" Stevie Rae asked.

"I'm using the word as a term of endearment," Damien said.

"And football players—don't forget there are Dark Sons, too," Erin said.

"Uh-huh, Twin. It is truly a crime and a shame that such seriously hot young lads get sucked in—"

"And she does mean that literally," said Erin with a naughty grin.

"By hags from hell," concluded Shaunee.

"Hello! Like I would forget the boys? I just keep getting interrupted."

The three girls gave him apologetic smiles. Stevie Rae pantomimed zipping her lips shut and throwing away the key. Erin and Shaunee mouthed "dork" at her, but they stayed quiet so Damien could finish.

I noticed that they'd played with the word "sucked," making me think that the little scene I'd witnessed hadn't been too unusual.

"But what the Dark Daughters really are is a group of stuck-up bitches who get off on lording power over everyone else. They want everyone to follow them, to conform to their freaky ideas of what it means to become a vamp. Most of all, they hate humans, and if you don't feel the same they don't want shit to do with you."

"Except to give you a hard time," Stevie Rae added. I could tell from her expression that she must have firsthand knowledge about the "hard time" part, and I remembered how pale and scared she'd looked when Aphrodite had shown me to our room. I made a mental note to remember to ask her later about what had happened.

"Don't let them scare you, though," Damien said. "Just watch your back around them and—"

"Hello, Zoey. Nice to see you again so soon."

I didn't have any trouble recognizing her voice this time. I decided it was like honey—slick and too darn sweet. Everyone at the table jumped, including me. She was wearing a sweater like mine, except that over her heart was embroidered the silver silhouette of three goddess-like women, one of them holding what looked like a pair of scissors. She had on a *very* short pleated black skirt, black tights that had silver sparkles in them, and knee-high black boots. Two girls were standing behind her, dressed in much the same way. One was black, with impossibly long hair (must be a really good weave), and the other was yet another blonde (who, on closer inspection of her brows, was probably, I decided, as much a natural blonde as I am).

"Hello, Aphrodite," I said when everyone else seemed too shocked to speak.

"Hope I'm not interrupting anything," she said insincerely.

"You're not. We were just discussing the trash that needs to be taken out tonight," Erin said with a big, fake smile.

"Well, you would certainly know about that," she said with a sneer, and then purposefully turned her back on Erin, who was curling her fists and looking as if she might leap over the table at Aphrodite. "Zoey, I should have said something to you earlier, but I guess it just slipped my mind. I want to issue an invitation for you to join the Dark Daughters in our own private Full Moon Ritual tomorrow night. I know it's unusual for someone who hasn't been here long to take part in a ritual so soon, but your Mark has clearly shown that you're, well, different than the average fledgling." She looked down her perfect nose at Stevie Rae. "I've already mentioned it to Neferet, and she agrees that it would be good for you to join us. I'll give you the details later, when you're not so busy with . . . uh . . . *trash.*" She gave the rest of the table her tight-lipped, sarcastic smile, flipped her long hair, and she and her entourage flitted off.

"Hag bitches from hell," Shaunee and Erin said together.

CHAPTER TEN

—

"I keep thinking that hubris is eventually going to bring Aphrodite down," Damien said.

"Hubris," Stevie Rae explained, "having godlike arrogance."

"I actually know that one," I said, still staring after Aphrodite and her mob. "We just finished reading *Medea* in English class. It's what brought Jason down."

"I'd love to knock the hubris right out of her bobble head," Erin said.

"I'll hold her for you, Twin," Shaunee said.

"No! Y'all know we've talked about this before. The penalty for fighting is bad. Really bad. It's not worth it."

I watched Erin and Shaunee pale at the same time and wanted to ask what could be so bad, but Stevie Rae went on talking, this time to me.

"Just be careful, Zoey. The Dark Daughters, and especially Aphrodite, can seem almost okay at times, and that's when they're most dangerous."

I shook my head. "Oh, nu uh. I'm not going to their full moon thing."

"I think you have to," Damien said softly.

"Neferet okayed it," Stevie Rae said as Erin and Shaunee nodded in agreement. "That means she'll expect you to go. You can't tell your mentor no."

"Especially when your mentor is Neferet, High Priestess of Nyx," Damien said.

"Can't I just say that I'm not ready for . . . for . . . whatever it is they want me to do, and ask Neferet if I can be—I dunno, what would you call it—excused from their full moon thingie this time?"

"Well, you could, but then Neferet would tell the Dark Daughters and they'd think that you're scared of them."

I thought about the major crap that had already passed between Aphrodite and me in such a short time. "Uh, Stevie Rae, I might already be scared of them."

"Don't ever let them know." Stevie Rae looked down at her plate, trying to hide her embarrassment. "That's worse than standing up to them."

"Honey," Damien said, patting Stevie Rae's hand, "stop beating yourself up about that."

Stevie Rae gave Damien a sweet, thank-you smile. Then she said to me, "Just go. Be strong and go. They won't do anything too awful at the ritual. It's here on campus; they wouldn't dare."

"Yeah, they do all their bad bullshit away from here, where it's harder for the vamps to catch them," Shaunee said. "Around here they pretend to be all sickeningly sweet so no one knows what they're really like."

"No one except us," Erin said, sweeping out her hand so that she included not just our little group, but everyone else in the room, too.

"I don't know, y'all, maybe Zoey will actually get along with some of them okay," Stevie Rae said without any touch of sarcasm or jealousy.

I shook my head. "Nope. I won't get along with them. I don't like their kind—the kind of people who try to control others and make them look bad just to feel better about themselves. And I don't want to go to their Full Moon Ritual!" I said firmly, thinking about my stepfather and his buddies, and how ironic it was that they seemed to have so much in common with a group of teenagers who called themselves the daughters of a goddess.

"I'd go with you if I could—any of us would—but unless you're one of the Dark Daughters you can only get in if you're invited," Stevie Rae said sadly.

"That's okay. I'll—I'll just deal with it." Suddenly I wasn't hungry anymore. I was just very, very tired, and I really wanted to change the subject. "So explain to me about the different symbols you wear here. You told me about ours—Nyx's spiral. Damien has a spiral, too, so that must mean he's a . . ." I paused to remember what Stevie Rae had called freshmen, "a third former. But Erin and Shaunee have wings, and Aphrodite had something else."

"You mean besides that cob stuck straight up her skinny anus?" Erin muttered.

"She means the three Fates," Damien interjected, beating Shaunee to whatever she was going to add. "The three Fates are children of Nyx. The sixth formers all wear the emblem of the Fates, with Atropos holding scissors to symbolize the end of school."

"And for some of us, the end of life," Erin added gloomily.

That shut everyone up. When I couldn't stand the uncomfortable silence anymore I cleared my throat and said, "So what about Erin and Shaunee's wings?"

"The wings of Eros, who is the child of Nyx's seed—"

"The *love* god," Shaunee said, adding a seated gyration of her hips.

Damien frowned at her and kept talking. "The golden wings of Eros are the fourth formers' symbol."

"'Cause we're the *love* class," Erin sang, raising her arms over her head and shimmying her hips.

"Actually, it's because we're supposed to be reminded of Nyx's capacity to love, and the wings symbolize our continuous movement forward."

"What's the symbol for fifth formers?" I asked.

"Nyx's golden chariot pulling a trail of stars," Damien said.

"I think it's the prettiest of the four symbols," Stevie Rae said. "Those stars sparkle like crazy."

"The chariot shows that we continue on Nyx's journey. The stars represent the magic of the two years that have already passed."

"Damien, you are a good little student," Erin said.

"I told you we should have gotten him to help us study for the human mythology test," Shaunee said.

"I thought *I* told *you* we needed his help, and—"

"Anyway," Damien shouted over their bickering, "that's about all there is to the four symbols of the classes. Easy-peasy, really," he looked pointedly at the now silent Twins. "That is, if you pay attention in class instead of writing notes and staring at guys you think are cute."

"You're really prudey, Damien," Shaunee said.

"Especially for a gay boy," Erin added.

"Erin, your hair's looking kinda frizzy today. Not to be mean or anything, but maybe you should think about switching products. You can't be too careful about those kinds of things. The next thing you know you'll be getting split ends."

Erin's blue eyes got huge and her hand went automatically to her hair.

"Oh, no no no. I do not believe you just said that, Damien. You know how crazy she is about her hair." Shaunee started to puff up like a mocha-colored blowfish.

Damien, meanwhile, just smiled and returned to his spaghetti—the perfect picture of innocence.

"Uh, y'all," Stevie Rae said quickly, standing up and pulling me with her by the elbow. "Zoey looks beat. Y'all remember what it was like when you first got here. We're going to go back to our room. I have to study for that vamp sociology test, so I probably won't see you until tomorrow."

"Okay, see ya," Damien said. "Zoey, it was really nice to meet you."

"Yeah, welcome to Hell High," Erin and Shaunee said together before Stevie Rae pulled me out of the room.

"Thanks. I really am tired," I told Stevie Rae as we backtracked through a hall that I was happy to recognize as the one that would lead to the main entrance to the central school building. We paused while a sleek, silver-gray cat chased a smaller, harassed-looking tabby across the hall in front of us.

"Beelzebub! Leave Cammy alone! Damien is going to rip your fur out!"

Stevie Rae made a grab for the gray cat and missed, but he did stop chasing the tabby and instead streaked back down the hall the way we had just come. Stevie Rae was frowning after him.

"Shaunee and Erin need to teach that cat of theirs some manners; he's always up to something." She glanced at me as we left the building and walked out into the soft, pre-dawn darkness. "That cute little Cameron is Damien's cat. Beelzebub belongs to Erin and Shaunee; he chose both of them—together. Yep. It's as strange as it sounds, but after a little while you'll be like the rest of us and start thinking that they must really be twins."

"They seem nice, though."

"Oh, they're great. They bicker a lot, but they're totally loyal and will never let anyone talk about you." She grinned. "Okay, *they* might talk about you, but that's different, and it won't be behind your back."

"And I really like Damien."

"Damien's sweet, and really smart. I just feel bad for him sometimes, though."

"How come?"

"Well, he had a roommate when he first got here about six months ago, but as soon as the guy found out Damien was gay—hello, it's not like the boy tries to hide it—he complained to Neferet and said he wasn't going to room with a fag."

I grimaced. I can't stand homophobes. "And Neferet actually put up with that attitude?"

"No, she made it clear that the kid—oh, he changed his name to Thor after he got here"—she shook her head and rolled her eyes—"doesn't that just figure? Anyway, Neferet let it be known that Thor was way out of line, and she gave Damien the option of moving into another room by himself or staying with Thor. Damien chose to move. I mean, wouldn't you?"

I nodded. "Yep. No way would I room with Thor the Homophobe."

"That's what we all think, too. So Damien has been in a room by himself since then."

"Aren't there any other gay kids here?"

Stevie Rae shrugged. "There're a few girls who are lesbians and totally out, but even though a couple of them are cool and hang with the rest of us they mostly stick together. They're way into the religious aspect of Goddess worship and spend most of their time in Nyx's Temple. And, of course, there are the moronic party girls who think it's cool to make out with each other, but usually only if some cute guys are watching."

I shook my head. "You know, I've never understood why girls

think making out with each other is the way to catch a boyfriend. You'd think it would be counterproductive."

"Like I want a boyfriend who only thinks I'm hot when I'm kissing some girl? Bleck."

"What about gay guys?"

Stevie sighed. "There are a few besides Damien, but they're mostly too weird and girly for him. I feel bad for him. I think he gets pretty lonely. His parents don't write or anything."

"The whole vampyre thing freaked them out?"

"No, they didn't really care about that. Actually, don't say anything to Damien because it hurts his feelings, but I think they were relieved when he was Marked. They didn't know what to do with a son who is gay."

"Why did they have to *do* anything? He's still their son. He just likes guys."

"Well, they live in Dallas, and his dad is big into the People of Faith. I think he's some kind of minister or something—"

I held up my hand. "Stop. You don't have to say another word. I totally get it." And I did. I was way too acquainted with the narrow-minded, "our way is the only right way" ideas of the People of Faith. Even thinking about it made me feel exhausted and depressed.

Stevie Rae opened the door to the dorm. The living-room area was empty except for a few girls who were watching *That '70s Show* reruns. Stevie Rae waved absently at them.

"Hey, do you want a pop or something to take upstairs with us?"

I nodded and followed her through the living room and into a smaller room off to the side that had four refrigerators, a big sink, two microwaves, lots of cabinets, and a pretty white wooden table that sat in the middle of it—just like a regular kitchen, only this one was weirdly refrigerator-friendly. Everything was neat and clean. Stevie Rae opened one of the fridges. I peeked over her shoulder to see that it was filled with all kinds of drinks—everything from pop to lots of juices and that fizzy water that tastes nasty.

"What do you want?"

"Any brown pop is fine," I said.

"This stuff is for all of us," she said as she handed me two Diet Cokes and grabbed two Frescas for herself. "There're fruit and veggies and stuff like that in those two fridges, and lean meat for sandwiches in the other one. They're kept full all the time, but the vamps are pretty obsessed with us eating healthy, so you won't find bags of chips or Twinkies or stuff like that."

"No chocolate?"

"Yeah, there's some really expensive chocolate in the cabinets. The vamps say chocolate in moderation is good for us."

Okay, so who the hell wants to eat chocolate in moderation? I kept the thought to myself as we walked back through the living room and headed upstairs to our room.

"So the, uh, vamps"—I kinda stumbled over the word—"are big on healthy eating?"

"Well, yeah, but I think basically just fledglings eating healthy. I mean, you don't see fat vamps, but you also don't see them chewing on celery and carrots and picking at salads. Mostly they eat together in their own dining room, and rumor has it that they eat well." She glanced at me and lowered her voice. "I heard that they eat a lot of red meat. A lot of *rare* red meat."

"Eeesh," I said, not liking the bizarre visual image I suddenly got of Neferet gnawing on a bloody steak.

Stevie Rae shivered, and went on: "Sometimes someone's mentor will sit with a fledgling at dinner, but they usually have just a glass or two of wine and don't eat with us."

Stevie Rae opened the door and with a sigh I sat on my bed and pulled off my shoes. God, I was tired. Rubbing my feet I wondered about why the adult vamps didn't eat with us, and then I decided I didn't really want to think about that long. I mean, it brought to mind too many questions like what are they really eating? And what will I have to eat when/if I become an adult vamp? Ugh.

And, part of my brain whispered that it also made me remember my reaction to Heath's blood yesterday. Had that been only yesterday? And also my more recent response to the blood of that guy in the hall. No. I definitely didn't want to think about either of them—at all. So I quickly refocused on the healthy-diet issue.

"Okay, they don't particularly care about eating healthy, so what's the big obsession with us eating healthy?" I asked Stevie Rae.

She met my eyes, looking worried and more than a little scared.

"They want us to eat healthy for the same reason they make us exercise every day—so that our bodies are as strong as possible, because if you start getting weak or fat or sick, that's the first sign that your body is rejecting the Change."

"And then you die," I said quietly.

"And then you die," she agreed.

CHAPTER ELEVEN

—

I didn't think I'd sleep. I figured I'd lay there and miss home and think about the bizarre twist my life had taken. Disturbing flashes of the guy in the hall's eyes drifted through my mind, but I was so tired I couldn't focus. Even Aphrodite's psycho hatefulness was something else that seemed sleepily far away. Actually, my last worries before I could remember nothing else were about my forehead. Was it feeling sore again because of the Mark and the cut over my temple—or was it because I was getting a ginormic zit? And would my hair look okay for my first day of vamp school tomorrow? But as I curled up with my comforter and inhaled the familiar smell of down feathers and home, I felt unexpectedly safe and warm . . . and was totally out.

I didn't have a nightmare, either. Instead I dreamed about cats. Go figure. Hot boys? No. Cool new vampire powers? Of course not. Just cats. There was one in particular—a small orange tabby who had little tiny paws and a pot belly with a pouch that looked kinda marsupial. She kept yelling at me in an old lady's voice and asking what had taken me so long to get here. Then her cat voice changed to an annoying buzzing beeping sound and I . . .

"Zoey, come on! Turn that stupid alarm clock off!"

"Wha—, huh?" Oh, hell. I hate mornings. My hand flailed about trying to find the off switch of my annoying alarm clock.

Have I mentioned that I am totally, completely blind without my contacts? I grabbed my nerdy glasses and peeked at the time. Six thirty P.M., and I was just waking up. Talk about bizarre.

"Do you want to take a shower first, or do you want me to?" Stevie Rae asked sleepily.

"I will, if you don't care."

"I don't . . . ," She yawned.

" 'Kay."

"We should hurry, though, 'cause, I don't know about you, but I have to eat breakfast or I feel like I'm going to starve to death before lunch."

"Cereal?" I suddenly perked up. I seriously adore cereal, and have an I ♥ CEREAL shirt somewhere to prove it. I especially love Count Chocula—yet another vampyre irony.

"Yeah, there're always lots of those tiny boxes of cereal and bagels and fruit and hard-boiled eggs and stuff."

"I'll hurry." Suddenly I was starving. "Hey, Stevie Rae, does it matter what I wear?"

"Nope," she yawned again. "Just pick one of the sweaters or jackets that show our third former symbol and you'll be fine."

I did hurry, even though I was really nervous about not looking right and I wished I could take hours doing and redoing my hair and makeup. I used Stevie Rae's makeup mirror while she was in the shower, and decided that under-doing was probably a better choice than over-doing. It was weird how my Mark seemed to change the whole focus of my face. I've always had nice eyes—big and round and dark, with lots of lashes. So much that Kayla used to whine about how unfair it was that I had enough lashes for three girls and she only had short little blond ones. (Speaking of . . . I did miss Kayla, especially this morning as I was getting ready to go to a new school without her. Maybe I'd call her later. Or e-mail her. Or . . . I remembered the comment Heath had made about the party, and decided maybe not.) Anyway, the Mark somehow made my eyes look even bigger and darker. I lined them with a smoky black shadow that had little sparkly flecks of silver in it. Not heavily like those loser girls who think that plastering on black eyeliner makes them look cool. Yeah, *right*. They look like scary raccoons. I smudged the line, added mascara, brushed some bronzing power over my face, and put on lip gloss (to hide the fact that I'd been nervously picking at my lips).

Then I stared at myself.

Thankfully my hair was acting right, and even my weird widow's peak wasn't sticking all up crazily like it did sometimes. I still looked . . . umm . . . different, but the same. The effect my Mark had on my face hadn't faded. It made everything that was ethnic about my features stand out: the darkness of my eyes, my high Cherokee cheekbones, my proud, straight nose, and even the olive color of my skin that was like my grandma's. The sapphire Mark of the Goddess seemed to have flipped a switch and spotlighted those features; it had freed the Cherokee girl within me and allowed her to shine.

"Your hair looks great," Stevie Rae said as she came into the room toweling dry her short hair. "I wish mine would act right when it's long. It doesn't. It just frizzes out and looks like a horse's tail."

"I like your short hair," I said, moving out of her way and grabbing my cute sparkly black ballet flats.

"Yeah, well, it makes me a freak here. Everybody has long hair."

"I noticed, but I don't really get it."

"It's one of the things that happens while we're going through the Change. Vamps' hair grows abnormally fast, just like their fingernails."

I tried not to shudder as I remembered Aphrodite's fingernail slashing through jeans and skin.

Thankfully, Stevie Rae was oblivious to my thoughts, and kept on talking.

"You'll see. After a while you won't have to look at their symbols to know what year they are. Anyway, you'll learn all about that kind of stuff in Vamp Sociology class. Oh! That reminds me." She rifled through some papers on her desk until she found what she was looking for and handed it to me. "Here's your schedule. We have third hour and fifth hour together. And check out the list of electives you have for second hour. You can choose from any of them."

My name was at the top of the schedule, printed in bold letters, Zoey Redbird, Entering Third Former, as well as the date, which was five (?!) days before the Tracker had Marked me.

1st hour—Vampyre Sociology 101. Rm. 215. Prof. Neferet
2nd hour—Drama 101. Performing Arts Center. Prof. Nolan
or
Sketching 101. Rm. 312. Prof. Doner
or
Intro to Music. Rm. 314. Prof. Vento
3rd hour—Lit 101. Rm. 214. Prof. Penthesilea
4th hour—Fencing. Gymnasium. Prof. D. Lankford

LUNCH BREAK

5th hour—Spanish 101. Rm. 216. Prof. Garmy
6th hour—Intro to Equestrian Studies. Field House. Prof. Lenobia

"No geometry?" I blurted, totally overwhelmed by the schedule, but trying to keep a positive attitude.

"No, thankfully. Next semester we'll have to take economics, though. But that couldn't be as bad."

"Fencing? Intro to Equestrian Studies?"

"I told you they like to keep us in shape. Fencing's okay, even though it's hard. I'm not very good at it, but you do get paired with upperclassmen a lot—kind of like peer instructors, and I'm just sayin', some of those boys are just plain hot! I'm not taking the horse class this semester—they put me in Tae Kwan Do. And I have to tell ya, I love it!"

"Really?" I said doubtfully. *Wonder what the horse class would be like?*

"Yep. Which elective are you going to pick?"

I glanced back down the list. "Which one are you taking?"

"Intro to Music. Professor Vento is cool, and I, uh . . ." Stevie Rae grinned and blushed. "I want to be a country music star. I mean, Kenny Chesney, Faith Hill, and Shania Twain are all vamps—and that's just three of them. Heck, Garth Brooks grew up right here in Oklahoma and you know he's the biggest vamp of them all. So I don't see why I can't be one, too."

"Makes perfect sense to me," I said. *Why not?*

"You want to take music with me?"

"That'd be fun if I could sing or play anything resembling an instrument. I can't."

"Oh, well, maybe not then."

"Actually, I was thinking about the drama class. I was in drama at SIHS, and I liked it okay. Do you know anything about Prof. Nolan?"

"Yeah, she's from Texas and has a major accent, but she studied drama in New York and everyone likes her."

I almost laughed out loud when Stevie Rae mentioned Prof. Nolan's accent. The girl twanged so bad she sounded like an ad for a trailer park, but no way was I gonna hurt her feelings by mentioning it.

"Well, then drama it is."

"Okay, grab your schedule and let's go. Hey," she said as we hurried out of the room and skipped down the stairs, "maybe you'll be the next Nicole Kidman!"

Well, I guess being the next Nicole Kidman wouldn't be bad (not that I plan on marrying and then divorcing a manic short guy). Now that Stevie Rae mentioned it, I hadn't really thought much about my future career since the Tracker had thrown my life into complete chaos, but now that I was actually thinking about it I still really wanted to be a veterinarian.

An obese long-haired black and white cat sprinted down the steps in front of us chasing a cat that looked like its clone. With all these cats you'd think that there would definitely be a need for vamp vets. (Hee hee . . . vamp vets . . . I could call my clinic Vamp Vets, and the ads would read: "We'll take your blood for free!")

The kitchen and living room were crowded with girls eating and talking and hurrying around. I tried to return some of the hellos I was getting as Stevie Rae introduced me to what seemed like an impossibly confusing stream of girls *and* keep my concentration on finding a box of Count Chocula. Just when I was starting to worry, I found it, hidden behind several massive boxes of Frosted Flakes (not a bad second choice, but, well, they're not chocolate and they don't have any yummy little marshmallows). Stevie Rae poured a quick bowl of Lucky Charms, and we perched at the kitchen table, eating fast.

"Hi, Zoey!"

That voice. I knew who it was before I saw Stevie Rae duck her head and stare into her cereal bowl.

"Hi, Aphrodite," I said, trying to sound neutral.

"In case I don't see you later I wanted to be sure you know where to go tonight. The Dark Daughters' Full Moon Ritual will start at four A.M., right after the school's ritual. You'll miss dinner, but don't worry about that. We'll feed you. Oh, it's in the rec hall over by the east wall. I'll meet you in front of Nyx's Temple before the school ritual so we can go in together, and then I can show you the way to the hall afterward."

"Actually, I already promised Stevie Rae that I'd meet her and we'd go to the school ritual together." I really hate pushy people.

"Yeah, sorry 'bout that." I was pleased to hear Stevie Rae lift her head and say.

"Hey, you know where the rec hall is, don't you?" I asked Stevie Rae in my most perkily clueless voice.

"Yep, I do."

"Then you can just show me how to get there, right? And that means Aphrodite doesn't have to worry about me getting lost."

"Anything I can do to help," Stevie Rae chirped, sounding like her old self.

"Problem solved," I said with a big smile at Aphrodite.

"Okay. Fine. I'll see you at four A.M. Don't be late." She twitched off.

"If she shakes her butt any more when she walks she's gonna break something," I said.

Stevie Rae snorted and almost spewed milk from her nose. Coughing, she said, "Don't do that while I'm eating!" Then she swallowed and smiled at me. "You didn't let her boss you around."

"Neither did you." I slurped the last spoonful of cereal. "Ready?"

"Ready. Okay, this'll be easy. Your first hour is right next to my first hour. All of the third former core classes are in the same hall. Come on—I'll point you in the right direction and you'll be set."

We rinsed off our dishes and stuffed them in one of the five dishwashers, then hurried outside into the darkness of a beautiful fall evening. Jeesh, it was weird going to school at night, even if my body was telling me that everything was normal. We followed the flow of students through one of the thick wooden doors.

"Third Former Hall is just over here," Stevie Rae said, guiding me around a corner and up a short flight of stairs.

"Is that a bathroom?" I asked as we hurried past water fountains situated between two doors.

"Yep," she said. "Here's my class, and there's yours right next door. See you after class!"

"Okay, thanks," I called.

At least the bathroom was close. If I had a case of raging nervous-stomach diarrhea I wouldn't have far to run.

CHAPTER TWELVE

—

"Zoey! Over here!"

I almost cried in relief when I heard Damien's voice and saw his hand waving at an empty desk next to him.

"Hi." I sat down and smiled gratefully at him.

"Are you ready for your first day?"

No.

I nodded. "Yep." I wanted to say more, but just then a bell gave five quick rings and as the echo of it died Neferet swept into the room. She was wearing a long black skirt slit up the side to show great stiletto boots, and a deep purple silk sweater. Over her left breast, embroidered in silver, was the image of a goddess with her arms upraised, hands cupping a crescent moon. Her auburn hair was pulled back into a thick braid. The series of delicate wavelike tattoos that framed her face made her look like an ancient warrior priestess. She smiled at us and I could see that the entire class was as caught as I was by her powerful presence.

"Good evening! I've been looking forward to beginning this unit. Delving into the rich sociology of the Amazons is one of my favorites." Then she gestured to me. "It is excellent timing that Zoey Redbird has joined us today. I am Zoey's mentor, so I'll expect my students to welcome her. Damien, would you please get Zoey a textbook? Her cabinet is next to yours. While you explain our locker system to her I want the rest of you to journal about what preconceived impressions you have of the ancient vampyre warriors who are known as the Amazons."

The typical paper rustling and student whispering commenced while Damien led me to the back of the classroom where there was a wall of cabinets. He opened one that had the number "12" in silver on it. The cabinet contained neat, wide shelves filled with textbooks and supplies.

"At the House of Night there aren't lockers, like at regular schools. Here, first hour is our homeroom and we each have a cabinet of our own. The room will always be open, so you come back here to get books and whatever, just like you would go to a locker in the hall. Here's the sociology book."

He handed me a thick leather book with the silhouette of a goddess stamped on the front of it along with the title, *Vampyre Sociology 101*. I grabbed a notebook and a couple of pens. When I shut the cabinet door I hesitated.

"Isn't there a lock or something?"

"No," Damien lowered his voice. "They don't need locks here. If someone steals something, the vamps know it. I don't even want to think about what would happen to someone stupid enough to do that."

We sat back down and I started to write about the only thing I knew about the Amazons—that they were warrior women who didn't have much use for men—but my mind wasn't on my work. Instead, I was wondering why Damien, Stevie Rae, and even Erin and Shaunee all freak out about getting in trouble. I mean, I'm a good kid—okay, not perfect, but still. I've only had detention once so far, and that wasn't my fault. Really. Some turd boy told me to suck his cock. What was I supposed to do? Cry? Giggle? Pout? *Umm . . . no . . .* So instead I bitch-slapped him (although I prefer just using the word smacked), and *I* got detention for it.

Anyway, detention wasn't actually that bad. I got all my homework done and started the new Gossip Girls book. Clearly detention at the House of Night entailed more than going to a teacher's classroom for forty-five minutes of "quiet time" after school. I'd have to remember to ask Stevie Rae . . .

"First, what pieces of the Amazon tradition do we still practice at the House of Night?" Neferet asked, drawing my attention back to class.

Damien raised his hand. "The bow of respect, with our fist over our heart, comes from the Amazons, and so does the way we shake hands—by gripping forearms."

"Correct, Damien."

Huh. That explained the funny handshake.

"So, what preconceived notions do you have about the Amazon warriors?" she asked the class.

A blonde who sat on the other side of the room said, "The Amazons were heavily matriarchal, as are all vampyre societies."

Jeesh, she sounded smart.

"That's true, Elizabeth, but when people discuss the Amazons, legend tends to add an additional layer to history. What do I mean by that?"

"Well, people—especially humans—think that the Amazons were man-haters," said Damien.

"Exactly. What we know is that just because a society is matriarchal, as ours is, it does not automatically mean that it is anti-male. Even Nyx has a consort, the god Erebus, to whom she is devoted. The Amazons were unique, though, in that they were a society of vampyre women who chose to be their own warriors and protectors. As most of you already know, our society today is still matriarchal, but we respect and appreciate the Sons of Night, and consider them our protectors and consorts. Now, open your text to Chapter Three and let's look at the greatest of the Amazon warriors, Penthesilea, but be careful to keep legend and history separate in your mind."

And from there Neferet launched into one of the coolest lectures I'd ever heard. I had no idea an hour had passed; the ringing bell was a total surprise. I'd just shoved my sociology book back into my cubbie (okay, I know that Damien and Neferet called them *cabinets,* but come on—they totally remind me of the cubbies we used to have in kindergarten) when Neferet called my name. I grabbed a notebook and a pen and hurried over to her desk.

"How are you?" she asked, smiling warmly.

"I'm okay. I'm good," I said quickly.

She lifted an eyebrow at me.

"Well, I suppose I'm nervous and confused."

"Of course you are. It's a lot to take in, and changing schools is always difficult—let alone changing schools and lives." She glanced over my shoulder. "Damien, would you walk Zoey to Drama class?"

"Sure," Damien said.

"Zoey, I'll see you tonight at Ritual. Oh, and has Aphrodite issued a formal invitation for you to join the Dark Daughters in their private ceremony afterward?"

"Yes."

"I wanted to double-check with you and make sure that you feel fine about attending. I would, of course, understand your reticence, but I encourage you to go; I want you to take advantage of every opportunity here, and the Dark Daughters is an exclusive organization. It is a compliment that they already seem interested in you as a possible pledge."

"I'm fine with going." I forced my voice and my smile to be nonchalant. Obviously she expected me to go, and the last thing I wanted was for Neferet to be disappointed in me. Plus, no way in hell was I going to do anything that might make Aphrodite think I was scared of her.

"Well done," Neferet said with enthusiasm. She squeezed my arm and I automatically smiled at her. "If you need me my office is in the same wing as the infirmary." She glanced at my forehead. "I see the stitches have almost completely dissolved. That's excellent. Does your head still hurt?"

My hand automatically found its way up to my temple. I could only feel the prickle of a stitch or two today when there had been at least ten yesterday. Very, very weird. And, even weirder, I hadn't thought about the cut once this morning.

I also realized I hadn't thought about my mom or Heath or even Grandma Redbird. . . .

"No," I said, suddenly realizing Neferet and Damien were waiting for me to answer. "No, my head doesn't hurt at all."

"Good! Well, you two better go before you're late. I know you'll love Drama. I think Professor Nolan has just begun working on monologues."

I was halfway down the hall, hurrying to keep up with Damien when it hit me.

"How did she know I was going to take Drama? I just decided it this morning."

"Adult vamps know way too much sometimes," Damien whispered. "Scratch that. Adult vamps know way too much *all* the time, especially when that vamp is a High Priestess."

In light of what I hadn't been telling Neferet I didn't want to think about that too long.

"Hey, y'all!" Stevie Rae rushed up. "How was Vamp Soc? Did y'all start the Amazons?"

"It was cool." I was glad to change the subject from the too mysterious vampyres. "I had no idea they really cut off their right breasts to keep them out of the way."

"They wouldn't have had to if they'd been as flat as me," said Stevie Rae, looking down at her own chest.

"Or me," sighed Damien dramatically.

I was still giggling when they pointed me to the Drama room.

Professor Nolan didn't ooze power like Neferet. Instead she oozed energy. She had an athletic, but somehow pear-shaped body. Her brunet hair was long and straight. And Stevie Rae had been right—she had a serious Texas twang.

"Zoey, welcome! Have a seat anywhere."

I said hi and sat beside the Elizabeth girl I recognized from Vamp Soc. She looked friendly enough and I already knew she was smart. (It never hurts to sit next to a smart kid.)

"We're just about to begin choosing the monologues that each of you will present to the class sometime next week. But first, I thought you'd like to have a demonstration of how a monologue should be performed, so I asked one of our talented upperclassmen to stop by and recite the famous monologue from *Othello*, written by the ancient vampyre playwright, Shakespeare." Professor Nolan paused and glanced out of the window in the door. "Here he is now."

The door opened and *oh my dear sweet lord* I do believe my heart totally stopped beating. I'm positive my mouth flopped open like a moron. He was the most gorgeous young lad I had ever seen. He was tall and had dark hair that did that adorably perfect Superman curl thing. His eyes were an amazing sapphire blue and . . .

Oh. Hell! Hell! Hell! It was the guy from the hall.

"Come on in, Erik. As usual, your entrance timing is perfect. We are ready for your monologue." She turned back to the class. "Most of you already know fifth former, Erik Night, and are aware that he won last year's worldwide House of Night monologue competition, the finals of which were held in London. He is also already creating a buzz in Hollywood as well as on Broadway for his performance last semester as Tony in our production of *West Side Story*. The class is all yours, Erik." Prof Nolan beamed.

As if my body were suddenly on automatic, I clapped with the rest of the class. Smiling and confident, Erik stepped up on the little stage that was situated front and center in the large, airy classroom.

"Hi. How are you guys doing?"

He spoke directly to me. I mean, *directly* to me. I could feel my face getting really hot.

"Monologues seem intimidating, but the key is to get your lines down, and then to imagine that you're actually acting *with* a full cast of actors. Trick yourself into thinking you're not up here all alone, like this . . ."

And he began the monologue from *Othello*. I don't know much about the play, except that it's one of Shakespeare's tragedies, but Erik's performance was amazing. He was a tall guy, probably at least six feet, but as he began to speak he seemed to get bigger and older and more powerful. His voice deepened and he took on an accent I couldn't place. His incredible eyes darkened and narrowed into slits, and when he said Desdemona's name it was like he was praying. It was obvious he loved her, even before he spoke the concluding lines:

She loved me for the dangers I had passed,
And I loved her that she did pity them.

As he said the last two lines his eyes locked with mine and, just like in the hall the day before, it seemed as if there was no one else in the room—no one else in the world. I felt a shiver deep inside of something very much like what I'd felt the two times I'd smelled blood since I'd been Marked, only no blood had been spilled in the room. There was only Erik. And then he smiled, touched his lips to his fingers as though he was sending me a kiss, and bowed. The whole class clapped like crazy, including me. Really. I couldn't help it.

"Now, that's how it's done," Professor Nolan said. "So, there are copies of monologues in the red bookshelves at the rear of the class. Each of you take several books and begin looking through them. What you're trying to find is a scene that means something to you—that touches some part of your soul. I'll be circulating and can answer any questions you have about individual monologues. Once you've chosen your pieces, I'll go through the steps you'll need to take as you prepare your own presentation." With an energetic smile and nod, she motioned for us to start looking through the zillions of monologue books.

I still felt flushed and short of breath, but I got up with the rest of the class, even though I couldn't help peeking at Erik over my shoulder. He was (unfortunately) leaving the room, but not before he turned and caught me gawking at him. I blushed (again). He met my eyes and smiled directly at me (again). And then he was gone.

"He's so f-ing hot," someone whispered in my ear. I turned and, shockingly, Ms. Perfect Student Elizabeth was staring after Erik and fanning herself.

"Doesn't he have a girlfriend?" I blurted like an idiot.

"Only in my dreams," Elizabeth said. "Actually, word has it that he and Aphrodite used to be hooked up, but I've been here for a few months and it's been over between them at least that long. Here ya go," she tossed a couple of monologue books at me. "I'm Elizabeth, no last name."

My face was a question mark.

She sighed. "My last name was Titsworth. Can you imagine? When I got here a few weeks ago and my mentor explained that I could change my name to whatever I wanted it to be, I knew I was going to get rid of the Titsworth part, but then the whole issue of picking a new last name just stressed me too much. So I decided I'd keep my first name and not hassle with a last name." Elizabeth No Last Name shrugged.

"Well, hi," I said. There were really some odd kids here.

"Hey," she said as we went back to our desks. "Erik was looking at you."

"He was looking at everyone," I said, even though I could feel my stupid face getting all hot and red again.

"Yeah, but he was *really* looking at you." She grinned and added, "Oh, I think your colored-in Mark is cool."

"Thanks." It probably looked weird as hell on my beet-red face.

"Any questions about choosing a monologue, Zoey?" Professor Nolan asked, making me jump.

"No, Professor Nolan. I've done them before in drama at SIHS."

"Very good. Let me know if I can clarify setting or character for you." She patted me on the arm and kept moving around the room. I opened up the first book and started to flip through the pages, trying (unsuccessfully) to forget about Erik and concentrate on monologues.

He *had* been looking at me. But why? He must have known that it had been me in the hall. So what kind of interest in me was he showing? And did I want a guy to like me who had been getting a blow job from the hateful Aphrodite? I probably shouldn't. I mean, I definitely wasn't going to take up where she left off. Or maybe he was just curious about my freakishly colored-in Mark, like practically everybody else was.

But it hadn't seemed like it . . . it had seemed like he'd been looking at *me*. And I'd liked it.

I glanced down at the book I'd been ignoring. The page was open to the subchapter: Dramatic Monologues for Women. The first monologue on the page was from *Always Ridiculous* by Jose Echegaray.

Well, hell. It was probably a sign.

CHAPTER THIRTEEN

—

I actually found my way to Lit class by myself. Okay, so it was just on the other side of Neferet's room, but still I felt a little more confident when I didn't have to ask to be led around like the helpless idiot new kid.

"Zoey! We saved a desk for ya!" Stevie Rae yelled the instant I got to class. She was sitting beside Damien, and practically hopping up and down with excitement. She looked like a happy puppy again, which made me smile. I was really glad to see her. "So, so, so! Tell me everything! How was Drama? Did you like it? Do you like Professor Nolan? Isn't her tattoo cool? It reminds me of a mask—kinda."

Damien grabbed Stevie Rae's arm. "Breathe and let the girl answer."

"Sorry," she said sheepishly.

"I guess Nolan's tattoos are cool," I said.

"You guess?"

"Well, I was distracted."

"What?" she said. Then her eyes narrowed. "Did someone embarrass you about your Mark? I swear people are just plain rude."

"No, that wasn't it. Actually that Elizabeth No Last Name girl said she thought it was cool. I was distracted because, well . . ." I was feeling my face get hot again. I'd decided that I was going to ask them about Erik, but now that I'd started talking I wondered whether I should say anything. Should I tell them about the hall?

Damien perked up. "I feel a juicy tidbit coming on. Come on, Zoey. You were distracted *becauuuuse?*" He drew the word out into a question.

"Okay, okay. I can sum it up in two words: Erik Night."

Stevie Rae's mouth dropped open and Damien did a little pretend swoon, which he had to straighten up from right away because at that moment the bell rang and Professor Penthesilea swept into the room.

"Later!" Stevie Rae whispered.

"Absolutely!" Damien mouthed.

I smiled innocently. If nothing else I was sure that I would love the fact that mentioning Erik would drive them crazy all hour.

Lit class was an experience. First of all, the classroom itself was totally different than any I'd ever seen. There were bizarrely interesting posters and paintings and what looked like original art work filling every inch of wall space. And hanging from the ceiling were wind chimes and crystals—lots of them. Professor Penthesilea (whose name I now recognized from Vamp Soc class as belonging to the most revered of all the Amazons, and who everyone called Prof P) was like something out of the movies (well, the ones on the Sci-Fi Channel). She had seriously long reddish-blond hair, big hazel eyes, and a curvy body that probably made all the guys drool (not that it's very hard to make teenage boys drool). Her tattoos were thin, pretty Celtic knots that traced their way down her face and around her cheekbones, making them look high and dramatic. She was wearing expensive-looking black slacks and a moss-colored silk cardigan sweater set that had the same goddess figure embroidered over her breast as Neferet had been wearing. And, now that I thought about it (and not Erik), I realized Prof

Nolan's blouse had the goddess embroidered on the breast pocket of her blouse, too. Hmmm . . .

"I was born in April of year 1902," Professor Penthesilea said, instantly grabbing our attention. I mean, please, she barely looked thirty. "So I was ten years old in April of 1912, and I remember the tragedy very well. About what am I speaking? Do any of you have any idea?"

Okay, I knew exactly what she was talking about, but it wasn't because I'm a hopeless history nerd. It's because when I was younger I thought I was in love with Leonardo DiCaprio, and my mom got me the entire DVD collection of his movies for my twelfth birthday. This particular movie I watched so many times I still have most of it memorized (and I can not tell you how many times I snot cried when he slipped off that board and floated away like an adorable Popsicle).

I looked around. No one else seemed to have a clue, so I sighed and raised my hand.

Prof P smiled and called on me, "Yes, Miss Redbird."

"The *Titanic* sank in April of 1912. It was struck by the iceberg late on Sunday night, the fourteenth, and sank just a few hours later on the fifteenth."

I heard Damien suck air beside me, and Stevie Rae's little *huh*. Jeesh, had I really been acting so stupid that they were shocked to hear me answer a question correctly?

"I do love it when a new fledgling knows something," Professor Penthesilea said. "Absolutely correct, Miss Redbird. I was living in Chicago at the time of the tragedy, and I will never forget the newsies shouting the tragic headlines from the street corners. It was a horrid event, especially because the loss of lives was so preventable. It also signaled the end of one age and the beginning of another, as well as bringing about many much-needed changes in shipping laws. We are going to study all of this, plus the deliciously melodramatic events of the night, in our next piece of literature, Walter Lord's meticulously researched book, *A Night to Remember*. Although Lord was not a vampyre—and it's really a shame he wasn't," she added under her breath, "I still find his take on the night compelling and his writing style and tone interesting and very readable. Okay, let's get started! The last person in each row, get books for the people in your row from the long cabinet in the back of the room."

Well, cool! This was definitely more interesting than reading *Great Expectations* (Pip, Estella, *who cares?!*). I settled in with *A Night to Remember* and my notebook opened to take, well, notes. Prof P started to read Chapter One aloud to us, and she was actually a good reader. Three class hours almost over and I'd liked all of them. Was it possible that this vamp school would actually be more than a boring place I went to every day because I had to and, besides that, all my friends were there? Not that *all* of the classes at SIHS had been boring, but we didn't get to study the Amazons and the *Titanic* (from a teacher who'd been alive when it sank!).

I glanced around at the other kids while Prof P read. There were about fifteen of us, which seemed about the average in my other classes, too. All of them had their books open and were paying attention.

Then my eye was caught by something red and bushy on the other side of the room near the rear of the class. I'd spoken too soon—not all of the kids were paying attention. This one had his head down on his arms and he was sound asleep, which I knew because his chubby, way-too-white-and-freckled face was turned in my direction. His mouth was open, and I think he might have been drooling a little. I wondered what Prof P would do to the kid. She didn't seem like the kind of teacher who would be cool with some slug sleeping in the back of the room, but she just kept on with her reading, interspersed with interesting firsthand facts about the early twentieth century, which I really liked (I loved hearing about the flappers—I would definitely have been a flapper if I'd lived in the 1920s). It wasn't until the bell was about to ring and Prof P had assigned the next chapter as homework, and then told us we could talk quietly amongst ourselves, that she acted as if she noticed the sleeping kid at all. He'd started to stir, finally lifting up his head to display the bright red sleeping circle that was on the side of his forehead and looked bizarrely out of place beside his Mark.

"Elliott, I need to see you," Prof P said from behind her desk.

The kid took his time getting up and then dragged his feet, scuffing his untied shoes, over to her desk.

"Yeah?"

"Elliott, you are, of course, failing Lit. But what's more important, you're failing life. Vampyre males are strong, honorable, and unique. They have been our warriors and protectors for countless generations. How do you expect to make the Change into a being who is more warrior than man if you do not practice the discipline it takes even to stay awake in class?"

He shrugged his soft-looking shoulders.

Her expression hardened. "I shall give you one opportunity to make up the zero for class participation you received today by writing a short paper on any issue that was important in America in the early twentieth century. The paper is due tomorrow."

Without saying anything, he started to turn away.

"Elliott," Prof P's voice had dropped and, thick with irritation, it made her sound way scarier than she'd seemed while she had been reading and lecturing. I could feel the power radiating from her, and it made me wonder why she would ever need a male anything to protect her. The kid stopped and turned back to face her.

"I did not excuse you. What is your decision about doing the work to make up today's zero?"

The kid just stood there without saying anything.

"That question calls for an answer, Elliott. Now!" The air around her crackled with the command, making the skin on my arms tingle.

Seemingly unaffected, he shrugged again. "I probably won't do it."

"That says something about your character, Elliott, and it's not something good. You're not only letting yourself down, but you're letting down your mentor, too."

He shrugged again and absently picked his nose. "The Dragon already knows how I am."

The bell rang and Prof P, with a disgusted look on her face, motioned for Elliott to leave the room. Damien, Stevie Rae, and I had just stood up and were starting to walk out the door when Elliott slouched by us, moving more quickly than I believed possible for someone so sloth-like. He bumped into Damien, who was ahead of us. Damien made an *oops* sound and stumbled a little.

"Fucking faggot, get outta my way," the loser kid snarled, pushing Damien with his shoulder so he could get through the door before him.

"I should smack the crap out of that jerk!" Stevie Rae said, hurrying up to Damien, who was waiting for us.

He shook his head. "Don't worry about it. That Elliott kid has major problems."

"Yeah, like having poopie for brains," I said, staring down the hall at the slug's back. His hair was certainly unattractive.

"*Poopie* for brains?" Damien laughed and linked one arm through mine and one through Stevie Rae's, leading us down the hall *Wizard of Oz* fashion. "That's what I like about our Zoey," he said. "She has such a way with vulgar language."

"Poopie's not vulgar," I said defensively.

"I think that's his point, honey," Stevie Rae laughed.

"Oh." I laughed, too, and I really, really liked how it sounded when he'd said "our" Zoey . . . like I belonged . . . like I might be home.

CHAPTER FOURTEEN

—

Fencing was totally cool, which was a surprise. Class was held in a huge room off the gym that looked like a dance studio, complete with a floor-to-ceiling wall of mirrors. Hanging from the ceiling along one side were weird life-sized manikins that reminded me of three-dimensional shooting targets. Everyone called Professor Lankford Dragon Lankford, or just Dragon. It didn't take me long to figure out why. His tattoo represented two dragons whose bodies, serpent-like, wrapped down over his jaw line. Their heads were over his brows and their mouths were open, breathing fire at the crescent moon. It was amazing and hard not to stare at. Plus, Dragon was the first male adult vampyre I'd seen up close. At first he confused me. I guess if you'd asked me what I expected from a male vampyre I would have said his opposite. Honestly, I had the movie-star vampyre stereotype in mind—tall, dangerous, handsome. You know, like Vin Diesel. Anyway, Dragon is short, has long blondish hair that he pulls back in a low ponytail, and (except for the fierce looking dragon tattoo) has a cute face with a warm smile

It was only when he began leading the class through its warm-up exercises that I began to realize his power. From the instant he held the sword (which I later found out was called an épée) in the traditional salute he seemed to become someone else—someone who moved with unbelievable quickness and grace. He feinted and lunged and effortlessly made the rest of the class—even the kids who were pretty good, like Damien—look like awkward puppets. When he finished leading the warm-ups, the Dragon paired everyone off and had them work on what he called "the standards." I was relieved when he motioned for Damien to be my partner.

"Zoey, it's good to have you join the House of Night," Dragon said, shaking my hand in the traditional Amazon vampyre greeting. "Damien can explain the different parts of the fencing uniform to you, and I'll get you a handout to study over the next few days. I am assuming you've had no previous instruction in the sport?"

"No, I haven't," I said, and then added nervously, "but I'd like to learn. I mean, the whole idea of using a sword is just cool."

Dragon smiled. "Foil," he corrected, "you'll be learning how to use a foil. It's the lightest weight of the three types of weapons we have here, and an excellent choice for women. Did you know that fencing is one of the very few sports where women and men can compete on entirely equal terms?"

"No," I said, instantly intrigued. How cool would it be to kick a guy's butt at a sport?!

"This is because the intelligent and focused fencer can successfully compensate for any perceived deficiencies he or she may have, and may even be able to turn those deficiencies—such as strength or reach—into assets. In other words, you may not be as strong or as fast as your opponent, but you could be smarter or able to remain focused better, which will tip the scales in your favor. Right, Damien?"

Damien grinned. "Right."

"Damien is one of the most focused fencers I've had the privilege to coach in decades, which makes him a dangerous opponent."

I snuck a sideways glance at Damien, who flushed with pride and pleasure.

"For the next week or so I'll have Damien drill you in the opening maneuvers. Always remember, fencing requires a mastery of skills that are sequential and hierarchical in nature. If one of the skills is not acquired, subsequent skills will be very difficult to master and the fencer will be at a permanent and serious disadvantage."

"Okay, I'll remember," I said. Dragon smiled warmly again before he moved off to work his way among each practicing pair.

"What he means is don't get discouraged or bored if I make you do the same exercise over and over."

"So what you're really saying is that you're going to be annoying, but there's a purpose behind it?"

"Yep. And part of that purpose will help lift that cute little butt of yours," he said sassily, tapping me with the side of his foil.

I slapped at him and rolled my eyes, but after twenty minutes of lunging and settling back into the beginning stance and lunging—over and over again—I knew he was right. My butt would be killing me tomorrow.

We took quick showers after class (thankfully, there were separate curtain-draped stalls for each of us in the girls' locker room and we didn't have to barbarically and tragically shower in a huge open area like we were prison inmates or whatever) and then I hurried with the rest of the crowd to the lunch room—better known as the dining hall. And I do mean hurry. I was starving.

Lunch was a huge build-your-own salad buffet, which included everything from tuna salad (eesh) to those weird mini-corns that are so confusing, and don't even taste like corn. (What exactly are they? Baby corn? Midget corn? Mutant corn?) I piled my plate high and got a big hunk of what looked and smelled like freshly baked bread, and slid into the booth beside Stevie Rae, with Damien following close behind me. Erin and Shaunee were already arguing over something to do with whose essay for their Lit class was better, even though they'd both gotten 96 on their papers.

"So, Zoey, give. What about Erik Night?" Stevie Rae asked the instant I'd forked a big bite of salad into my mouth. Stevie Rae's words immediately shut up the Twins and focused the entire table's attention on me.

I'd thought about what I was going to say about Erik, and decided that I wasn't ready to tell anyone about the unfortunate blow-job scene. So I just said, "He kept looking at me." When they frowned at me I realized that through my salad mouth what I'd really said was "He keffft looookn at mmm." I swallowed and tried again. "He kept looking at me. In Drama class. It was just, I dunno, confusing."

"Define 'looking at me,'" Damien said.

"Well, it happened the second he came into class, but it was especially noticeable when he was giving us an example of a monologue. He did this thing from *Othello,* and when he said the line about love and such, he stared straight at me. I would have thought it was just an accident or something, but he looked at me before he started the monologue, and then again as he was leaving the room." I sighed and squirmed a little, uncomfortable with their way too piercing looks. "Never mind. It was probably just part of his act."

"Erik Night is the hottest damn thing at this entire school," Shaunee said.

"Forget that—he's the hottest damn thing on this planet," Erin said.

"He's not hotter than Kenny Chesney," Stevie Rae said quickly.

"Okay, just please with your country obsession!" Shaunee frowned at Stevie Rae before turning her attention back to me. "Do *not* let this opportunity pass you by."

"Yeah," Erin echoed. "Do *not*."

"Pass me by? What am I supposed to do? He didn't even say anything to me."

"Uh, Zoey honey, did you smile back at the boy?" Damien asked.

I blinked. Had I smiled back at him? Ah, crap. I bet I hadn't. I bet I just sat there and stared like a moron and maybe even drooled. Okay, well, I might not have drooled, but still. "I dunno," I said instead of the sad truth, which didn't fool Damien at all.

He snorted. "Next time smile at him."

"And maybe say hi," Stevie Rae said.

"I thought Erik was a just pretty face," Shaunee said.

"And body," Erin added.

"Until he dumped Aphrodite," Shaunee continued. "When he did that I realized the boy might have something going on upstairs."

"We can already tell he has it going on downstairs!" Erin said, waggling her eyebrows.

"Uh-huh!" Shaunee said, licking her lips like she was contemplating eating a big piece of chocolate.

"You two are gross," Damien said.

"We only meant that he has the cutest butt in town, Miss Priss," Shaunee said.

"As if you haven't noticed," Erin said.

"If you started talking to Erik it would really piss off Aphrodite." Stevie Rae said.

Everyone turned and stared at Stevie Rae as if she'd just parted the Red Sea or something.

"It's true," Damien said.

"Very true," Shaunee said while Erin nodded.

"So the rumor is he used to go out with Aphrodite," I said.

"Yep," Erin said.

"The rumor is grotesque but true," Shaunee said. "Which makes it even better that now he likes you!"

"Guys, he was probably just staring at my weird Mark," I blurted.

"Maybe not. You're really cute, Zoey," Stevie Rae said with a sweet smile.

"Or maybe your Mark made him look, and then he thought you were cute so he kept looking," Damien said.

"Either way, his looking will definitely piss Aphrodite off," Shaunee said.

"Which is a good thing," Erin said.

Stevie Rae waved away their comments. "Just forget about Aphrodite and your Mark and all that other stuff. Next time he smiles at you, say hi. That's all."

"Easy," Shaunee said.

"Peasy," Erin said.

"Okay," I mumbled and went back to my salad, wishing desperately that the whole Erik Night issue was as easy-peasy as they thought it was.

One thing about lunch at the House of Night was the same as lunch at SIHS or any other school I'd ever eaten at—it was over too soon. And then Spanish class was a blur. Profesora Garmy was like a little Hispanic whirlwind. I liked her right away (her tattoos looked oddly like feathers, so she reminded me of a little Spanish bird), but she ran the class speaking entirely in Spanish. Entirely. I should probably mention here that I haven't had Spanish since eighth grade, and I freely admit to not paying much attention to it then. So I was pretty lost, but I wrote down the homework and promised myself that I'd study the vocab words. I hate being lost.

Intro to Equestrian Studies was held in the Field House. It was a long, low brick building over by the south wall, attached to a huge indoor riding arena. The whole place had that sawdusty, horsey smell that mixed with leather to form something that was pleasant, even though you know that part of the "pleasant" scent was poopie—horse poopie.

I stood nervously with a small group of kids just inside the corral where a tall, stern-faced upperclassman had directed us to wait. There were only about ten of us, and we were all third formers. Oh, (great) that annoying redheaded Elliott kid was slouching against the wall kicking at the sawdust floor. He raised enough dust to make the girl standing closest to him sneeze. She threw him a dirty look and moved a few steps away. God, did he irritate *everyone*? And why couldn't he use some product (or perhaps a comb) on that nappy hair?

The sound of hooves drew my attention from Elliott and I looked up in time to see a magnificent black mare pounding into the corral at full gallop. She slid to a stop a couple feet in front of us. While we all gawked like fools, the mare's rider dismounted gracefully. She had thick hair that reached to her waist and was so blond it was almost white, and eyes that were a weird shade of slate gray. Her body was tiny, and the way she stood reminded me of those girls who obsessively take dance classes so that even when they're not in ballet they stand like they have something stuck way up their butts. Her tattoo was an intricate series of knots entwined around her face—within the sapphire design I was sure I could see plunging horses.

"Good evening. I am Lenobia, and *this*," she pointed at the mare and gave our group a contemptuous look before finishing the sentence, "is a horse." Her voice rang against the walls. The black mare blew through her nose as if to punctuate her words. "And you are my new group of third formers. Each of you has been chosen for my class because we believe you might possibly have an aptitude for riding. The truth is that less than half of you will last the semester, and less than half of those who last will actually develop into decent equestrians. Are there any questions?" She didn't pause long enough for anyone to ask anything. "Good. Then follow me and you shall begin." She turned and marched back into the stable. We followed.

I wanted to ask who the "we" were who thought I might have an aptitude for riding, but I was scared to say anything and just scrambled after her like everyone else. She came to a halt in front of a row of empty stalls. Outside of them were pitchforks and wheelbarrows. Lenobia turned to face us.

"Horses are not big dogs. Nor are they a little girl's romanticized dream image of a perfect best friend who will always understand you."

Two girls standing beside me fidgeted guiltily and Lenobia skewered them with her gray eyes.

"Horses are work. Horses take dedication, intelligence, and time. We'll begin with the work part. In the tack room down this hall you'll find mucking boots. Choose a pair quickly, while we all get gloves. Then each of you take your own stall and get busy."

"Professor Lenobia?" said a chubby girl with a cute face, who raised her hand nervously.

"Lenobia will do. The name I chose in honor of the ancient vampyre queen needs no other title."

I didn't have a clue who Lenobia was, and made a mental note to look it up.

"Go on. You have a question, Amanda?"

"Yeah, uh, yes."

Lenobia raised one brow at the girl.

Amanda swallowed noisily. "Get busy doing what, Profes—, I mean, Lenobia, ma'am?"

"Cleaning out stalls, of course. The manure goes in the wheelbarrows. When your barrow is full you can dump it in the compost area on the wall side of the stables. There is fresh sawdust in the storage room beside the tack room. You have fifty minutes. I'll be back in forty-five to inspect your stalls."

We all blinked at her.

"You may commence. Now."

We commenced.

Okay. Really. I know it's going to sound weird, but I didn't mind cleaning out my stall. I mean, horse poopie just isn't that gross. Especially because it was obvious that these stalls were cleaned out like every other instant of the day. I grabbed the mucking boots (which were big rubber galoshes—totally ugly, but they did cover my jeans all the way up to my knees) and a pair of gloves and got to work. There was music playing through excellent loudspeakers— something that I was pretty sure was Enya's latest CD (my mom used to listen to Enya before she married John, but then he decided that it might be witch music so she quit, which is why I'll always like Enya). So I listened to the haunting Gaelic lyrics and pitch-forked up poopie. It didn't seem that hardly any time had passed when I was dumping the wheelbarrow and then filling it with clean sawdust. I was just smoothing it around the stall when I got that prickly feeling that someone was watching me.

"Good job, Zoey."

I jumped and whirled around to see Lenobia standing just outside my stall. In one hand she was holding a big, soft curry brush. In the other she was holding the lead rope of a doe-eyed roan mare.

"You've done this before," Lenobia said.

"My grandma used to have a really sweet gray gelding I named Bunny," I said before I realized how stupid I sounded. Cheeks hot, I hurried on, "Well, I was ten, and his color reminded me of Bugs Bunny, so I started calling him that and it stuck."

Lenobia's lips tilted up in the barest hint of a smile. "It was Bunny's stall you cleaned?"

"Yeah. I liked to ride him, and Grandma said that no one should ride a horse unless they clean up after one." I shrugged. "So I cleaned up after him."

"Your grandmother is a wise woman."

I nodded.

"And did you mind cleaning up after Bunny?"

"No, not really."

"Good. Meet Persephone," Lenobia nodded her head at the mare beside her. "You've just cleaned her stall."

The mare came into the stall and walked straight up to me, sticking her muzzle in my face and blowing gently, which tickled and made me giggle. I rubbed her nose and automatically kissed the warm velvet of her muzzle.

"Hi there, Persephone, you pretty girl."

Lenobia nodded in approval as the mare and I got to know each other.

"There are only about five minutes left before the bell rings for school to end, so it is not necessary that you stay as part of today's class, but if you'd like, I believe you have earned the privilege of brushing Persephone."

Surprised, I looked up from patting the horse's neck. "No problem, I'll stay," I heard myself saying.

"Excellent. You can return the brush to the tack room when you've finished. I'll see you tomorrow, Zoey." Lenobia handed me the brush, patted the mare, and left us alone in the stall.

Persephone stuck her head in the metal rack that held fresh hay, and got to work chewing, while I got to work brushing. I'd forgotten how relaxing it was to groom a horse. Bunny had died of a sudden and very scary heart attack two years ago, and Grandma had been too upset to get another horse. She'd said that "the rabbit" (which is what she used to call him) couldn't be replaced. So it had been two years since I'd been around a horse, but it came back to me instantly—all of it. The smells, the warm, soothing sound of a horse eating, and the gentle *shoosh* the curry brush made as it slid over the mare's slick coat.

At the edge of my attention I vaguely heard Lenobia's voice, sharp and angry, as she totally chewed out a student I guessed was the annoying redheaded kid. I peeked over Persephone's shoulder and took a quick look down the stall line. Sure enough, the red-headed kid was slouched in front of his stall. Lenobia stood beside him, hands on her hips. Even from the side view I could see she was mad as hell. Was it that kid's mission to piss off every teacher here? And his mentor was Dragon? Okay, the guy looked nice, un-til he picked up a sword—uh, I mean *foil*—then he shifted from nice guy to deadly-dangerous-vampyre-warrior-guy.

"That redheaded slug kid must have a death wish," I told Persephone as I returned to her grooming. The mare twitched an ear back at me and blew through her nose. "Yep, I knew you'd agree. Wanta hear my theory about how my generation could single-handedly wipe out slugs and loser kids from America?" She seemed receptive, so I launched into my Don't Procreate with Losers speech. . . .

"Zoey! There you are!"

"Ohmygod! Stevie Rae! You scared the poo out of me!" I pat-ted and reassured Persephone, who had shied when I'd squealed.

"What in the world are ya doin'?"

I waggled the curry brush in her direction. "What does it look like I'm doing, Stevie Rae, getting a pedicure?"

"Stop messing around. The Full Moon Ritual is gonna start in like two minutes?"

"Ah, hell!" I gave Persephone one more pat and hurried out of the stall to the tack room.

"You forgot all about it, didn't you?" Stevie Rae said, holding my hand to help me balance while I kicked my feet out of the rubber boots and put my cute little ballet slippers back on.

"No," I lied.

Then I realized that I'd also forgotten all about the Dark Daughters' ritual afterward.

"Ah, *hell!*"

CHAPTER FIFTEEN

—

About halfway to Nyx's Temple I realized that Stevie Rae was being unusually quiet. I glanced sideways at her. Was she also looking pale? I got a creepy walk-over-your-grave feeling.

"Stevie Rae, is something wrong?"

"Yeah, well, it's sad and kinda scary."

"What is? The Full Moon Ritual?" My stomach started to hurt.

"No, you'll like that—or at least you'll like this one." I knew she meant, versus the Dark Daughters' ritual I had to go to afterward, but I didn't want to talk about that. Stevie Rae's next words made the whole issue of the Dark Daughters seem like a small, secondary problem. "A girl died last hour."

"What? How?"

"How they all die. She didn't make the Change, and her body just . . ." Stevie Rae paused, shuddering. "It happened near the end of Tae Kwan Do class. She'd been coughing, like she was short of breath at the beginning of our warmup exercises. I didn't think anything of it. Or maybe I did, but I put it out of my mind."

Stevie Rae gave me a small, sad smile and she looked ashamed of herself.

"Is there any way to save a kid? After, you know, they start—" I broke off and made a vague, uncomfortable gesture.

"No. There's no way you can be saved if your body starts to reject the Change."

"Then don't feel bad about not wanting to think about the girl who was coughing. There's nothing you could have done anyway."

"I know. I just . . . it was awful. And Elizabeth was so nice."

I felt a sharp jolt somewhere in the middle of my body. "Elizabeth No Last Name? She's the girl who died?"

Stevie Rae nodded, blinking hard and obviously trying not to cry.

"That's horrible," I said, my voice so weak it was almost a whisper. I remembered how considerate she'd been about my Mark, and how she'd noticed Erik looking at me. "But I just saw her in Drama class. She was fine."

"That's how it happens. One second the kid sitting next to you looks perfectly normal. The next . . ." Stevie Rae shivered again.

"And everything's going to go on like normal? Even though someone at the school just died?" I remembered that last year, when a group of sophomores from SIHS had been in a car accident one weekend and two of them had been killed, extra counselors had been called in to school on Monday and all the athletic events had been cancelled for that week.

"Everything goes on like normal. We're supposed to get used to the idea that it might happen to anyone. You'll see. Everyone will act like nothing happened, especially upperclassmen. It's just third formers and good friends of Elizabeth, like her roommate, who will show any reaction at all. The third formers—that's us—are supposed to act right and get over it. Elizabeth's roommate and best friends will probably keep to themselves for a couple days, but then they'll be expected to get it together." She lowered her voice, "Truthfully, I don't think the vamps think of any of us as *real* until we actually Change."

I thought about this. Neferet didn't seem to treat me like I was temporary—she'd even said that it was an excellent sign that my Mark was colored in already, not that I was as confident as she seemed to be about my future. But I absolutely was not going to say anything that might sound as if Neferet was giving me special treatment. I didn't want to be "the weird one." I just wanted to be Stevie Rae's friend and fit in with my new group.

"That's really awful," was all I said.

"Yeah, but at least if it happens, it happens fast."

Part of me wanted to know the details, and part of me was too scared even to ask the question.

Thankfully, Shaunee interrupted before I could make myself ask what I was really too freaked out to want to know.

"Just please with the taking so long," Shaunee called from the front steps of the temple. "Erin and Damien are already inside saving a place in the circle for us, but you know that once the ritual starts they won't let anyone else in. Hurry up!"

We rushed up the steps, and with Shaunee leading us, hurried into the temple. Sweet, smoky incense engulfed me as I entered the dark arched foyer of Nyx's Temple. Automatically, I hesitated. Stevie Rae and Shaunee turned to me.

"It's okay. There's nothing to be nervous or scared about." Stevie Rae met my eyes and added, "At least nothing in there."

"The Full Moon Ritual is great. You'll like it. Oh, when the vamp traces the pentagram on your forehead and says 'blessed be' all you have to do is say 'blessed be' back to her," Shaunee explained. "Then follow us over to our place in the circle." She smiled reassuringly at me and hurried ahead into the dimly lit interior room.

"Wait." I grabbed Stevie Rae's sleeve. "I don't want to sound stupid, but isn't a pentagram a sign of evil or something like that?"

"That's what I thought, too, until I got here. But all that evil stuff is bull that the People of Faith want you to believe so that . . . Heck," she said with a shrug, "I'm not even sure why they're so set on people—well, humans that is—believing that it's an evil sign. The truth is that for like a zillion years the pentagram has stood for wisdom, protection, perfection. Good stuff like that. It's just a five-pointed star. Four of the points stand for the elements. The fifth, the one that points up, stands for the spirit. That's all it is. No boogieman there."

"Control," I muttered, glad we had a reason to quit talking about Elizabeth and death.

"Huh?"

"The People of Faith want to control everything, and part of that control is that everyone has to always believe exactly the same. That's why they want people to think the pentagram is bad." I shook my head in disgust. "Never mind. Come on. I'm readier than I thought I was. Let's go in."

We walked deeper into the foyer and I heard running water. We passed a beautiful fountain, and then the entryway curved gently to the left. Within a thick, arched stone doorway stood a vampyre I didn't recognize. She was dressed entirely in black—a long skirt and a silky, bell-sleeved blouse. The only decoration she had on was the silver embroidered goddess figure over her breast. Her hair was long and the color of wheat. Sapphire-colored spirals radiated from her crescent moon tattoo to down around her flawless face.

"That's Anastasia. She teaches the Spells and Rituals class. She's also Dragon's wife," Stevie Rae whispered quickly before she stepped up to the vampyre and respectfully placed her fist over her heart.

Anastasia smiled and dipped her finger in a rock bowl she was holding. Then she traced a five-pointed star on Stevie Rae's forehead.

"Blessed be, Stevie Rae," she said.

"Blessed be," Stevie Rae responded. She gave me an encouraging look before she disappeared into the smoky room beyond.

I took a deep breath and made a conscious decision to put all thoughts of Elizabeth and death and what-ifs out of my mind—at least during this ritual. I moved purposefully into the space in front of Anastasia. Mimicking Stevie Rae, I placed my closed fist over my heart.

The vampyre dipped her finger in what I could now see was oil. "Merry meet, Zoey Redbird, welcome to the House of Night and your new life," she said as she traced the pentagram on my forehead over my Mark. "And blessed be."

"Blessed be," I murmured, surprised at the electric shiver that passed through my body when the damp star had taken form on my forehead.

"Go on in and join your friends," she said kindly. "There's no need to be nervous, I believe the Goddess is already looking after you."

"Th-thank you," I said, and hurried into the room. There were candles everywhere. Huge white ones suspended from the ceiling in iron chandeliers. Big candle trees held more of them and were lined along the walls. In the temple, sconces didn't burn oil tamely in lanterns, like in the rest of the school. Here the sconces were *real*. I knew that this place used to be a People of Faith church dedicated to St. Augustine, but it looked like no church I'd ever seen before. Besides being lit only by candlelight, there were no pews. (And, by the way, I really dislike pews—could they be any more uncomfortable?) Actually, the only furniture in the big room was an antique wooden table situated in the center that was kinda like the one in the dining hall—only this one wasn't just loaded with food and wine and such. This one also held a marble statue of the Goddess, arms upraised and looking a lot like the embroidered design the vamps wore. There was a huge candelabrum on the table, its fat white candles burning brightly, as well as several thick sticks of smoking incense.

Then my eyes were caught by the open flame burning from out of a recess in the stone floor. It flickered wildly, its yellow fire almost waist high. It was beautiful, in a controlled danger kind of a way, and it seemed to draw me forward. Thankfully, Stevie Rae's waving hands snagged my attention before I could follow my impulse to approach the flame, and then I noticed, wondering how I could have failed to see this from the beginning, that there was a huge circle of people—students as well as adult vamps— stretching around the edges of the room. Feeling nervous and awestruck at the same time, I made my feet move so I could take my place in the circle beside Stevie Rae.

"Finally," Damien said under his breath.

"Sorry we're late," I said.

"Leave her alone. She's nervous enough as it is," Stevie Rae told him.

"*Sssh!* It's starting," Shaunee hissed.

Four forms seemed to materialize from within the darkened corners of the room to become women who made their way to four spots just within the living circle, like the directions on a compass. Two more entered from the doorway through which I'd just come. One was a tall man—well, scratch that—male vampyre (all of the adults were vamps), and, ohmygod, he was hot. Now, here was an excellent example of the stereotype of the gorgeous vamp guy, up close and personal. He was over six feet tall and looked like he belonged on the big screen.

"And *there* is the only reason I'm taking that damn Poetry elective," Shaunee whispered.

"I'm with you there, Twin," Erin breathed dreamily.

"Who is he?" I asked Stevie Rae.

"Loren Blake, Vamp Poet Laureate. He's the first male Poet Laureate in two hundred years. Literally," she whispered. "*And* he's only like twenty-something, and that's in real years, not just in looks."

Before I could say anything else, he started to speak and my mouth was too busy flopping open at the sound of his voice for me to do anything but listen.

She walks in beauty, like the night
Of cloudless climes and starry skies . . .

As he spoke he moved slowly toward the circle. As if his voice was music, the woman who had entered the room with him began to sway, and then to dance gracefully around the outside of the living circle.

And all that's best of dark and bright
Meet in her aspect and her eyes . . .

The dancing woman had everyone's attention. With a jolt I realized that it was Neferet. She was wearing a long silk dress that had tiny crystal beads sewn all over it, so that the candlelight caught each of her movements and made her shimmer like the star-filled night sky. Her movements seemed to call alive the words of the old poem (at least my mind was still working well enough that I recognized it as Lord Byron's "She Walks in Beauty").

Thus mellowed to that tender light
Which heaven to gaudy day denies.

Somehow both Neferet and Loren managed to end up in the center of the circle as he finished reciting the stanza. Then Neferet took a goblet from the table and lifted it, as if offering a drink to the circle.

"Welcome Nyx's children to the Goddess's celebration of the full moon!"

The adult vamps chorused, "Merry meet."

Neferet smiled and put the goblet back on the table and picked up a long white taper that was already lit and sitting in a single candlestick holder. Then she walked across the circle to face a vamp I didn't know who was standing at what must be the head of the circle. The vamp saluted her, hand over breast, before turning around so that her back was to Neferet.

"*Psst!*" Stevie Rae whispered. "We all face each of the four directions as Neferet evokes the elements and casts Nyx's circle. East and air come first."

Then everyone, including me even though I was kinda slow, turned to face east. Out of the corner of my eye I could see Neferet raise her arms over her head as her voice rang against the stone walls of the temple.

"From the east I summon air and ask that you carry to this circle the gift of knowledge that our ritual will be filled with learning."

The instant Neferet began speaking the invocation I felt the air change. It moved around me, ruffling my hair and filling my ears with the sound of wind sighing through leaves. I looked around, expecting to see that everyone else had been caught in a mini-whirlwind, but didn't notice anyone else's hair getting messed up. Weird.

The vamp who was standing in the east pulled a thick yellow candle from the folds of her dress, and Neferet lit it. She lifted it into the air, and then placed it, flickering, at her feet.

"Turn to the right, for fire," Stevie Rae whispered again.

We turned and Neferet continued. "From the south I summon fire and ask that you light in this circle the gift of strength of will, so that our ritual will be binding and powerful."

The wind that had been blowing softly against me was replaced by a sensation of heat. It wasn't exactly uncomfortable; it was more like the flush you feel when you step into a hot tub, but it was warm enough to make a light sweat break out over my body. I glanced at Stevie Rae. She had her head raised slightly and her eyes were closed. There was no sign of sweat on her face. The intensity of the heat suddenly jumped up a notch, and I looked back at Neferet. She had lit a large red candle that Penthesilea was holding. Then, as the east-facing vamp had done, Penthesilea lifted it up in offering before placing it by her feet.

This time I didn't need Stevie Rae's nudging to turn again to my right and face west. Somehow, I knew not just that we needed to turn, but that the next element to be summoned would be water.

"From the west I summon water and ask that you wash this circle in compassion, that the light of the full moon can be used to bestow healing to our group as well as understanding."

Neferet lit the west-facing vamp's blue candle. The vamp lifted it, and placed it at her feet as the sound of waves filled my ears and the salty scent of the sea filled my nose. Eagerly, I completed the circle by facing north and knew I'd be embracing earth.

"From the north I summon earth and ask that you grow within this circle the gift of manifestation, that the wishes and prayers from tonight will come to fruition."

Suddenly I could feel the softness of a grassy meadow under my feet, and I smelled hay and heard birdsong. A green candle was lit and placed at "earth"'s feet.

I should have probably been afraid of the odd sensations breaking over me, but they filled me with an almost unbearable lightness—*I felt good!* So good that when Neferet faced the flame that burned in the middle of the room and the rest of us turned to the interior of the circle I had to press my lips tightly together to keep from laughing out loud. The drop-dead gorgeous poet was standing across the fire from Neferet and I could see that he was holding a big purple candle in his hands.

"And last, I summon spirit to complete our circle and ask that you fill us with connection, so that as your children we may prosper together."

Unbelievably, I felt my own spirit leap, like there were bird wings fluttering around inside my chest, as the poet lit the candle from the huge flame and then placed it on the table. Then Neferet began to move around within the circle, speaking to us, meeting our eyes, including us in her words.

"This is the time of the fullness of the moon. All things wax and wane, even Nyx's children, her vampyres. But on this night the powers of life, of magick, and of creation are at their brightest—as is our Goddess's moon. This is the time of building . . . of doing."

My heart was beating hard as I watched Neferet speak, and I realized with a little start that she was actually giving a sermon. This was a worship service, but the casting of the circle and Neferet's words coupled to touch me like no other sermon had ever even begun to do. I glanced around. Maybe it was the setting. The room was misty with incense and magical in the flickering candlelight. Neferet was everything a High Priestess should be. Her beauty was a flame of its own, and her voice was a magic that held everyone's attention. No one was slumped down in a pew sleeping or sneakily doing sudoku.

"This is a time when the veil between the mundane world and the strange and beautiful realms of the Goddess become thin indeed. On this night may one transcend the boundaries of the worlds with ease, and know the beauty and enchantment of Nyx."

I could feel her words wash against my skin and close my throat. I shivered and the Mark on my forehead suddenly felt warm and tingly. Then the poet began to speak in his deep, powerful voice.

"This is a time for weaving the ethereal into being, of spinning the strands of space and time to bring forth Creation. For life is a circle as well as a mystery. Our Goddess understands this, as does her consort, Erebus."

As he spoke I felt better about Elizabeth's death. Suddenly it didn't seem so scary, so horrible. It seemed more like a part of the natural world, a world that we all had a place in.

"Light . . . dark . . . day . . . night . . . death . . . life . . . all is tied together by spirit and the touch of the Goddess. If we keep the balance and look to the Goddess we can learn to weave a spell of moonlight and fashion with it a fabric of pure magical substance to keep with us all the days of our lives."

"Close your eyes, Children of Nyx," Neferet said "and send a secret desire to your Goddess. Tonight, when the veil between the worlds is thin—when magic is afoot within the mundane—perhaps Nyx will grant your petitions and dust you with the gossamer mist of dreams fulfilled."

Magic! They actually were praying for magic! Would it work—could it work? Was there *really* magic in this world? I remembered the way my spirit had been able to see words and how the Goddess had called me with her visible voice down into the crevasse and then kissed my forehead and changed my life forever. And how, just moments ago, I'd felt the power of Neferet's calling of the elements. I hadn't imagined it—I *couldn't* have imagined it.

I closed my eyes and thought about the magic that seemed to surround me, and then I sent up my wish into the night. *My secret wish is that I belong . . . that I have finally found a home no one can take away from me.*

Despite the unusual warmth of my Mark, my head felt light and unimaginably happy as Neferet called for us to open our eyes and, in a voice that was at the same time soft and powerful—woman and warrior combined—she continued the ritual.

"This is a time of traveling unseen in the full moonlight. A time to listen for music not fashioned by human or vampyre hands. It is a time for oneness with the winds that caress us"— Neferet bowed her head slightly to the east—"and the bolt of lightning that mimics the spark of first life." She tilted her head to the south. "It is a time to revel in the eternal sea and the warm rains that soothe us, as well as the verdant land that surrounds and keeps us." She acknowledged the west and north in turn.

And each time Neferet named an element it felt as though a jolt of sweet electricity sizzled through my body.

Then the four women who personified the elements moved as one to the table. With Neferet and Loren, each of them lifted a goblet.

"All hail, O Goddess of Night and the full moon!" Neferet said. "All hail Night, from whom our blessings come. On this night we give thanks to thee!"

Still holding the goblets, the four women scattered back to their places in the circle.

"In the mighty name of Nyx," Neferet said.

"And of Erebus," the poet added.

"We ask from within your sacred circle that you give us the knowledge to speak the language of the wilds, to fly with the freedom of the bird, to live the power and grace of the feline, and to find an ecstasy and joy in life that would stir the very heights of our being. Blessed be!"

I couldn't stop grinning. I'd never heard stuff like this in church before, and I sure as hell had never felt so energized there, either!

Neferet drank from the goblet she held, and then she offered it to Loren, who drank from it and said "blessed be." Mirroring their actions, the four women moved quickly around the circle, allowing each person, fledgling and adult, to drink from a goblet. When it was my turn I was happy to see the familiar face of Penthesilea offer me a drink and a blessing. The wine was red and I expected it to be bitter, like the sip of my mom's hidden Cabernet I tried once (and definitely did not like), but it wasn't. It was sweet and spicy and it made my head feel even lighter.

When everyone had been given a drink, the goblets were returned to the table.

"Tonight I want each of us to spend at least a moment or two alone in the light of the full moon. Let its light refresh you and help you to remember how extraordinary you are . . . or you are becoming." She smiled at some of the fledglings, including me. "Bask in your uniqueness. Revel in your strength. We stand separate from the world because of our gifts. Never forget that, because you may be sure the world never will. Now let us close the circle and embrace the night."

In reverse order, Neferet thanked each element and sent them away as each candle was blown out, and as she did so I felt a little twinge of sadness, like I was saying good-bye to friends. Then she completed the ritual by saying, "This rite is ended. Merry meet and merry part and merry meet again!"

The crowd echoed: "Merry meet and merry part and merry meet again!"

And that was it. My first ritual of the Goddess was over.

The circle broke up quickly—more quickly than I would have liked it to. I wanted to stand there and think about the amazing things I had felt, especially during the calling of the elements, but that was impossible. I was carried out of the temple on a tide of chatter. I was glad that everyone was so busy talking that no one noticed how quiet I was; I didn't think I could explain to them what had just happened to me. Hell! I couldn't even explain it to myself.

"Hey, you think they'll have Chinese food again tonight? I just loved it last full moon when they had that yummy moo goo stuff afterward," Shaunee said. "Not to mention, my fortune cookie said 'You will make a name for yourself,' which is way cool."

"I'm so starved I don't care what they feed us as long as they feed us," Erin said.

"Me too," Stevie Rae said.

"For once we are in perfect agreement," Damien said, linking arms with Stevie Rae and me. "Let's eat."

And suddenly, that reminded me. "Uh, guys." That nice tingly feeling the ritual had given me was gone. "I can't go. I have to—"

"We're morons." Stevie Rae thumped herself on the forehead hard enough to make a smacking sound. "We totally forgot."

"Ah, crap!" Shaunee said.

"The hags from hell," Erin said.

"Want me to save you a plate of something?" Damien asked sweetly.

"No. Aphrodite said they're going to feed me."

"Probably raw meat," Shaunee said.

"Yeah, from some poor kid she caught in her nasty spider web," Erin said.

"By that she means the one between her legs," Shaunee explained.

"Stop, you're freaking Zoey out," Stevie Rae said as she started nudging me toward the door. "I'll show her where the rec hall is, then I'll meet you guys at our table."

Outside I said, "Okay, tell me that they're kidding about the raw meat."

"They're kidding?" Stevie Rae said unconvincingly.

"Great. I don't even like my steak rare. What am I going to do if they really do try to feed me raw meat?" I refused to think about what kind of raw meat it might be.

"I think I have a Tums somewhere in my purse. Do you want it?" Stevie Rae asked.

"Yeah," I said, already feeling nauseous.

CHAPTER SIXTEEN

"That's it." Stevie Rae had stopped, looking uncomfortable and apologetic in front of the steps that led to a round brick building situated on a little hill overlooking the eastern part of the wall surrounding the school. Huge oaks wrapped it in darkness within darkness, so I could barely make out flickers of either gas or candles lighting up the entrance. Not one speck of light was coming from the darkened windows that were long and arched and seemed to be made of stained glass.

"Okay, well, thanks for the Tums." I tried to sound brave. "And save a place for me. This really can't take that long. I should be able to get done here and join you guys for dinner."

"Don't rush. Really. You might meet someone you like and want to hang out. Don't worry about it if you do. I won't be mad and I'll just tell Damien and the Twins that you're reconnoitering."

"I'm not going to become one of them, Stevie Rae."

"I believe you," she said, but her eyes looked suspiciously big and round.

"So I'll see you soon."

" 'Kay. See you soon," she said, and started to follow the sidewalk back to the main building.

I didn't want to watch her walk away—she looked all forlorn and spanked puppylike. Instead I climbed up the steps and told myself that this was going to be no big deal—nothing worse than the time my Barbie sister talked me into going to cheerleading camp with her (I don't know what the hell I'd been thinking). At least this fiasco wouldn't last a week. They'll probably cast another circle, which was actually very cool, do some unusual praying like Neferet did, and then break for dinner. That would be my cue to smile nicely and slip out. Easy-peasy.

The torches on either side of the thick wooden door were lit by gas and not the raw flame sconces used in Nyx's Temple. I reached my hand toward the heavy iron knocker, but, with a sound that was disturbingly like a sigh, it opened away from my touch.

"Merry meet, Zoey."

Oh. My. God. It was Erik. He was wearing all black, and his dark, curly hair and his insanely blue eyes reminded me of Clark Kent—well, okay, without the dorky glasses and the nerdy slicked-back hair . . . so . . . I supposed that would mean he actually reminded me (again) of Superman—well, without the cape or tights or the big S . . .

Then the babble in my mind totally shut itself up when his oil-dampened finger slid over my forehead, tracing the five points of the pentagram.

"Blessed be," he said.

"Blessed be," I replied, and would be eternally grateful that my voice didn't croak or crack or squeak. Ah, man, he smelled *good*, but I couldn't place what he smelled like. It wasn't any of the tired, overused colognes guys apply by the gallon. He smelled like . . . he smelled like . . . the forest at night just after it's rained . . . something earthy and clean and . . .

"You can come on in," he was saying.

"Oh, uh, thanks," I said brilliantly. I stepped inside. And then I stopped. The interior was all one big room. The circular-shaped walls were draped in black velvet, totally blocking the windows and the silver moonlight. I could see that under the heavy curtains there were weird shapes, which started to freak me out until I realized that—hello—it's a rec room. They must have shoved the TVs and game stuff to the sides of the room and covered them so everything would look, well, creepier. Then my attention was captured by the circle itself. It was situated in the middle of the room and made up entirely of candles in tall red glass containers, like the prayer candles you can buy in the Mexican foods section of the grocery store that smell like roses and old ladies. There must have been more than a hundred of them and they lit up the kids who were standing in a loose circle behind them talking and laughing with a ghostly light that was tinted red. The kids were all wearing black and I noticed right away that none of them were wearing any embroidered rank insignias, but each had a thick silver chain that glittered around their necks from which an odd symbol dangled. It looked like two crescent moons positioned back to back against a full moon.

"There you are, Zoey!"

Aphrodite's voice slid across the room just ahead of her body. She was wearing a long black dress that flashed with onyx beading, reminding me weirdly of a dark version of Neferet's beautiful gown. She had on the same necklace as the others, but hers was bigger and outlined in red jewels that might have been garnets. Her blond hair was loose and draped around her like a gold veil. She was entirely too pretty.

"Erik, thanks for making Zoey welcome. I can take it from here." She sounded normal, and she even rested her manicured fingertips on Erik's arm for a second in what the uninformed might think of as just a friendly gesture, but her face told a different story. It was set and cold, and her eyes seemed to blaze into his.

Erik barely gave her a look, and he definitely moved his arm away from her touch. Then he gave me a quick smile and, without glancing at Aphrodite again, walked away.

Great. Exactly what I didn't need was to get in the middle of a nasty breakup. But I couldn't seem to help the fact that my eyes followed him across the room.

Stupid me. Again. Sigh.

Aphrodite cleared her throat, and I tried (unsuccessfully) not to look like I'd been caught doing something I shouldn't have been doing. Her slick, mean smile said there was absolutely no doubt that she'd noticed my interest in Erik (and his interest in me). And, again, I wondered if she knew it had been me in the hall the day before.

Well, it wasn't like I could ask her.

"You need to hurry, but I brought something for you to change into." Aphrodite was talking quickly as she motioned for me to follow her to the girls' restroom. She threw me a disgusted look over her shoulder. "It's not like you can come to a Dark Daughters' ritual dressed like that." Once we were in the bathroom she brusquely handed me a dress that had been hanging from one of the partitions and kinda pushed me into the stall. "You can put your clothes on the hanger and carry them back to the dorm like that."

There didn't seem to be any arguing with her and, anyway, I felt like an outsider enough as it was. Being dressed differently made me feel like I'd shown up at a party dressed like a duck, but no one had told me it wasn't a costume party so everyone else was wearing jeans.

I quickly got out of my clothes and slid the black dress over my head, sighing with relief when it fit. It was simple but flattering. The material was the soft clingy stuff that never wrinkles. It had long sleeves and a round neckline that showed most of my shoulders (good thing I'd worn my black bra). All around the neckline, the edge of the long sleeves, and the hem, which was right above my knee, were sewn little red sparkly beads. It really was pretty. I slipped my shoes back on thinking, happily, that a nice pair of ballet flats can go with just about any outfit, and stepped out of the stall.

"Well, at least it fits." I said.

But I noticed Aphrodite wasn't looking at the dress. She was looking at my Mark, which bugged the crap out of me. Okay, my Mark is colored in—get over it already! I didn't say anything, though. I mean, this was her "party" and I was a guest. Translation: I was totally outnumbered, so I better be good.

"I'll be leading the ritual, of course, so I'm gonna be too busy to hold your hand through it."

Okay, I should've just kept my mouth shut, but she was wearing on my last nerve. "Look, Aphrodite, I don't need you to hold my hand."

Her eyes narrowed and I braced myself for another psycho girl scene. Instead she smiled a totally non-nice smile that made her look like a snarling dog. Not that I was calling her a bitch, but the analogy seemed scarily accurate.

"Of course you don't need your hand held. You'll just breeze right through this little ritual like you've breezed through everything else here. I mean, after all, you *are* Neferet's new favorite."

Wonderful. On top of the Erik issue and the weirdness over my Mark issue, she was jealous that Neferet was my mentor.

"Aphrodite, I don't think I'm Neferet's new favorite. I'm just new." I tried to sound reasonable, and I even smiled.

"Whatever. So, are you ready?"

I gave up trying to reason with her and nodded, wishing this whole ritual thing would hurry up and be over.

"Fine. Let's go." She led me out of the rest room and over to the circle. I recognized the two girls we walked up to as two of the "hags from hell" who had followed her around in the cafeteria. Only instead of wearing pursed-face, I-just-ate-a-lemon expressions, they were smiling warmly at me.

No. I wasn't fooled. But I made my face smile, too. When in enemy territory it's best to blend in and look inconspicuous and/or stupid.

"Hi, I'm Enyo," said the taller of the two. She was, of course, blonde, but her long, flowing locks were more the color of waving wheat than gold. Although in the candlelight it was hard to be sure which cliché was a more appropriate description. And I still didn't believe she was a natural blonde.

"Hi," I said.

"I'm Deino," said the other girl. She was obviously mixed and had a gorgeous combination of really pretty, coffee-with-lots-of-cream skin and excellent thick, curly hair, which probably had never had the nerve to nap up on her for an instant, no matter the humidity.

The two of them were freakishly perfect.

"Hi," I said again. Feeling more than a little claustrophobic, I moved into the space they'd created between them.

"You three enjoy the ritual," Aphrodite said.

"Oh, we will!" Enyo and Deino said together. The three of them shared a look that made my skin crawl. I turned my attention away from them before my better judgment won out over my pride and I bolted from the room.

I had a good view of the inner area of the circle now, and again it was similar to the one in Nyx's Temple, except this one had a chair pulled up beside the table and there was someone sitting in it. Well, kinda sitting. Actually, the whoever was slumped down with the hood of a cloak covering his or her head.

Well . . . hmmm . . .

Anyway, the table was draped with the same black velvet as the walls, and there was a Goddess statue on it, a bowl of fruit and bread, several goblets, and a pitcher. And a knife. I squinted to be sure I was seeing right. Yep. It was a knife—it had a bone handle and a long, wicked curving blade that looked entirely too sharp to be used for cutting fruit or bread safely. A girl I thought I recognized from the dorm was lighting several fat sticks of incense that sat in ornately carved incense holders on the table, and totally ignoring whoever was slumped in the chair. Jeesh, was the kid asleep?

Immediately the air began to fill with smoke that I swear was green-tinged and curled, ghostlike, around the room. I expected it to smell sweet, like the incense at Nyx's Temple, but when a feathery wisp of smoke reached me and I breathed it in I was surprised by its bitterness. It was kinda familiar and I frowned, trying to figure out what it reminded me of . . . crap, what was it? It was almost like bay leaf, with a clovey middle. (I had to remember to thank Grandma Redbird later for teaching me about spices and their smells.) I sniffed again, intrigued, and my head felt a little woozy. Weird. Okay, the incense was odd. It seemed to change as it filled the room, like expensive perfume that changes with each person who wears it. I breathed in again. Yep. Clove and bay, but there was something at the end of it; something that made the scent finish tangy and bitter . . . dark and mystic and alluring in its . . . naughtiness.

Naughtiness? Then I knew.

Well, hell! They were filling the room with pot smoke mixed with spices. Unbelievable. I'd stood up to peer pressure and for years said no to even the most polite offers to try one of those gross-looking homemade joints that get passed around at parties and whatnot. (I mean, please. Is that even sanitary? And just exactly why would I want to do a drug that made me want to obsessively eat fattening snack foods?) And now here I stood, immersed in pot smoke. Sigh. Kayla would never believe it.

Then, feeling paranoid (probably another side effect of the pot invasion) I looked around the circle, sure I'd see a professor who was ready to leap in and haul us all away to . . . to . . . I dunno, something unspeakably horrid, like the boot camp Maury sends all of his troubled teen guests to.

But, thankfully, unlike the circle in Nyx's Temple, there were no adult vamps here, and only about twenty kids. They were talking quietly and acting like the totally illegal marijuana incense was no big deal. (Pot heads.) Trying to breathe shallowly, I turned to the girl to my right. When in doubt (or panic), make small talk.

"So . . . Deino is a, well, different name. Does it mean something special?"

"Deino means terrible," she said, smiling sweetly.

From my other side the tall blonde chimed in perkily, "And Enyo means warlike."

"Huh," I said, trying hard to be polite.

"Yeah, Pemphredo, which means wasp, is the one lighting the incense," explained Enyo. "We got the names from Greek mythology. They were the three sisters of the Gorgon and Scylla. Myth says they were born as hags who shared an eye, but we decided that was probably just bullshit male-dominant propaganda written by human men who wanted to keep strong women down."

"Really?" I didn't know what else to say. Really.

"Yeah," Deino said. "Human men suck."

"They should all die," Enyo said.

On that lovely thought the music suddenly started, making it impossible (thankfully) to talk.

Okay, the music was disturbing. It had a deep, pulsing beat that was ancient as well as modern. Like someone had mixed one of those nasty bootie-humping songs with a tribal mating dance. And then, much to my shock, Aphrodite began to dance her way around the circle. Yes, I suppose you could say she was hot. I mean, she had a good body and she moved like Catherine Zeta-Jones in *Chicago*. But somehow it didn't work for me. And I don't mean because I'm not gay (even though I'm not gay). It didn't work because it seemed like a crude imitation of Neferet's dance to "She Walks in Beauty." If this music was a poem it would be more like "Some Ho Grinds Her Bootie."

During Aphrodite's crotch-flailing display everyone was, naturally, staring at her, so I looked around the circle, pretending that I wasn't really looking for Erik, until . . . oh, crap . . . I found him almost directly opposite me. And he was the one kid in the room not watching Aphrodite. He was watching me. Before I could figure out whether I should look away, smile at him or wave or whatever (Damien had said to smile at the kid, and Damien was a self-proclaimed expert on guys), the music stopped and I looked from Erik to Aphrodite. She was standing in the middle of the circle in front of the table. Purposefully, she picked up a big purple pillar candle in one hand, and the knife in another. The candle was lit, and she carried it, holding it in front of her like a beacon, to the side of the circle where I now noticed one yellow candle nestled amongst the red ones. I didn't need any prodding from Warlike or Terrible (yeesh) to turn to the east. As wind ruffled my hair, from the corner of my vision I could see that she had lit the yellow candle and now she raised the knife, slashing a pentagram in the air as she spoke:

O winds of storm, in Nyx's name I do call thee forth,
cast thy blessing, I do ask,
upon the magic which shall be worked here!

I will admit that she was good. Though not as powerful as Neferet, it was obvious that she'd practiced voice control and the silky sound of her words carried easily. We turned to the south and she approached the large red pillar candle among the other red ones, and I could feel what I was already recognizing as the power of the fire and the magic circle wash over my skin.

> *O fire of lightning, in Nyx's name I do call thee forth,*
> *bringer of storms and power of magic,*
> *I ask your aid in the spell I do here work!*

We turned again and, along with Aphrodite, I felt flushed and unexpectedly drawn to the blue candle that nestled within the red ones. Even though it thoroughly freaked me out, I had to keep myself from stepping from circle and joining her in the invocation of water.

> *O torrents of rain, in Nyx's name I do call thee forth.*
> *Join me with your drowning strength, in performing this*
> *most powerful of rituals!*

What in the hell was wrong with me? I was sweating and instead of feeling just a little warm, like during the earlier ritual, the Mark on my forehead was hot—burning hot—and I swear I could hear the roar of the sea in my ears. Numbly, I turned again to the right.

> *O earth, deep and damp, in Nyx's name I do call thee forth,*
> *that I may feel the earth herself move in the roar of the storm*
> *of power*
> *which doth come when you aid me in this rite!*

Aphrodite sliced the air again, and I could feel the palm of my right hand tingle, as if it ached to hold the knife and cut the air.

I smelled cut grass and heard the cry of a whippoorwill, like it was nesting invisibly in the air beside me. Aphrodite moved back to the center of the circle. Placing the still-burning purple candle back on its place in the middle of the table she completed the casting.

O spirit, wild and free, in Nyx's name I do call thee to me!
Answer me! Stay with me during this mighty ritual
and grant me thy Goddess's power!

And somehow I knew what she was going to do next. I could hear the words inside my mind—inside my own spirit. When she raised the goblet and began walking around the circle I felt her words, and even though she didn't have the poise and power of Neferet what she said ignited within me, like I was burning from the inside out.

"This is the time of the fullness of our Goddess's moon. There is magnificence to this night. The ancients knew the mysteries of this night, and used them to strengthen themselves . . . and to split the veil between worlds and have adventures we only dream about today. Secret . . . mysterious . . . magical . . . true beauty and power in vampyre form—not tainted by human rules or law. We are *not* humans!" With this, her voice did ring against the walls, very much as Neferet's had earlier. "And all your Dark Daughters and Sons ask tonight in this rite is what we have petitioned each full moon for the past year. Free the power within us so that, like the mighty felines of the wild, we know the lithe suppleness of our animal brethren and we are not bound by human chains or caged by their ignorant weaknesses."

Aphrodite had stopped right in front of me. I knew I was flushed and breathing hard, just as she was. She raised the goblet and offered it to me.

"Drink, Zoey Redbird, and join us in asking Nyx for what is ours by the right of blood and body and the Mark of the great Change—the Mark that she has already touched you with."

Yes, I know. I should have probably said no. But how? And suddenly I didn't want to. I definitely didn't like or trust Aphrodite, but wasn't what she was saying basically true? My mother and stepfather's reactions to my Mark came back hard and clear in my memory, along with Kayla's look of fear and Drew's and Dustin's revulsion. And how no one had called me, or even text-messaged me, since I'd been gone. They'd just let me be dumped here to deal with a new life all on my own.

It made me sad, but it also made me mad.

I grabbed the goblet from Aphrodite and took a big drink. It was wine, but it didn't taste like the wine in the other moon ritual. This one was sweet, too, but there was a spice to it that tasted like nothing I'd ever experienced before. It caused an explosion of sensation in my mouth that traveled with a hot, bittersweet trail down my throat and filled me with a dizzy desire to drink more and more and more of it.

"Blessed be," Aphrodite hissed at me as she jerked the goblet from me, sloshing some of the red liquid over my fingers. Then she gave me a tight, triumphant smile.

"Blessed be," I replied automatically, head still reeling with the taste of the wine. She moved to Enyo, offering her the goblet, and I couldn't stop myself from licking my fingers to get one more taste of the wine that had spilled there. It was beyond delicious. And it smelled . . . it smelled familiar . . . but through the whoosh of dizziness in my head I couldn't concentrate enough to figure out where I'd smelled something that incredible before.

It hardly took any time for Aphrodite to travel around the circle, giving each of the kids a taste from the goblet. I watched her closely, wishing I could have more as she returned to the table. She lifted the goblet again.

"Great and magical Goddess of Night and of the full moon, she who rides through the thunder and the tempest, leading the spirits and the Elder Ones, beautiful and awesome one, who even those most ancient must obey, aid us in what we ask. Fill us with your power and magic and strength!"

Then she upended the goblet, and I watched, jealously, as she drank until she drained the last drops. When she finished drinking, the music started up again. In time with it she made her way back around the circle, dancing and laughing as she blew out each candle and told each element good-bye. And somehow, as she was moving around the circle, my vision got all screwed up because her body rippled and changed and it suddenly seemed as if I was watching Neferet again—only now she was a younger, rawer version of the High Priestess.

"Merry meet and merry part and merry meet again!" she finally said. We all responded while I blinked my vision clear and the weird image of Aphrodite-as-Neferet faded, as did the burning of my Mark. But I could still taste the wine on my tongue. It was way strange. I don't like alcohol. Seriously. I just don't like the way it tastes. But there was something about this wine that was delicious beyond . . . well, beyond even Godiva dark chocolate truffles (I know, it's hard to believe). And I still couldn't figure out why it somehow seemed familiar.

Then everyone started to talk and laugh as the circle broke up. The gaslights came on overhead, making us blink from their brightness. I looked across the circle, trying to see if Erik might still be watching me, and a movement at the table caught my eye. The person who had been slumped and motionless during the entire ritual was finally moving. He kinda jerked around, awkwardly pulling himself more into a sitting position. The hood on the dark cloak fell back, and I was shocked to see bright orange-red, bushy, unattractive hair and a pudgy too-white and freckled face.

It was that annoying Elliott kid! Very, very odd that he was here. What could the Dark Daughters and Sons want with him? I looked around the room again. Yep, as I'd suspected, there wasn't one ugly, dorky-looking kid present. Everyone, and I do mean everyone, except Elliott was attractive. He definitely didn't belong.

He was blinking and yawning and looked like he'd been sniffing way too much of the incense. He lifted his hand to wipe something off his nose (probably one of the boogers he liked to go spelunking after) and I saw the white of thick bandages that were wrapped around his wrists. What the . . . ?

A terrible, crawly feeling worked its way up my spine. Enyo and Deino were standing not far from me, talking animatedly to the girl they'd called Pemphredo. I walked over to them and waited till there was a lull in the conversation. Pretending that my stomach wasn't trying to squeeze itself to death, I smiled and nodded in the general direction of Elliott.

"What's that kid doing here?"

Enyo glanced at Elliott and then rolled her eyes. "He's nothing. Just the refrigerator we used tonight."

"What a loser," Deino said, dismissing Elliott with a sneer.

"He's practically *human*," Pemphredo said in disgust. "No wonder all he's good for is a snack bar."

My stomach felt like it was being turned inside out. "Wait, I don't get it. Refrigerator? Snack bar?"

Deino the Terrible turned her haughty, chocolate-colored eyes on me. "That's what we call humans—refrigerators and snack bars. You know—breakfast, lunch, and dinner."

"Or any of the meals in between," warlike Enyo practically purred.

"I still don't—" I started, but Deino interrupted me.

"Oh, come on! Don't pretend that you couldn't tell what was in the wine, and that you didn't *love* the taste of it."

"Yeah, admit it, Zoey. It was obvious. You would have downed the whole thing—you wanted it even more than we did. We saw you licking it off your fingers," Enyo said, leaning forward all into my personal space as she stared at my Mark. "That makes you some kind of freak, doesn't it? Somehow you're fledgling and vamp, all in one, and you wanted more of that kid's blood than just a taste."

"Blood?" I didn't recognize my own voice. The word "freak" kept echoing round and round in my head.

"Yes, *blood,*" Terrible said.

I felt hot and cold at once and looked away from their knowing faces, and right into Aphrodite's eyes. She was standing across the room from me talking to Erik. Our eyes locked and slowly, purposefully, she smiled. She was holding the goblet again, and she raised it in an almost imperceptible salute to me before taking a drink from it and turning back to laugh at something Erik had just said.

Holding myself together, I made a lame excuse to Warlike, Terrible, and the Wasp, and walked calmly from the room. The instant I closed the thick wooden door of the rec hall behind me I ran like a crazy blind person. I didn't know where I was going, except that I wanted to be away.

I drank blood—that horrid Elliott kid's blood—and I'd liked it! And worse, the delicious smell had been familiar because I'd smelled it before when Heath's hands had been bleeding. It hadn't been a new cologne I'd been drawn to; it had been his blood. And I'd smelled it again in the hall yesterday when Aphrodite had slit Erik's thigh and I had wanted to lick up his blood, too.

I was a freak.

Finally, I couldn't breathe and I collapsed against the cool stone of the school's protective wall, gasping for air and puking my guts up.

CHAPTER SEVENTEEN

—

Shakily, I wiped the back of my hand across my mouth and then stumbled away from the puke spot (I refused to even consider what I puked up and how it must have looked) until I came to a giant oak that had grown so close to the wall that half of its branches hung over the other side of it. I leaned against the tree, concentrating on not getting sick again.

What had I done? What was happening to me?

Then, from somewhere in the limbs of the oak I heard a meow. Okay, it wasn't really your normal, average, catlike meow. It was more like a grumpy, "me-eeh-uf-me-eef-uf-*snort.*"

I looked up. Perched on a limb that was resting against the wall was a small orange cat. She was staring at me with huge eyes and she definitely looked disgruntled.

"How did you get up there?"

"Me-uf," she said, sneezed, and inched her way along the branch, clearly trying to get closer to me.

"Well, come on kitty-kitty-kitty," I coaxed.

"Me-eeh-uf-ow," she said, creeping forward about half one of her little paw lengths.

"That's it, come on, baby girl. Move your little tiny paddies this way." Yes, I was displacing my freak-out and channeling it into saving the cat, but the truth was that I couldn't think about what had just happened. Not now. It was too soon. Too fresh. So the cat was an excellent distraction. Plus, she looked familiar. "Come on baby girl, come on . . ." I kept up a conversation with her as I hooked the toe of my flats into the rough brick of the wall and managed to pull myself up far enough so I could grab onto the lowest part of the branch the cat was on. Then I was able to use the branch as a kind of rope to climb farther up the wall, the whole time talking to the cat, while she kept complaining at me.

Finally I got within touching range of her. We stared at each other for a long time, and I started to wonder if she knew about me. Could she tell that I'd just tasted (and liked) blood? Did I have blood puke breath? Did I look different? Had I grown fangs? (Okay, that last question was ridiculous. Adult vamps don't have fangs, but still.)

She "me-eeh-uf-owed" at me again, and moved a little closer. I reached out and scratched the top of her head so that her ears went down and she closed her eyes, purring.

"You look like a little lioness," I told her. "See how much nicer you are when you're not complaining?" Then I blinked in surprise, realizing why she seemed so familiar. "You were in my dream." And a little happiness pushed through the wall of sickness and fear inside me. "You're my cat!"

The cat opened her eyes, yawned, and sneezed again, as if to comment on why it had taken me so long to figure it out. With a grunt of effort I scrambled up so that I was sitting on the wide top of the wall beside the branch where the cat was perched. With a kitty sigh, she jumped delicately off the branch, onto the top of the wall, and walked on tiny white paws over to me to crawl into my lap. There didn't seem to be anything for me to do except to scratch her on the head some more. She closed her eyes and purred loudly. I petted the cat and tried to still the tumult in my mind. The air smelled like it might rain, but the night was unusually warm for the end of October, and I put my head back, breathing deeply and letting the silver moonlight that peeked through the clouds calm me.

I looked at the cat. "Well, Neferet said that we should sit in the moonlight. I glanced up at the night sky again. "It would be better if the stupid clouds would blow away, but still . . ."

I had only just spoken the words and a gust of wind whistled around me, suddenly blowing away the wispy clouds.

"Well, thanks," I called aloud to nothing in particular. "That was a very convenient wind." The cat muttered, reminding me that I'd had the nerve to quit scratching her ears. "I think I'll call you Nala because you are a little lioness," I told her, resuming my scratching. "You know, baby girl, I'm so glad I found you today; I really needed something good to happen to me after the night I've had. You would not believe—"

A weird smell drifted up to me. It was so odd that I broke off what I was saying. What was that? I sniffed and wrinkled my nose. It was a dry, old smell. Like a house that had been closed up for too long, or somebody's scary old basement. It wasn't a good smell, but it also wasn't so gross that it made me want to gag. It was just wrong. Like it didn't belong out here in the open at night.

Then something caught at the corner of my eyesight. I looked down the long, winding brick wall. Standing there, half turned away from me like she wasn't sure which way she wanted to go, was a girl. The light from the moon, and my new and improved fledgling ability to see well at night, let me see her even though there were no outside lights near this part of the wall. I felt myself tense. Had one of those hateful Dark Daughters followed me? No way did I feel like dealing with any more of their crap tonight.

I must have actually voiced the frustrated groan I thought I had made in my mind, because the girl looked up toward where I was sitting on top of the wall.

I gasped in shock and felt fear skitter through me.

It was Elizabeth! The Elizabeth No Last Name kid who was supposed to be dead. When she saw me her eyes, which were a weird, glowing red, widened and then she made an odd shrieking sound before whirling around and disappearing with inhuman speed into the night.

At the same instant, Nala arched her back and hissed with such ferocity that her little body shook.

"It's okay! It's okay!" I said over and over, trying to calm the cat and me. Both of us were shaking and Nala was still growling low in her throat. "It couldn't have been a ghost. It couldn't have been. It was just . . . just . . . a weird kid. I probably scared her and she—"

"Zoey! Zoey! Is that you?"

I jumped and almost fell off the wall. It was too much for Nala. She gave another tremendous hiss and leaped neatly from my lap to the ground. Completely and utterly freaked out, I grabbed the branch for balance and squinted out into the night.

"Who—who is it?" I called over the pounding of my heart. Then I was blinded by the beams of two flashlights aimed directly at me.

"Of course it's her! Like I couldn't recognize my own best friend's voice? Jeesh, she hasn't been gone *that* long!"

"Kayla?" I said, trying to shield my eyes from the glare of the flashlights with my hand, which was shaking like crazy.

"Well, I told you we'd find her," a guy's voice said. "You always want to give up too soon."

"Heath?" Maybe I was dreaming.

"Yep! Whoo-hoo! We found ya, baby!" Heath yelled, and even in the awful flashlight glare I could see him hurl himself at the wall and then start to scramble up like a tall, blond, football-playing monkey.

Incredibly relieved it was him and not a boogie monster, I called down to him, "Heath! Be careful. If you fall you're going to break something." Well, unless he landed on his head—then he'd probably be okay.

"Not me!" he said, pulling himself up and over so that he was sitting beside me, straddling the wall. "Hey, Zoey, check it out— look at me; I'm king of the world!" He yelled, throwing out his arms, grinning like a total fool, and breathing alcohol-scented air all over me.

No wonder I'd refused to go out with him.

"Okay, there's no need to *forever* make fun of my unfortunate *ex*-infatuation with Leonardo." I glared at him, feeling more like myself than I had in hours. "Actually, it's kinda like my unfortunate *ex*-infatuation with you. Only it didn't last as long, and you didn't make a bunch of cheesy but cool movies."

"Hey, you're not still mad about Dustin and Drew are you? Forget them! They're retards." Heath said, giving me his puppy-dog look, which used to be really cute when he was in eighth grade. Too bad the cuteness had stopped working for him about two years ago. "And, anyway, we came all the way over here to bust you out."

"What?" I shook my head and squinted at him. "Wait. Turn those flashlights off. They're killing my eyes."

"If we turn them off we can't see," Heath said.

"Fine. Then turn them away. Uh, point them out there or something," I gestured out away from the school (and me). Heath turned the beam of the one he'd been clutching out into the night, and so did Kayla. I was able to drop my hand, which I was pleased to see had quit shaking, and stop squinting. Heath's eyes widened when he saw my Mark.

"Check it out! It's colored in now. Wow! It's like . . . like . . . on TV or something."

Well, it was nice to see that some things never change. Heath was still Heath—cute, but not the brightest Crayola in the pack.

"Hey! What about me? I'm here too, ya know!" Kayla called. "Someone help me get up there, but be careful. Let me put my new purse down. Oh, and I better take off these shoes. Zoey, you would not believe the sale you missed yesterday at Bakers. All of their summer shoes totally on closeout. I mean, *serious* closeout. Seventy percent off. I got five pairs for . . ."

"Help her up," I told Heath. "Now. It's the only way she'll stop talking."

Yep. Some things just didn't change.

Heath scooted around till he was on his belly, and then leaned down to offer his hands to Kayla. Giggling, she grabbed them and let him haul her up on top of the wall with us. And it was while she was giggling and he was hauling that I saw it—the unmistakable way Kayla grinned and giggled and blushed at Heath. I knew it as well as I knew I would never be a mathematician. Kayla liked Heath. Okay, not liked. She *liked* Heath.

Suddenly Heath's guilty comment about messing around on me at the party I'd missed made perfect sense.

"So how's Jared?" I asked abruptly, totally stopping K-babble's giggles.

"Okay, I guess," she said without meeting my eyes.

"You guess?"

She moved her shoulders and I saw that under her very cute leather jacket she was wearing the tiny little cream lace cami we used to call the Boob Shirt, because not only did it show a lot of cleavage, but it was the color of skin, so it looked like it was showing even more than it actually was.

"I dunno. We haven't really talked much the past couple days or so."

She still wouldn't look at me, but she did glance at Heath, who looked clueless—but that was really his only look. So my best friend was going after my boyfriend. Now that pissed me off, and for a second I wished it wasn't such a nice warm night. I wished it was cold and Kayla would freeze her over-developed boobies right off.

From the north the wind whipped around us suddenly, viciously, bringing an almost frightening chill.

Trying not to look obvious, Kayla pulled her jacket closed and giggled again, this time nervously instead of flirtatiously, and I got another big whiff of beer, and something else. Something that had been so recently imprinted into my senses that I was surprised I hadn't smelled it right away.

"Kayla you've been drinking *and* smoking?"

She shivered and blinked at me like a very slow rabbit. "Just a couple. Beers, I mean. And, well, um, Heath had one little bitty joint and I was really, really scared to come here, so I just had a couple tiny hits off it."

"She needed some fortification," Heath said, but he's never been good with words over two syllables, so it sounded like fort-fi-ka-shun.

"Since when have you started smoking pot?" I asked Heath.

He grinned. "It's no big deal, Zo. I just have a joint once in a while. They're safer than cigarettes."

I really hated it when he called me Zo.

"Heath," I tried to sound patient. "They are not safer than cigarettes, and even if they are that's not saying much. Cigarettes are disgusting and they kill you. And, seriously, the biggest losers at school smoke pot. Besides the fact that you really can not afford to kill any more brain cells." I almost added "or sperms," but I didn't want to go there. Heath would definitely get the wrong idea if I made a reference to his man parts.

"Nu uh," Kayla said.

"What Kayla?"

She was still clutching her jacket against the chill. Her eyes had changed from pitiful rabbit to sly, tail-twitchy cat. I recognized the change. She did it constantly with people she didn't consider part of her girlfriend group. It used to drive me crazy and I would yell at her and tell her she shouldn't be so mean. Now she was turning that crap on me?

"I said nu uh because not just losers smoke—at least not just once in a while. You know those two really hot running backs who play for Union, Chris Ford and Brad Higeons? I saw them at Katie's party the other night. They smoke."

"Hey, they're not that hot," Heath said.

Kayla ignored him and kept talking. "And Morgan smokes sometimes."

"Morgan, as in Morgie who's a Tigette?" Yes, I was pissed at K, but good gossip is good gossip.

"Yeah. She also just got her tongue and her"—K broke off and mouthed the word "clit"—"pierced. Can you imagine how much that must have hurt?"

"What? What did she get pierced?" Heath said.

"Nothing," K and I said together, for a moment sounding eerily like the best friends we used to be.

"Kayla, you're not staying on subject. Again. The Union football players have always been drug-happy. Hello! Please recall their steroid use, which is why it took sixteen years for us to beat them."

"Go, Tigers! Yeah, we kicked Union's ass!" Heath said.

I rolled my eyes at him.

"And Morgan has clearly begun losing her mind, which is why she's piercing her . . ." I glanced at Heath and reconsidered. "Her body *and* smoking. Tell me someone normal who's smoking."

K thought for a second. "Me!"

I sighed. "Look, I just don't think it's smart."

"Well, you don't always know *everything*." The hateful glint was back in her eyes.

I looked from her to Heath, and then back to her again. "Clearly, you're right. I don't know *everything*."

Her mean look turned startled and then flattened out to mean again, and I suddenly couldn't help comparing her to Stevie Rae, who, even though I'd only known for a couple days, I was absolutely, totally sure would not ever go after my boyfriend, whether he was an almost-ex or not. I also didn't think she would run away from me and treat me like I was a monster when I needed her the most.

"I think you should leave," I said to Kayla.

"Fine," she said.

"It's probably not a good idea for you to come back again, either."

She shrugged one shoulder so that her jacket fell open and I could see the thin strap of the cami slip down her shoulder, making it clear she wasn't wearing a bra.

"Whatever," she said.

"Help her get down, Heath."

Heath was generally pretty good at following simple directions, so he hoisted Kayla down. She grabbed the flashlight and looked back up at us.

"Hurry up, Heath. I'm getting really cold." Then she spun around and started marching off toward the road.

"Well . . . ," Heath said a little awkwardly. "It did get cold all of a sudden."

"Yeah, it can quit now," I said absently, and didn't pay much attention when the wind suddenly stopped.

"Hey, uh, Zo. I really did come to bust you out."

"No."

"Huh?" Heath said.

"Heath, look at my forehead."

"Yeah, you have that half moon thing. And it's colored in, which is weird because it wasn't colored in before."

"Well, it is now. Okay, Heath, focus. I've been Marked. That means that my body is going through the Change to become a vampyre."

Heath's eyes went from my Mark and traveled down my body. I saw them hesitate at my boobs and then my legs, which made me realize that they were showing all naked almost up to my crotch because my skirt had hiked up when I climbed on top of the wall.

"Zo, whatever's happening to your body is cool with me. You look seriously hot. You've always been beautiful, but now you look like a real goddess." He smiled at me and touched my cheek gently, reminding me why I've liked him so much for such a long time. Despite his faults, Heath could be really sweet, and he always made me feel completely beautiful.

"Heath," I said softly. "I'm sorry, but things have changed."

"Not with me they haven't." Taking me completely by surprise he leaned forward, slid a hand up over my knee and kissed me.

I jerked back and grabbed his wrist. "Stop it Heath! I'm trying to talk to you."

"How about you talk, and I kiss?" he whispered.

I started to tell him no again.

Then I felt it.

His pulse under my fingers.

It was beating hard and fast. I swear I could hear it, too. And as he leaned into me to kiss me again I could see the vein that ran along his neck. It moved, beating strong as the blood pumped through his body. Blood . . . His lips touched mine and I remembered the taste of the blood in the goblet. That blood had been cold and mixed with wine, and from a weak, loser kid who was a nothing. Heath's blood would be hot and rich . . . sweet . . . sweeter than Elliott the Refrigerator. . . .

"Ow! Damn, Zoey. You scratched me!" He jerked his wrist from my hand. "Shit, Zo, you made me bleed. If you didn't want me to kiss you, all you had to do was say so."

He lifted his bleeding wrist to his mouth and sucked at the drop of blood that was glistening there. Then he raised his eyes to meet mine, and he froze. He had blood on his lips. I could smell it—it was like the wine, only better, worlds better. The scent of it wrapped around me and made the hair on my arms rise.

I wanted to taste it. I wanted to taste it more than anything I'd ever wanted in my life.

"I want . . ." I heard myself whisper in a voice I didn't know.

"Yes . . . ," Heath answered like he was in a trance. "Yes . . . whatever you want. I'll do whatever you want."

This time I leaned into him and touched my tongue to his lip, taking the drop of blood into my mouth where it exploded— heat, sensation, and a rush of pleasure I'd never known.

"More," I rasped.

Like he'd lost the ability to speak and could only nod, Heath lifted his wrist to me. It was barely bleeding, and when I licked the tiny scarlet line Heath moaned. The touch of my tongue seemed to do something to the scratch, because instantly it started dripping blood, faster . . . faster . . . My hands were shaking as I raised his wrist to my mouth and pressed my lips against his warm skin. I shivered and moaned in pleasure and—

"Oh my *God!* What are you doing to him!" Kayla's voice was a scream that pierced through the scarlet fog in my brain.

I dropped Heath's wrist as though it had burned me.

"Get away from him!" Kayla was shrieking. "Leave him alone!" Heath didn't move.

"Go," I told him. "Go and don't ever come back."

"No," he said, looking and sounding oddly sober.

"Yes. Get out of here."

"Let him go!" Kayla yelled.

"Kayla, if you don't shut up I'll fly down there and suck every last bit of blood from your stupid cheating cow body!" I spit the words at her.

She squealed and took off. I turned back to Heath, who was still staring at me.

"Now you need to go, too."

"I'm not scared of you, Zo."

"Heath, I'm scared of me enough for both of us."

"But I don't mind what you did. I love you, Zoey. More now than I ever have."

"Stop it!" I didn't mean to yell, but I caused him to flinch at the power that had filled my words. I swallowed hard and calmed my voice. "Just go. Please." Then, searching for some way to make him leave I added, "Kayla's probably going to get the cops right now. Neither of us needs that."

"Okay, I'll go. But I won't stay away." He kissed me hard and quick. I felt a white-hot stab of pleasure when I tasted the blood that was still on our lips. Then he slid down the wall and disappeared into the darkness until all I could see of him was the little dot of light from his flashlight, and then, finally, not even that.

I wouldn't let myself think. Not yet. Moving methodically, like a robot, I used the branch to steady myself as I climbed down. My knees were shaking so badly that I was able to walk only the couple of feet to the tree where I sank down on the ground, pressing my back against the security of its ancient bark. Nala materialized, hopping into my lap as if she'd been my cat for years instead of minutes, and as my sobs started she crawled from my lap to my chest to press her warm face against my wet cheek.

After what seemed like a long time my sobs turned to hiccups and I wished I hadn't run out of the rec hall without my purse. I could really use a Kleenex.

"Here. You look like you need this."

Nala complained as I jumped in surprise at the voice, and blinked up through my tears to see someone handing me a tissue.

"Th-thanks," I said, taking it and wiping my nose.

"No problem," Erik Night said.

CHAPTER EIGHTEEN

—

"Are you okay?"

"Yeah, I'm okay. Totally. Fine." I lied.

"You don't look fine," Erik said. "Mind if I sit down?"

"No, go ahead," I said listlessly. I knew my nose was bright red. I'd definitely been snotting on myself when he walked up, and I had the sneaking suspicion he'd witnessed at least part of the nightmare between Heath and me. The night was just getting worse and worse. I glanced at him and decided, *What the hell, I might as well continue the trend.* "In case you didn't realize it, it was me who saw that little scene between you and Aphrodite in the hall yesterday."

He didn't even hesitate. "I know, and I wish you hadn't. I don't want you to get the wrong idea about me."

"And what idea would that be?"

"That there's more going on between Aphrodite and me than there really is."

"Not my business," I said.

He shrugged. "I just want you to know that she and I are not going out anymore."

I almost said that it sure looked like Aphrodite wasn't aware of that, but then I thought about what had just happened between

Heath and me, and with a sense of surprise I realized that maybe I shouldn't judge Erik too harshly.

"Okay. You guys aren't going out," I said.

He sat quietly beside me for a little while, and when he spoke again I thought he sounded almost angry. "Aphrodite didn't tell you about the blood in the wine."

He hadn't said it like a question, but I answered anyway. "Nope."

He shook his head and I saw his jaw tighten. "She told me she was going to. She said she'd let you know while you were changing your clothes so that if you weren't okay with it you could skip drinking from the goblet."

"She lied."

"Not a big surprise," he said.

"Ya think?" I could feel my own anger building inside me. "This whole thing has just been wrong. I get pressured into going to the Dark Daughters' ritual where I'm tricked into drinking blood. Then I meet up with my almost-ex-boyfriend who just happens to be one hundred percent human, and no-damn-body bothered to explain to me that the tiniest speck of his blood would turn me into . . . into . . . a monster." I bit my lip and held on to my anger so I wouldn't start crying again. I also decided I wouldn't say anything about thinking I saw Elizabeth's ghost— that was too much weird to admit for one night.

"No one explained it to you because it's something that shouldn't have started to effect you until you were a sixth former," he said quietly.

"Huh?" I was back to being dazzlingly articulate.

"Bloodlust doesn't usually begin until you're a sixth former and you're almost completely Changed. Once in a while you'll hear about a fifth former who has to deal with it early, but that doesn't happen very often."

"Wait—what are you saying?" My mind felt like bees were buzzing around in it.

"You start having classes about bloodlust and other things mature vamps have to deal with during your fifth form, and then, in your final year, that's mostly what school focuses on—that and whatever you've decided to major in."

"But I'm a third former—barely I mean, I've only been Marked a few days."

"Your Mark is different; *you're* different," he said.

"I don't want to be different!" I realized I was shouting and got my voice under control. "I just want to figure out how to get through this like everybody else."

"Too late, Z," he said.

"So what now?"

"I think you'd better talk to your mentor. It's Neferet, isn't it?"

"Yeah," I said miserably.

"Hey, cheer up. Neferet's great. She hardly ever takes on fledglings to mentor anymore, so she must really believe in you."

"I know, I know. It's just that this makes me feel . . ." How *did* I feel about talking to Neferet about what had happened tonight? Embarrassed. Like I was twelve years old again and I had to tell our male gym teacher that I'd started my period and had to go to the locker room to change my shorts. I peeked sideways at Erik. There he sat, gorgeous and attentive and perfect. Hell. I couldn't tell him that. So instead I blurted, "Stupid. It makes me feel stupid." Which wasn't actually a lie, but mostly what it made me feel, besides embarrassed and stupid, was scared. I didn't want this thing that made it impossible for me to fit in.

"Don't feel stupid. You're actually way ahead of the rest of us."

"So . . . ," I hesitated, then took a deep breath and barreled on, "did you like the way the blood in the goblet tasted tonight?"

"Well, here's the deal with that: My first Full Moon Ritual with the Dark Daughters was at the end of my third former year. Except for the 'refrigerator' that night, I was the only third former there—just like you tonight." He gave a small, humorless laugh. "They only invited me because I'd finaled in the Shakespeare soliloquy contest and was being flown to London for the competition the next day." He glanced at me and looked a little embarrassed. "No one from this House of Night had ever made it to London. It was a big deal." He shook his head self-mockingly. "Actually, I thought *I* was a big deal. So the Dark Daughters invited me to join them, and I did. I knew about the blood. I was given the opportunity to turn it down. I didn't."

"But did you like it?"

This time his laugh was real. "I gagged and puked my guts up. It was the most disgusting thing I'd ever tasted."

I groaned. My head dropped forward and I put my face in my hands. "You're not helping me."

"Because you thought it was good?"

"Better than good," I said, my face still in my hands. "You say it was the most disgusting thing you'd ever tasted? I thought it was the most delicious. Well, the most delicious until I—" I stopped, realizing what I had been about to say.

"Until you tasted fresh blood?" he asked gently.

I nodded my head, afraid to speak.

He tugged at my hands, making me unbury my face. Then he put his finger under my chin and forced me to look straight at him.

"Don't be embarrassed or ashamed. It's normal."

"Loving the taste of blood is *not* normal. Not for me."

"Yes, it is. All vampyres have to deal with their lust for blood," he said.

"I am not a vampyre!"

"Maybe you're not—yet. But you're also definitely not the

average fledgling, and there's nothing wrong with that. You're special, Zoey, and special can be amazing."

Slowly, he took his finger from my chin and, as he had earlier that night, he traced the shape of a pentagram softly over my darkened Mark. I liked the way his finger felt against my skin— warm and a little rough. I also liked that being near him didn't set off all the weird reactions I'd had to being close to Heath. I mean, I couldn't hear Erik's blood beating or see the pulse in his neck jumping. Not that I'd mind if he kissed me. . . .

Hell! Was I becoming a vampyre slut? What was next? Would no male of any species (which might even include Damien) be safe around me? Maybe I should avoid all guys until I figured out what was going on with me and knew I could control myself.

Then I remembered that I had been trying to avoid everyone, which is why I was out here in the first place.

"What are you doing out here, Erik?"

"I followed you," he said simply.

"Why?"

"I figured I knew what Aphrodite had pulled in there and I thought you might need a friend. You're rooming with Stevie Rae, right?"

I nodded.

"Yeah, I thought about finding her and sending her out here to you, but I didn't know if you'd want her to know about . . ." He paused and made a vague gesture back in the direction of the rec hall.

"No! I—I don't want her to know." I stumbled over the words, I said them so fast.

"That's what I thought. So, that's why you're stuck with me." He smiled and then looked kinda uncomfortable. "I really didn't mean to listen in between you and Heath. Sorry about that."

I focused on petting Nala. So, he'd watched Heath kiss me, and then saw the whole blood thing. God, how embarrassing . . . Then a thought struck me and I glanced up at him, smiling ironically. "I guess that makes us even. I didn't mean to listen in between you and Aphrodite, either."

He smiled back at me. "We're even. I like that."

His smile made my stomach do funny things. "I wouldn't really have flown down and sucked Kayla's blood," I managed to say.

He laughed. (He had a really nice laugh.) "I know that. Vampyres can't fly."

"It freaked her out, though," I said.

"From what I saw, she deserved it." He waited a beat and then said, "Can I ask you something? It's kinda personal."

"Hey, you've seen me drink blood from a cup and like it, puke, kiss a guy, lick his blood like I'm a puppy, and then bawl my eyes out. And I've seen you turn down a blow job. I think I can manage to answer a kinda personal question."

"Was he really in a trance? He looked like it and he sounded like it."

I squirmed uncomfortably and Nala complained at me till I petted her quiet.

"It seemed like he was," I finally managed to say. "I don't know if it was a trance or not—and I totally didn't mean to put him under my power or anything freaky like that—but he did change. I dunno. He'd been smoking and drinking. He might have just been high." I heard Heath's voice again, rising from my memory like a cloying mist: *Yes . . . whatever you want . . . I'll do whatever you want.* And I saw that intense look he'd given me. Hell, I hadn't even known Heath the Jock was capable of that kind of intensity (at least off the football field). I knew for sure he couldn't spell the word (intensity, not football).

"Had he been like that the whole time, or just after you . . . um . . . started to—"

"Not the whole time. Why?"

"Well, that rules out two things that could have been making him act weird. One—if he was just high then he would have been like that the whole time. Two—he might have been acting like that because you're really pretty, and that alone could make a guy feel like he's in a trance around you."

His words made something flutter low in my stomach again— something that no guy had made me feel before. Not Heath the Jock, or Jordon the Sloth, or Jonathan the Stupid Band Kid (my dating history isn't long, but it's colorful).

"Really?" I said like a moron.

"Really." He smiled very unmoronically.

How could this guy like me? I'm a blood-drinking dork.

"But that wasn't it either, because he should have noticed how hot you look even before you kissed him, and what you're saying is that he didn't seem entranced until after blood came into the picture."

(*Entranced*—hee hee—he actually said *entranced*.) I was too busy grinning stupidly at his use of complex vocab to think before I answered him. "Actually, it happened when I started to hear his blood."

"Say again?"

Ah, crap. I hadn't meant to say that. I cleared my throat. "Heath started to change when I heard the blood pounding through his veins."

"Only adult vamps can hear that." He paused and then, with a quick smile added, "And Heath sounds like the name of a gay soap opera star."

"Close. He's BA's star quarterback."

Erik nodded and looked amused.

"Uh, by the way, I like what you changed your name to. Night is a cool last name," I said, trying to hold up my end of the conversation and say something even slightly insightful.

His smile widened. "I didn't change it. Erik Night is the name I was born with."

"Oh, well. I like it." Why didn't someone just shoot me?

"Thanks."

He glanced at his watch and I could see that it was almost six thirty—in the A.M., which still seemed freaky.

"It'll be getting light soon," he said.

Guessing that this was our cue for us to go our separate ways, I started to gather my feet under me and get a better hold on Nala so I could stand up, and I felt Erik's hand under my elbow, steadying me. He helped me up and then just stood there, so close that Nala's tail was brushing against his black sweater.

"I'd ask if you wanted to get something to eat, but the only place serving food right now is the rec hall, and I don't think you want to go back there."

"No, definitely not. But I'm not hungry anyway." Which, I realized as soon as I said it, was a big lie. At the mention of food I was suddenly starving.

"Well, do you mind if I walk you back to your dorm?" he asked.

"Nope," I said, trying to be nonchalant.

Stevie Rae, Damien, and the Twins would totally die if they saw me with Erik.

We didn't say anything as we started walking, but it wasn't an awkward, uncomfortable silence. Actually, it was nice. Once in a while our arms would brush against each other and I thought about how tall and cute he was and how much I'd like him to hold my hand.

"Oh," he said after a while, "I didn't finish answering your question before. The first time I tasted blood at one of the Dark Daughters' rituals I hated it, but it got better and better each time. I can't say I think it's delicious, but it's grown on me. And I definitely like the way it makes me feel."

I looked sharply at him. "Dizzy and kinda weak-kneed? Like you're drunk, only you're not."

"Yeah. Hey, did you know it's impossible for a vamp to get drunk?" I shook my head. "It's something about what the Change does to our metabolism. It's even tough for fledglings to get wasted."

"So drinking blood is the way vamps get wasted?"

He shrugged. "I suppose. Anyway, drinking human blood is forbidden for fledglings."

"Well then why hasn't anyone clued the teachers in on what Aphrodite's up to?"

"She's not drinking human blood."

"Uh, Erik, I was there. Blood was definitely in the wine and it came from that Elliott kid." I shuddered. "And what a gross choice he was, too."

"But he's not human," Erik said.

"Wait—it's forbidden to drink human blood," I said slowly. (Oh, hell! That's what I'd just done.) "But it's okay to drink an-other fledgling's blood?"

"Only if it's consensual."

"That makes no sense."

"Sure it does. It's normal for our bloodlust to develop as our bodies Change, so we need an outlet. Fledglings heal quickly, so there's no real chance of someone getting hurt. And there aren't any aftereffects, like when a vamp feeds off a living human."

What he was saying was banging through my head like the annoying, too-loud music that blared in Wet Seal, and I grasped the first thing I could think clearly about. "*Living* human?" I squeaked. "Tell me you don't mean versus feeding off a corpse." I was feeling a little nauseous again.

He laughed. "No, I mean versus drinking blood harvested from the vamps' blood donors."

"Never heard of such a thing."

"Most humans haven't. You won't learn about it until you're a fifth former."

Then some more of what he'd said broke through the confusion that was my mind. "What did you mean by aftereffects?"

"We just started learning about it in Vamp Sociology 312. Seems that when an adult vampyre feeds from a living human, there can be a very strong bond formed. It's not always on the part of the vamp, but humans become infatuated pretty easily. It's dangerous for the human. I mean, think about it. The blood loss alone isn't a good thing. Then add that to the fact that we outlive humans by decades, sometimes even centuries. Look at it from a human's point of view; it would really suck to be totally in love with someone who never seems to age while you get old and wrinkled and then die."

Again I thought about the dazed but intense way Heath had looked at me, and I knew that, no matter how hard it might be, I'd have to tell Neferet everything.

"Yep, that would suck," I said faintly.

"Here we are."

I was surprised to see that we'd stopped in front of the girl's dorm. I looked up at him.

"Well, thanks for following me—I think," I said, with a wry smile.

"Hey, any time you want someone to butt in when he's not invited, I'm the guy for you."

"I'll keep that in mind," I said. "Thanks." I hefted Nala up on my hip and started to open the door.

"Hey, Z," he called.

I turned back.

"Don't give back the dress to Aphrodite. By her including you in the circle tonight she formally offered you a position in the Dark Daughters, and it's tradition that the High Priestess in training gives a gift to the new member on her first night. I don't imagine you'll want to join, but you still have the right to keep the dress. Especially because you look so much better in it than she ever did." He reached forward and took my hand (the one that wasn't clutching my cat), and turned it over so that my wrist faced up. Then he took his finger and traced the vein that was close to the surface there, making my pulse jump crazily.

"And you should also know that I'm the guy for you if you decide you might like to try another sip of blood. Keep that in mind, too."

Erik bent and, still looking in my eyes, he lightly bit the pulse point at my wrist before kissing the spot softly. This time the fluttery feeling in my stomach was more intense. It made the inside of my thighs tingle and my breathing deepen. His lips still on my wrist he met my eyes and I felt a shiver of desire pass through my body. I knew he could feel me tremble. He let his tongue flick against my wrist, which made me shiver again. Then he smiled at me and walked away into the pre-dawn light.

CHAPTER NINETEEN

—

My wrist was still tingling from Erik's totally unexpected kiss (and bite and lick), and I wasn't sure I could speak yet, so I was relieved that there were only a few girls in the big entry room, and they did little more than glance at me before they went back to watching what sounded like *America's Next Top Model*. I hurried into the kitchen and plunked Nala down on the floor, hoping she wouldn't run off while I made a sandwich. She didn't; actually she followed me around the room like a little orange dog, complaining at me in her weird non-meow. I kept telling her "I know" and "I understand" because I figured she was yelling at me about what a moron I'd been tonight, and, well, she was right. Sandwich made, I grabbed a bag of pretzels (Stevie Rae had been right, I couldn't find any decent junk food in any of the cabinets), some brown pop (I don't really care what kind, just so that it's brown and not diet—eesh), and my cat, and I slipped up the stairs.

"Zoey! I've been so worried about you! Tell me everything." Curled up in bed with a book, Stevie Rae was obviously waiting up for me. She was wearing her pajamas that had cowboy hats all over the drawstring cotton pants, and her short hair was sticking out on one side as if she'd fallen asleep on it. I swear she looked about twelve years old.

"Well," I said brightly. "Looks like we have a pet." I turned so that Stevie Rae could see Nala squished against my hip. "Here, help me before I drop something. If it's the cat she'll probably never stop complaining."

"She's adorable!" Stevie Rae leaped up and rushed over to try to take Nala from me, but the cat clung to me as though someone would kill her if she let go, so Stevie Rae took my food instead and set it on my bedside table.

"Hey, that dress is amazing."

"Yeah, I changed before the ritual." Which reminded me that I was going to have to give it back to Aphrodite. Fine. I was not keeping the "gift," even though Erik had said I should. Anyway, returning it seemed like a good time to "thank" her for "forgetting" to clue me in about the blood. Hag bitch.

"So . . . how was it?"

I sat on my bed and gave Nala a pretzel, which she promptly started batting around (at least she'd stopped complaining), then I took a big bite of sandwich. Yes, I was hungry, but I was also buying time. I didn't know what I should tell Stevie Rae, and what I shouldn't. The blood thing was just so confusing—and so gross. Would she think I was awful? Would she be scared of me?

I swallowed and decided to steer the conversation to a safer topic. "Erik Night walked me home."

"Get out!" She bobbed up and down on the bed like a country jack-in-the-box. "Tell me *everything*."

"He kissed me," I said, crinkling my eyebrows at her.

"You have got to be kidding! Where? How? Was it good?"

"He kissed my hand." I decided quickly to lie. I didn't want to explain the whole wrist/pulse/blood/bite thing. "It was when he said good night. We were right in front of the dorm. And, yes, it was good." I grinned at her around another mouthful of sandwich.

"I'll bet Aphrodite shit puppies when you left the rec hall with him."

"Well, actually, I left before him and he caught up with me. I'd, uh, gone for a walk along the wall, which is where I found Nala," I scratched the cat's head. She curled up next to me, closed her eyes, and started purring. "Actually, I think *she* found *me*. Anyway, I had climbed up on the wall because I thought she needed rescuing, and then—and you will *not* believe this—I saw something that looked like Elizabeth's ghost, and then my almost-ex-boyfriend from SIHS, Heath, and my ex–best friend showed up."

"What? Who? Slow down. Start with Elizabeth's ghost."

I shook my head and chewed. Through bites of sandwich I explained. "It was really creepy and really weird. I was sitting up there on the wall petting Nala, and something caught my attention. I looked down and there was this girl standing not too far away from me. She looked up at me, with red glowing eyes, and I swear it was Elizabeth."

"No way! Were you totally freaked?"

"Totally. The second she saw me she gave this horrible shriek and then ran off."

"I would have been scared shitless."

"I was, only I hardly had time to think about it when Heath and Kayla showed up."

"What do you mean? How could they be here?"

"No, not *here*, they were outside the wall. They must have heard me trying to settle Nala down after she completely freaked at Elizabeth's ghost, because they came running up."

"Nala saw her, too?"

I nodded.

Stevie Rae shivered. "Then she must have really been there."

"Are you sure she's dead?" My voice was almost a whisper.

"There couldn't have been some mistake made and she's still alive but wandering around the school?" It sounded ridiculous, but not much more ridiculous than me seeing an actual ghost.

Stevie Rae swallowed hard. "She's dead. I saw her die. Everyone in class did."

She looked like she was going to cry and the whole subject was creeping me out, so I shifted to a less scary topic. "Well, I could be wrong. Maybe it was just some kid with weird eyes who looked like her. It was dark, and then Heath and Kayla were suddenly there."

"What was that all about?"

"Heath said they came to 'bust me out.'" I rolled my eyes. "Can you imagine?"

"Are they stupid?"

"Apparently. Oh, and then Kayla, my ex–best friend, made it obvious that she's after Heath!"

Stevie Rae gasped. "Slut!"

"No kidding. Anyway, I told them to leave and not come back, and then I got upset, which is when Erik found me."

"Aww! Was he sweet and romantic?"

"Yeah, he was, kinda. And he called me Z."

"Ooooh, a nickname is a seriously good sign."

"That's what I thought."

"So then he walked you back to the dorm?"

"Yeah, he said that he'd take me to get something to eat, but the only thing that was still open was the rec hall, and I didn't want to go back there." Ah, crap. I knew right away that I shouldn't have said that much.

"Were the Dark Daughters awful?"

I looked at Stevie Rae with her big deer-like eyes, and knew I couldn't tell her about drinking blood. Not yet. "Well, you know how Neferet was sexy and beautiful *and* classy?"

Stevie Rae nodded.

"Aphrodite did basically what Neferet did, but she looked like a ho."

"I've always thought that she was really nasty," Stevie Rae said, shaking her head in disgust.

"Tell me about it." I looked at Stevie Rae and blurted, "Yesterday, right before Neferet took me here to the dorm I saw Aphrodite trying to give Erik a blow job."

"No way! Jeesh, she's disgusting. Wait, you said she was *trying* to do it. What's up with that?"

"He was telling her no and pushing her away. He said he didn't want her anymore."

Stevie Rae giggled. "I'll bet that made her lose what little of her mind she has left."

I remembered how she'd been all over him, even when he was clearly telling her no. "Actually, I would have felt sorry for her if she hadn't been so . . . so . . ." I struggled to put it into words.

"Hag from hell–like?" Stevie Rae offered helpfully.

"Yeah, I guess that's it. She has this attitude, like it's her right to be as mean and nasty as she wants to be, and we should all just bow down and accept her."

Stevie Rae nodded. "That's how her friends are, too."

"Yeah, I met the awful triplets."

"You mean Warlike, Terrible, and Wasp?"

"Exactly. What were they thinking when they took those horrid names?" I said, popping pretzels in my mouth.

"They were thinking exactly what that entire group of hers thinks—that they are better than everyone else and untouchable because nasty Aphrodite is going to be the next High Priestess."

I spoke the next words as they whispered through my mind. "I don't think Nyx will allow that."

"What do you mean? They are already the 'in' group, and

Aphrodite has been leader of the Dark Daughters since her affinity became obvious during her fifth former year."

"What's her affinity?"

"She gets visions, like of future tragedies," Stevie Rae scowled.

"Do you think she fakes them?"

"Oh, heck no! She's amazingly accurate. What I think, and Damien and the Twins agree with me, is that she only tells about the visions if she has one when she's around people outside her little group."

"Wait, are you saying she knows about bad things that are going to happen in time to stop them, but she doesn't do anything about it?"

"Yep. Last week she had a vision during lunch, but the hags closed ranks around her and started leading her out of the dining hall. If Damien hadn't run right into them because he was late and hurrying in to lunch, making them scatter so that he could see that Aphrodite was in the middle of a vision, no one would ever have known. And a whole plane full of people would probably be dead."

I choked on a pretzel. Between coughs I sputtered, "A plane full of people! What the hell?"

"Yeah, Damien could tell Aphrodite was having a vision, so he got Neferet. Aphrodite had to tell her the vision, which was seeing a jet crash just after takeoff. Her visions are so clear that she could describe the airport and read the numbers on the tail of the plane. Neferet took that info and contacted the Denver airport. They double-checked the plane and found some problem that they hadn't noticed before, and said that if they hadn't fixed it the plane would have crashed immediately after takeoff. But I know darn well Aphrodite wouldn't have said a word if she hadn't been caught, even though she made up a big lie about her friends leading her from the dining hall because they knew she'd want to be taken to Neferet right away. Total b.s."

I started to say that I couldn't believe that even Aphrodite and her hags would purposefully allow the death of hundreds of people, but then I remembered the hateful stuff they'd said that night—*Human men suck . . . They should all die*—and I realized they hadn't just been talking; they'd been serious.

"So why didn't Aphrodite lie to Neferet? You know, tell her a different airport or switch the numbers of the plane around or something?"

"Vamps are almost impossible to lie to, especially when they ask you a direct question. And, remember, Aphrodite wants to be a High Priestess more than anything. If Neferet believed she was as twisted as she is, it would seriously hurt her future plans."

"Aphrodite has no business being a High Priestess. She's selfish and hateful, and so are her friends."

"Yeah, well, Neferet doesn't think so, and she was her mentor."

I blinked in surprise. "You've got to be kidding! And she doesn't see through Aphrodite's crap?" That couldn't be right; Neferet is way smarter than that.

Stevie Rae shrugged. "She acts different around Neferet."

"But still . . ."

"And she does have a powerful affinity, which has to mean that Nyx has special plans for her."

"Or she's a demon from hell, and she gets her power from the dark side. *Hello!* Has no one seen *Star Wars*? It was hard to believe Anakin Skywalker would turn, and look what happened there."

"Uh, Zoey. That's like total fiction."

"Still, I think it makes a good point."

"Well, try telling that to Neferet."

I chewed my sandwich and thought about it. Maybe I should. Neferet did seem way too smart to fall for Aphrodite's games. She probably already knew something was up with the hags. Maybe all she needed was someone to stand up and say something to her.

"So, has anyone ever tried to tell Neferet about Aphrodite?" I asked.

"Not that I know of."

"Why not?"

Stevie Rae looked uncomfortable. "Well, I think it seems kinda tattletale-like. Anyway, what would we tell Neferet? That we *think* Aphrodite *might* hide her visions, but that the only proof we have is that she's a hateful bitch." Stevie Rae shook her head. "No, I can't see that going over very well with Neferet. Plus, if by some miracle she believed us, what would Neferet do? It's not like she's going to kick her out of the school so she can cough herself to death on the streets. She'd still be here with her pack of hags and all those guys who would do anything for her if she snapped her little clawed fingers at them. I guess it's just not worth it."

Stevie Rae had a point, but I didn't like it. I really, really didn't like it.

Things might be different if a more powerful fledgling took Aphrodite's place as leader of the Dark Daughters.

I jumped guiltily, and covered it by taking a big gulp of pop. What was I thinking? I wasn't power hungry. I didn't want to be a High Priestess or get caught up in a pain-in-the-ass battle with Aphrodite and half the school (the more attractive half, at that). I just wanted to find a place for myself in this new life, a place that felt like home—a place where I fit in and was like the rest of the kids.

Then I remembered the electric jolts I'd felt during the casting of both circles, and how the elements had seemed to sizzle through my body, and also how I had had to force myself to stay in the circle and not join Aphrodite in the casting.

"Stevie Rae, when a circle's being cast, do you feel anything?" I asked abruptly.

"What do you mean?"

"Well, like when fire's called to the circle. Do you ever feel hot?"

"Nah. I mean, I really like the circle stuff, and sometimes when Neferet is praying I feel a zap of energy traveling through the circle itself, but that's it."

"So you've never felt a breeze when wind's called, or smelled rain with water, or felt grass under your feet with earth?"

"No way. Only a High Priestess with a major affinity for the elements would—" She broke off suddenly and her eyes got huge. "Are you saying that *you* felt that stuff? Any of that stuff?"

I squirmed. "Maybe."

"Maybe!" she squeaked. "Zoey! Do you have any idea what this could mean?"

I shook my head.

"Just last week in Soc class we were studying about the most famous vamp High Priestesses in history. There hasn't been a priestess with an affinity for all four of the elements for hundreds of years."

"Five," I said miserably.

"All five! You felt something with spirit, too!"

"Yeah, I think so."

"Zoey! This is amazing. I don't think there's ever been a High Priestess who felt all five of the elements." She nodded at my Mark. "It's that. It means you're different, and you really are."

"Stevie Rae, can we just keep this between us for a while? I mean, not even tell Damien or the Twins? I just—I just want to try to figure this out on my own a little. I feel like everything's happening too fast."

"But Zoey, I—"

"And I might be wrong," I interrupted quickly. "What if I was just excited and nervous because I'd never been in a ritual before? Do you know how embarrassed I'd be if I told people 'hey, I'm the only fledgling ever to have an affinity for all the elements' and it turned out to be nerves?"

Stevie Rae chewed her cheek. "I dunno, I still think you should tell someone."

"Yeah, then Aphrodite and her herd could be right there to gloat if it turned out that I was imagining things."

Stevie Rae paled. "Oh, man. You're totally right. That would be really awful. I won't say anything till you're ready. Promise."

Her reaction reminded me. "Hey, what is it Aphrodite did to you?"

Stevie Rae looked down at her lap, clasped her hands together, and hunched her shoulders as if she suddenly felt a chill. "She invited me to a ritual. I hadn't been here very long, only about a month or so, and I was kinda excited that the 'in' group wanted me." She shook her head, still not looking at me. "It was stupid of me, but I didn't really know anyone very well yet, and I thought maybe they would be my friends. So I went. But they didn't want me to be one of them. They wanted me to be a—a—blood donor for their ritual. They even called me 'refrigerator,' like I wasn't good for anything except holding blood for them. They made me cry and when I said no they laughed at me and kicked me out. That's how I met Damien, and then Erin and Shaunee. They were hanging out together and they saw me run out of the rec hall, so they followed me and told me not to worry about it. They've been my friends ever since." She finally looked up at me. "I'm sorry. I would have said something to you before, except I knew they wouldn't try that with you. You're too strong, and Aphrodite is too curious about your Mark. Plus, you're beautiful enough to be one of them."

"Hey, so are you!" I felt sick to my stomach thinking about Stevie Rae being slumped in the chair like Elliott . . . about drinking Stevie Rae's blood.

"No, I'm just kinda cute. I'm not them."

"I'm not them, either!" I yelled, causing Nala to wake up and mutter restlessly at me.

"I know you're not. That's not what I meant. I just meant that I knew they would want you in their group, so they wouldn't try to use you like that."

No, they managed to trick me and tried their best to freak me out. But why? Wait! I knew what they'd been up to. Erik said that the first time he drank blood he'd hated it, and had run out puking. I'd been here only two days. They'd wanted to do something that would disgust me so badly that I'd be scared away from them and their ritual forever.

They didn't want me to be part of the Dark Daughters, but they also didn't want to tell Neferet they didn't want me. Instead, they wanted *me* to refuse to join *them*. For whatever twisted reason, bully Aphrodite wanted to keep me out of the Dark Daughters. Bullies have always pissed me off, which meant, unfortunately, I knew what I had to do.

Ah, crap. I was going to join the Dark Daughters.

"Zoey, you're not mad at me, are you?" Stevie Rae said in a small voice.

I blinked, trying to clear my thoughts. "Of course not! You were right; Aphrodite didn't try to get me to do anything like giving blood." I popped the last bite of sandwich into my mouth, chewing fast. "Hey, I'm really beat. Do you think you could help me find a litter box for Nala so that I can get some sleep?"

Stevie Rae instantly brightened, and hopped off the bed with her usual perkiness. "Check this out." She practically skipped to the side of the room and held up a big green bag that had FELICIA'S SOUTHERN AGRICULTURE STORE, 2616 S. HARVARD, TULSA printed in bold white letters across it. From it she dumped onto the floor a litter box, food and water dishes, a box of Friskies cat food (with extra hairball protection), and a sack of kitty litter.

"How did you know?"

"I didn't. It was sitting in front of our door when I got back from dinner." She reached into the bottom of the bag and pulled out an envelope and an adorable pink leather collar that had miniature silver spikes all around it.

"Here, this is for you."

She handed me the envelope, which I could now see had my name printed on it, while she coaxed Nala into her collar. Inside, written in a beautiful, flowing script on expensive bone-colored stationery was one line.

Skylar told me she was coming.

It was signed with a single letter: N.

CHAPTER TWENTY

—

I was going to have to talk to Neferet. I thought about it as Stevie Rae and I rushed through breakfast the next morning. I didn't want to tell her anything about my supposed strange reaction to the elements—I mean, I hadn't been lying to Stevie Rae. I could have imagined the entire thing. What if I tell Neferet and she makes me take some kind of weird affinity test (in this school, who knew?) and she finds out that I don't have anything other than an overactive imagination? No way did I want to go through something like that. I'd just keep my mouth shut until I knew more about it. I also didn't want to say anything to her about thinking I might have seen Elizabeth's ghost. Like I wanted Neferet to think I was psycho? Neferet was cool, but she was an adult, and I could almost hear the "it was just your imagination because you'd been through so many changes" lecture I would get if I admitted to seeing a ghost. But I did need to talk to her about the bloodlust thing. (Yeesh—if I liked it so much why did the thought of it still make me feel queasy?)

"Ya think she's going to follow you to class?" Stevie Rae said, pointing to Nala.

I looked down at my feet where the cat lay curled, purring contentedly. "Can she?"

"Do you mean, is she allowed?"

I nodded.

"Yeah, cats can go anywhere they want."

"Huh," I said, reaching down to scratch the top of her head. "I guess she might follow me around all day then."

"Well, I'm glad she's yours and not mine. From what I saw when the alarm when off, she's a serious pillow-hogger."

I laughed. "You're right about that. How such a petite girl could push me off my own pillow, I do not know." I gave her head one more scratch. "Let's go. We're gonna be late."

I stood up with my bowl in my hand, and almost ran smack into Aphrodite. She was, as usual, flanked by Terrible and Warlike. Wasp was nowhere to be seen (maybe she'd taken a shower this morning and melted when the water touched her—hee hee). Aphrodite's nasty smile reminded me of a piranha I'd seen at the Jenks Aquarium when my biology class went there last year on a field trip.

"Hi, Zoey. Gosh, you left in such a hurry last night I didn't get a chance to say bye. Sorry you didn't have a good time. It's too bad, but the Dark Daughters isn't for everyone." She glanced at Stevie Rae and curled her lip.

"Actually, I had a great time last night, and I absolutely love the dress you gave me!" I gushed. "Thank you for inviting me to join the Dark Daughters. I accept. Totally."

Aphrodite's feral smile flattened. "Really?"

I grinned like an utterly clueless fool. "Really! When's the next meeting or ritual or whatever—or should I just ask Neferet? I'm going to see her this morning. I know she'll be happy to hear how welcome you made me feel last night and that I'm now a Dark Daughter."

Aphrodite hesitated for just a moment. Then she smiled again and matched my clueless tone of voice perfectly. "Yes, I bet Neferet will be glad to hear you've joined us, but I am the leader of the Dark Daughters and I know our schedule by heart, so there's no need to bother her with silly questions. Tomorrow is our Samhain celebration. Wear *your* dress," she emphasized the word, and my smile widened. I'd meant to get to her and I had. "And meet at the rec hall right after dinner, four thirty A.M., sharp."

"Great. I'll be there."

"Good, what a nice surprise," she said slickly. Then, followed by Terrible and Warlike (who looked vaguely shell-shocked), the three of them left the kitchen.

"Hags from hell," I muttered under my breath. I glanced at Stevie Rae, who was staring at me with a stricken expression frozen on her face.

"You're joining them?" she whispered.

"It's not what you think. Come on, I'll tell you on the way to class." I put our breakfast dishes in a dishwasher and herded the too quiet Stevie Rae out of the dorm. Nala padded after us, occasionally hissing at any cat who dared wander too close to me on the sidewalk. "I'm reconnoitering, just like you said last night," I explained.

"No. I don't like it," she said, shaking her head so hard she made her short hair bounce crazily.

"Have you never heard of the old saying 'keep your friends close and your enemies closer'?"

"Yeah, but—"

"That's all I'm doing. Aphrodite gets away with too much crap. She's mean. She's selfish. She can't be what Nyx wants for a High Priestess."

Stevie Rae's eyes got huge. "You're going to stop her?"

"Well, I'm gonna try." And as I spoke I felt the sapphire crescent moon on my forehead tingle.

* * *

"Thanks for the cat things you got for Nala," I said.

Neferet looked up from the paper she was grading and smiled. "Nala—that's a good name for her, but you should thank Skylar, not me. He's the one who told me she was coming." Then she glanced at the orange ball of fur that was impatiently twining between my legs. "She's really attached to you." Her eyes lifted again to meet mine. "Tell me, Zoey, do you ever hear her voice inside your head, or know exactly where she is, even when she's not in the same room as you?"

I blinked. Neferet thought I might have an affinity for cats! "No, I—I don't hear her in my head. But she does complain at me a lot. And I wouldn't know about whether or not I know where she is when she's not with me. She's always with me."

"She is delightful." Neferet crooked a finger at Nala and said, "Come to me, child."

Instantly, Nala padded over and jumped up on Neferet's desk, scattering papers everywhere.

"Oh, gosh, I'm sorry, Neferet." I grabbed for Nala, but Neferet waved me away. She scratched Nala's head, and the cat closed her eyes and purred.

"Cats are always welcome, and papers are easily reorganized. Now, what is it you really wanted to speak with me about, Zoeybird?"

Her use of my grandma's nickname for me made my heart hurt, and I suddenly missed her with an intensity that had me blinking tears from my eyes.

"Are you missing your old home?" Neferet asked softly.

"No, not really. Well, except for Grandma, but I've been so busy that I guess I just now realized it," I said guiltily.

"You don't miss your mother and father."

It wasn't like she'd said it as a question, but I felt that I needed to answer her. "No. Well, I don't really have a dad. He left us when I was little. My mom remarried three years ago and, well . . ."

"You can tell me. I give you my word that I will understand," Neferet said.

"I hate him!" I said with more anger than I'd expected to feel. "Since he joined our *family*"—I said the word sarcastically—"nothing has been right. My mom totally changed. It's like she can't be his wife and my mother anymore. It hasn't been my home for a long time."

"My mother died when I was ten years old. My father did not remarry. Instead, he began to use me as his wife. From the time I was ten until Nyx saved me by Marking me when I was fifteen, he abused me." Neferet paused and let the shock of what she was saying settle into me before she continued. "So you see, when I say that I understand what it is to have your home become an unbearable place I am not just spouting platitudes."

"That's awful." I didn't know what else to say.

"It was then. Now it is simply another memory. Zoey, humans in your past, and even in your present and future, will become less and less important to you until, eventually, you will feel very little for them. You'll understand this more as you continue to Change."

There was a cold flatness to her voice that made me feel odd, and I heard myself saying, "I don't want to stop caring about my grandma."

"Of course you don't." She was back to being warm and caring again. "It's only nine P.M., why don't you call her? You can be late to Drama class; I'll let Professor Nolan know that you are excused."

"Thank you, I'd like that. But it's not what I wanted to talk to you about." I took a deep breath. "I drank blood last night."

Neferet nodded. "Yes, the Dark Daughters often mix fledgling blood with their ritual wine. It's something the young like to do. Did it upset you greatly, Zoey?"

"Well, I didn't know about it until afterward. Then, yes, it did upset me."

Neferet frowned. "It wasn't ethical of Aphrodite not to tell you before. You should have had a choice about partaking. I'll speak with her."

"No!" I said a little too quickly, and then I forced myself to sound calmer. "No, there's really no need. I'll take care of it. I've decided to join the Dark Daughters, so I don't want to start off by looking like I set out to get Aphrodite in trouble."

"You're probably right. Aphrodite can be rather temperamental, and I trust that you can take care of it yourself, Zoey. We do like to encourage fledglings to solve the problems they have with each other among themselves whenever possible." She studied me, concern obvious in her face. "It's normal for the first few tastes of blood to be less than appetizing. You'd know that if you had been with us longer."

"It's not that. It—it tasted really good. Erik told me that mine was an unusual reaction."

Neferet's perfect brows shot up. "It is, indeed. Did you also feel dizzy or exhilarated?"

"Both," I said softly.

Neferet glanced at my Mark. "You are unique, Zoey Redbird. Well, I think it would be best to pull you out of this section of Sociology, and move you into a Sociology 415."

"I'd really rather you didn't do that," I said quickly. "I already feel like enough of a freak with everyone staring at my Mark and watching to see if I'll do something weird. If you move me into a class with kids who have been here for three years, they'll really think I'm bizarre."

Neferet hesitated, scratching Nala's head while she considered.

"I understand what you mean, Zoey. I haven't been a teenager for over one hundred years, but vampyres have long, accurate memories, and I do recall what it was like to go through the Change." She sighed. "Okay, how about a compromise? I'll allow you to stay in the third former Soc class, but I want to give you the text we use in the upper-level class, and have you agree to read a chapter a week, and promise that you'll discuss any questions you have with me."

"Deal," I said.

"You know, Zoey, as you Change, you literally are becoming an entirely new being. A vampyre is not a human, although we are humane. It may sound reprehensible to you now, but your desire for blood is as normal for your new life as your desire for"—she paused and smiled—"brown pop has been in your old life."

"Jeesh! Do you know everything?"

"Nyx has gifted me generously. Besides my affinity for our lovely felines and my abilities as a healer, I am also an intuitive."

"You can read my mind?" I asked nervously.

"Not exactly. But I can pick up bits and pieces of things. For instance, I know that there's something else you need to tell me about last night."

I drew a deep breath. "I was upset after I found out about the blood, so I ran out of the rec hall. That's how I found Nala. She was in a tree that was real close to the school's wall. I thought she was stuck up there, so I climbed up on the wall to get her and, well, while I was talking to her two kids from my old school found me."

"What happened?" Neferet's hand had stilled; she was no longer petting Nala, and I had all of her attention.

"It wasn't good. They—they were wasted, high and drunk." Okay, I hadn't meant to blurt that!

"Did they try to hurt you?"

"No, nothing like that. It was my ex–best friend and my almost-ex-boyfriend."

Neferet raised her brow at me again.

"Well, I'd quit going out with him, but he and I still had a thing for each other."

She nodded as though she understood. "Go on."

"Kayla and I kinda fought. She sees me differently now and I guess I see her differently, too. Neither one of us likes the new view." As I said it I realized it was true. It wasn't that K had changed—actually, she'd been exactly the same. It was just that the little things I used to ignore, like her nonsensical babble and her mean side, were now suddenly too irritating to deal with. "Anyway, she left and I was alone with Heath." I stopped there, not sure how to say the rest of it.

Neferet's eyes narrowed. "You experienced bloodlust for him."

"Yes," I whispered.

"Did you drink his blood, Zoey?" Her voice was sharp.

"I just tasted a drop of it. I'd scratched him. I hadn't meant to, but when I heard his pulse pounding it—it made me scratch him."

"So you didn't actually drink from the wound?"

"I started to, but Kayla came back and interrupted us. She totally freaked, and that's how I finally got Heath to leave."

"He didn't want to?"

I shook my head. "No. He didn't want to." I felt like I was going to cry again. "Neferet, I'm so sorry! I didn't mean to. I didn't even know what I was doing until Kayla screamed."

"Of course you didn't realize what was happening. How could a newly Marked fledgling be expected to know about bloodlust?" She touched my arm in a reassuring, mom-like gesture. "You probably didn't Imprint with him."

"Imprint?"

"It's what often happens when vampyres drink directly from humans, especially if there is a bond that has been established between them prior to the blood-letting. This is why it is forbidden for fledglings to drink the blood of humans. Actually, it's strongly discouraged for adult vampyres to feed from humans, too. There's an entire sect of vampyres who consider it morally wrong and would like to make it illegal," she said.

I watched her eyes darken as she talked. The expression in them suddenly made me very nervous and I shivered. Then Neferet blinked and her eyes changed back to normal. Or had I just imagined their weird darkness?

"But that's a discussion best left for my sixth form sociology class."

"What do I do about Heath?"

"Nothing. Let me know if he tries to see you again. If he calls you, don't answer. If he began Imprinting even the sound of your voice will effect him and work as a lure to draw him to you."

"It sounds like something out of *Dracula*," I muttered.

"It's nothing like that wretched book!" she snapped. "Stoker vilified vampyres, which has caused our kind endless petty troubles with humans."

"I'm sorry, I didn't mean—"

She waved her hand dismissively. "No, I shouldn't have taken out my frustration about that old fool's book on you. And don't worry about your friend Heath. I'm sure he'll be fine. You said that he was smoking and drinking? I assume you mean marijuana?"

I nodded. "But I don't smoke," I added. "Actually, he didn't used to and neither did Kayla. I don't get what's happening to them. I think they're hanging with some of those druggie football players from Union, and none of them have enough sense to just say no."

"Well, his reaction to you might have had more to do with his level of intoxication than a possible Imprint." She paused, pulling a scratch pad out of her desk drawer, and handing me a pencil. "But just in case, why don't you write down your friends' full names and where they live. Oh, and add the names of the Union football players, too, if you know them."

"Why would you need all of their names?" I felt my heart fall into my shoes. "You're not going to call their parents, are you?"

Neferet laughed. "Of course not. The misbehavior of human teenagers is no concern of mine. I only ask so that I can focus my thoughts on the group and perhaps pick up any vestiges of a possible Imprint among them."

"What happens if you do? What happens to Heath?"

"He's young and the Imprint will be weak, so time and distance should make it fade eventually. If he actually Imprinted in full, there are ways to break it." I was about to say that maybe she should just go ahead and do whatever she did to break an Imprinting when she continued. "None of the ways are pleasant."

"Oh, okay."

I wrote the names and addresses for Kayla and Heath. I didn't have a clue where the Union guys lived, but I did remember their names. Neferet got up and went to the back of the classroom to retrieve a thick textbook whose title in silver letters read *Sociology 415*.

"Begin with Chapter One and work your way through this entire book. Until you've finished it, let's consider it your homework instead of the work I assign to the rest of the Soc 101 class."

I took the book. It was heavy and the cover felt cool in my hot, nervous grip.

"If you have any questions, any at all, come see me right away. If I'm not here you can come to my apartment in Nyx's Temple. Go in the front door and follow the stairs on your right. I am the only priestess at the school right now, so the entire second floor belongs to me. And don't worry about disturbing me. You're my fledgling—it's your job to disturb me," she said with a warm smile.

"Thank you, Neferet."

"Try not to worry. Nyx has touched you and the goddess cares for her own." She hugged me. "Now, I'm going to go tell Professor Nolan what's been keeping you. Go ahead and use the phone at my desk to call your grandma." She hugged me again and then closed the classroom door gently behind her as she left.

I sat down at her desk and thought about how great she was, and how long it'd been since my mom had hugged me like that. And for some reason, I started to cry.

CHAPTER TWENTY-ONE

—

"Hi Grandma, it's me."

"Oh! My Zoeybird! Are you okay, honey?"

I smiled into the phone and wiped my eyes. "I'm good, Grandma. I just miss you."

"Little bird, I miss you, too." She paused and then said, "Has your mom called you?"

"No."

Grandma sighed. "Well, honey, maybe she doesn't want to bother you while you're settling into your new life. I did tell her that Neferet had explained to me that your days and nights will be flip-flopped."

"Thanks, Grandma, but I don't think that's why she hasn't called me."

"Maybe she has tried and you just missed her call. I called your cell yesterday, but I only got your voicemail."

I felt a twinge of guilt. I hadn't even checked my phone for messages. "I forgot to plug my cell phone in. It's back in the room. Sorry I missed your call, Grandma." Then, to make her feel better (and to get her to quit talking about it), I said, "I'll check my phone when I get back to my room. Maybe Mom did call."

"Maybe she did, honey. So, tell me, how is it there?"

"It's good. I mean, there are a lot of things I like about it.

My classes are cool. Hey, Grandma, I'm even taking fencing and an equestrian class."

"That's wonderful! I remember how much you liked to ride Bunny."

"And I got a cat!"

"Oh, Zoeybird, I'm so glad. You've always loved cats. Are you making friends with the other kids?"

"Yeah, my roommate, Stevie Rae, is great. And I already like her friends, too."

"So, if everything is going so well, why the tears?"

I should have known I couldn't hide anything from my grandma. "It's just . . . just that some of the things about the Change are really hard to deal with."

"You're well, aren't you?" Worry was thick in her voice. "Is your head okay?"

"Yeah, it's nothing like that. It's—" I stopped. I wanted to tell her; I wanted to tell her so bad I could explode, but I didn't know how. And I was afraid—afraid she wouldn't love me anymore. I mean, Mom had quit loving me, hadn't she? Or, at the very least, Mom had traded me in for a new husband, which in some ways was worse than quitting loving me. What would I do if Grandma walked away from me, too?

"Zoeybird, you know you can tell me anything," she said gently.

"It's hard, Grandma." I bit my lip to keep from crying.

"Then let me make it easier. There is nothing you could say that would make me stop loving you. I'm your Grandma today, tomorrow, and next year. I'll be your Grandma even after I join our ancestors in the spirit world, and from there I'll still love you, Little Bird."

"I drank blood and I liked it!" I blurted.

Without any hesitation, Grandma said, "Well, honey, isn't that what vampyres do?"

"Yeah, but I'm not a vampyre. I'm just a few-days-old fledgling."

"You're special, Zoey. You always have been. Why should that change now?"

"I don't feel special. I feel like a freak."

"Then remember something. You're still you. Doesn't matter that you've been Marked. Doesn't matter that you're going through the Change. Inside, your spirit is still *your* spirit. On the outside you might look like a familiar stranger, but you need only look inside to find the you you've known for sixteen years."

"The familiar stranger . . . ," I whispered. "How did you know?"

"You're my girl, Honey. You're daughter of my spirit. It's not hard to understand what you must be feeling—it's very much like what I imagine I'd be feeling."

"Thank you, Grandma."

"You are welcome, *u-we-tsi-a-ge-ya*."

I smiled, loving how the Cherokee word for daughter sounded—so magical and special, like it was a Goddess-given title. Goddess-given . . .

"Grandma, there's something else."

"Tell me, Little Bird."

"I think I feel the five elements when a circle is cast."

"If that is the truth, you have been given great power, Zoey. And you know that with great power comes great responsibility. Our family has a rich history of Tribal Elders, Medicine Men, and Wise Women. Have a care, Little Bird, to think before you act. The Goddess would not have granted you special powers on a whim. Use them carefully, and make Nyx, as well as your ancestors, look down and smile on you."

"I'll try my best, Grandma."

"That's all I would ever ask of you, Zoeybird."

"There's a girl here who also has special powers, too, but she's

awful. She's a bully and she lies. Grandma, I think . . . I think . . ."
I took a deep breath and said what had been brewing in my mind
all morning. "I think I'm stronger than she is and I think that
maybe Nyx Marked me so that I can get her out of the position
she's in. But—but that would mean that I have to take her place,
and I don't know if I'm ready for that, not now. Maybe not ever."

"Follow what your spirit tells you, Zoeybird." She hesitated,
then said, "Honey, do you remember the purification prayer of
our people?"

I thought about it. I couldn't count the times I'd gone with her
to the little stream behind Grandma's house and watched her
bathe ritualistically in the running water and speak the purification prayer. Sometimes I stepped into the stream with her and
said the prayer, too. The prayer had been entwined throughout
my childhood, spoken at the change of seasons, in thanks for the
lavender harvest, or in preparation for the coming winter, as well
as whenever Grandma was faced with hard decisions. Sometimes
I didn't know why she purified herself and spoke the prayer.
It simply had always been.

"Yes," I said. "I remember it."

"Is there running water inside the school grounds?"

"I don't know, Grandma."

"Well, if there isn't then get something to use as a smudge stick.
Sage and lavender mixed together are best, but you can even use
fresh pine if you have no other choice. Do you know what to do,
Zoeybird?"

"Smudge myself, starting at my feet and working my way up
my body, front and back," I recited, as if I was a small child again
and Grandma was drilling me in the ways of our people. "And
then face the east and speak the purification prayer."

"Good, you do remember. Ask for the Goddess's help, Zoey.

I believe that she will hear you. Can you do this before sunrise tomorrow?"

"I think so."

"I will perform the prayer, too, and add a grandmother's voice to ask the Goddess to guide you."

And suddenly I felt better. Grandma was never wrong about these sorts of things. If she believed it would be okay, then it really would be okay.

"I'll speak the purification prayer before dawn. I promise."

"Good, Little Bird. Now this old woman had better let you go. You are in the middle of a school day right now, aren't you?"

"Yeah, I'm on my way to Drama class. And, Grandma, you'll never be old."

"Not as long as I can hear your young voice, Little Bird. I love you, *u-we-tsi-a-ge-ya.*"

"I love you, too, Grandma."

Talking to Grandma had lifted a terrible weight from my heart. I was still scared and freaked out about the future, and I wasn't wild about the thought of bringing down Aphrodite. Not to mention that I really didn't have a clue how to go about it. But I did have a plan. Okay, maybe it wasn't a "plan," but at least it was something to do. I'd complete the purification prayer, and then . . . well . . . then I'd figure out what to do after that.

Yeah, that would work. Or at least that's what I kept telling myself through my morning classes. By lunch I'd decided on the place for my ritual—under the tree by the wall where I'd found Nala. I thought about it while I made my way through the salad bar behind the Twins. Trees, especially oaks, were sacred to the Cherokee people, so that seemed to be a good choice. Plus, it was secluded and easy to get to. Sure, Heath and Kayla had found me over there, but I wasn't planning on sitting on top of the wall again, and I couldn't imagine Heath showing up at dawn two days in a row, whether he had been Imprinted or not. I mean, this was the guy who slept till two in the afternoon in the summer, *every day*. It took two alarm clocks and his mother shrieking at him to get him up for school. The kid was not going to be up at pre-dawn again. It would probably take him months to recover from yesterday. No, actually, he'd probably snuck out of the house and met K (sneaking out had always been easy for her, her parents were totally clueless), and they'd been up all night. Which meant that he'd missed school *and* would be playing sick and sleeping in for the next two days. Anyway, I wasn't worried about him showing up.

"Don't you think baby corns are scary? There's just something wrong about their midget bodies."

I jumped and almost dropped the ladle of ranch dressing into the vat of white liquid, and looked up into Erik's laughing blue eyes.

"Oh, hi," I said. "You scared me."

"Z, I think I'm making a habit of sneaking up on you."

I giggled nervously, very aware that the Twins were watching every move we made.

"You look like you've recovered from yesterday."

"Yeah, no problem. I'm fine. And this time I'm not lying."

"And I heard you joined the Dark Daughters."

Shaunee and Erin sucked air together. I was careful not to look at them.

"Yep."

"That's cool. That group needs some new blood."

"You say 'that group' like you don't belong to it. Aren't you a Dark Son?"

"Yeah, but it's not the same as being a Dark Daughter. We're just ornamental. Kinda the opposite of how it is in the human world. All the guys know that we're just there to look good and keep Aphrodite amused."

I looked up at him, reading something else in his eyes. "And is that what you're still doing, amusing Aphrodite?"

"As I said last night, not anymore, which is one reason I don't really consider myself a member of the group. I'm sure they'd officially kick me out if it wasn't for that little acting thing I do."

"You mean 'little' as in Broadway and LA already being interested in you."

"That's what I mean." He grinned at me. "It's not real, you know. Acting is all pretend. It's not what I really am." He bent down to whisper in my ear. "Really, I'm a dork."

"Oh, please. Does that line work for you?"

He exaggerated a look of being offended. "Line? No, Z. That's no line, and I can prove it."

"Sure you can."

"I can. Come to the movies with me tonight. We'll watch my favorite DVDs of all time."

"How does that prove anything?"

"It's *Star Wars*, the original ones. I know all the lines for all the parts." He leaned closer and whispered again. "I can even do Chewbacca's parts."

I laughed. "You're right. You are a dork."

"Told you."

We'd come to the end of the salad bar and he walked with me over to the table where Damien, Stevie Rae, and the Twins were already seated. And, no, they weren't making any attempt to hide the fact that they were all totally gawking at the two of us.

"So, will you go . . . with me . . . tonight?"

I could hear the four of them holding their breaths. Literally.

"I'd like to, but I can't tonight. I—uh—I already have plans."

"Oh. Okay. Well . . . next time. See ya." He nodded at the table and walked away.

I sat down. They were all staring at me. "What?" I said.

"You have lost every last bit of your mind," Shaunee said.

"My exact thoughts, Twin," Erin said.

"I hope you have a really good reason for blowing him off," Stevie Rae said. "It was obvious you hurt his feelings."

"Think he'd let me comfort him?" Damien asked, still gazing dreamily after Erik.

"Give it up," Erin said.

"He doesn't play for your team," Shaunee said.

"Shush!" Stevie Rae said. She turned to look me straight in the eyes. "Why did you tell him no? What could be more important than a date with him?"

"Getting rid of Aphrodite," I said simply.

CHAPTER TWENTY-TWO

—

"She has a point," Damien said.

"She joined the Dark Daughters," Shaunee said.

"What!" Damien squeaked, his voice going up about twenty octaves.

"Leave her alone," Stevie Rae said, instantly coming to my defense. "She's reconnoitering."

"Reconnoitering, hell! If she joined the Dark Daughters she's engaging the enemy full on," Damien said.

"Well, she joined," Shaunee said.

"We heard her," Erin said.

"Hello! I'm still right here," I said.

"So what are you going to do?" Damien asked me.

"I don't really know," I said.

"You better get a plan and get one quick or those hags are gonna have you for lunch," Erin said.

"Yep," Shaunee said, biting viciously into her salad for effect.

"Hey! She doesn't have to figure this out on her own. She has us." Stevie Rae crossed her arms over her chest and glared at the Twins.

I smiled my thanks to Stevie Rae. "Well, I kinda have an idea."

"Good. Tell us and we'll brainstorm," said Stevie Rae.

Everyone looked expectantly at me. I sighed. "Well. Um . . . ,"

I started hesitantly, afraid I was sounding like a moron, and then I decided I might as well tell them what had been on my mind since I talked to Grandma, so I finished in a rush. "I thought I'd perform an ancient purification prayer based on Cherokee ritual and ask Nyx to help me come up with a plan."

The silence at the table seemed to last forever. Then Damien finally said, "Asking for Nyx's help isn't a bad idea."

"Are you Cherokee?" Shaunee asked.

"You look Cherokee," Erin said.

"Hello! Her last name is Redbird. She's Cherokee," Stevie Rae said with finality.

"Well, that's good," Shaunee said, but she looked doubtful.

"I just think that Nyx might actually hear me and—maybe— give me some kind of clue as to what I should do about horrid Aphrodite." I looked at each of my friends. "Something inside me says it's just wrong to let her get away with all the crap she's getting away with."

"Let me tell them!" Stevie Rae suddenly said. "They won't tell anyone. Really. And it'd help if they knew."

"What the F?" Erin said.

"Okay, now you have no choice," Shaunee said, pointing at Stevie Rae with her fork. "She knew if she said that we would pester the crap outta you till you told us whatever it is she's talking about."

I frowned at Stevie Rae, who shrugged her shoulders sheepishly and said, "Sorry."

Reluctantly, I lowered my voice and leaned forward. "Promise you won't tell anyone."

"Promise," they said.

"I think I can feel the five elements when a circle is cast."

Silence. They just stared. Three of them shocked, Stevie Rae smug.

"So, you still think she can't take down Aphrodite?" Stevie Rae said.

"I *knew* there was more to your Mark than falling down and hitting your head!" Shaunee said.

"Wow," Erin said. "Talk about good gossip."

"No one can know!" I said quickly.

"Please," Shaunee said. "We're just sayin' that someday this is gonna be great gossip."

"We know how to wait for great gossip," Erin said.

Damien ignored both of them. "I don't think there's a record of any High Priestess who has had an affinity with all five elements." Damien's voice got more excited as he spoke. "Do you know what that means?" He didn't give me a chance to respond. "It means you could potentially be the most puissant High Priestess the vampyres have ever known."

"Huh?" I said. *Puissant?*

"Strong—powerful," he said impatiently. "You might actually be able to take out Aphrodite!"

"Now, that's some seriously good news," Erin said, as Shaunee nodded in enthusiastic agreement.

"So when and where are we doing the purification thingie?" Stevie Rae said.

"We?" I said.

"You're not in this alone, Zoey," she said.

I opened my mouth to protest—I mean, I wasn't even sure what I was going to do. I didn't want to get my friends mixed up in something that might be—actually, would probably be—a total mess. But Damien didn't give me time to tell them no.

"You need us," he said simply. "Even the most puissant High Priestess needs her circle."

"Well, I hadn't really thought about casting a circle. I was just gonna do a kind of purification prayer thing."

"Can't you cast a circle and then pray the prayer and ask for Nyx's help?" Stevie Rae asked.

"Seems logical," Shaunee said.

"Plus, if you really do have an affinity for the five elements, I'll bet we'll be able to sense it when you cast your own circle. Right, Damien?" Stevie Rae said. Everyone looked at the gay scholar of our group.

"Sounds like good logic to me," he said.

I was still going to argue, even though everything inside of me felt relieved and happy and grateful that my friends would be there with me, that they wouldn't let me face all of this uncertainty alone.

Value them; they are pearls of great price.

The familiar voice floated through my mind, and I realized that I shouldn't question the new instinct within me that seemed to have been born when Nyx kissed my forehead and permanently changed my Mark and my life.

"Okay, I'm going to need a smudge stick." They looked at me blankly, and I went on to explain. "It's for the purification part of the ritual because I don't have any running water handy. Or do I?"

"You mean like a stream or a river or something like that?" Stevie Rae asked.

"Yeah."

"Well, there's a little stream that runs through the courtyard outside the dining hall and disappears somewhere under the school," Damien said.

"That's no good; it's too public. We'll need to use the smudge stick. What works best is dried lavender and sage mixed together, but if I have to I can use pine."

"I can get the sage and lavender," Damien said. "They have that kind of stuff in the school supplies store for the fifth and sixth former's Spells and Rituals class. I'll just say I'm helping out an upperclassman by picking some up for him. What else do you need?"

"Well, in the purification ritual Grandma always thanked the seven sacred directions the Cherokee people honor: north, south, east, west, sun, earth, and self. But I think I want to make the prayer more specific to Nyx." I chewed my lip, thinking.

"I think that's smart," Shaunee said.

"Yeah," Erin added. "I mean, Nyx isn't allied with the sun. She's Night."

"I think you should follow your gut," Stevie Rae said.

"Trusting herself is one of the first things a High Priestess learns to do," Damien said.

"Okay, then I'll also need a candle for each of the five elements," I decided.

"Easy-peasy," Shaunee said.

"Yeah, the temple is never locked and there are zillions of circle candles in there."

"Is it okay to take them?" Stealing from Nyx's Temple definitely did not feel like a good idea.

"It's fine as long as we bring them back," Damien said. "What else?"

"That's it." I think. Hell, I wasn't sure. It's not like I actually knew what I was doing.

"When and where?" Damien asked.

"After dinner. Let's say five o'clock. And we can't go together. The last thing we need is for Aphrodite or any of the other Dark Daughters to think we're having some kind of meeting and get curious about us. So let's meet at a huge oak tree by the eastern wall." I smiled crookedly at them. "It's easy to find if you pretend that you've just run out of one of the Dark Daughter's rituals in the rec hall, and you want to get the hell away from the hags."

"That doesn't take much pretending," Shaunee said.

Erin snorted.

"Okay, we'll bring the stuff," Damien said.

"Yeah, we'll bring the stuff; you bring the puissantness," Shaunee said, giving Damien a smartass look.

"That is not the correct form of that word. You know, you really should do more reading. Maybe your vocabulary would improve," Damien said.

"Your *mom* needs to read more," Shaunee said, and then she and Erin dissolved in giggles at the really bad "your mom" joke.

I, for one, was glad that they shifted the subject away from me and I could eat my salad and think in relative privacy while they bickered back and forth. I was chewing and trying to remember all the words to the purification prayer when Nala hopped up on the bench beside me. She looked at me with her big eyes and then leaned into me and started to purr like a jet engine. I don't know why, but she made me feel better. And when the bell rang and we all hurried off to class, each of my four friends smiled at me, gave me a secret wink, and said, "Later, Z." They made me feel better, too, even though their easy adoption of Erik's nickname for me gave my heart a twinge.

Spanish class zoomed by: a whole lesson on learning how to say that we like things or don't like things. Profe Garmy was cracking me up. She said it would change our lives. *Me gusta gatos.* (I like cats.) *Me gusta ir de compras.* (I like shopping.) *No me gusta cocinar.* (I don't like to cook.) *No me gusta lavantar el gato.* (I don't like to wash the cat.) Those were Profe Garmy's favorites, and we spent the hour coming up with our own favorites.

I tried not to scribble things like *me gusta Erik* . . . and *no me gusta el hag-o Aphrodite.* Okay, so I'm sure *el hag-o* is not how you say "hag" in Spanish, but still. Anyway, class was fun and I actually understood what we were saying. Equestrian class didn't quite zoom by. Mucking stalls was good for thinking—I went over and over the purification prayer—but the hour definitely seemed to take an hour. This time Stevie Rae didn't have to come get me. I was way too anxious to lose track of time. As the bell rang I was quickly putting up the curry combs, happy that Lenobia had let me groom Persephone again, and preoccupied because she had also told me that starting next week she thought I might actually begin riding her. I hurried out of the stables, wishing that the hour wasn't so late back in the "real" world. I'd have loved to call Grandma and tell her how well I was doing with the horses.

"I know what's going on."

I swear I almost choked. "God, Aphrodite! Could you make a sound or something! What are you, part spider? You scared the hell outta me."

"What's wrong?" she purred. "Guilty conscience?"

"Uh, when you sneak up behind people, you scare them. Guilt has nothing to do with it."

"So you're not guilty?"

"Aphrodite, I don't know what you're talking about."

"I know what you're planning for tonight."

"And yet I still don't know what you're talking about." *Ah, crap! How could she have found out?*

"Everyone thinks you're so damn cute and so damn innocent and they're so damn impressed by that freakish Mark of yours. Everyone but me." She turned to face me, and we stopped in the middle of the sidewalk. Her blue eyes narrowed and her face twisted until it was scarily haggish. Huh. I wondered (briefly) if the Twins realized how accurate their nickname for her was. "No matter what bullshit you've heard he's still mine. He'll always be mine."

My eyes widened and I felt a wash of relief so intense it made me laugh. She was talking about Erik, not about the purification prayer! "Wow, you sound like Erik's mom. Does he know you're checking up on him?"

"Did I look like Erik's mom when you watched me suck his dick in the hall?"

So she did know. Whatever. I suppose it was inevitable that we would have this conversation. "No, you didn't look like Erik's mom. You looked like what you are—desperate—while you pathetically tried to throw yourself at a guy who was clearly telling you he didn't want you anymore."

"Fucking bitch! Nobody talks to me like that!"

She raised her hand and, clawlike, moved to slash at my face. Then it seemed that the world stopped, leaving the two of us in a little bubble of slow-motion. I caught her wrist, stopping her easily—too easily. It was like she was a small, sick child who had struck out in anger, but was really too weak to do any harm. I held her there for a moment, meeting her hateful eyes.

"Don't ever try to hit me again. I'm not one of the kids you can bully. Get this, and get this now. I am not scared of you." Then I flung her wrist away from me, and was totally shocked to see her stagger back several feet.

Rubbing her wrist, she glared at me. "Don't bother showing up tomorrow. Consider yourself uninvited and no longer a Dark Daughter."

"Really?" I felt unbelievably calm. I knew I held the trump card on this and I pulled it. "So you want to explain to my mentor, High Priestess Neferet, the vamp whose idea it was for me to join the Dark Daughters in the first place, that you kicked me out because you're jealous that your ex-boyfriend likes me?"

Her face paled.

"Oh, and you may be very sure that I'll be totally, completely upset when Neferet asks me about it." I sniffed and sobbed a little like I was fake crying.

"Do you know what it's like to be a part of something and have *no one* else in the group want you there?" she snarled between her clenched teeth.

I felt my stomach clench and had to force myself not to let her see she'd struck a nerve. Yes, I knew exactly what it was like to be a part of something—a supposed family—and have it feel like *no one* else wanted me there, but Aphrodite wasn't going to know it. Instead I smiled, and in my sweetest voice I said, "Why, whatever do you mean, Aphrodite? Erik is part of the Dark Sons and just today at lunch he told me how happy he was that I'd joined the Dark Daughters."

"Come to the ritual. Pretend you're part of the Dark Daughters. But you'd better remember something. They're *my* Dark Daughters. You're the outsider; the one who is not wanted. And remember this, too. Erik Night and I have a bond that you'll never understand. He's not my *ex* anything. You didn't stay to see the end of our little game in the hall. He was then and he is now exactly what I want him to be. Mine." Then she tossed her very big, very blond hair and stalked away.

About two breaths later Stevie Rae stuck her head out from behind an old oak that was not far from the sidewalk and said, "Is she gone?"

"Thankfully." I shook my head at Stevie Rae. "What are you doing back there?"

"Are you kidding? I'm hiding. She scares the bejezzus outta me. I was coming to meet you and saw the two of you arguing. Man, she actually tried to hit you!"

"Aphrodite has some serious anger-management issues."

Stevie Rae laughed.

"Uh, Stevie Rae, you can come out from behind there now."

Still laughing, Stevie Rae practically skipped over to me and linked her arm with mine. "You really stood up to her!"

"I really did."

"She really, *really* hates your guts."

"She really, *really* does."

"You know what that means?" Stevie Rae said.

"Yep. I don't have any choice now. I'm going to have to take her down."

"Yep."

But I knew that I'd had no choice even before Aphrodite tried to scratch my eyes out. I hadn't had any choice since Nyx had placed her Mark on me. As Stevie Rae and I walked together in the gaslight-illuminated richness of the night, the Goddess's words repeated over and over through my mind: *You are old beyond your years, Zoeybird. Believe in yourself and you will find a way. But remember, darkness does not always equate to evil, just as light does not always bring good.*

CHAPTER TWENTY-THREE

—

"I hope the rest of them can find it," I said, glancing around me while Stevie Rae and I waited by the big oak tree. "It didn't seem this dark last night."

"It wasn't. It's really cloudy tonight, so the moon's having trouble shining through. But don't worry, the Change is doing really cool things for our night vision. Heck, I think I can see as good as Nala." Stevie Rae scratched the cat affectionately on her head and Nala closed her eyes and purred. "They'll find us."

I leaned against the tree and worried. Dinner had been good— seriously yummy broiled chicken, seasoned rice, and baby snow peas (one thing I could say for this place, they could really cook)—yeah, everything had been great. Until Erik had come by our table and said hi. Okay, it wasn't really a "hi, Z, I still like you" hi. It was a "hi, Zoey." Period. Yep. That was it. He'd gotten his food and was walking with a couple other guys the Twins called hotties. I will admit that I didn't even notice them. I was too busy noticing Erik. They came to our table. I looked up and smiled. He met my eyes for a millisecond, said, "Hi, Zoey," and walked on. And all of a sudden the chicken didn't taste nearly as good.

"You just hurt his ego. Be nice to him and he'll ask you out again," Stevie Rae said, bringing me and my thoughts back to the present under the tree.

"How'd you know I was thinking about Erik?" I asked. Stevie Rae had quit petting Nala, so I reached down to scratch the cat on top of her head before she started complaining at me.

" 'Cause that's what I'd be thinking about."

"Well, I should be thinking about the circle I have to cast but have never cast before in my entire life, and the purification ritual I have to perform, and not some boy."

"He's not 'some boy.' He's some *fiiine* boy," Stevie Rae drawled, making me laugh.

"You must be talking about Erik," Damien said, stepping out of the shadow of the wall. "Don't worry. I saw the way he was looking at you at lunch today. He'll ask you out again."

"Yeah, take it from him," Shaunee said.

"He is our group expert on All Things Penile," Erin said as they joined them under the tree.

"Quite true," Damien said.

Before they could make my head hurt I changed the subject. "Did you get the stuff we need?"

"I had to mix the dried sage and lavender together myself. I hope it's okay that I tied them like this." Damien pulled the smudge stick of dried herbs out of his jacket sleeve and handed it to me. It was thick and almost a foot long, and right away I smelled the familiar sweetness of lavender. He'd wrapped the bundle tightly together on one end with what looked like extra-thick thread.

"It's perfect." I smiled at him.

He looked relieved, and then said, a little shyly, "I used my cross-stitch thread."

"Hey, I told you before you shouldn't be ashamed that you like to cross-stitch. I think it's a cute hobby. Plus, you're really good at it," Stevie Rae said.

"I wish my dad thought so," Damien said.

I hated hearing the sadness in his voice. "I wish you'd teach me sometime. I've always wanted to learn how to cross-stitch," I lied, and was glad to see Damien's face brighten.

"Anytime, Z," he said.

"How about the candles?" I asked the Twins.

"Hey, we told you. Easy . . ." Shaunee opened her purse and pulled out green, yellow, and blue votives in correspondingly colored thick glass cups.

"Peasy." From her purse Erin took a red and purple votive in the same kind of colored containers.

"Good. Okay, let's see. Let's move over here, a little way from the trunk, but close enough that we're still standing under the branches." They followed me as I walked a few paces from the tree. I looked at the candles. What should I do? Maybe I should . . . And as I thought about it, I knew. Without stopping to wonder how or why or question the intuitive knowledge that had suddenly come to me, I simply acted on it. "I'm going to give each of you a candle. Then, just like the vamps in Neferet's Full Moon Ritual, you're going to represent that element. I'll be spirit." Erin handed me the purple votive. "I'm the center of the circle. The rest of you take your places around me." Without hesitation I took the red candle from Erin and handed it to Shaunee. "You'll be fire."

"Sounds good to me. I mean, everyone knows how hot I am." She grinned and shimmied to the southern edge of the circle.

The green candle was next. I turned to Stevie Rae. "You're earth."

"And green's my favorite color!" she said, happily moving to stand across from Shaunee.

"Erin, you're water."

"Good. I used to like to lay out, which involves swimming when I needed to cool off." Erin moved to the western position.

"So I must be air," Damien said, taking the yellow candle.

"You are. Your element opens the circle."

"Kinda like I wish I could open people's minds," he said, moving to the eastern position.

I smiled warmly at him. "Yep. Kinda like that."

"Okay. What's next?" Stevie Rae asked.

"Well, let's use the smoke from the smudge stick to purify ourselves." I set the purple candle at my feet so I could concentrate on the smudge stick. Then I rolled my eyes. "Well, hell. Did anyone remember matches or a lighter or whatever?"

"Naturally," Damien said, pulling a lighter from his pocket.

"Thanks, air," I said.

"Don't mention it, High Priestess," he said.

I didn't say anything, but when he called me that a shiver of excitement tingled through my body.

"Here's how you use the smudge stick," I said, glad that my voice sounded way calmer than I felt. I stood in front of Damien, deciding that I should begin where the circle would be started. Realizing that I was eerily echoing my Grandma and the lessons of my childhood, I began explaining the process to my friends. "Smudging is a ritual way to cleanse a person, place, or an object of negative energies, spirits, or influences. The smudging ceremony involves the burning of special, sacred plants and herbal resins, then, either passing an object through the smoke, or fanning the smoke around a person or place. The spirit of the plant purifies whatever is being smudged." I smiled at Damien. "Ready?"

"Affirmative," he said in typical Damien fashion.

I lit the smudge stick and let the fire burn the dry herbs for a little while, and then I blew them out so that all that was left was a nicely smoking ember. Then, starting at Damien's feet, I wafted smoke up his body while I continued my explanation of the ancient ceremony.

"It's really important to remember that we're asking the spirits of the sacred plants we're using to help us, and we should show them proper respect by acknowledging their powers."

"What do lavender and sage do?" Stevie Rae asked from across the circle.

While I smudged my way up Damien's body I answered Stevie Rae. "White sage is used a lot in traditional ceremonies. It drives out negative energies, spirits, and influences. Actually, desert sage does the same thing, but I like white sage better because it smells sweeter." I'd made it to Damien's head and I grinned at him. "Good choice, Damien."

"Sometimes I think I might be a little psychic," Damien said.

Erin and Shaunee snorted, but we ignored them.

"Okay, now turn clockwise and I'll finish up with your back," I told him. He turned and I continued. "My grandma always uses lavender in all of her smudge sticks. I'm sure part of the reason is that she owns a lavender farm."

"Cool!" Stevie Rae said.

"Yeah, it's an awesome place." I smiled over my shoulder at her, but I kept smudging Damien. "The other part of the reason she uses lavender is because it is able to restore balance and create a peaceful atmosphere. It also draws loving energy and positive spirits." I tapped Damien's shoulder so he'd turn around. "You're done." Then I moved around the circle to Shaunee, who was representing the element fire, and I began smudging her.

"Positive spirits?" Stevie Rae said, sounding young and scared. "I didn't know we'd be calling anything more than the elements to the circle."

"Please. Just please, Stevie Rae," Shaunee said, frowning through the smoke to Stevie Rae. "You can not be a vampyre and be afraid of ghosts."

"Nope. It doesn't even sound right," Erin said.

I glanced across the circle at Stevie Rae and our eyes met

briefly. We were both thinking about my encounter with what might have been Elizabeth's ghost, but neither of us seemed willing to talk about it.

"I'm *not* a vampyre. Yet. I'm just a fledgling. So it's okay for me to be scared of ghosts."

"Wait, isn't Zoey talking about Cherokee spirits? They probably won't pay much attention to a ceremony done by a bunch of vampyre fledglings whose non–Native American-ness outweighs our High Priestess's Cherokee-ness four to one," Damien said.

I finished with Shaunee and moved on to Erin. "I don't think it matters that much what we are on the outside," I said, instantly feeling the rightness of what I was saying. "I think what matters is our intent. It's kinda like this: Aphrodite and her group are some of the best looking, most talented kids at this school, and the Dark Daughters should be an awesome club. But instead we call them the hags and they're basically a bunch of bullies and spoiled brats." Wonder how Erik fit into all of that? Was he really just 'whatever' about the group, like he told me, or was he into it more deeply than that, as Aphrodite implied?

"Or kids who have been bullied into joining and who are just along for the ride," Erin said.

"Exactly." I mentally shook myself. Now was not the time to daydream about Erik. I finished smudging Erin and walked over to stand in front of Stevie Rae. "What I mean is that I do think the spirits of my ancestors can hear us, just like I think the spirits of the sage and the lavender are working for us. But I don't think you have anything to be afraid of, Stevie Rae. Our intention is not to call them here so that we can use them to kick Aphrodite's ass." I paused in my smudging and added, "Even though the girl definitely needs a good ass-kicking. And I don't think there will be any scary ghosts hanging around tonight," I said firmly, then handed Stevie Rae the smudge stick and said, "Okay, now you do me." She began mimicking my actions and I relaxed into the familiar sweet smoke as it drifted around me.

"We're not going to ask them to help us kick her ass?" Shaunee definitely sounded disappointed.

"Nope. We're purifying ourselves so that we can ask for Nyx's guidance. I don't want to beat Aphrodite up." I remembered how good it'd felt to toss her away from me and tell her off. "Well, okay, I might enjoy it, but the truth is that doesn't solve the problem of the Dark Daughters."

Stevie Rae was done smudging me and I took the stick from her and carefully rubbed it out on the ground. Then I returned to the center of the circle where Nala was curled contentedly in a little orange ball beside the spirit candle. I looked around at my friends. "It's true that we don't like Aphrodite, but I think it's important not to focus on negatives like kicking her ass or pushing her out of the Dark Daughters. That's what she would do in our place. What we want is what's right. More like justice than revenge. We're different than her, and if we somehow manage to take her place in the Dark Daughters, that group will be different, too."

"See, that's why you'll be the High Priestess and Erin and I will just be your very attractive sidekicks. Because we are shallow and we just want to knock her bobble-head off her shoulders," Shaunee said while Erin nodded.

"Positive thoughts only, please," Damien said sharply. "We are in the middle of a purification ritual."

Before Shaunee could do anything more than glare at Damien, Stevie Rae chirped, " 'Kay! I'm thinkin' only positive things, like how great it would be if Zoey was leader of the Dark Daughters."

"Good idea, Stevie Rae," Damien said. "I'm thinking the same."

"Hey! That's my happy thought, too," Erin said. "Peter Pan with me, Twin," she called to Shaunee, who stopped scowling at Damien and said, "You know I'm always up for some happy thoughts. And it would be damn nice if Zoey was in charge of the Dark Daughters and on her way to being High Priestess for real."

High Priestess for real . . . I wondered briefly whether it was a good or bad thing that those words made me feel as if I might need to puke. Again. Sighing, I lit the purple candle. "Ready?" I asked the four of them.

"Ready!" they said together.

"Okay, pick up your candles."

Without hesitating (which meant I also wasn't giving myself time to chicken out), I carried the candle over to Damien. I wasn't experienced and brilliant like Neferet, or seductive and confident like Aphrodite. I was just me. Just Zoey—that familiar stranger who had gone from being an almost normal high school kid to a truly unusual vampyre fledgling. I took a deep breath. As my grandma would say, all I could do was try my best.

"Air is everywhere, so it only makes sense that it is the first element to be called into the circle. I ask that you hear me, air, and I summon you to this circle." I lit Damien's yellow candle with my purple one and instantly the flame began to flicker crazily. I watched Damien's eyes get big and round and startled-looking as wind suddenly whipped in a mini-whirlwind around our bodies, lifting our hair and brushing softly against our skin.

"It's true," he whispered, staring at me. "You can actually manifest the elements."

"Well," I whispered back, feeling lightheaded, "one of them at least. Let's try for two."

I walked over to Shaunee. She raised her candle eagerly and made me smile when she said, "I'm ready for fire—bring it on!"

"Fire reminds me of cold winter nights and the warmth and safety of the fireplace that heats my grandma's cabin. I ask that you hear me, fire, and I summon you to this circle." I lit the red candle and the flame blazed, much brighter than should have been possible for an ordinary votive. The air around Shaunee and me was suddenly filled with the rich, woody scent and homey warmth of a roaring fireplace.

"Wow!" Shaunee exclaimed, her dark eyes dancing with the reflection of the candle's shimmering flame. "Now, that's cool!"

"That's two," I heard Damien say.

Erin was grinning when I took my place in front of her. "I'm ready for water," she said quickly.

"Water is relief on a hot Oklahoma summer day. It's the amazing ocean that I really would like to see someday, and it's the rain that makes the lavender grow. I ask that you hear me, water, and I summon you to this circle."

I lit the blue candle and felt instant coolness against my skin, as well as smelled a clean, salty scent that could only be the ocean I'd never seen.

"Awesome. Really, really awesome," Erin said, drawing in a deep breath of ocean air.

"That's three," Damien said.

"I'm not scared anymore," Stevie Rae said when I stood in front of her.

"Good," I said. Then I focused my mind on the fourth element, earth. "Earth supports and surrounds us. We wouldn't be anything without her. I ask that you hear me, earth, and I summon you to this circle." The green candle lit easily, and suddenly Stevie Rae and I were overwhelmed with the sweet scent of freshly cut grass. I heard the rustle of the oak's leaves and we looked up to see the great oak literally bowing its branches over us as though it would shield us from all harm.

"Totally amazing," Stevie Rae breathed.

"Four," Damien said, his voice filled with excitement.

I walked quickly to the center of the circle and lifted my purple candle.

"The last element is one that fills everything and everyone. It makes us unique and it breathes life into all things. I ask that you hear me, spirit, and I summon you to this circle."

Incredibly, it seemed that I was suddenly surrounded by the four elements, that I was in the middle of a whirlpool made up of air and fire, water and earth. But it wasn't scary, not at all. It filled me with peace, and at the same time I felt a surge of white-hot power and had to press my lips tightly together to keep from laughing with pure joy.

"Look! Look at the circle!" Damien shouted.

I blinked my vision clear and instantly felt the elements settle down, as if they were playful kittens who were sitting around me, waiting happily for me to call them to bat at string and whatnot. I was smiling at the comparison when I saw the glowing light that wrapped around the circumference of the circle, joining Damien, Shaunee, Erin, and Stevie Rae. It was bright and clear, and the luminous silver of a full moon.

"And that makes five," Damien said.

"Holy crap!" I blurted, very un–High Priestess-like, and the four of them laughed, filling the night with the sounds of happiness. And I understood, for the first time, why Neferet and Aphrodite had danced during the rituals. I wanted to dance and laugh and shout with happiness. *Another time,* I told myself. Tonight there was more serious work to be done.

"Okay, I'm going to speak the purification prayer," I told my four friends. "And while I say the prayer I'm going to face each of the elements, one at a time."

"What do you want us to do?" Stevie Rae asked.

"Focus on the prayer. Concentrate. Believe that the elements will carry it to Nyx, and that the Goddess will answer it by helping me to know what I should do," I said with way more certainty than I felt.

Once again I faced east. Damien smiled encouragement to me. And I began to recite the ancient purification prayer I'd said so many times with my grandma—with just a few changes I'd decided on earlier.

Great Goddess of Night, whose voice I hear in the wind, who breathes the breath of life to Her children. Hear me; I need your strength and wisdom.

I paused briefly as I turned to the south.

Let me walk in beauty, and make my eyes ever behold the red and purple sunset that comes before the beauty of your night. Make my hands respect the things you have made and my ears sharp to hear your voice. Make me wise so that I may understand the things you have taught your people.

I turned again to the right, and my voice felt stronger as I fell into the rhythm of the prayer.

Help me to remain calm and strong in the face of all that comes toward me. Let me learn the lessons you have hidden in every leaf and rock. Help me seek pure thoughts and act with the intention of helping others. Help me find compassion without empathy overwhelming me.

I faced Stevie Rae, whose eyes were squeezed shut as though she was concentrating with all of her might.

I seek strength, not to be greater than others, but to fight my greatest enemy, the doubts within myself.

I walked back to the center of the circle and finished the prayer, and for the first time in my life, I felt a flush of sensation as the power of the ancient words rushed from me to what I hoped with all my heart and soul was my listening Goddess.

Make me always ready to come to you with clean hands and straight eyes. So when life fades, as the fading sunset, my spirit may come to you without shame.

Technically, that was the conclusion of the Cherokee prayer my grandma had taught me, but I felt the need to add: "And Nyx, I don't understand why you Marked me and why you have given me the gift of an affinity for the elements. I don't even have to know. What I want to ask is that you help me know the right thing to do, and then give me the courage to do it." And I finished the prayer the way I remembered Neferet completed her ritual: "Blessed be!"

CHAPTER TWENTY-FOUR

—

"That was truly the most prodigious circle-casting I've ever experienced!" Damien gushed after the circle had been closed and we were gathering up the candles and smudge stick.

"I thought 'prodigious' meant 'big,'" Shaunee said.

"It also can show exciting wonder and can refer to something stupendous and monumental," Damien said.

"For once I'm not going to argue with you," Shaunee said, surprising everyone except Erin.

"Yeah, the circle was *prodigious*," Erin said.

"Do you know I actually could feel earth when Zoey called it?" Stevie Rae said. "It was like I was suddenly surrounded by a growing wheat field. No, it was more than being surrounded by it. It was like I was suddenly a part of it."

"I know exactly what you mean. When she called flame it was like the fire exploded through me," Shaunee said.

I tried to understand what I was feeling while the four of them talked happily together. I was definitely happy, but overwhelmed and more than a little confused. So it was true, I did have some kind of affinity with all five of the elements.

Why?

Just to bring down Aphrodite? (Which, by the by, I still didn't have a clue how to do.) No, I didn't think so. Why would Nyx touch me with such unusual power just so that I could kick a spoiled bully out of the leadership of a club?

Okay, the Dark Daughters were more than a student council or whatever, but still.

"Zoey, are you all right?"

The concern in Damien's voice made me look up from Nala, and I realized that I was sitting in the middle of what used to be the circle, with my cat on my lap, completely engrossed in my own thoughts as I scratched her head.

"Oh, yeah. Sorry. I'm fine, just a little distracted."

"We should get back. It's getting late," Stevie Rae said.

"Okay. You're right," I said, and got up, still holding Nala. But I couldn't make my feet follow them as they started to head back to the dorms.

"Zoey?"

Damien, the first to notice my hesitation, stopped and called back to me, and then my other friends stopped, looking at me with expressions that ranged from worried to confused.

"Uh, why don't you guys go ahead? I'm going to stay out here for just a little while longer."

"We could stay with you and—" Damien began, but Stevie Rae (bless her little bumpkin heart) interrupted him.

"Zoey needs to do some thinkin' on her own. Wouldn't you if you just found out you were the only fledgling in known history to have an affinity for all five elements?"

"I suppose," Damien said reluctantly.

"But don't forget that it'll be getting light soon," Erin said.

I smiled reassuringly at them. "I won't. I'll be back at the dorm soon."

"I'll make a sandwich for you and try to scare up some chips to go with your brown non-diet pop. It's important that a High

Priestess eats after she performs a ritual," Stevie Rae said with a smile and a wave as she pulled the rest of the four along with her.

I called thanks to Stevie Rae as they disappeared into the darkness. Then I walked over to the tree and sat down, resting my back against its thick trunk. I closed my eyes and petted Nala. Her purr was normal and familiar and incredibly soothing, and it seemed to help ground me.

"I'm still me," I whispered to my cat. "Just like Grandma said. All the other stuff can change, but what's really Zoey—what's been Zoey for sixteen years—is still Zoey."

Maybe if I repeated it over and over enough to myself, I'd actually believe it. I rested my face in one hand and scratched my cat with the other, and told myself that I was still me . . . still me . . . still me . . .

"See how she leans her cheek upon her hand! O, that I were a glove upon that hand, that I might touch that cheek!"

Nala "me-eeh-uf-owed" in complaint as I jumped in surprise.

"Seems like I keep finding you by this tree," Erik said, smiling down at me and looking like a god.

He made me feel all fluttery in my stomach, but tonight he also made me feel something else. Just exactly why did he keep "finding" me? And just exactly how long had he been watching this time?

"What are you doing out here, Erik?"

"Hi, it's nice to see you, too. And, yes, I would like to have a seat, thank you," he said and started to sit beside me.

I stood up, making Nala mutter at me again.

"Actually, I was just going to go back to the dorm."

"Hey, I didn't mean to intrude or whatever. I just couldn't concentrate on my homework so I went for a walk. I guess my feet carried me this way without me telling them to, 'cause next thing

I knew here I was and here you are. I'm really not stalking you. Promise."

He stuck his hands in his pockets and looked totally embarrassed. Well, totally cute and embarrassed, and I remembered how much I had wanted to say yes to him earlier when he asked me to watch dorky movies with him. And now here I was, rejecting him and making him uncomfortable again. It's a wonder the kid ever talked to me. Clearly, I was taking this High Priestess thing way too seriously.

"So how about walking me back to my dorm? Again," I asked.

"Sounds good."

This time Nala complained when I tried to carry her. Instead she trotted along after us while Erik and I fell into step together as easily as we had before. We didn't say anything for a while. I wanted to ask him about Aphrodite, or at the very least tell him what she'd said to me about him, but I couldn't come up with a good way of saying something that I probably didn't have any business questioning him about.

"So what were you doing out here this time?" he asked.

"Thinking," I said, which technically wasn't a lie. I had been thinking. A lot. Before, during, and after the circle-casting I was conveniently not going to mention.

"Oh. Are you worried about that Heath kid?"

Actually, I hadn't thought about Heath or Kayla since I'd talked to Neferet, but I shrugged, not wanting to get specific about what I'd been thinking.

"I mean, I guess it's probably hard to break up with someone just because you got Marked," he said.

"I didn't break up with him because I got Marked. He and I were pretty much finished before that. The Mark just made it more final." I looked at Erik and took a deep breath. "What about you and Aphrodite?"

He blinked in surprise. "What do you mean?"

"I mean today she told me that you'll never be her ex because you'll always be hers."

His eyes narrowed and he looked truly pissed. "Aphrodite has a serious problem with telling the truth."

"Well, not that it's any of my business, but—"

"It *is* your business," he said quickly. And then, totally and utterly shocking me, he took my hand. "At least I'd like it to be your business."

"Oh," I said. "Okay, well, okay." Once again, I was sure I was astounding him with my witty conversation skills.

"So you weren't just avoiding me tonight; you really had some thinking to do?" he asked slowly.

"I wasn't avoiding you. There's just . . . ," I hesitated, not sure how the hell to explain something I was pretty sure I shouldn't explain to him. "There's a lot of stuff going on with me right now. This whole Change thing is pretty confusing sometimes."

"It gets better," he said, squeezing my hand.

"Somehow, for me, I doubt it," I muttered.

He laughed and tapped my Mark with his finger. "You're just ahead of some of the rest of us. That's hard at first, but, believe me, it'll get easier—even for you."

I sighed. "I hope so." But I doubted it.

We stopped in front of the dorm, and he turned to me, his voice suddenly low and serious. "Z, don't believe the crap Aphrodite says. She and I haven't been together in months."

"But you used to be," I said.

He nodded and his face looked strained.

"She's not a very nice person, Erik."

"I know that."

And then I realized what had really been bothering me and decided, oh, well, what the hell, I'd just say it.

"I don't like it that you'd be with someone who's so mean. It makes me feel funny about wanting to be with you." He opened up his mouth to say something and I kept talking, not wanting to hear excuses I wasn't sure that I should or could believe. "Thanks for walking me home. I am glad you found me again."

"I'm glad I found you, too," he said. "I'd like to see you again, Z, and not just by accident."

I hesitated. And wondered why I was hesitating. I did want to see him again. I needed to forget Aphrodite. Seriously, she *is* really pretty and he *is* a guy. He probably fell into her haggish (and hot) clutches before he knew what was happening. I mean, she did kinda remind me of a spider. I should be glad that she hadn't bitten his head off, and give the guy a chance.

"Okay, how about I watch those dorky DVDs with you Saturday?" I said before I could freakishly talk myself out of going out with the most gorgeous guy at this school.

"It's a date," he said.

Obviously giving me time to pull away if I wanted to, Erik slowly bent down and kissed me. His lips were warm and he smelled really good. The kiss was soft and nice. Honestly, it made me want him to kiss me more. Too soon it was over, but he didn't move away from me. We were standing close, and I realized that I had my hands on his chest. His were resting lightly on my shoulders. I smiled up at him.

"I'm glad you asked me out again," I said.

"I'm glad you finally said yes," he said.

Then he kissed me again, only this time he wasn't hesitant. The kiss deepened, and my arms went up around his shoulders. I felt, more than heard, him moan and as he kissed me long and hard it was like he flipped a switch somewhere deep inside me, and hot, sweet, electric desire flashed through me. It was crazy and amazing, and more than anyone else's kisses had ever made me feel.

I loved the way my body fitted his, hard against soft, and I pressed myself against him, forgetting about Aphrodite and the circle I'd just cast and the entire rest of the world. This time when we broke off the kiss we were both breathing hard, and we stared at each other. As my sense started to return to me I realized that I was totally smushed against him and that I'd been standing there in front of the dorm making out like a slut. I started to pull out of his arms.

"What's wrong? Why do you suddenly look different?" he said, tightening his arms around me.

"Erik, I'm not like Aphrodite." I pulled harder and he let me go.

"I know you're not. I wouldn't like you if you were like her."

"I don't just mean my personality. I mean standing out here making out with you isn't normal behavior for me."

"Okay." He reached one hand toward me as though he wanted to pull me back into his arms, but then he seemed to change his mind and his hand fell to his side. "Zoey, you make me feel different than anyone has ever made me feel before."

I felt my face getting hot and I couldn't tell if it was from anger or embarrassment. "Don't patronize me, Erik. I saw you in the hall with Aphrodite. You've clearly felt this kind of stuff before, and more."

He shook his head and I saw hurt in his eyes. "What Aphrodite made me feel was all physical. What you make me feel is about touching my heart. I know the difference, Zoey, and I thought you did, too."

I stared at him—at those gorgeous blue eyes that had seemed to touch me the first time he looked at me. "I'm sorry," I said softly. "That was mean of me. I do know the difference."

"Promise me that you won't let Aphrodite come between us."

"I promise." It scared me, but I meant it.

"Good."

Nala materialized out of the dark and started winding around my legs and complaining. "I better get her inside and put her to bed."

"Okay." He smiled and gave me a quick kiss. "See you Saturday, Z."

My lips tingled all the way up to my room.

CHAPTER TWENTY-FIVE

—

The next day started with what I looked back on later as suspicious normalcy. Stevie Rae and I ate breakfast, still whispering good gossip about how hot Erik was and trying to figure out what I'd wear on our date Saturday. We didn't even see Aphrodite or the hag triplets, Warlike, Terrible, and Wasp. Vamp Soc class was so interesting—we'd moved from the Amazons to learning about an ancient Greek vampyre festival called Correia—that I'd stopped thinking about the Dark Daughters ritual planned for that evening, and for a little while I'd actually quit worrying about what I was going to do about Aphrodite. Drama class was good, too. I decided to do one of Kate's soliloquies from *The Taming of the Shrew* (I've loved that play ever since I saw the old movie starring Elizabeth Taylor and Richard Burton). Then as I was leaving class Neferet snagged me in the hall and asked how far I'd read in the upper level Vamp Soc book. I'd had to tell her that I really hadn't read much (translation: I hadn't read any) yet, and I was totally distracted by her obvious disappointment in me when I hurried into English class. I'd just taken my seat between Damien and Stevie Rae when all hell broke loose, and everything vaguely resembling anything normal about the day ended.

Penthesilea was reading "You Go and I'll Stay a While," Chapter Four of *A Night to Remember*. It's a really good book, and we were all listening, as usual, then that stupid Elliott kid started coughing. Jeesh, the kid was totally and completely annoying.

Somewhere in the middle of the chapter and the obnoxious coughing I started to smell something. It was rich and sweet, delicious, and elusive. Automatically, I inhaled deeply, still trying to concentrate on the book.

Elliott's coughing got worse, and with the rest of the class, I turned to give him a dirty look. I mean, please. Could he not get a cough drop or a drink or whatever?

And then I saw the blood.

Elliott wasn't in his usual slouched and sleeping position. He was sitting straight up, staring at his hand, which was covered with fresh blood. As I watched him, he coughed again, making a nasty, wet sound that reminded me of the day I'd been Marked. Only when Elliott coughed, bright scarlet blood spewed from his mouth.

"Wh—?" he gurgled.

"Get Neferet!" Penthesilea snapped the command as she jerked open one of her desk drawers, yanked out a neatly folded towel, and moved quickly down the aisle to Elliott. The kid who was sitting closest to the door took off.

In utter silence we watched Penthesilea make it to Elliott just in time for his next bloody cough, which she caught in the towel. He clutched the towel to his face, hacking and spitting and gagging. When he finally looked up, bloody tears were running down his pale, round face, and blood was running from his nose like it was a faucet someone had left on. When he turned his head to look up at Penthesilea, I could see that there was a red stream coming from his ear, too.

"No!" Elliott said with more emotion than I'd ever heard him show. "No! I don't want to die!"

"Sssh," Penthesilea soothed, smoothing his orange hair back from his sweaty face. "Your pain will end soon."

"But—but, no I—" He started to protest again, in a whiny voice that sounded more like his own, then he was interrupted by another round of hacking coughs. He gagged again, this time puking blood into the already soaked towel.

Neferet entered the room with two tall, powerful-looking vampyre men close behind her. They carried a flat stretcher and a blanket; Neferet was carrying only a vial filled with milky-colored liquid. Not two breaths behind them, Dragon Lankford burst into the room.

"That's his mentor," Stevie Rae whispered almost soundlessly. I nodded, remembering when Penthesilea had chastised Elliott for letting Dragon down.

Neferet handed Dragon the vial she'd been holding. Then she stood behind Elliott. She put her hands on his shoulders. Instantly, his gagging and coughing subsided.

"Drink this quickly, Elliott," Dragon told him. When he started to weakly shake his head no, he added gently, "It will make your pain end."

"Will—will you stay with me?" Elliott gasped.

"Of course," Dragon said. "I won't let you be alone for even a moment."

"Will you call my mom?" Elliott whispered.

"I will."

Elliott closed his eyes for a second, and then, with shaking hands he held the vial to his lips and drank. Neferet nodded to the two men, and they picked him up and lay him on the stretcher as if he was a doll and not a dying kid. With Dragon by his side, they hurried from the room. Before Neferet followed them she turned to face the shocked classroom of third formers.

"I could tell you that Elliott will be fine—that he will recover, but that would be a lie." Her voice was serene, but filled with commanding strength. "The truth is his body has rejected the

Change. In minutes he will die the permanent death and will not mature into a vampyre. I could tell you not to worry, that it won't happen to you. But this would be a lie, too. On average, one out of every ten of you will not make the Change. Some fledglings die early in their third former year, as is Elliott. Some of you will be stronger and last until your sixth former year, and then sicken and die suddenly. I tell you this not so that you will live in fear. I tell you for two reasons. First, I want you to know that as your High Priestess I will not lie to you, but will help ease your passing into the next world if that time comes. And second, I want you to live as you would be remembered if you would die tomorrow, because you might. Then if you do die your spirit can rest peacefully knowing that you leave behind an honorable memory. If you do not die, then you will have set the foundation for a long life rich with integrity." She looked straight into my eyes as she finished, saying, "I ask that Nyx's blessing comfort you today, and that you remember death is a natural part of life, even a vampyre life. For someday we all must return to the bosom of the Goddess." She closed the door behind her with a sound that seemed to echo finality.

Penthesilea worked quickly and efficiently. Matter-of-factly she cleaned up the spatters of blood that stained Elliot's desk. When all evidence of the dying kid was gone, she returned to the front of the class and led us in a moment of silence for Elliott. Then she picked up the book and began reading where she'd left off. I tried to listen. I tried to block out the vision of Elliott bleeding out through his eyes and ears and nose and mouth. And I also tried not to think about the fact that the delicious smell I'd noticed had been, without a doubt, Elliott's lifeblood pouring from his dying body.

* * *

I know things are supposed to go on as usual after a fledgling dies, but apparently it was unusual for two kids to die so close together, and everyone was unnaturally quiet for the rest of the day. Lunch was silent and depressing, and I noticed that most of the food was picked at rather than eaten. The Twins didn't even bicker with Damien, which might have been a nice change if I hadn't known the awful reason behind it. When Stevie Rae made some lame excuse to leave lunch early and go back to the room before fifth hour started, I was more than happy to say I'd go with her.

We walked along the sidewalk in the thick dark of another cloudy night. Tonight the gaslights didn't feel cheerful and warm. Instead they seemed cold and not bright enough.

"No one liked Elliott, and somehow I think that makes it worse," Stevie Rae said. "It was weirdly easier with Elizabeth. At least we could feel honestly sorry she was gone."

"I know what you mean. I feel upset, but I know I'm really upset that I saw what can happen to us and now I can't get it out of my mind, and not upset that the kid's dead."

"At least it happens fast," she said softly.

I shivered. "I wonder if it hurts."

"They give you something—that white stuff Elliott drank. It makes it stop hurting, but it lets you be conscious till the end. And Neferet always helps with the actual dying."

"It's scary, isn't it?" I said.

"Yeah."

We didn't say anything for a while. Then the moon peeped through the clouds, painting the leaves of the tree with an eerie silver watercolor, and reminding me suddenly of Aphrodite and her ritual.

"Any chance Aphrodite will cancel the Samhain ritual tonight?"

"No way. The Dark Daughters' rituals are never cancelled."

"Well, hell," I said. Then I glanced at Stevie Rae. "He was their refrigerator."

She gave me a startled look. "Elliott?"

"Yeah, it was really gross, and he acted all drugged and weird. He must have been starting to reject the Change even then." There was an uncomfortable silence, and then I added, "I didn't want to say anything to you before, especially after you told me about . . . well . . . you know. Are you sure Aphrodite won't cancel tonight? I mean, what with Elizabeth and now Elliott."

"It won't matter. And the Dark Daughters don't care about the kid they use as a refrigerator. They'll just get someone else." She hesitated. "Zoey, I've been thinking. Maybe you shouldn't go tonight. I heard what Aphrodite said to you yesterday. She's going to make sure no one accepts you. She'll be really, really mean."

"I'll be okay, Stevie Rae."

"No, I have a bad feeling about it. You don't have a plan yet, do you?"

"Well, no. I'm still in the reconnoitering stage," I said, trying to lighten up the conversation.

"Reconnoiter later. Today's been too awful. Everyone's upset. I think you should wait."

"I can't just not show up, especially after what Aphrodite said to me yesterday. She'll think she told me and now she can intimidate me."

Stevie Rae took a deep breath. "Well, then I think you should take me with you." I started to shake my head but she kept right on talking. "You're a Dark Daughter now. Technically, you can invite people to the rituals. So invite me. I'll go and watch your back."

I thought about drinking blood and liking it so much that it was obvious, even to Warlike and Terrible. And I tried, and failed, not to think about the scent of blood—Heath's and Erik's and even Elliott's. Stevie Rae would find out someday how blood affected me, but it wouldn't be tonight. Actually, if I could help it, it wouldn't be anytime soon. I didn't want to chance losing her or the Twins or Damien—and I was afraid I would. Yes, they knew I was "special," and they accepted me because that uniqueness meant High Priestess to them, and that was good. My bloodlust was not so good. Would they accept it as easily?

"No way, Stevie Rae."

"But, Zoey, you shouldn't go into that hag pack alone."

"I won't be alone. Erik will be there."

"Yeah, but he used to be Aphrodite's boyfriend. Who knows how good he'll be at standing up to her if she gets real hateful with you."

"Honey, I can stand up for myself."

"I know, but—" She broke off and gave me a funny look. "Z, are you vibrating?"

"Huh? Am I what?" And then I heard it, too, and started laughing. "It's my cell phone. I stuck it in my purse after it charged up last night." I pulled it out of my purse, glancing at the time on the face dial. "It's past midnight, who the heck . . ." Flipping the phone open I was shocked to see that I had fifteen new text messages and five missed calls. "Jeesh, someone's been calling and calling, and I didn't even notice." I checked the text messages first, and felt my stomach start to clench as I read them.

Zo call me
I stl luv u
Zo call me plz
Got 2 see u
U & Me
Will u call?

I wnt 2 tlk 2 u
Zo!
Call me bak

I didn't need to read any more of them. They were all basically the same. "Ah, crap. They're all from Heath."

"Your ex?"

I sighed. "Yeah."

"What does he want?"

"Apparently, me." Reluctantly, I keyed in the code to access my voice messages, and Heath's cute, dopey voice shocked me with how loud and animated he sounded.

"Zo! Call me. Like, I know it's late, but . . . wait. It's not late to you, but it's late to me. But that's okay 'cause I don't care. I just want you to call me. Okay. So. Bye. Call me."

I groaned and deleted it. The next one sounded even more manic.

"Zoey! Okay. You need to call me. Really. And don't be mad. Hey, I don't even like Kayla. She's lame. I still love you, Zo, only you. So call me. I don't care when. I'll just wake up."

"Man oh man," Stevie Rae said, easily overhearing Heath's gushing. "The boy's obsessed. No wonder you dumped him."

"Yeah," I mumbled, quickly deleting the second message. The third was much like the first two, only more desperate. I turned the volume down and tapped my foot impatiently while I went through all five messages, not listening except to see when I could delete and move on to the next one. "I gotta go see Neferet," I said, more to myself than to Stevie Rae.

"How come? You need to block him from calling or something?"

"No. Yeah. Something like that. I just need to talk to her about, well, about what I should do." I avoided Stevie Rae's curious gaze.

"I mean, he's already showed up here once. I don't want him to come by again and cause any trouble."

"Oh, yeah, that's true. It'd be bad if he ran into Erik."

"It'd be awful. Okay, I better hurry and try to catch Neferet before fifth hour. I'll see you after school."

I didn't wait for Stevie Rae's good-bye, but took off in the direction of Neferet's room. Could this day get any worse? Elliott dies and I'm attracted to his blood. I have to go to the Samhain ritual tonight with a bunch of kids who hate me and want to make sure I know it, and I've probably Imprinted my ex-almost-boyfriend.

Yep. Today really, really sucked.

CHAPTER TWENTY-SIX

—

If Skylar's hissing and growling hadn't caught my attention, I would never have seen Aphrodite slumped in the little alcove down the hall from Neferet's room.

"What is it, Skylar?" I held my hand out gingerly, remembering what Neferet had said about her cat being a known biter. I was also sincerely glad that Nala wasn't tagging long after me as usual—Skylar would probably eat my poor little cat for lunch. "Kitty-kitty," the big orange tom gave me a considering look (probably considering whether or not to bite the crap out of my hand). Then he made his decision, un-puffed himself, and trotted over to me. He rubbed around my legs, then he gave the alcove one more good hiss before he took off, disappearing down the hall in the direction of Neferet's room.

"What the hell was his problem?" I looked hesitantly into the alcove, wondering what would make a mean cat like Skylar puff up and hiss, and I felt a jolt of shock. She was sitting right on the floor, hard to see in the shadow under the ledge that held a pretty statue of Nyx. Her head was tilted back, and her eyes were rolled so that only their whites were showing. She scared the total crap out of me. I felt frozen, expecting any second to see blood pouring down her face. Then she moaned and muttered something I couldn't understand while her eyeballs shifted around behind her closed lids as though she was watching a scene. I realized what must be happening. Aphrodite was having a vision. She'd probably felt it coming on and hidden in the alcove so no one would find her and she could keep her info about the death and destruction she could prevent to her hateful self. Cow. Hag.

Well, I was done letting her get away with that crap. I bent down and grabbed her under the arms, pulling her to her feet. (Let me tell you, she's a lot heavier than she looks.)

"Come on," I groaned, half carrying her while she lurched blindly forward with me. "Let's take a little trip down the hall and see what kind of tragedy you want to keep quiet about."

Thankfully, Neferet's room wasn't far away. We staggered in and Neferet jumped up from behind her desk and rushed to us.

"Zoey! Aphrodite! What?" But as soon as she got a good look at Aphrodite, her alarm changed to calm understanding. "Help me bring her over here to my chair. She'll be more comfortable there."

We led Aphrodite to Neferet's big leather chair, and let her sink into it. Then Neferet crouched beside her and took her hand.

"Aphrodite, with the Goddess's voice I beseech you to tell her Priestess what it is you see." Neferet's voice was soft, but compelling, and I could feel the power in her command.

Aphrodite's eyelids instantly began to flicker, and she drew a deep, gasping breath. Then they opened suddenly. Her eyes looked huge and glassy.

"So much blood! There's so much blood coming out of his body!"

"Who, Aphrodite? Center yourself. Focus and clear the vision," Neferet commanded.

Aphrodite drew another gasping breath. "They're dead! No. No. That can't be! Not right. No. Not natural! I don't understand . . . I don't . . ." She blinked her eyes again, and her gaze seemed to clear. She looked around the room, like she didn't recognize anything. Her eyes touched me. "You . . . ," she said faintly. "You know."

"Yeah," I said, thinking that I sure did know that she was trying to hide her vision, but all I said was, "I found you in the hall and—" Neferet's raised hand stopped me.

"No, she's not finished. She shouldn't be coming to so soon. The vision is still too abstract," Neferet told me quickly, and then she lowered her voice again and assumed the compelling, commanding tone. "Aphrodite, go back. See what it is you were meant to witness, and what you were meant to change."

Ha! Got you now. I couldn't help being a little smug. After all, she had tried to scratch my eyes out yesterday.

"The dead . . ." Getting more and more difficult to understand, Aphrodite murmured something that sounded like "Tunnels . . . they kill . . . someone there . . . I don't . . . I can't . . ." She was frantic, and I almost felt sorry for her. Clearly, whatever she was seeing was freaking her out. Then her searching eyes found Neferet, and I saw recognition flash through them and I started to relax. She was coming around and this whole weirdness would be cleared up. And just as I thought that, Aphrodite's eyes, which seemed to be locked on Neferet, widened unbelievably. A look of pure terror blanked her face and she screamed.

Neferet clamped her hands on Aphrodite's trembling shoulders. "Awaken!" She spared hardly a glance over her shoulder at me to say, "Go now, Zoey. Her vision is confused. Elliott's death has upset her. I need to be certain she is herself once more."

I didn't need to be told twice. Heath's obsession forgotten, I got the hell outta there and headed to Spanish class.

I couldn't concentrate on school. I kept replaying the weird scene with Neferet and Aphrodite over and over in my head. She'd obviously been having a vision about people dying, but from Neferet's reaction it hadn't behaved like a normal vision (if there was such a thing). Stevie Rae had said that Aphrodite's visions were so clear that she could direct people to the right airport and even the specific plane she'd seen crashing. Yet today, all of a sudden, nothing was clear. Well, nothing but seeing me and saying weird stuff, and then screaming her brains out at Neferet. It so didn't make sense. I was almost looking forward to seeing how she'd act tonight. Almost.

I put away Persephone's curry brushes and picked up Nala, who'd been perched on top of the horse's feeder watching and making her weird me-eeh-uf-ows at me, and started slowly back to the dorm. This time Aphrodite didn't hassle me, but when I rounded the corner by the old oak Stevie Rae, Damien, and the Twins were huddled together doing a lot of talking—that suddenly shut up when I came into view. They all looked guiltily at me. It was pretty easy to guess who they'd been talking about.

"What?" I said.

"We were just waiting for you," Stevie Rae said. Her usual perkiness was missing.

"What's wrong with you?" I asked.

"She's worried about you," Shaunee said.

"We're worried about you," Erin said.

"What's going on with your ex?" Damien asked.

"He's buggin', that's all. If he didn't bug, he wouldn't be my ex." I tried to speak nonchalantly, without looking any of the four of them in the eye too long. (I've never been a particularly good liar.)

"We think I should go with you tonight," Stevie Rae said.

"Actually, we think *we* should go with you tonight," Damien corrected.

I frowned at them. No possible way I wanted all four of them to watch me drink whatever loser kid's blood they managed to mix into the wine tonight.

"No."

"Zoey, it's been a really bad day. Everyone's stressed. Plus, Aphrodite is out to get you. It makes sense that we should stick together tonight," Damien said logically.

Yeah, it was logical, but they didn't know the whole story. I didn't want them to know the whole story. Yet. The truth was, I cared too much about them. They made me feel accepted and safe—they made me feel like I fit in here. I couldn't risk losing that right now, not when all of this was still so new and so scary. So I did what I had learned to do too well at home when I was scared and upset and didn't know what else to do—I got pissed and defensive.

"You guys say that I have powers that will someday make me your High Priestess?" They all nodded eagerly and smiled at me, which squeezed my heart. I gritted my teeth and made my voice real cold. "Then you need to listen to me when I say no. I don't want you there tonight. This is something I have to deal with. Alone. And I don't want to talk about it anymore."

And then I stomped away from them.

Naturally, within half an hour I was sorry I'd been so awful. I paced back and forth under the big oak that had somehow become my sanctuary, annoying Nala and wishing that Stevie Rae would show up so I could apologize. My friends didn't know why I didn't want them there. They were just looking out for me. Maybe . . . maybe they would understand about the blood thing. Erik seemed to understand. Okay, sure, he was a fifth former, but still. We were all supposed to go through it. We were all supposed to start craving blood—or we died. I brightened a little and scratched Nala's head.

"When the alternative is death, blood drinking doesn't seem so bad. Right?"

She purred, so I took that as a yes. I checked the time on my watch. Crap. I had to go back to the dorm, change my clothes, and go meet the Dark Daughters. Listlessly, I started following the wall back. It was a cloudy night again, but I didn't mind the darkness. Actually, I was starting to like the night. I should. It was going to be my element for a very long time. If I lived. As though she could read my morbid thoughts, Nala "me-eeh-uf-owed" grumpily at me as she trotted along beside me.

"Yeah, I know. I shouldn't be so negative. I'll work on that right after I—"

Nala's low growl surprised me. She'd stopped. Her back was arched and her hair was standing on end, making her look like a fat little puffball, but her slitted eyes were no joke, and neither was the ferocious hiss that snaked from her mouth. "Nala, what . . ."

A terrible chill fingered its way down my spine even before I turned to look in the direction my cat was staring. Later, I couldn't figure out why I didn't scream. I remember my mouth opening so I could gulp air, but I was absolutely silent. It seemed I'd gone numb, but that was impossible. If I'd been numb there's no way I could have been so thoroughly petrified.

Elliott was standing not ten feet from me in the darkness that shadowed the space next to the wall. He must have been heading in the same direction Nala and I were walking. Then he'd heard Nala, and half turned back toward us. She hissed again at him and, with a frighteningly quick movement he whirled around to fully face us.

I swear I couldn't breathe. He was a ghost—he had to be, but he looked so solid, so real. If I hadn't watched his body rejecting the Change, I would have thought he was just looking especially pale and . . . and . . . *weird.* He was abnormally white, but there was more wrong about him than that. His eyes had changed. They reflected what little light there was and they glowed a terrible rust red, like dried blood.

Exactly as the ghost of Elizabeth's eyes had glowed.

There was something else different about him, too. His body looked strange—thinner. How was that possible? The smell came to me then. Old and dry and out of place, like a closet that hadn't been opened in years or a creepy basement. It was the same smell I'd noticed just before I'd seen Elizabeth.

Nala growled and Elliott dropped into an odd, half crouch and hissed back at her. Then he bared his teeth, and I could see that *he had fangs!* He took a step toward Nala as if he was going to attack her. I didn't think, I just reacted.

"Leave her alone and get the hell out of here!" It amazed me that I sounded like I wasn't doing anything more exciting than yelling at a bad dog, because I was definitely scared totally shitless.

His head swiveled in my direction and the glow of his eyes touched me for the first time. *Wrong!* The intuitive voice inside me that had become familiar was screaming. *This is an abomination!*

"You . . ." His voice was horrible. It was raspy and guttural, as if something had damaged his throat. "I will have you!" And he began to come toward me.

Raw fear engulfed me like a bitter wind.

Nala's battle yowl rent the night as she hurled herself at Elliott's ghost. In complete shock I watched, expecting the cat to go spitting and clawing through empty air. Instead she landed on his thigh, claws extended, scratching and howling like an animal three times her size. He screamed, grabbed her by the scruff of her neck, and threw her away from him. Then, with impossible speed and strength he literally leaped to the top of the wall, and disappeared into the night that surrounded the school.

I was shaking so hard that I stumbled. "Nala!" I sobbed. "Where are you, little girl?"

Puffed up and growling, she padded over to me, but her slitted eyes were still focused on the wall. I crouched beside her, and with shaking hands checked to make sure she felt all in one piece. She felt unbroken, so I scooped her up and began jogging away from the wall as fast as I could.

"It's okay. We're okay. He's gone. What a brave girl you were." I kept talking to her. She perched halfway over my shoulder so that she could see behind us, and she continued to growl.

When I got to the first gaslight, not far from the rec hall, I stopped and shifted Nala's position so that I could look more closely to see that she was really okay. What I found made my stomach clench so hard I thought I was going to throw up. On her paws was blood. Only it wasn't Nala's. And it didn't smell delicious like other blood had smelled. Instead it carried the scent of musty dryness, old basements. I forced myself not to retch as I wiped her paws on the winter grass. Then I picked her up again and hurried down the sidewalk that led to the dorm. Nala never stopped looking behind us and growling.

Stevie Rae, the Twins, and Damien were all conspicuously absent from the dorm. They weren't watching TV—they weren't in the computer room or the library, and they weren't in the kitchen, either. I climbed quickly up the stairs, hoping desperately that at least Stevie Rae would be in our room. No such luck.

I sat on my bed, petting the still distraught Nala. Should I try to find my friends? Or should I just stay here? Stevie Rae would eventually come back to our room. I looked at her gyrating Elvis clock. I had about ten minutes to get changed and to the rec hall. But how could I go on to the ritual after what had just happened?

What *had* just happened?

A ghost had tried to attack me. No. That wasn't right. How

could ghosts bleed? But had it been blood? It didn't smell like blood. I had no idea what was going on.

I should go directly to Neferet and tell her what had happened. I should get up right now and take myself and my freaked-out cat to Neferet and tell her about Elizabeth last night and now Elliott tonight. I should . . . I should . . .

No. This time it wasn't a scream within me. It was the strength of certainty. I could not tell Neferet, at least not at that moment.

"I have to go to the ritual." I said aloud the words that were echoing through my mind. "I have to be at this ritual."

As I pulled on the black dress and searched around the closet for my ballet flats I felt myself becoming very calm. Things here didn't play by the same rules as they did in my old world—in my old life—and it was time I accepted that and started getting used to it.

I had an affinity for the five elements, which meant that I had been gifted with incredible powers by an ancient goddess. As Grandma had reminded me, with great power comes great responsibility. Maybe I was being allowed to see things—like ghosts that didn't act or look or smell like ghosts should—for a reason. I didn't know what that meant yet. Actually, I didn't know much besides the two thoughts that were clearest in my mind: I couldn't tell Neferet, and I had to go to the ritual.

Hurrying to the rec hall I tried to at least think positively. Maybe Aphrodite would not show up tonight, or be there but forget to harass me.

It turned out, as my luck would have it, neither was the case.

CHAPTER TWENTY-SEVEN

—

"Nice dress, Zoey. It looks just like mine. Oh, wait! It used to be mine." Aphrodite laughed a throaty, I'm-so-grown-up-and-you're-just-a-kid laugh. I really hate it when girls do that. I mean, yes, she's older, but I have boobs, too.

I smiled, purposefully putting an extra dose of cluelessness into my voice and launched into a gihugic lie, which I think I pulled off pretty well considering I'm a bad liar, I had just been attacked by a ghost, and everybody was staring at us and listening in.

"Hi, Aphrodite! Gosh, I was just reading the chapter in the Soc 415 book Neferet gave me about how important it is for the leader of the Dark Daughters to make every new member of the group feel welcome and accepted. You must be proud that you're doing your job so well." Then I stepped a little closer to her and lowered my voice so she alone could hear me. "And I must say you look better than you did the last time I saw you." I watched her pale and was sure fear flickered through her eyes. Surprisingly, it didn't make me feel victorious and smug. It just made me feel mean and shallow and tired. I sighed. "Sorry. I shouldn't have said that."

Her face hardened. "Fuck off, freak," she hissed. Then she laughed as though she'd just made a huge joke (at my expense), turned her back on me, and with a hateful flip of her hair walked to the middle of the rec hall.

Okay, I didn't feel bad anymore. Hateful cow. She raised one slim arm, and everyone who had been gawking at me now turned their attention (thankfully) to her. Tonight she had on an antique-looking red silk dress that fit her as if it had been painted on. I'd like to know just exactly where she got her clothes. Goth ho store?

"A fledgling died yesterday, and then another one died today."

Her voice was strong and clear, and sounded almost compassionate, which surprised me. For a second she really did remind me of Neferet, and I wondered whether she was going to say something profound and leader-like.

"We all knew both of them. Elizabeth had been nice and quiet. Elliott had been our refrigerator for the past several rituals." She smiled suddenly; it was feral and mean, and any resemblance she might have had to Neferet ended. "But they were weak, and vampyres do not need weakness in their coven." She shrugged her scarlet-covered shoulders. "If we were humans we'd call it survival of the fittest. Thank the Goddess we're not humans, so let's just call it Fate, and be happy tonight that it didn't kick any of our asses."

I was totally grossed out to hear sounds of general agreement. I hadn't really known Elizabeth, but she'd been nice to me. Okay, I admit that I hadn't liked Elliott—no one had. The kid was annoying and unattractive (and his ghost or whatever seemed to be carrying on those traits), but I was not glad he died. *If I'm ever leader of the Dark Daughters I won't make fun of the death of a fledgling, no matter how insignificant.* I made the promise to myself, but I was also conscious of sending it out like a prayer. I hoped Nyx heard me, and I hoped she approved.

"But enough gloom and doom," Aphrodite was saying. "It's Samhain! The night when we celebrate the end of the harvest season and, even better, it is the time when we remember our ancestors—all the great vampyres who have lived and died before us." The tone of her voice was creepy, like she was getting into the show she was putting on way too much, and I rolled my eyes as she continued. "It's the night when the veil between life and death is thinnest and when spirits are most likely to walk the earth." She paused and looked around the audience, being careful to ignore me (like everyone else was). I had a moment to wonder about what she'd just said. Could what have happened with Elliott have something to do with the veil between life and death being thinnest, and the fact that he had died on Samhain? I didn't have time to wonder any more about it because Aphrodite raised her voice and shouted, "So what are we going to do?"

"Go out!" the Dark Daughters and Sons yelled back.

Aphrodite's laugh was way too sexual to be appropriate, and I swear she touched herself. Right there in front of everyone. Jeesh, she was nasty.

"That's right. I've chosen an awesome place for us tonight, and we even have a new little refrigerator waiting for us there with the girls."

Ugh. By "the girls" did she mean Warlike, Terrible, and Wasp? I glanced quickly around the room. Didn't see them anywhere. Great. I could only imagine what those three plus Aphrodite would consider "awesome." And I didn't even want to think about the poor kid who had somehow been talked into being their new refrigerator.

And, yes, I was going to be in total denial about the fact that my mouth watered when Aphrodite mentioned that there was a refrigerator waiting for us, which meant I was going to get to drink blood again.

"So let's get out of here. And remember, be silent. Focus your minds on being invisible, and any human who happens to still be awake will simply not see us." Then she looked right at me. "And may Nyx have mercy on anyone who gives us away, because we certainly won't." She smiled silkily back at the group. "Follow me, Dark Daughters and Sons!"

In silent pairs and small groups, everyone followed Aphrodite out the back door of the rec hall. Naturally, they ignored me. I almost didn't follow them. I really didn't want to. I mean, I'd had enough excitement for one night. I should go back to the dorm and apologize to Stevie Rae. Then we could find the Twins and Damien, and I could tell them about Elliott (I paused to consider whether my gut feeling was warning me against telling my friends, but it stayed silent). Okay. So. I could tell them. That sounded like a better idea than following bitchy Aphrodite and a group of kids who couldn't stand me. But my intuition, which had been quiet when I'd thought about talking to my friends, suddenly reared up again. I had to go to the ritual. I sighed.

"Come on, Z. You don't want to miss the show, do you?"

Erik was standing by the back door, looking like Superman with his blue eyes smiling at me.

Well, hell.

"Are you kidding? Hateful girls, totally cliquish drama-trauma, and the possibility for embarrassment and bloodletting. What's not to love? I wouldn't miss a minute of it." Together Erik and I followed the group out the door.

Everyone was walking quietly to the wall behind the rec hall, which was too close to where I'd seen Elizabeth and Elliott for me to feel comfortable. And then, weirdly, the kids seemed to disappear into the wall.

"What the—?" I whispered.

"It's just a trick. You'll see."

I did. It was actually a trap door. Like the kind you see in those old murder movies, only instead of a door in a library wall or inside a fireplace (as in one of the Indiana Jones movies—yes, I'm a dork), this trap door was a small section of the thick, otherwise solid-looking school wall. Part of it swung out, leaving an open space just big enough for one person (or fledgling or vamp or possibly even a freakishly solid ghost or two) to slip through. Erik and I were the last ones through. I heard a soft *whoosh,* and looked back in time to see the wall closing seamlessly.

"It's on an automatic keypad, like a car door," Erik whispered.

"Huh. Who all knows about this?"

"Anyone who's ever been a Dark Daughter or Son."

"Huh." I suspected that was probably most of the adult vamps. I glanced around. I didn't see anyone watching us, or following us.

Erik noticed my look. "They don't care. It's school tradition that we sneak out for some of the rituals. As long as we don't do anything too stupid, they pretend like they don't know we're going." He shrugged. "It works out okay, I guess."

"As long as we don't do anything too stupid," I said.

"Shush!" Someone in front of us hissed. I closed my mouth and decided to concentrate on where we were going.

It was about four thirty A.M. Uh, no one was awake. Big surprise. It was weird to be walking through this really cool part of Tulsa—a neighborhood filled with mansions built by old oil money—and have nobody notice us. We were cutting through amazingly landscaped yards and no dogs were even barking at us. It was as if we were shadows . . . or ghosts. . . . The thought gave me a creepy chill. The moon that earlier had been mostly obscured by clouds was now shining silver-white in an unexpectedly clear sky. I swear that even before I was Marked I could have read by its light. It was cold, but that didn't bother me like it would have just a week ago. I tried not to think about what that meant about the Change that was going on inside my body.

We crossed a street, then slid soundlessly between two yards. I heard running water before I saw the little footbridge. The moonlight lit up the stream as though someone had spilled mercury across the top of it. I felt captured by its beauty, and I automatically slowed down, reminding myself that night was my new day. I hoped that I would never get used to the dark majesty of it.

"Come on, Z," whispered Erik from the other side of the bridge.

I looked up at him. He was silhouetted against an incredible mansion that stretched up the hill behind him with its huge, terraced lawn and pond and gazebo and fountains and waterfalls (these people clearly had entirely too much money), and he reminded me of one of those romantic heroes out of history, like . . . like . . . Well, the only two heroes I could think of were Superman and Zorro, and neither of them were truly historical. But he did look very knight-like and romantic. And then it registered on me exactly which amazing mansion we were trespassing on, and I hurried across the bridge to him.

"Erik," I whispered frantically, "this is the Philbrook Museum! We're really going to get in trouble if they catch us messing around here."

"They won't catch us."

I had to scramble to keep up with him. He was walking fast, much more eager than me to catch up with the silent, ghostlike group.

"Okay, this isn't just some rich guy's house. This is a *museum*. There are twenty-four-hour security guards here."

"Aphrodite will have drugged them."

"What!"

"Ssssh. It doesn't hurt them. They'll be groggy for a while and then go home and not remember anything. No big deal."

I didn't reply, but I really didn't like that he was so 'whatever' about drugging security guards. It just didn't seem right, even though I could understand the need for it. We were trespassing. We didn't want to get caught. So the guards needed to be drugged. I got it. I just didn't like it, and it sounded like yet another thing that was begging to be changed about the Dark Daughters and their holier-than-thou attitudes. They reminded me more and more of the People of Faith, which was not a flattering comparison. Aphrodite wasn't God (or Goddess, for that matter), despite what she called herself.

Erik had stopped walking. We stepped up to join the group where it had formed a loose circle around the domed gazebo situated at the bottom of the gentle slope that led up to the museum. It was close to the ornamental fishpond that ended right before the terraces leading up to the museum began. It really was an incredibly beautiful place. I'd been there two or three times on field trips, and once, with my Art class, I'd even been inspired to sketch the gardens, even though I definitely can not draw. Now the night had changed it from a place with pretty, well-tended gardens and marble water features into a magical fairy kingdom all washed in the light of the moon and shaded by layers of grays and silvers and midnight blues.

The gazebo itself was amazing. It sat on the top of huge round stairs, throne-like, so that you had to climb up to it. It was made of carved white columns, and the dome was lit from beneath, so that it looked like something that could have been found in ancient Greece, and then restored to its original glory and lit for the night to see.

Aphrodite climbed the stairs to take her place in the middle of the gazebo, which immediately sucked some of the magic and beauty from it. Naturally, Warlike, Terrible, and Wasp were there, too. Another girl was with them, who I didn't recognize. Of course I could have seen her a zillion times and wouldn't have remembered—she was just another Barbie-like blond (although her name probably meant something like Wicked or Hateful). They'd set up a little table in the middle of the gazebo and draped it with black cloth. I could see that there were a bunch of candles on it, and some other stuff, including a goblet and a knife. Some poor kid was slumped with his head down on the table. A cloak had been pulled around him, so that it covered his body, and he looked a lot like Elliott on the night he'd been the refrigerator.

It must really take a lot out of a kid to have his blood drained for Aphrodite's rituals, and I wondered whether that had anything to do with bringing on Elliott's death. I blocked from my mind the fact that my mouth started watering when I thought about the kid's blood being mixed with the wine in the goblet. Weird how something could totally gross me out and make me want it really bad at the same time.

"I will cast the circle and call the spirits of our ancestors to dance within it with us," Aphrodite said. She spoke softly, but her voice traveled around us like a poisonous mist. It was spooky to think about ghosts being drawn to Aphrodite's circle, especially after my own recent experiences with ghosts, but I have to admit that it intrigued me almost as much as it scared me. Maybe I was so certain I had to be here because I was meant to get some clue about Elizabeth and Elliott tonight. Plus, this ritual was obviously something the Dark Daughters had been doing for a while. It couldn't be that scary or dangerous. Aphrodite played all big and cool, but I had a feeling that it was an act. Underneath she was what all bullies are—insecure and immature. Also, bullies tended to avoid anyone tougher than them, so it was only logical that if Aphrodite was going to call spirits into a circle it meant that they were harmless, probably even nice. Aphrodite was definitely not going to face down a big, bad, boogie monster.

Or anything as truly freaky as what Elliott had become.

I started to relax into welcoming what was already becoming a familiar hum of power as the four Dark Daughters took candles that corresponded to the element they were representing, and then moved to the correct area of the mini-circle in the gazebo. Aphrodite summoned wind, and my hair lifted gently in a breeze that only I could feel. I closed my eyes, loving the electricity that tingled across my skin. Actually, in spite of Aphrodite and the stuck-up Dark Daughters, I was already enjoying the beginning of the ritual. And Erik was standing beside me, which helped me not to care that no one else there would talk to me.

I relaxed more, certain suddenly that the future wasn't going to be that bad. I'd make up with my friends, we'd figure out together what the hell was going on with the weird ghosts, and maybe I'd even get a totally hot boyfriend. Everything would be okay. I opened my eyes and watched Aphrodite move around the circle. Each element sizzled through me, and I wondered how Erik could stand so close to me and not notice it. I even snuck a peek at him, half expecting him to be staring at me as the elements played over my skin, but, like everyone else, he was looking at Aphrodite. (Which was actually annoying—wasn't he supposed to be sneaking looks at me, too?) Then Aphrodite began the ritual of summoning of the ancestral spirits, and even I couldn't keep my attention from her. She stood at the table, holding a long braid of dried grass over the purple spirit flame, so that it lit quickly. She allowed it to burn for a little while, and then blew it out. She waved it gently around her as she began to speak, filling the area with tendrils of smoke. I sniffed, recognizing the scent of sweet grass, one of the most sacred of ceremonial herbs because it attracted spiritual energy. Grandma used it often in her prayers. Then I frowned and felt a tendril of worry. Sweet grass should be used only after sage has been burned to cleanse and purify the area; if not, it might attract any energy—and "any" didn't always mean good. But it was too late to say anything, even if I could have stopped the ceremony. She had already begun calling to the spirits, and her voice had taken on an eerie, singsong quality that was somehow intensified by the smoke that curled thickly around her.

On this Samhain night, hear my ancient call all you spirits of our ancestors. On this Samhain night, let my voice carry with this smoke to the Otherworld where bright spirits play in the sweet grass mists of memory. On this Samhain night I do not call the spirits of our human ancestors. No, I let them sleep; I have no need for them in life or in death. On this Samhain night I call magical ancestors— mystical ancestors—those who were once more than human, and who, in death, are more than human.

Completely entranced, I watched with everyone else as the smoke swirled and changed and began to take on forms. At first I thought I was seeing things, and I tried to blink my vision clear, but soon I understood what I was seeing had nothing to do with blurry vision. There *were* people forming within the smoke. They were indistinct, more like the outlines of bodies than actual bodies themselves, but as Aphrodite continued to wave the sweet grass they grew more substantial, and then suddenly the circle was filled with spectral figures that had dark, cavernous eyes and open mouths.

They didn't look anything like Elizabeth or Elliott. Actually, they looked exactly as I imagined ghosts would—smoky and transparent and creepy. I sniffed the air. Nope, I definitely didn't smell any old basement yuckiness.

Aphrodite put down the still-smoking grass and picked up the goblet. Even from where I was watching, it seemed that she looked unusually pale, as though she had taken on some of the physical characteristics of the ghosts. Her red dress was almost painfully bright within the circle of smoke and gray and mist.

"I greet you, ancestral spirits, and ask that you accept our offering of wine and blood so that you may remember what it is to taste life." She lifted the goblet, and the smoky shapes churned and roiled with obvious excitement. "I greet you, ancestral spirits, and within the protection of my circle I—"

"Zo! I knew I'd find you if I tried hard enough!"

Heath's voice sliced through the night, cutting off Aphrodite's words.

CHAPTER TWENTY-EIGHT

—

"Heath! What in the hell are you doing here!"

"Well, you didn't call me back." Oblivious to everyone else, he hugged me. I didn't need the bright light of the moon for me to see his bloodshot eyes. "I missed you, Zo!" he blurted, wafting beer breath all over me.

"Heath. You need to go—"

"No. Let him stay," Aphrodite interrupted me.

Heath's gaze swiveled up to her, and I imagined what she must look like through his eyes. She stood in the pool of light made by the gazebo's spotlights shining through the sweet grass smoke, illuminating her almost as though she was underwater. Her red silk dress clung to her body. Her blond hair was thick and heavy down her back. Her lips were tilted up in a mean-looking smile, which I'm sure Heath would misunderstand and think she was being nice. Actually, he probably wouldn't even notice the smoky ghosts that had stopped hovering around the goblet and had now turned their blank eyes toward him. He also wouldn't notice that Aphrodite's voice had a weird, hollow sound to it and that her eyes were glassy and staring. Hell, knowing Heath he wouldn't notice anything except her big boobies.

"Cool, a vampyre chick," Heath said, totally proving me right.

"Get him out of here." Erik's voice was tight with worry.

Heath tore his eyes from Aphrodite's boobs to glare at Erik. "Who're you?"

Ah, crap. I recognized that tone. It was the one Heath used when he was getting ready to have a jealous fit. (Another reason he was my ex.)

"Heath, you need to get out of here," I said.

"No." He stepped closer to me and put his arm possessively around my shoulders, but he didn't look at me. He kept staring down Erik. "I came to see my girlfriend, and I'm gonna see my girlfriend."

I ignored the fact that I could feel Heath's pulse where his arm rested against my shoulders. Instead of doing something utterly gross and disturbing, like biting into his wrist, I shrugged off his arm and then yanked at it so he had to face me and not Erik.

"I am *not* your girlfriend."

"Aw, Zo, you're just sayin' that."

I gritted my teeth. God, he was dumb. (Yet *another* reason he was my ex.)

"Are you stupid?" Erik said.

"Look, you bloodsucking fuck, I'm—" Heath began to say, but Aphrodite's strangely echoing voice drowned him out.

"Come up here, human."

Like our eyes were magnets to her freaky attraction, Heath, Erik, and I (and, for that matter, the rest of the Dark Daughters and Sons) stared up at her. Her body looked weird. Was it pulsing? How could it? She flipped back her hair and ran one hand down her body like a nasty stripper, cupping her breast and then moving down to rub between her legs. Her other hand lifted and she curled her finger, beckoning Heath.

"Come to me, human. Let me taste you."

This was bad; this was wrong. Something terrible was going to happen to Heath if he went up there and stepped within that circle.

Totally entranced by her, Heath lurched forward without any hesitation (or common sense). I grabbed one of his arms, and was pleased to see Erik grab his other.

"Stop it, Heath! I want you to go. Now. You don't belong here."

With an effort, Heath pulled his eyes from Aphrodite. He jerked his arm from Erik's grip and practically growled at him. Then he turned on me.

"You're cheating on me!"

"Can you not listen? It's impossible for me to cheat on you. We are not together! Now get out of—"

"If he refuses our summons, then we shall go to him."

My head jerked up to see Aphrodite's body convulse as gray wisps seeped out of her. She let out a gasp that was a cross between a sob and a scream. The spirits, including the ones that had obviously been possessing her, rushed to the edge of the circle, pressing against it in an effort to break free and get to Heath.

"Stop them, Aphrodite. If you don't they'll kill him!" Damien shouted as he stepped out from behind an ornamental hedge that framed the pond.

"Damien, what—" I began, but he shook his head.

"No time to explain," he told me quickly before turning his attention back to Aphrodite. "You know what they are," he called up to her. "You have to contain them in the circle or he'll die."

Aphrodite was so pale she looked like a ghost herself. She moved away from the smoky shapes that were still trying to push against the invisible boundary of the circle, until she was pressed against one edge of the table.

"I won't stop them. If they want him, they can have him. Better him than me—or any of the rest of us," Aphrodite said.

"Yeah, we don't want any part of this kind of shit!" said Terrible before dropping her candle, which sputtered and went out. Without another word, she ran out of the circle and down the gazebo stairs. The other three girls who were supposed to be personifying the elements followed her lead, disappearing quickly into the night and leaving their candles overturned and unlit.

Horrified, I watched one of the gray shapes begin to melt through the circle. The smoke that was his spectral body began seeping down the stairs, reminding me of a snake as it slithered in our direction. I felt the Dark Daughters and Sons stir and glanced around me. They were nervously backing away, looks of fear twisting their faces.

"It's up to you, Zoey."

"Stevie Rae!"

She was standing unsteadily in the middle of the circle. She'd thrown off the cape that had covered her, and I could see the white linen bandages on her wrists.

"I told you we needed to stick together." She smiled weakly at me.

"Better hurry," Shaunee said.

"Those ghosts are scaring the shit right outta your ex," Erin said.

I looked over my shoulder to see the Twins standing beside the white-faced, open-mouthed Heath, and I felt a jolt of pure happiness. They hadn't abandoned me! I wasn't alone!

"Let's get this done," I said. "Keep him here," I told Erik, who was staring at me with obvious shock.

Without needing to look back to be sure my friends were following me, I hurried up the steep stairs to the ghost-filled gazebo. When I reached the boundary of the circle I hesitated for a second. The spirits were slowly dissolving through it, their attention completely focused on Heath. I took a deep breath and stepped inside the invisible barrier, feeling an awful chill as the dead brushed restlessly against my skin.

"You have no right to be here. This is *my* circle," Aphrodite said, pulling herself together enough to wrinkle her lip at me and block my way to the table and the spirit candle, which was the only one still lit.

"*Was* your circle. Now you need to shut up and move," I told her.

Aphrodite narrowed her eyes at me.

Ah, crap. I really didn't have time for this.

"Bobble-head, you need to do what Zoey says. I have been dying to kick the shit outta you for two years," Shaunee said, moving up to stand beside me.

"Me, too, you nasty ho bag," Erin said, stepping up to my other side.

Before the Twins could pounce on her, Heath's scream shattered the night. I whirled around. Mist was crawling up Heath's legs, leaving long, thin tears in his jeans that instantly began to weep blood. Panicked, he was kicking and shrieking. Erik hadn't run away, but was hitting at the mist, too, even though whenever some of it stuck on him it ripped his clothes and tore open his skin.

"Fast! Take your places," I yelled before the seductive smell of their blood could mess with my concentration.

My friends ran to the deserted candles. Hastily they picked them up and waited in the proper positions.

I moved around Aphrodite, who was staring at Heath and Erik, with her hand pressed against her mouth as if to hold back her screams. I grabbed the purple candle and rushed over to Damien.

"Wind! I summon you to this circle," I yelled, touching the purple candle to the yellow one. I wanted to cry with relief when the familiar whirlwind suddenly sprang up, swirling around my body and lifting my hair crazily.

Shielding the purple candle with my hand I ran to Shaunee.

"Fire! I summon you to this circle!" Heat flared with the whirling air as I lit the red candle. I didn't pause, but kept moving clockwise around the circle. "Water! I summon you to this circle!" The sea was there, salty and sweet at the same time. "Earth! I summon you to this circle!" I touched the flame to Stevie Rae's candle, trying not to flinch at the bandages that covered her wrists. She was abnormally pale, but she grinned when the air filled with the scent of freshly cut hay.

Heath screamed again, and I rushed back to the center of the circle and lifted the purple candle. "Spirit! I summon you to this circle!" Energy sizzled into me. I glanced around at the boundary of my circle and, sure enough, I could see the ribbon of power marking its circumference. I closed my eyes for an instant. *Oh, thank you, Nyx!*

Then I put the candle down on the table and grabbed the goblet of bloody wine. I turned to face Heath and Erik and the ghostly horde.

"Here is your sacrifice!" I yelled, sloshing the liquid in the goblet in a messy arc around me, so that it made a blood-colored circle on the gazebo floor. "You weren't called here to kill. You were called here because it's Samhain and we wanted to honor you." I spilled more wine, trying hard to ignore the seductive scent of fresh blood mixed with wine.

The ghosts paused in their attack. I focused on them, not wanting to distract myself with the terror in Heath's eyes and the pain in Erik's.

"We prefer this warm young blood, Priestess." The eerie voice echoed up to me, sending chills over my skin. I swear I could smell his rotting flesh-scented breath.

I swallowed hard. "I understand that, but those lives aren't yours to take. Tonight is a night for celebration, not for death."

"And yet we choose death—it is dearest to us." Ghostly laughter

floated through the air with the tainted smoke of sweet grass, and the spirits began to converge again on Heath.

I threw down the goblet and raised my hands. "Then I'm not asking anymore; I'm telling you. Wind, fire, water, earth, and spirit! I command in Nyx's name that you close this circle, pulling back to it the dead who have been allowed to escape. Now!"

Heat surged through my body and shot from my outstretched hands. In a rush of salt-scented wind that was burning hot, a shining green mist whooshed from me down the stairs to whip around Heath and Erik, making their clothes and hair flap like mad. The magical wind caught the smoky shapes and tore them from their victims, and with a deafening roar, it sucked them back into the boundary of my circle. Suddenly I was surrounded by ghostly shapes, from which I could feel danger and hunger pulsing, as clearly as I had felt Heath's blood earlier. Aphrodite was curled up on the chair, cowering from the specters. One of them brushed against her and she let out a little shriek, which seemed to stir them up even more, and they pressed violently around me.

"Zoey!" Stevie Rae cried my name, her voice shrill with fear. I saw her take a hesitant step toward me.

"No!" Damien snapped. "Don't break the circle. They can't hurt Zoey—they can't hurt any of us, the circle is too strong. But only if we don't break it."

"We're not going anywhere," Shaunee called.

"Nope. I like it right here," Erin said, sounding only a little breathless.

I felt their loyalty and trust and acceptance like a sixth element. It filled me with confidence. I straightened my spine and looked at the swirling, angry ghosts.

"So—we're not leaving. Which means you guys have got to go."

I pointed down at the spilled blood and wine. "Take your sacrifice and get out of here. It's all the blood that is owed to you tonight."

The smoky horde paused in their seething. I knew I had them. I drew a deep breath and finished it.

"With the power of the elements I command you: Go!"

Suddenly, as though an invisible giant slapped them down, they dissolved into the wine-soaked floor of the gazebo, somehow absorbing the blood-tinged liquid and making it disappear with them.

I breathed a long, ragged sigh of relief. Automatically, I turned to Damien.

"Thank you, wind. You may depart." He started to blow out his candle, but didn't need to, a little puff of wind, which felt surprisingly playful, did it for him. Damien grinned at me. And then his eyes got huge and round.

"Zoey! Your Mark!"

"What?" I lifted my hand to my forehead. It tingled, as did my shoulders and my neck (which figured, I always get shoulder/neck-aches when I'm over-stressed), plus my whole body was still humming with the aftereffects of elemental power, so I hadn't even noticed it.

His shocked look changed to happiness. "Finish closing the circle. Then you can use one of Erin's many mirrors to see what's happened."

I turned to Shaunee to say good-bye to fire.

"Wow . . . amazing," Shaunee said, staring at me.

"Hey, how did you know I have more than one mirror in my purse?" Erin was complaining from across the circle at Damien when I turned to her and sent water away. Her eyes got big when she caught a good look at me, too. "Holy shit!" she said.

"Erin, you really shouldn't curse in a sacred circle. Y'all know it's not—" Stevie Rae was saying in her sweet Okie twang when I turned to say good-bye to earth, and her words were suddenly cut off as she gasped, "Oh, my *goodness!*"

I sighed. *Hell, what now?* I went back to the table and lifted the spirit candle.

"Thank you, spirit. You may depart," I said.

"Why?" Aphrodite stood up so abruptly that she knocked over the chair. Like everyone else, she was staring at me with a ridiculously shocked expression. "Why you? Why not me?"

"Aphrodite, what are you talking about now?"

"She's talking about this." Erin handed me a compact she pulled out of the chic leather purse she always had slung over her shoulder.

I opened it and looked. At first I didn't understand what I was seeing—it was too foreign, too surprising. Then, from my side, Stevie Rae whispered, "It's beautiful . . ."

And I realized she was right. It was beautiful. My Mark had been added to. A delicate swirl of lace-like sapphire tattooing framed my eyes. Not as intricate and large as an adult vamp, but unheard of in a fledgling. I let my fingers trace the curling design, thinking that it looked like something that should decorate the face of an exotic foreign princess . . . or maybe the High Priestess of a goddess. And I stared hard at the me that wasn't really me—this stranger who was becoming more and more familiar.

"And that's not all Zoey. Look at your shoulder," Damien said softly.

I glanced down at the deep, off-the-shoulder neckline of my cool dress and felt a jolt of shock surge through my body. My shoulder was tattooed, too. Stretching from my neck, down my shoulder and back, were sapphire tattoos in a swirling pattern much like that on my face, only the blue marks on my body looked even more ancient, even more mysterious, because they were interspersed with letterlike symbols.

My mouth opened, but words wouldn't come out.

"Z, he needs help." Erik broke through my shock and I looked up from my shoulder to see him stumbling into the gazebo, half carrying an unconscious Heath.

"Whatever. Leave him here," Aphrodite said. "Someone will find him in the morning. We need to get out of here before the guards wake up."

I whirled on her. "And you ask why me and not you? Maybe because Nyx is sick and tired of you being selfish, spoiled, indulged, hateful . . ." I paused, so pissed I couldn't think of any more adjectives.

"Nasty!" Erin and Shaunee added together.

"Yeah, and a nasty bully." I took a step closer to her and got all in her face. "This whole Change is hard enough without someone like you. Unless we want to be your"—I glanced up at Damien and smiled—"your sycophants, you make us feel like we don't belong—like we're nothing. That's over, Aphrodite. What you did tonight was totally, completely wrong. You almost caused Heath to die. And maybe even Erik and who knows who else, and it was all because of your selfishness."

"It wasn't my fault your boyfriend tracked you here," she yelled.

"No, Heath wasn't your fault, but that's the only thing that wasn't your fault tonight. It was your fault that your so-called friends wouldn't stand by you and keep the circle strong. And it was your fault that negative spirits found the circle to begin with." She looked confused, which pissed me off even more. "Sage, you hateful hag! You're supposed to use sage to clear out negative energy before you use sweet grass. And it's not surprising that you drew such horrid spirits."

"Yeah, 'cause you're horrid," Stevie Rae said.

"You don't have shit to say about it, refrigerator," Aphrodite sneered.

"No!" I put my finger in her face. "This refrigerator crap is the first thing that's ending."

"Oh, so now you're going to pretend that you don't crave the taste of blood more than any of us?"

I glanced up at my friends. They met my eyes without flinching. Damien smiled encouragement. Stevie Rae nodded at me. The Twins winked. And I realized that I'd been a fool. They weren't going to shun me. They were my friends; I should have trusted them more, even if I hadn't learned to trust myself yet.

"We'll all eventually crave blood," I said simply. "Or we'll die. But that doesn't make us monsters, and it's time the Dark Daughters stopped acting the part. You're finished, Aphrodite. You're no longer leader of the Dark Daughters."

"And I suppose you think that now you're the leader?"

I nodded. "I am. I didn't come to the House of Night asking for these powers. All I wanted was a place to fit in. Well, I guess this is Nyx's way of answering my prayer." I smiled at my friends and they grinned back at me. "Clearly, the Goddess has a sense of humor."

"You stupid bitch, you can't just take over the Dark Daughters. Only a High Priestess can change their leadership."

"Convenient, then, that I am here, isn't it?" Neferet said.

CHAPTER TWENTY-NINE

—

Neferet stepped from the shadows and into the gazebo, moving quickly to Heath and Erik. First, she touched Erik's face and checked the bloody slash marks on his arms from where he'd struggled futilely to try to pull the ghosts off Heath. As she passed her hands over his wounds I could actually see the blood drying. Erik breathed a sigh of relief, like his pain had disappeared.

"These will heal. Come to the infirmary when we get back to school and I'll give you some salve that will lessen the sting from your wounds." She patted his cheek and he blushed bright red. "You showed the bravery of a vampyre warrior when you stayed to protect the boy. I am proud of you, Erik Night, as is the Goddess."

I felt a rush of pleasure at her approval; I was proud of him, too. Then I heard murmured agreement all around me and realized that the Dark Daughters and Sons had returned and were crowding the stairs of the gazebo. How long had they been watching? Neferet turned her attention to Heath, and I forgot about everyone else. She lifted the torn legs of his jeans and examined the bloody marks there and on his arms. Then she cupped his pale, rigid face in her hands and closed her eyes. I watched his body stiffen even more and convulse, and then he sighed and, like Erik, he relaxed. After a moment, he looked like he was sleeping peacefully instead of fighting silently against death. Still on her knees beside him, Neferet said, "He will recover, and he will remember nothing of this night except that he got drunk and then lost trying to find his ex-almost-girlfriend." She looked up at me as she said the last of it, her eyes kind and filled with understanding.

"Thank you," I whispered.

Neferet nodded slightly to me, before she stood to confront Aphrodite.

"I am as responsible for what happened here tonight as you are. I have known for years of your selfishness, but I chose to overlook it, hoping that age and the touch of the Goddess would mature you. I was wrong." Neferet's voice took on the clear, powerful quality of a command. "Aphrodite, I officially release you from your position as leader of the Dark Daughters and Sons. You are no longer in training for High Priestess. You are now no different than any other fledgling." With one swift movement, Neferet reached out, grasped the silver and garnet necklace of rank that dangled between Aphrodite's breasts, and tore it from her neck.

Aphrodite didn't make a sound but her face was chalky and she stared unblinkingly at Neferet.

The High Priestess turned her back on Aphrodite and approached me. "Zoey Redbird, I knew you were special from the day Nyx let me foresee that you would be Marked." She smiled at me and put a finger under my chin, lifting my head so that she could get a better look at the new addition to my Mark. Then she brushed my hair aside so that the tattoos that had appeared on my neck, shoulders, and back could also be seen. I heard the Dark Daughters and Sons gasp as they, too, got their first look at my unusual Marks. "Extraordinary, truly extraordinary," she breathed, letting her hand fall back to her side as she continued. "Tonight you showed the wisdom of the Goddess's choice in gifting you with special powers. You have earned the position of Leader of the

Dark Daughters and Sons and High Priestess in training, through your Goddess-given gifts as well as through your compassion and wisdom." She handed me Aphrodite's necklace. It felt heavy and warm in my hands. "Wear this more wisely than did your predecessor." Then she made a truly amazing gesture. Neferet, High Priestess of Nyx, saluted me, fist crossed over her heart, head bowed formally, with the vampyre sign of respect. Everyone around us except Aphrodite mimicked her. Tears blurred my vision as my four friends grinned at me and bowed with the other Dark Daughters and Sons.

But even in the midst of such perfect happiness I felt the shadow of confusion. How could I have ever doubted that I could tell Neferet anything?

"Go back to the school. I'll take care of what needs to be done here," Neferet told me. She hugged me quickly and whispered into my ear, "I am so very proud of you, Zoeybird." Then she gave me a little push in the direction of my friends. "Welcome the new Leader of the Dark Daughters and Sons!" she said.

Damien, Stevie Rae, Shaunee, and Erin led the cheering. And then everyone surrounded me and it seemed that I was washed from the gazebo in an exuberant wave of laughter and congratulations. I nodded and smiled at my new "friends," but I wasn't a fool. Silently I reminded myself that only moments before they had been agreeing with everything Aphrodite had said.

It would definitely take a while to change things.

We got to the bridge and I reminded my new charges that we'd have to be quiet as we made our way back through the neighborhood to the school, and I motioned for them to go on ahead of me. When Stevie Rae, Damien, and the Twins started to cross the bridge I whispered, "No, you guys walk with me."

Grinning so broadly they looked goofy, the four of them stood around me. I met Stevie Rae's bright gaze. "You shouldn't have volunteered to be the refrigerator. I know how scared you were." Stevie Rae's grin faded at the reprimand in my voice.

"But if I hadn't, we wouldn't have known where the ritual was going to be, Zoey. I did it so I could text-message Damien, and he and the Twins could meet me here. We knew you'd need us."

I held up my hands and she stopped talking, but she looked like she was going to cry. I smiled gently at her. "You didn't let me finish. I was going to say that you shouldn't have done it, but I'm so glad you did!" I hugged her, and smiled through tears at the other three of them. "Thank you—I'm glad you were all there."

"Hey, Z, that's what friends do," Damien said.

"Yep," said Shaunee.

"Exactly," said Erin.

And they closed around me in a giant, smothering group hug—which I totally loved.

"Hey, can I get in on this?"

I looked up to see Erik standing nearby.

"Well, yes, you absolutely may," Damien said brightly.

Stevie Rae dissolved into giggles, and Shaunee sighed and said, "Give it up, Damien. Wrong team, remember?" Then Erin pushed me out of the center of the group and toward Erik. "Give the guy a hug. He did try to save your boyfriend tonight," she said.

"My *ex*-boyfriend," I said quickly, stepping into Erik's arms, more than a little overwhelmed by the mixture of the scent of the fresh blood still clinging to him and the fact that he was, well, *hugging* me. Then, to add to everything else, Erik kissed me so hard that I swear I thought the top of my head would spin off.

"Please, just please," I heard Shaunee say.

"Get a room!" Erin said.

Damien giggled as I stepped self-consciously out of Erik's arms.

"I'm starving," Stevie Rae said. "This refrigerator stuff makes you hungry."

"Well, let's go get you something to eat," I said.

My friends started over the bridge and I could hear Shaunee bickering with Damien about whether we should have pizza or sandwiches.

"Mind if I walk with you?" Erik asked.

"Nah, I'm getting used to it," I said, smiling up at him.

He laughed and walked onto the bridge. Then from the darkness behind me I heard a very distinct, very annoyed, "me-eeh-uf-ow!"

"Go on, I'll catch up with you guys in a minute," I told Erik and then I walked back into the shadows at the edge of the Philbrook's lawn. "Nala? Kitty, kitty, kitty . . . ," I called. And, sure enough, a disgruntled ball of fur trotted out of the bushes, complaining the entire time. I bent down and picked her up and she instantly started to purr. "Well, silly girl, why did you follow me all the way out here if you don't like walking that far? Like you haven't been through enough tonight already," I murmured, but before I could head back to the bridge, Aphrodite stepped out of the shadows and blocked my way.

"You might have won tonight, but this isn't over," she told me.

She made me feel really tired. "I wasn't trying to 'win' anything. I was just trying to make things right."

"And that's what you think you did?" Her eyes darted nervously back and forth from me to the path that led to the gazebo, as if someone had followed her. "You don't really know what happened here tonight. You were just being used—we were all just being used. We're puppets, that's all we are." She angrily wiped at her face and I realized she was crying.

"Aphrodite, it doesn't have to be like this between us," I said softly.

"Yes it does!" she snapped. "It's the parts we're supposed to play. You'll see . . . you'll see. . . ." Aphrodite started to walk away.

A thought drifted unexpectedly from my memory. It was of Aphrodite, during her vision. As if it was happening again, I could hear her say, *They're dead! No. No. That can't be! Not right. No. Not natural! I don't understand . . . I don't . . . You . . . you know.* Her scream of terror echoed eerily through my mind. I thought of Elizabeth . . . of Elliott . . . the fact that they had appeared to *me*. Too much of what she said made sense.

"Aphrodite, wait!" She looked over her shoulder at me. "The vision you had today in Neferet's office, what was it really about?"

Slowly, she shook her head. "It's only beginning. It's going to get much worse." She turned and suddenly hesitated. Her way was blocked by five kids—my friends.

"It's okay," I told them. "Let her go."

Shaunee and Erin parted. Aphrodite lifted her head, shook back her hair, and marched past them as if she owned the world. I watched her walk over the bridge, my stomach clenching. Aphrodite knew something about Elizabeth and Elliott, and eventually I was going to have to find out what it was.

"Hey," Stevie Rae said.

I looked at my roommate and new best friend.

"Whatever happens, we're in it together."

I felt the knot in my stomach release. "Let's go," I said.

Surrounded by my friends, we all went home.

BETRAYED

We would like to dedicate this book to (Aunty) Sherry Rowland, friend and publicist. Thank you, Sher, for taking care of us. Even when we're high maintenance and annoying (and especially when you give us "treaties"). We heart you very much.

ACKNOWLEDGMENTS

As usual, we want to thank Dick L. Cast, Dad/Grandpa, for knowing everything biological and helping us with stuff.

Thank you to our amazing agent, Meredith Bernstein, who came up with the fabulous idea that began this series.

We would like to thank our St. Martin's team, Jennifer Weis and Stefanie Lindskog, for helping us create such a wonderful series. In particular a big WE HEART YOU to the talented artists who designed such beautiful covers.

And we'd like to note a special acknowledgment to Street Cats, a cat rescue and adoption service in Tulsa. We support Street Cats (and actually adopted Nala from them!) and appreciate their dedication to and love for cats. Please visit their Web site at www.streetcatstulsa.org for more information. If you're interested in giving to a pet rescue charity we promise that they are an excellent choice!　　　　　　　　　　　　　　—P. C. & KRISTIN

I would like to send thanks out to my high school students who 1) beg to be put in these books and then killed off, 2) provide constant comedic fodder for me, 3) and will actually leave me alone sometimes so I can write.

NOW GO DO YOUR HOMEWORK. Oh, and expect a quiz.

　　　　　　　　　　　　　　—MISS CAST

CHAPTER ONE

"New kid. Check it out," Shaunee said as she slid into the big boothlike bench we always claim as ours for every school meal served in the dining hall (translation: high-class school cafeteria).

"Tragic, Twin, just tragic." Erin's voice totally echoed Shaunee's. She and Shaunee had some kind of psychic link that made them bizarrely similar, which is why we'd nicknamed them "the Twins," even though Shaunee is a café latte–colored Jamaican American from Connecticut and Erin is a blond-haired, blue-eyed white girl from Oklahoma.

"Thankfully, she's Sarah Freebird's roommate." Damien nodded toward the petite girl with seriously black hair who was showing the lost-looking new kid around the dining hall, his sharp, fashion-wise gaze checking out the two girls and their outfits—from shoes to earrings—in one fast glance. "Clearly her fashion sense is better than Sarah's, despite the stress of being Marked and changing schools. Maybe she'll be able to help Sarah out with her unfortunate ugly shoe propensity."

"Damien," Shaunee said. "*Again* you are getting on my damn—"

"—last nerve with your unending vocab bullshit," Erin finished for her.

Damien sniffed, looking offended and superior and gayer than he usually looked (even though he is definitely gay). "If your vocabulary wasn't so abysmal you wouldn't have to carry a dictionary around with you to keep up with me."

The Twins narrowed their eyes at him and sucked air to begin a new assault, which, thankfully, my roommate interrupted. In her thick Oklahoma accent, Stevie Rae twanged the two definitions as if she was giving clues for a spelling bee. "Propensity—an often intense natural preference. Abysmal—absolutely horrible. There. Now would y'all quit bickering and be nice? You know it's almost time for parent visitation, and we shouldn't be acting like retards when our folks show up."

"Ah, crap," I said. "I'd totally forgotten about parent visitation."

Damien groaned and dropped his head down on the table, banging it not-so-gently. "I'd totally forgotten, too." The four of us gave him sympathetic looks. Damien's parents were cool with him being Marked, moving to the House of Night, and beginning the Change that would either turn him into a vampyre or, if his body rejected the transformation, kill him. They were not okay with him being gay.

At least Damien's parents were okay with something about him. My mom and her current husband—my step-loser, John Heffer—on the other hand, hated absolutely everything about me.

"My 'rentals aren't coming. They came last month. This month they're too busy."

"Twin, once again we prove our twin-ness," Erin said. "My 'rentals sent me an e-mail. They aren't coming either 'cause of some Thanksgiving cruise they decided to take to Alaska with my Aunt Alane and Uncle Liar Lloyd. Whatever." She shrugged— apparently as unbothered as Shaunee by her parents' absence.

"Hey, Damien, maybe your mama and daddy won't show either," Stevie Rae said with a quick smile.

He sighed. "They'll be here. It's my birthday month. They'll bring presents."

"That doesn't sound so bad," I said. "You were talking about needing a new sketch pad."

"They won't get me a sketch pad," he said. "Last year I asked for an easel. They got me camping supplies and a subscription to *Sports Illustrated.*"

"Eeesh!" said Shaunee and Erin together while Stevie Rae and I wrinkled our noses and made sympathetic noises.

Clearly wanting to change the subject, Damien turned to me. "This'll be your parents' first visit. What're you expecting?"

"Nightmare," I sighed. "Total, absolute, and complete nightmare."

"Zoey? I thought I'd bring my new roommate over to meet you. Diana, this is Zoey Redbird—the leader of the Dark Daughters."

Glad to be diverted from having to talk about my own horrid parental issues, I looked up, smiling, at the sound of Sarah's tentative, nervous voice.

"Wow, it's really true!" the new girl blurted before I could even say hi. As per usual she was staring at my forehead and blushing bright red. "I mean, uh . . . sorry. I didn't mean to be rude or anything . . ." she trailed off, looking miserable.

"That's okay. Yeah, it is true. My Mark is filled in and added to." I kept my smile in place, trying to make her feel better, even though I truly hated that it seemed like I was the main attraction at a freak show. Again.

Thankfully, Stevie Rae chimed in before Diana's staring and my silence could get any more uncomfortable.

"Yeah, Z got that cool lacy spiral tattoo thing on her face and down along her shoulders when she saved her ex-boyfriend from some scary-assed vampyre ghosts," Stevie Rae said cheerily.

"That's what Sarah told me," Diana said tentatively. "It just sounded so unbelievable that, well, I uh . . ."

"You didn't believe it?" Damien said helpfully.

"Yeah. Sorry," she repeated, fidgeting and picking at her fingernails.

"Hey, don't worry about it." I worked up a fairly authentic smile. "It seems pretty bizarre to me sometimes, and I was there."

"And kicking butt," Stevie Rae said.

I gave her my you-are-so-not-helping-me look, which she ignored. Yes, I might someday become their High Priestess, but I'm not exactly the boss of my friends.

"Anyway, this whole place can seem pretty strange at first. It gets better," I told the new kid.

"Thanks," she said with genuine warmth.

"Well, we better go so I can show Diana to where her fifth hour class will be," Sarah said, and then she totally embarrassed me by getting all serious and formal and saluting me with the traditional vampyre sign of respect, closed fist over her heart and bowed head, before she left.

"I really hate it when they do that," I muttered, picking at my salad.

"I think it's nice," Stevie Rae said.

"You deserve to be shown respect," Damien said in his schoolteacher voice. "You're the only third former ever to have been made leader of the Dark Daughters *and* the only fledgling or vampyre in history who has shown an affinity for all five of the elements."

"Face it, Z," Shaunee said around a bite of salad while she gestured at me with her fork.

"You're special." Erin finished for her (as usual).

A third former is what the House of Night called freshmen—so a fourth former is a sophomore, et cetera. And, yes, I am the only third former to be made leader of the Dark Daughters. Lucky me.

"Speaking of the Dark Daughters," Shaunee said. "Have you decided what you want the new requirements for membership to be?"

I stifled the urge to shriek, *Hell no, I still can't believe I'm in charge of this thing!* Instead I just shook my head, and decided—with what I hoped was a stroke of brilliance—to put some of the pressure back on them.

"No, I don't know what the new requirements should be. Actually, I was hoping you guys would help me. So, do you have any ideas?"

As I suspected, all four of them got quiet. I opened my mouth to thank them very much for their muteness, but our High Priestess's commanding voice came over the school intercom. For a second I was happy about the interruption, and then I realized what she was saying and my stomach started to clench.

"Students and professors, please make your way to the reception hall. It is now time for this month's parent visits."

Well, hell.

"Stevie Rae! Stevie Rae! Ohmygosh I have missed you!"

"Mama!" Stevie Rae cried and flew into the arms of a woman who looked just like her, only fifty pounds heavier and twenty-some years older.

Damien and I stood awkwardly just inside the reception hall, which was starting to fill up with uncomfortable-looking human parents, a few human siblings, a bunch of fledgling students, and several of our vampyre professors.

"Well, there're my parents," Damien said with a sigh. "Might as well get this over with. See ya."

"See ya," I mumbled and watched him join two totally ordinary people who were carrying a wrapped present. His mom gave him a quick hug and his dad shook his hand with exuberant masculinity. Damien looked pale and stressed.

I made my way over to the long, linen-draped table that ran the length of one wall. It was filled with expensive cheese and meat platters, desserts, coffee, tea, and wine. I'd been at the House of Night for a month, and it still was a little shocking to me that wine is served so readily here. Part of the reason they do is simple—the school is modeled after the European Houses of Night. Apparently, in Europe wine with meals is like tea or Coke with meals here—so no big deal. The other part is a genetic fact— vampyres don't get drunk—fledglings can barely get buzzed (at least on alcohol—blood, unfortunately, is a whole other issue). So wine literally is no big deal here, although I thought it would be interesting to check out how Oklahoma parents reacted to booze at school.

"Mama! You have to meet my roommate. Remember I told you about her? This is Zoey Redbird. Zoey this is my mama."

"Hi, Mrs. Johnson. It's good to meet you," I said politely.

"Oh, Zoey! It is just so nice to meet you! And, *oh my!* Your Mark is as pretty as Stevie Rae said it was." She surprised me with a soft mom hug and whispered, "I'm glad you're taking care of my Stevie Rae. I worry about her."

I squeezed her back and whispered, "No problem, Mrs. Johnson. Stevie Rae's my best friend." And even though it was totally unrealistic, I suddenly wished my mom would hug me and worry about me like Mrs. Johnson worried about her daughter.

"Mama, did you bring me any chocolate chip cookies?" Stevie Rae asked.

"Yes, baby, I did, but I just realized that I left them in the car." Stevie Rae's mom twanged in an Okie accent that was identical to her daughter's. "Why don't you come out with me and help me carry them inside. I made a little extra for your friends this time."

She smiled kindly at me. "You're more than welcome to come on out with us, too, Zoey."

"Zoey."

I heard my voice spoken like a frozen echo of Mrs. Johnson's warm kindness, and looked over her shoulder to see my mom and John coming into the hall. My heart fell into my stomach. She'd brought him. Why the hell couldn't she have come alone and let it be just her and me for a change? But I knew the answer to that. He would never allow it. And his not allowing it meant that she wouldn't do it. Period. End of subject. Since she'd married John Heffer my mom didn't have to worry about money. She lived in a gihugic house in a quiet suburban neighborhood. She volunteered for the PTA. She was majorly active in church. But during the past three years of her "perfect" marriage she'd completely and utterly lost herself.

"Sorry, Mrs. Johnson. I see my parents now, so I better go."

"Oh, honey, I'd love to meet your mama and daddy." And, like we were at any normal high school function, Mrs. Johnson turned, smiling, to meet my parents.

Stevie Rae looked at me, and I looked at her. *Sorry,* I mouthed to her. I mean, I wasn't absolutely sure anything bad would happen, but with my step-loser closing the distance between us as if he were some testosterone-filled general leading a death march, I figured the odds were probably good for a nightmare scene.

Then my heart lifted way out of my stomach and everything suddenly got much, much better when my favorite person in the world stepped around John and held her arms out to me.

"Grandma!"

She enfolded me in her arms and the sweet scent of lavender that always moved with her, as if she carried a piece of her beautiful lavender farm everywhere she went.

"Oh, Zoeybird!" She held tight to me. "I have missed you, *u-we-tsi a-ge-hu-tsa*."

I smiled through my tears, loving the sound of the familiar Cherokee word for daughter—it meant security and love and unconditional acceptance. Things I hadn't felt in my home for the past three years—things that before I'd come to the House of Night I'd only found at my grandma's farm.

"I've missed you, too, Grandma. I'm so glad you came!"

"You must be Zoey's grandmamma," Mrs. Johnson said when we'd quit clinging to each other. "It's so good to meet you. You have a fine girl, here."

Grandma smiled warmly and started to reply, but John interrupted in his usual I'm-so-superior voice.

"Well, actually, that would be *our* fine girl you would be complimenting."

As if on a Stepford Wives cue, my mother finally managed to speak. "Yes, we're Zoey's parents. I'm Linda Heffer. This is my husband, John, and my mother, Sylvia Red—" Then, in the middle of her oh-so-polite introductions, she bothered to actually look at me and her voice came to a breath-gulping halt midword.

I made my face smile, but it felt hot and hard, like it was poured plaster and had been sitting in the summer sun and would crack all to pieces if I wasn't careful.

"Hi, Mom."

"For the love of God what have you done to that Mark?" Mom said the word *Mark* like she'd say the word cancer or pedophile.

"She saved the life of a young man and tapped into a Goddess-given affinity for the elements. In return Nyx has touched her with several unusual Marks for a fledgling," Neferet said in her smooth musical voice as she walked into the middle of our awkward little group, hand extended directly to my step-loser. Neferet was what most adult vampyres are, stunningly perfect. She was tall, with long waves of dark auburn hair and brilliant, almond-shaped eyes an unusual shade of moss green. She moved with a grace and confidence that was clearly not human, and her skin was so spectacular that it looked like someone had turned a light on inside her. Today she was wearing a sleek, royal blue silk suit with silver spiral earrings (representing the path of the Goddess, but it's not like most parents knew that). A silver form of the Goddess with upraised hands was embroidered over her left breast, as it was over all the other professors' breasts. Her smile was dazzling. "Mr. Heffer, I am Neferet, High Priestess of the House of Night, although it might be easier if you would just think of me as you would any ordinary high school's principal. Thank you for coming to parent visitation night."

I could tell that he took her hand automatically. I was sure he would have refused it if she hadn't caught him by surprise. She shook his hand quickly and then turned to my mom.

"Mrs. Heffer, it is a pleasure to meet Zoey's mother. We are so pleased that she has joined the House of Night."

"Well, uh, thank you!" my mom said, clearly disarmed by Neferet's beauty and charm.

When Neferet greeted my grandma, her smile widened and became more than just polite. I noticed that they shook hands in the traditional vampyre greeting style, grasping each other's forearms.

"Sylvia Redbird, it is always a pleasure to see you."

"Neferet, it makes my heart glad to see you, too, and I thank you for honoring your oath to look after my granddaughter."

"It is an oath that is not a burden to fulfill. Zoey is such a special girl." Now Neferet's smile included me in its warmth. Then she turned to Stevie Rae and her mother. "And this is Zoey's roommate, Stevie Rae Johnson, and her mother. I hear that the two of them are practically inseparable, and that even Zoey's cat has taken to Stevie Rae."

"Yeah, it's true. She actually sat on my lap while we watched TV last night," Stevie Rae said laughingly. "And Nala doesn't like anyone except Zoey."

"Cat? I don't remember anyone giving permission for Zoey to get a cat," John said, making me want to retch. Like anyone except Grandma had bothered to talk to me for an entire month!

"You misunderstand, Mr. Heffer, at the House of Night cats roam free. They choose their owners, not the other way around. Zoey didn't need permission when Nala chose her," Neferet said smoothly.

John made a snorting noise, which I was relieved to see everyone ignored. Jeesh, he's such an ass.

"May I offer you some refreshment?" Neferet waved graciously at the table.

"Oh, golly! That reminds me of the cookies I left in the car. Stevie Rae and I were just on our way out there. It was really nice to meet y'all." With a quick hug for me and a wave for everyone else, Stevie Rae and her mom escaped, leaving me there, even though I wished I were anywhere else.

I stayed close to Grandma, lacing my fingers through hers as we walked over to the refreshment table, thinking how much easier this would be if it was just she who had come to visit me. I snuck a look at my mom. A permanent frown seemed to have been painted on her face. She was looking around at the other kids, and hardly even glanced in my direction. *Why come at all?* I wanted to scream at her. *Why seem like you might actually care—might actually miss me—and then show so obviously that you don't?*

"Wine, Sylvia? Mr. and Mrs. Heffer?" Neferet offered.

"Thank you, red please," Grandma said.

John's tight lips registered his displeasure. "No. We don't drink."

With a superhuman effort I didn't roll my eyes. Since when

didn't he drink? I would bet the last fifty dollars in my savings account that there was a six-pack of beer in the fridge at home right now. And my mom used to drink red wine like Grandma. I even saw her throw Grandma a narrow-eyed, envious look as she sipped the rich wine Neferet had poured for her. But *no* they didn't drink. At least not in public. Hypocrites.

"So, you were saying that the addition to Zoey's Mark happened because she did something special?" Grandma squeezed my hand. "She told me that she'd been made leader of the Dark Daughters, but she didn't tell me how exactly that happened."

I felt myself tense up again. I really didn't want to deal with the scene it would cause if my mom and John found out that what had actually happened was that the ex-leader of the Dark Daughters had cast a circle on Halloween night (known at the House of Night as Samhain, the night the veil between our world and the world of spirits is thinnest), conjured some very scary vampyre spirits, and then lost control of them when my human ex-boyfriend, Heath, stumbled up looking for me. And I so didn't want anyone to *ever* mention what only a couple of people knew—that Heath was looking for me because I'd tasted his blood and he was fast becoming fixated on me, something humans do pretty easily when they get involved with vamps—even vamp fledglings, for that matter. So the then leader of the Dark Daughters, Aphrodite, totally lost control of the ghosts and they were going to eat Heath. Literally. Worse—they were also acting like they wanted to take a chomp out of the rest of us, too, including totally hot Erik Night, the vamp kid who I can happily report is definitely not my *ex*-boyfriend, but who I've sorta been dating this past month so he's my *almost*-boyfriend. Anyway, I had to do something, so with some help from Stevie Rae, Damien, and the Twins, I cast my own circle, tapping into the power of the five elements: wind, fire, water, earth, and spirit. Using my affinity for the elements, I managed to banish the ghosts back to wherever it is they live (or unlive?). When they were gone I had these new tattoos, a delicate collection of lacelike sapphire swirls that framed my face—totally unheard of for a mere fledgling to have—and matching Marks interspersed with cool runelike-looking symbols on my shoulders, something no fledgling or vamp has ever had. Then Aphrodite was exposed as the rotten-assed leader she was, causing Neferet to fire her and put me in her place. Consequently, I'm also in training to be a High Priestess of Nyx, the vampyre Goddess, who is Night personified.

None of that would go over well with ultra-religious, ultra-judgmental Mom and John.

"Well, there was a small accident. Zoey's quick thinking and bravery made sure no one got hurt, and at the same time she connected with a special affinity she has been given to draw energy from the five elements." Neferet's smile was proud and I felt a wash of happiness at her approval. "The tattooing is simply an outward sign of the favor she's found with the Goddess."

"What you're saying is blasphemy." John spoke in a tight, strained voice that managed to sound condescending and angry at the same time. "You are putting her immortal soul in danger."

Neferet turned her moss-colored eyes on him. She didn't look angry. Actually, she looked amused.

"You must be one of the Elders of the People of Faith."

His birdlike chest swelled up. "Well, yes, yes I am."

"Then let us come to an understanding quickly, Mr. Heffer. I would not think of coming into your home, or into your church, and belittling your beliefs, though I disagree profoundly with them. Now, I do not expect you to worship as I do. In truth, I would never even think to attempt to sway you to my beliefs, even though I have a deep and abiding commitment to my Goddess. So all I insist upon is that you show me the same courtesy

I have already awarded you. When you are in my 'home,' you respect my beliefs."

John's eyes had become mean little slits and I could see his jaw clenching and unclenching.

"Your way of life is sinful and wrong," he said fiercely.

"Thus says a man who admits to worshipping a God who vilifies pleasure, relegates women to roles that are little more than servants and broodmares, though they are the backbone of your church, and seeks to control his worshippers through guilt and fear." Neferet laughed softly, but the sound was humorless and the unspoken warning in it made the hair on my forearms prickle. "Have a care for how you judge others; perhaps you should look to cleaning your own house, first."

His face reddening, John sucked in a breath and opened his mouth for what I knew would be an ugly lecture on how right his beliefs are and how wrong everyone else's are, but before he could respond Neferet cut him off. She hadn't raised her voice, but it was suddenly filled with the power of a High Priestess and I shivered in fear, even though her wrath was not directed at me.

"You have two choices. You may visit the House of Night as its invited guest, which means you will respect our ways and keep your displeasure and judgment to yourself. Or you may leave and not return. Ever. *Decide now.*" The last two words washed against my skin and I had to force myself not to cringe. I noticed that my mom was staring with wide, glassy eyes at Neferet, her face pale as milk. John's face had gone the opposite color. His eyes were narrow and his cheeks were flushed a very unattractive red.

"Linda," he said through his teeth. "Let's go." Then he looked at me with such disgust and hatred that I literally took a step back. I mean, I knew he didn't like me, but until that moment I hadn't realized how much. "This place is what you deserve. Your mother and I won't be back. You're on your own now." He spun around and started for the door. My mom hesitated, and for a second I thought she might actually say something nice—like she was sorry about him—or that she missed me—or that I shouldn't worry, she'd be back no matter what he said.

"Zoey, I can't believe what you've gotten yourself into now." She shook her head and, as usual, followed John's lead and left the room.

"Oh, sweetheart, I'm so sorry." Grandma was there, instantly hugging me and whispering reassurance. "I'll be back, my little bird. I promise. And I'm so proud of you!" She held me by my shoulders and smiled through her tears. "Our Cherokee ancestors are proud of you, too. I can feel it. You have been touched by the Goddess, and you have the loyalty of good friends," she glanced up at Neferet and added, "and wise teachers. Someday you might even learn to forgive your mother. Until then remember that you are the daughter of my heart, *u-we-tsi a-ge-hu-tsa.*" She kissed me. "I must leave, too. I drove your little car here, and I will leave it for you, so I must ride back with them." She handed me the keys to my vintage Bug. "But remember always that I love you, Zoeybird."

"I love you, too, Grandma," I said, and kissed her back, hugging her hard and taking deep breaths of her scent like I could hold her in my lungs and exhale her slowly over the next month as I missed her.

"Bye, sweetheart. Call me when you get a chance." She kissed me again and then left.

I watched her leave, and didn't realize I was crying until I felt the tears drip from my face onto my neck. I'd actually forgotten Neferet was still standing beside me, so I jumped a little in surprise when she handed me a tissue.

"I am sorry for that, Zoey," she said quietly.

"I'm not." I blew my nose and wiped my face before I looked at her. "Thanks for standing up to him."

"I did not mean to send your mother away, too."

"You didn't. She chose to follow him. Just like she's been doing for over three years now." I felt the hotness of tears threaten the back of my throat and spoke quickly, willing them away. "She used to be different. It's stupid, I know, but I keep expecting her to turn back into what she was before. It never happens, though. It's like he's killed my mom and put a stranger in her body."

Neferet put her arm around me. "I like what your grandma said—that maybe someday you can find the ability to forgive your mother."

I stared at the door the three of them had just disappeared through. "That someday is far away."

Neferet squeezed my shoulder sympathetically.

I looked up at her, so glad she was there with me, and I wished—for about the zillionth time—that she was my mom. Then I remembered what she had told me almost a month ago, that her mom had died when she was a little girl, and her dad had abused her, physically and mentally, until she had been saved by being Marked.

"Did you ever forgive your father?" I asked tentatively.

Neferet looked down at me and blinked several times, as if she were slowly coming back from a memory that had taken her far, far away. "No. No I didn't ever forgive him, but when I think of him now it is as if I'm remembering someone else's life. The things he did to me he did to a human child, not a High Priestess and vampyre. And to a High Priestess and vampyre he, like most humans, is completely inconsequential."

Her words sounded strong and sure, but as I looked into the depths of her beautiful green eyes I saw a flicker of something old and painful and definitely not forgotten, and wondered how honest she was being with herself . . .

CHAPTER TWO

I was incredibly relieved when Neferet said there was no reason for me to stay in the reception hall. After the scene with my family I felt like everyone was staring at me. I was, after all, the girl with the freaky Marks *and* the nightmare family. I took the shortest way out of the reception hall—the sidewalk that led outside through the pretty little courtyard that the windows of the dining hall looked out onto.

It was a little after midnight, which was—yes—a totally weird time for a parent open house, but the school begins classes at 8:00 P.M., and finishes up at 3:00 A.M. On the surface it seemed to make more sense to have parent visitation begin at 8:00, or maybe even an hour or so before school started, but Neferet had explained to me that the point was that parents accept their child's Change, and understand that days and nights would forever be different for them. On my own I decided that another plus of making the time inconvenient is that it gave a lot of parents the excuse they needed not to come, without outright telling their kid, *Hey—I don't want anything to do with you now that you're turning into a bloodsucking monster.*

Too bad my parents hadn't taken that out.

I sighed and slowed down, taking my time following one of the winding paths through the courtyard. It was a cool, clear November night. The moon was almost full, and its bright silver light was a pretty contrast to the antique gaslights that illuminated the court-yard with their soft yellow glows. I could hear the fountain that sat in the middle of the garden, and I automatically changed direction so that I was heading toward it. Maybe the soothing tinkle of the water would help my stress level . . . and help me forget.

When I rounded the curve that led to the fountain I was walking slowly, and daydreaming a little about my new almost-boyfriend, the totally delicious Erik. He was away from the school for the yearly Shakespeare monologue competition. Naturally, he'd finished first at our school, and had advanced easily to the Houses of Night international competition. It was Thursday, and he'd only been gone since Monday, but I missed him like crazy and couldn't wait till Sunday when he was supposed to get back. Erik was the hottest guy at our school. Hell, Erik Night might be the hottest guy at any school. He was tall, dark, and handsome—like an old-time movie star (without the latent homosexual ten-dencies). He was also incredibly talented. Someday soon he was going to join the rank of other vamp movie stars like Matthew McConaughey, James Franco, Jake Gyllenhaal, and Hugh Jack-man (who is totally gorgeous for an old guy). Plus, Erik was truly a nice guy—which only added to his hotness.

So I will admit to being preoccupied with visions of Erik as Tristan and me as Isolde (only our passionate love story would have a happy ending), and didn't notice that there were other people in the courtyard until a raised male voice shocked me with how mean and disgusted it sounded.

"You are one disappointment after another, Aphrodite!"

I froze. Aphrodite?

"It was bad enough that your getting Marked meant that you couldn't go to Chatham Hall, especially after everything I did to be sure you were accepted," said a woman in a brittle, cold voice.

"Mother, I know. I said I was sorry."

Okay, I should leave. I should turn around and walk quickly and quietly out of the courtyard. Aphrodite was probably my least favorite person at school. Actually, Aphrodite was probably my least favorite person anywhere, but purposefully listening in on what was clearly an ugly scene with her parents was just wrong wrong wrong.

So I tiptoed a few feet off the path where I could hide more easily behind a big ornamental bush *and* have a decent view of what was going on. Aphrodite was sitting on the stone bench closest to the fountain. Her parents were standing in front of her. Well, her mom was standing. Her dad was pacing.

Man, her parents were really pretty people. Her dad was tall and handsome. The kind of guy who kept in shape, kept all of his hair, and had really good teeth. He was dressed in a dark suit that looked like it cost a zillion dollars. He also looked weirdly familiar, and I was sure I'd seen him on TV or something. Her mom was totally gorgeous. I mean, Aphrodite was blond and perfect-looking, and her mom was an older, richly dressed, well-groomed version of her. Her sweater was obviously cashmere, and her pearls were long and real. Every time she gestured with her hands the gihugic pear-shaped diamond on her ring finger flashed a light as cold and beautiful as her voice.

"Have you forgotten that your father is the mayor of Tulsa?" Aphrodite's mom snapped viciously.

"No, no, of course not, Mother."

Her mom didn't seem to hear her. "Spinning a decent slant on the fact that you're here instead of on the East Coast preparing for Harvard was difficult enough, but we consoled ourselves with the fact that vampyres can attain money and power and success, and we expected you to excel in this"—she paused and grimaced distastefully—"rather unusual venue. And now we hear that you're no longer leader of the Dark Daughters and have been ejected from High Priestess training, which makes you no different than any of the other riffraff at this wretched school." Aphrodite's mother hesitated, as if she needed to calm herself before continuing. When she spoke again I had to strain to hear her hissing whisper. "Your behavior is unacceptable."

"As usual, you disappoint us," her father repeated.

"You already said that, Dad," Aphrodite said, sounding like her usual smart-ass self.

Like a striking snake, her mom slapped Aphrodite across her face, so hard that the crack of skin against skin made me jump and wince. I expected Aphrodite to leap off the bench and go after her mom's throat (please—we don't call her a hag from hell for nothing), but she didn't. She just pressed her own palm against her cheek and bowed her head.

"Do not cry. I've told you before, tears mean weakness. At least do this one thing right and don't cry," her mom snapped.

Slowly Aphrodite raised her head and took her hand from her cheek. "I didn't mean to disappoint you, Mother. I'm really sorry."

"Saying you're sorry doesn't fix anything," her mom said. "What we want to know is what you're going to do about getting your position back."

In the shadows I held my breath.

"I—I can't do anything about it," Aphrodite said, sounding hopeless and suddenly very young. "I messed up. Neferet caught me. She took the Dark Daughters away from me and gave them to someone else. I think she's even considering transferring me to a different House of Night completely."

"We already know that!" Her mom raised her voice, clipping her words so that they seemed to be made of ice. "We talked with Neferet before we saw you. She was going to transfer you to another school, but we interceded. You will remain at this school. We also tried to reason with her about giving you your position back after perhaps some period of restriction or detention."

"Oh, Mother, you didn't?"

Aphrodite sounded horrified, and I couldn't blame her. I could only imagine the impression these cold, pretending-to-be-perfect parents made on our High Priestess. If Aphrodite had ever had even the slightest chance of getting back in Neferet's favor, her creepy parents had probably ruined it for her.

"Of course we did! Did you expect us to just sit by while you destroyed your future by becoming a vampyre nobody at some nondescript foreign House of Night?" her mom said.

"More than you already have," her dad added.

"But it's not about me being on some kind of high school re-striction," Aphrodite said, obviously trying to control her frustra-tion and reason with them. "I messed up. Big time. That's bad enough, but there's a girl here whose powers are stronger than mine. Even if Neferet gets over being mad at me, she's not going to give me back the Dark Daughters." Then Aphrodite said something that totally shocked me. "The other girl is a better leader than I am. I realized that on Samhain. She deserves to be head of the Dark Daughters. I don't."

Ohmygod. Did hell just freeze over?

Aphrodite's mom took a step closer to her and I flinched with her, sure she was going to get smacked again. But her mother didn't hit her. She bent so that her beautiful face was staring right into her daughter's. From where I was standing they looked so similar that it was scary.

"Don't you *ever* say someone deserves something more than you. You're my daughter, and you will always deserve the best." Then she straightened again and ran her hand through her per-fect hair, even though I was pretty sure it wouldn't dare get messed up. "We couldn't convince Neferet to give you back your position, so you're going to have to convince her."

"But, Mother, I already told you—" she started, but her dad cut her off.

"Get the new girl out of the way, and Neferet will be more likely to give you back your position."

Ah, crap. "The new girl" was me.

"Discredit her. Cause her to make mistakes, and then be sure it's someone else who tells Neferet about them and not you. It'll look better that way." Her mom spoke matter-of-factly, like she was talking about which outfit Aphrodite should wear tomorrow instead of plotting against me. Jeesh, talk about a hag from hell!

"And watch yourself. Your behavior has to be beyond reproach. Maybe you should be more forthcoming about your visions, at least for a while," her father said.

"But you've told me for years to try to keep the visions to myself, that they are the source of my power."

I could hardly believe what I was hearing! A month ago Damien had told me that several of the kids thought that Aphrodite was trying to hide some of her visions from Neferet, but they thought it was because she hated humans—and Aphrodite's visions were always about a future tragedy where humans died. When she shared her visions with Neferet, the High Priestess was almost always able to stop the tragedy from happening and save lives. So Aphrodite purposefully keeping her visions to herself was one of the things that made me decide that I had to take her position as leader of the Dark Daughters. I'm not power hungry. I didn't really want the position. Hell, I still wasn't sure what to do with it. I'd just known that Aphrodite was bad news, and that I had to do something to stop her. Now I was hearing that some of the crap she'd been doing was because she let her hateful parents boss her around! Her mom and dad actually thought it was okay to keep quiet about information that could save lives. And her father was the mayor of Tulsa! (No wonder he looked familiar.) It was so bizarre it was making my head hurt.

"The visions aren't your *source* of power!" her dad was saying. "Do you never listen? I said that your visions could be used to *gain* power for you because information is always power. The source of your visions is the Change that's taking place inside your body. It's genetics, that's all."

"It's supposed to be a gift from the Goddess," Aphrodite said softly.

Her mother's laugh was cold. "Don't be stupid. If there was such thing as a goddess, why would she grant *you* powers? You're just a ridiculous child, and one who is prone to making mistakes, as this last little escapade of yours has once again proven. So be smart for a change, Aphrodite. Use your visions to gain favor back, but act humble about it. You have to make Neferet believe that you're sorry."

I almost didn't hear Aphrodite's whispered, "I am sorry . . ."

"We'll expect much better news next month."

"Yes, Mother."

"Good, now walk us back to the reception hall so that we can mingle with the others."

"Can I please stay here for a little while? I'm really not feeling very well."

"Absolutely not. What would people say?" her mother said. "Pull yourself together. You'll escort us back to the hall and you'll be gracious about it. Now."

Aphrodite was slowly standing up from the bench, and heart beating so hard I was afraid it would give me away, I hurried back down the path till I came to the fork that would take me out of the courtyard. Then I practically ran from the garden.

I thought about what I'd overheard all the way back to the

dorm. I believed that I had nightmare parents, but they were like *The Brady Bunch* mom and dad (hello—I watch Nickelodeon reruns like everyone else) compared to Aphrodite's hateful, power-freak parents. Much as I hated to admit it, what I saw tonight made me understand why Aphrodite acted like she did. I mean, what would I be like if I hadn't had Grandma Redbird to love me and support me and help me grow a backbone these past three years? And that was something else, too. My mom had been normal. Sure, she'd been stressed out and overworked, but she'd been normal for the first thirteen of my almost seventeen years of life. It was only after she married John that she changed. So I'd had a good mom and a fantastic grandma. What if I hadn't? What if all I'd ever known was how it had been for the past three years—me being an unwanted outsider in my own family?

I might have turned out like Aphrodite, and I might still be letting my parents control me because I was hoping desperately that I would be good enough, make them proud enough, so that someday they would really love me.

It made me see Aphrodite with totally new eyes, which I wasn't particularly thrilled about.

CHAPTER THREE

"Yeah, Zoey, I understand what you're sayin' and all, but hello! Part of what you overheard was that Aphrodite is gonna try to set you up so that she can get you kicked out of the Dark Daughter leadership, so don't go feeling too darn sorry for her," Stevie Rae said.

"I know—I know. I'm not getting all warm and fuzzy about her. I'm just saying that after overhearing her with her psycho parents I understand why she is like she is."

We were walking to first hour. Well, actually, Stevie Rae and I were practically running to first hour. As usual, we were almost late. I knew I shouldn't have had that second bowl of Count Chocula.

Stevie Rae rolled her eyes. "And you say I'm too nice."

"I'm not being nice. I'm being understanding. But understanding doesn't change the fact that Aphrodite acts like a hag bitch from hell."

Stevie Rae made a snorting noise and shook her head, causing her blond curls to bounce like she was a little girl. Her short cut was odd at the House of Night where everyone, even most of the guys, had ridiculously long, thick hair. Okay, my hair has always been long, but still—it was really weird when I first got here and was bombarded with hair hair hair. Now it made perfect sense.

Part of the physical Change that happens as we become vampyres is that our hair and nails grow abnormally fast. After a little practice, you can tell what year a fledgling is without checking the crest on her jacket. Vampyres looked different than humans (not bad different—just different), so it's only logical that as a fledgling passes through more and more of the Change her body looks different, too.

"Zoey, you're so not paying attention."

"Huh?"

"I said, don't let your guard down about Aphrodite. Yes, she has nightmare parents. Yes, they're controlling and manipulating her. Whatever. She's still hateful and mean and vindictive. Watch out for her."

"Hey, don't worry. I will."

"Okay, good. I'll see you third hour."

"See ya," I called to her back. Jeesh, she was such a worrier.

I hurried into class and had just taken my seat in the desk next to Damien, who raised an eyebrow at me and said, "Another two-bowl morning?" when the bell rang and Neferet swept into the room.

Okay, I know it's bordering on weird (or maybe queer is the better word choice) to continually notice how gorgeous a woman is when you're a woman, too, but Neferet is so damn beautiful that it's like she has the ability to focus all the light in the room on herself. She was wearing a simple black dress and totally to die for black boots. She had on her silver Goddess path earrings and, as always, the silver embroidered Goddess rested over her heart. She didn't exactly look like the Goddess Nyx—who I swear I'd seen in a vision the day I was Marked—but she had the Goddess's aura of strength and confidence. I'll just admit it. I wanted to be her.

Today was unusual. Instead of lecturing for most of the hour (and, no, amazingly enough Neferet was never a boring lecturer) she gave us an essay assignment on the Gorgon, who we had been studying all week. We learned that actually she had not been a monster who turned men to stone with a glance. She had been a famous vampyre High Priestess whose Goddess-given gift was an affinity, or a special connection, for the earth, which is probably where the "turn to stone" myth came from. I'm pretty sure if a vamp High Priestess got pissed enough and had a magical connection with the earth (stones *do* come from the earth), she could easily zap someone into granite. So today's assignment was to write an essay on human myth and symbolism, and the meaning behind the fictionalization of the Gorgon's story.

But I was too restless to write. Plus, I had all weekend to finish the essay. I was way more worried about the Dark Daughters. The full moon was Sunday. I would be expected to lead the ritual for the Dark Daughters. I realized everyone was also expecting me to make an announcement about changes I planned to make. Uh, I needed to have a clue about those changes. Surprisingly, I did have an idea, but it definitely needed help.

I ignored Damien's curious look as I quickly gathered up my notebook and went up to Neferet's desk.

"Problem, Zoey?" she asked.

"No. Uh, yes. Well, actually, if you would let me go to the media center for the rest of the hour, my problem would probably go away." I realized I was nervous. I'd only been at the House of Night for a month, and I still wasn't sure about the protocol for being excused from class. I mean, there were only two kids in the entire month who'd gotten sick. And they'd died. Both of them. Their bodies had rejected the Change, one had happened right in front of me during Lit class. It had been totally gross. But other than the occasional dying kid students rarely missed class. Neferet was watching me, and I remembered that she was an intuitive and she could probably sense the ridiculous babble going on in my head. I sighed. "It's Dark Daughters stuff. I want to come up with some new leadership ideas."

She looked pleased. "Anything I can help you with?"

"Probably, but I need to do some research and get my ideas straight first."

"Very well, come to me when you're ready. And feel free to spend as much time in the media center as you need," Neferet said.

I hesitated. "Do I need a pass?"

She smiled. "I am your mentor and I have given you permission, what more could you need?"

"Thanks," I said, and hurried out of the classroom feeling stupid. I would be so glad when I'd been at the school long enough to know all the little inside rules. And, anyway, I don't know what I'd been so worried about. The halls were deserted. Unlike my old high school (South Intermediate High School in Broken Arrow, Oklahoma—which is a totally boring suburb of Tulsa) there were no Napoleon Complex, overly tanned vice principals with nothing better to do than to prowl the halls harassing kids. I slowed down and told myself to relax—jeesh, I'd been stressed out lately.

The library was in the front center area of the school in a cool multilevel room that had been built to mimic the turret of a castle, which fit in well with the theme of the rest of the school. The whole thing looked like something out of the past. That was probably one of the reasons it had attracted the attention of the vamps five years ago. Then it had been a stuck-up rich kids' prep school, but it had originally been built as a monastery for the Saint Augustine People of Faith monks. I remember that when I asked how the prep school had been talked into selling to the vamps Neferet had told me that they'd made them a deal they couldn't refuse. The memory of the dangerous tone her voice had taken still made my skin crawl.

"Me-eeh-uf-ow!"

I jumped and almost peed on myself. "Nala! You scared the crap outta me!"

Unconcerned, my cat launched herself into my arms, and I had to juggle notebook, purse, and small (but chubby) orange cat. All the while Nala complained at me in her grumpy old lady cat voice. She adored me, and she'd definitely chosen me as her own, but that didn't mean that she was always pleasant. I shifted her, and pushed open the door to the media center.

Oh—what Neferet had told my stupid step-loser John had been the truth. Cats do roam free all over the school. They often followed "their" kid to class. Nala, in particular, liked to find me several times a day. She'd insist I scratch her head, complain a little at me, and then take off and go do whatever cats did with their free time. (Plot world domination?)

"Do you need help with her?" the media specialist asked. I had only met her briefly during my orientation week, but I remembered her name was Sappho. (Uh, she wasn't the *real* Sappho—that vampyre poet had died like a thousand years ago—right now we were studying her work in Lit class.)

"No, Sappho, but thank you. Nala doesn't really like anyone except me."

Sappho, a tiny dark-haired vamp whose tattoos were elaborate symbols Damien had told me were Greek alphabet glyphs, smiled fondly at Nala. "Cats are such wonderfully interesting creatures, don't you think?"

I moved Nala to my other shoulder and she grumbled in my ear. "They're definitely not dogs," I said.

"Thank the Goddess for that!"

"Do you mind if I use one of the computers?" The media center was lined with row after row of books—thousands of them—but it also had a very cool, up-to-date computer lab.

"Of course, make yourself at home and feel free to call on me if you can't find what you need."

"Thanks."

I picked a computer that sat on a nice big desk and clicked into the Internet. This was something else that was way different than my old school. Here there were no passwords and no Internet filtering program that restricted sites. Here students were expected to show some sense and act right—and if they didn't it's not like the vamps, who were almost impossible to lie to, wouldn't find out. Just thinking about trying to lie to Neferet made my stomach hurt.

Focus and stop messing around. This is important.

Okay, so an idea had been milling around in my head. It was time to see if there was anything to it. I pulled up Google and typed in "private preparatory schools." Zillions came up. I started narrowing. I wanted exclusive and upper class (none of those stupid "alternative academies" that were really just holding pens for future criminals—ugh). I also wanted old schools, ones that had been around for generations. I was looking for something that had passed the test of time.

I easily found Chatham Hall, which was the school Aphrodite's parents had thrown in her face. It was an exclusive East Coast prep school and, man, did it look stuck-up. I clicked out. Any place Aphrodite's freak parents approved of would not be something I wanted to use as a role model. I kept searching . . . Exeter . . . Andover . . . Taft . . . Miss Porter's (really—hee hee—that's the school's name) . . . Kent . . .

"Kent. I've heard that name before," I told Nala, who had curled up on top of the desk so that she could watch me sleepily. I clicked into it. "It's in Connecticut—that's why it's familiar. This is where Shaunee had been going when she was Marked." I browsed through the site, curious to see where Shaunee had spent the first part of her freshman (or third former) year. It was a pretty school—there was no denying that. Stuck-up, sure, but there was something about it that seemed more welcoming than the other prep schools. Maybe it was just because I knew Shaunee. I kept going through the site—and suddenly sat up straighter. "This is it," I muttered to myself. "This is the kind of stuff I need."

I pulled out my pen and notebook paper and got busy taking notes. Lots of notes.

If Nala hadn't hissed a warning, I would have jumped out of my skin when a deep voice spoke behind me.

"You look completely engrossed in that."

I glanced over my shoulder—and froze. Ohmygod.

"Sorry, I didn't mean to interrupt you. It was just so unusual to see a student writing feverishly in longhand, rather than pecking away at the computer keys, that I thought you might be writing poetry. You see, I prefer to write poetry longhand. The computer is just too impersonal."

Stop being such a moron! Speak to him! My mind screamed at me. "I—uh—I'm not writing poetry." God, that was brilliant.

"Oh, well. Doesn't hurt to check. Nice talking with you."

He smiled and started to turn away and my mouth finally managed to work a little more correctly. "Uh, I think computers are impersonal, too. I've never really written poetry, but when I write something that's important to me I like to do it like this." Totally dorklike, I held up my pen.

"Well, maybe you should try writing poetry. Sounds like you might have the soul of a poet." He held out his hand. "Usually about this time of day I come by and give Sappho a break. I'm not a full-time professor because I'm only here for one school year. I just teach two classes, so I have extra time. I'm Loren Blake, Vampyre Poet Laureate."

I grasped his forearm in the traditional vampyre greeting, trying not to think about how warm his arm was, how strong he felt, and how alone we were in the empty media center.

"I know," I said. Then I wanted to slit my throat. What an idiotic thing to say! "What I mean is I know who you are. You're the first male Poet Laureate they've named in two hundred years." I realized I was still grasping his arm and let go of him. "I'm Zoey Redbird."

His smile made my heart flop around inside my chest. "I know who you are, too." His gorgeous eyes, so dark they looked black and bottomless, sparkled mischievously. "You're the first fledgling to have a colored-in, expanded Mark, as well as the only vamp, fledgling or adult, to have an affinity for all five of the elements. It's nice to finally meet you face-to-face. Neferet's told me a lot about you."

"She has?" I was mortified that my voice squeaked.

"Of course she has. She's incredibly proud of you." He nodded at the empty seat beside me. "I don't want to interrupt your work, but do you mind if I sit with you a little while?"

"Yeah, sure. I need a break. I think my butt's asleep." Oh, God, just kill me now.

He laughed. "Well then, would you like to stand while I sit?"

"No, I'll—uh—just shift my weight." And then I'll hurl myself out the window.

"So, if it's not too personal, may I ask what you're working so diligently on?"

Okay, I needed to think and talk. Be normal. Forget that he was easily the most heart-stoppingly beautiful man I'd ever been near in my entire life. He's a professor at the school. Just another teacher. That's all. Yeah, right. Just another teacher who looked like every woman's dream of The Perfect Man. And I did mean Man. Erik was hot and handsome and very cool. Loren Blake was a whole other universe. A totally off-limits, impossibly sexy universe I was not allowed access to. As if he saw me as anything but a kid anyway. Please. I'm sixteen. Okay, almost seventeen, but still. He's probably at least twenty-one or something. He was just being nice. More than likely he wanted a closer look at my freaky Marks. He could be collecting research for a highly embarrassing poem about the—

"Zoey? If you don't want to tell me what you're working on, that's fine. I really didn't mean to bother you."

"No! It's okay." I drew a deep breath and got myself together. "Sorry—guess I was still thinking about my research," I lied, hoping that he was a young enough vamp that he didn't have the incredible lie detector powers the older profs had. I blundered quickly on. "I want to change the Dark Daughters. I think it needs a foundation—some clear rules and guidelines. Not just to join, but once you're in there should be standards. You shouldn't be given a free pass to be as big a jerk as you want to be, and still get the privilege of being a Dark Daughter or Son." I paused and I could feel my face getting hot and red. What the hell was I babbling on about? I must sound like the school idiot.

But instead of laughing at me or, worse, saying something patronizing and taking off, he seemed to be considering what I said.

"So what have you come up with?" he asked.

"Well, I like the way this private school called Kent runs their student leadership group. Look—" I clicked on the right link and read from the text. "The Senior Council and Prefect System is an integral part of life at Kent. These students are chosen as leaders who vow to be role models and to manage all aspects of student life at Kent." I used my pen to point at the computer screen. "See, there are several different Prefects, and they are elected to each yearly Council by votes of the students and the faculty, but the final choice is made by the Headmaster—which would be Neferet—and the Senior Prefect."

"Which would be you," he said.

I could feel my face getting hot. Again. "Yeah. It also says every May new Council members are 'Tapped' as possible appointees for the next school year, and there's a big service held to celebrate." I smiled, and said, more to myself than him, "Sounds like a new ritual Nyx would approve of." As I said the words I felt the rightness of them deep within me.

"I like it," Loren said. "I think it's a great idea."

"Really? You're not just saying that?"

"There's something about me that you should know. I don't lie."

I stared into his eyes. They seemed bottomless. He was sitting so close to me that I could feel the heat from his body, which made me suppress a shiver from a sudden rush of forbidden desire. "Well, thanks then," I said softly. Feeling suddenly bold, I continued. "I want the Dark Daughters to stand for more than just a social group. I want them to set examples—do the right things. So I thought that each of us would have to swear to uphold five ideals representing the five elements."

His brows went up. "What did you have in mind?"

"The Dark Daughters and Sons should swear to be authentic for air, faithful for fire, wise for water, empathetic for earth, and sincere for spirit." I finished without looking at my notes. I already knew the five ideals by heart. So I watched his eyes instead. He didn't say anything for a moment. Then, slowly, he reached out and traced one finger over the fluid line of my tattoo. I wanted to tremble under his touch, but I couldn't move.

"Beautiful and intelligent and innocent," he whispered. Then his incredible voice recited, *"The best part of beauty is that which no picture can express."*

"So sorry to interrupt, but I really do need to check out the next three books in this series for Professor Anastasia."

Aphrodite's voice broke the spell between Loren and me, as well as almost giving me a heart attack. Actually, Loren looked as shaken as I felt. He dropped his hand from my face and walked quickly to the checkout counter. I sat where I was like I'd grown to my chair, trying to look oh-so-busy scribbling more notes (which were actually, well, scribble). I heard Sappho come back in and take over checking out Aphrodite's books from Loren. I could hear him leaving, and almost as if I couldn't help it, I turned and looked at him. He was walking out the door and not paying the least bit of attention to me.

But Aphrodite was staring straight at me with a wicked smile curving her perfect lips.

Well, hell.

CHAPTER FOUR

I wanted to tell Stevie Rae about what had happened with Loren, and about Aphrodite busting in on us, but I wasn't up to going into it in front of Damien and the Twins. Not that they weren't my friends, too, but I had hardly had time to process what had happened, and the thought of the three of them chattering like crazy about it made me cringe. Especially since the Twins had rearranged their school schedules to get into Loren's poetry elective, where they freely admitted they spent the entire hour every day just staring at him. They would totally lose their minds when I told them what had happened. (Plus, had anything happened? I mean, the guy had just touched my face.)

"What's wrong with you?" Stevie Rae asked.

The attention that the four of them had been focusing on trying to figure out if there was a hair in Erin's salad or if it was just one of those weird string things from a piece of celery shifted instantly to me.

"Nothin', I'm just thinking about the Full Moon Ritual Sunday." I looked at my friends. They were watching me with eyes that said that they totally believed I'd come up with something and not make an ass out of myself. I wish I had their confidence in me.

"So what are you going to do? Have you decided?" Damien asked.

"I think so. Actually, what do you guys think of this idea . . ." I launched into the whole Council and Prefect idea, and realized about halfway through explaining it to them that it really was a pretty good plan. I finished with the five ideals that were each allied with an element.

No one said anything. I was just starting to worry when Stevie Rae threw her arm around me and hugged me hard.

"Oh, Zoey! You're going to be an awesome High Priestess."

Damien was all misty-eyed and his voice cracked adorably. "I feel like I'm in the court of a great queen."

"Or you could just be a great queen," Shaunee said.

"Her Majesty Damien . . . hee hee," Erin said, giggling.

"Y'all . . ." Stevie Rae warned.

"Sorry," the Twins said together.

"It was just so hard to resist," Shaunee said. "But seriously, we love the idea."

"Yeah, sounds like an excellent way to keep the hags out," Erin said.

"Well, that's another thing I needed to talk to you guys about." I took a deep breath. "I think seven is a good number for the Council. That way it's a decent size, and it's impossible to have a tie vote." They nodded. "So, everything I've been reading—not just about the Dark Daughters, but about student leadership groups in general—says that the Council members are upperclassmen. Actually the Senior Prefect, which would be me, is a, well, senior, and not a freshman."

"I like the title third former better. It sounds older," Damien said.

"Whatever we call it, it's still abnormal that we're so young. Which means we need two older kids on the Council with us."

There was a pause, and then Damien said, "I nominate Erik Night."

Shaunee rolled her eyes.

Erin said, "Okay, how many times do we have to explain this to you—the boy is not on your team. He likes breasts and vaginas, not penises and anu—"

"Stop!" I absolutely did not want to get off on this subject. "I think Erik Night is a good choice, and *not* because he likes me or, well . . ."

"Girl parts?" Stevie Rae offered.

"Yes, girl parts versus boy parts. I think he has the qualities we're looking for. He's talented, well liked, and he's really a good guy."

"And he's totally drop dead . . ." Erin said.

". . . gorgeous," Shaunee finished.

"It's true; he is. But we're absolutely not basing membership on appearance."

Shaunee and Erin frowned, but didn't argue with me. They're actually not real shallow; they're just kinda shallow.

I drew a deep breath. "And I think the seventh member of the Council needs to be one of the seniors who was part of Aphrodite's inside group. That is, if one of them petitions to join our Council."

This time there was no bedazzled silence. Erin and Shaunee, as usual, spoke at the same time.

"One of the hags from hell!"

"No f-ing way!"

Damien spoke while the Twins were taking breaths so they could shriek again. "I don't see how that could be a good idea."

Stevie Rae just looked upset and picked at her lip.

I held up my hand, and was pleased (and surprised) when they actually shut up.

"I didn't take over the Dark Daughters to start a war at school. I took over because Aphrodite was a bully, and she had to be stopped. Now that I'm in charge I want the Dark Daughters to be a group kids are honored to belong to. And I don't mean just a little select clique of kids, like when Aphrodite was the leader. The Dark Daughters and Sons should be hard to get into and it should be select. But not because only the current leader's friends have a chance to get in. I want the Dark Daughters and Sons to be something everyone is proud of, and I think by allowing one of the old group on my Council I'll be sending the right message."

"Or you'll be letting a viper into our midst," Damien said quietly.

"Correct me if I'm wrong, Damien, but aren't snakes closely allied with Nyx?" I spoke quickly, following the intuitive feeling that was prompting me. "Haven't they gotten a bad reputation because historically they've been symbols of female power, and men wanted to take that power away from women and make it something disgusting and scary instead?"

"No, you're right," he said reluctantly, "but that doesn't mean letting one of Aphrodite's gang into our Council is a good idea."

"See, that's the point. I don't want it to just be *our* Council. I want it to be something that becomes a tradition with the school. Something that lasts beyond us."

"So you mean if any of us don't make it through the Change, founding this new kind of Dark Daughters will be like we've lived on," Stevie Rae said, and I could see that she'd captured the interest of the rest of them.

"That's exactly what I meant—even though I don't think I realized it until this second," I said in a rush.

"Well, I like that part of it, even though I have no intention of drowning in my own bloody lungs," Erin said.

"Of course you won't, Twin. It's a much too unattractive way to die."

"I don't want to even think about not making it through the Change," Damien said, "but if—if something awful were to happen to me, I would want something about me to live on here at the school."

"Could we have plaques?" Stevie Rae asked, and I noticed she was suddenly looking unusually pale.

"Plaques?" I had no clue what she was talking about.

"Yeah. I think we should have a plaque or something that records the names of the . . . the . . . what did you call them?"

"Prefects," Damien said.

"Yeah, Prefects. The plaque, or whatever, could have the names of each year's Prefect Council, and it'll be displayed for ever and ever."

"Yeah," said Shaunee, warming to the idea. "But not just a plaque. We need something cooler than just a plain old plaque."

"Something that's unique—like us," Erin said.

"Handprints," Damien said.

"Huh?" I asked.

"Our handprints are unique. What if we made cement casts of each of our handprints, then signed our names below them," Damien said.

"Like the stars do in Hollywood!" Stevie Rae said.

Okay, it seemed kinda cheesy, which meant I couldn't help but like it. The idea was like us—unique—cool—and bordering on tacky.

"I think handprints are an excellent idea. And you know where the perfect place for them is?" They looked at me with bright, happy eyes, their worry about one of Aphrodite's friends joining us, as well as the pretty much constant fear of sudden death we all carried around with us, temporarily forgotten. "The courtyard is the perfect place."

The bell rang, calling us back to class. I asked Stevie Rae to tell our Spanish teacher, Proffe Garmy, that I had gone to see Neferet, so I'd be late. I really wanted to tell her about my ideas while they were still fresh in my mind. It wouldn't take long—I'd just give her a basic outline and see if she liked the direction I was heading. Maybe . . . maybe I'd even ask her to come to the Full Moon Ritual Sunday, and be there when I announced the new selection process for membership to the Dark Daughters and Sons. I was thinking about how nervous I'd be if Neferet was there, watching me cast a circle and lead my own ritual, and was telling myself sternly that I'd have to get rid of my nerves . . . that it was the best thing for the Dark Daughters if Neferet was there showing her support of my new ideas and—

"But that's what I saw!" Aphrodite's voice, carrying from the cracked door of Neferet's classroom, jarred my thoughts and made me stop short. She sounded awful—totally upset and maybe even scared.

"If your sight is no better than that, then perhaps it's time you quit sharing what you see with others." Neferet's voice was ice, terrifying, cold, and hard.

"But, Neferet, you asked! All I did was tell you what I saw."

What was Aphrodite talking about? Ah, hell. Could she have run to Neferet about seeing Loren touch my face? I looked around the deserted hall. I should get out of here, but no damn way I was going to leave if that hag was talking about me—even if it seemed Neferet wasn't believing anything she was saying. So instead of leaving (like a smart girl), I walked quickly and quietly into the shadowed corner near the partially opened door. And then, thinking fast, I took off one of my silver hoop earrings and tossed it into the corner. I come and go from Neferet's classroom a lot—it's not beyond all reason that I'd be looking for a lost earring outside her door.

"You know what I want you to do?" Neferet's words were so filled with anger and power that I could feel them crawl across my skin. "I want you to learn to not speak of things that are *ques-*

tionable." She drew the word out. Was she talking about gossiping about Loren and me?

"I—I just wanted you to know." Aphrodite had started crying, and she choked the words between sobs. "I th-thought there might be something you could do to stop it."

"Perhaps it would be wiser for you to think that because of your selfish actions in the past, Nyx is withholding her power from you because you are no longer in her favor and that what you are now seeing are false images."

I'd never heard the kind of cruelty that filled Neferet's voice. It didn't even sound like her, and it scared me in a way that was hard for me to define. The day I'd been Marked, I'd had an accident before I got to the House of Night. When I was unconscious I'd had an out-of-body experience, which ended with me meeting Nyx. The Goddess told me that she had special plans for me, and then she kissed my forehead. When I woke up my Mark had been filled in. I had a powerful connection with the elements (although I didn't realize that till much later), and I also had a weird new gut feeling that sometimes told me to say or do certain things—and sometimes told me very clearly to keep my mouth shut. Right now my gut feeling was telling me that Neferet's anger was all wrong, even if it was in response to Aphrodite's malicious gossip about me.

"Please don't say that, Neferet!" Aphrodite sobbed. "Please don't tell me that Nyx has rejected me!"

"I don't have to tell you anything. Search within your soul. What is it telling you?"

If Neferet had spoken the words gently, they might have been nothing more than a wise teacher, or priestess, giving someone who was troubled some direction—as in look inside yourself to find, and fix, the problem. But Neferet's voice was cold and sneering and cruel.

"It's—it's telling me that I've—I've, uh, made m-mistakes, but not that the Goddess hates me."

Aphrodite was crying so much that she was getting harder and harder to understand.

"Then you should look closer."

Aphrodite's sobs were wrenching. I couldn't listen anymore. Leaving my earring, I followed my gut and got the hell out of there.

CHAPTER FIVE

My stomach hurt all through the rest of Spanish class, so much so that I even figured out how to ask Proffe Garmy, *"puedo ir al bano,"* and spent so much time in the bathroom that Stevie Rae followed me in there asking what was wrong.

I know I was worrying the hell out of her—I mean, if a fledgling starts looking sick, that tends to mean that she's dying. And I'm positive I looked awful. I told Stevie Rae that I was getting my period and the cramps were killing me—although not literally. She didn't seem convinced.

I was incredibly glad to get to my last class of the week, Equestrian Studies. Not only did I love the class, but it always calmed me. This week I'd graduated to actually cantering Persephone, the horse that Lenobia (no prof title for her, she said the name of the ancient vampyre queen was title enough) had assigned to me the first week of class, and practiced changing leads. I worked with the beautiful mare until both of us were sweating and my stomach felt a little better, then I took my time cooling her off and grooming her, not caring that the bell had signaled the end of the school day a good half an hour before I emerged from her stall. I went to the immaculately kept tack room to put away the curry combs, and was surprised to see Lenobia sitting on a chair outside the door. She was rubbing saddle soap into what looked like an already spotlessly clean English saddle.

Lenobia was striking-looking, even for a vampyre. She had amazing hair that reached her waist and was so blond it was almost white. Her eyes were a weird color of gray, like a stormy sky. She was tiny, and carried herself like a prima ballerina. Her tattoo was an intricate series of knots entwining around her face—within the sapphire design horses plunged and reared.

"Horses can help us work through our problems," she said without looking up from the saddle.

I wasn't sure what to say. I liked Lenobia. Okay, when I started her class she had scared me; she was tough and sarcastic, but after I got to know her (and proved I understood horses were not just big dogs), I'd come to appreciate her wit and her no-nonsense attitude. Actually, next to Neferet, she was my favorite teacher, but she and I hadn't ever talked about anything except horses. So, hesitantly, I finally said, "Persephone makes me feel calm, even when I don't feel calm. Does that make any sense?"

She looked up at me then, her gray eyes shadowed with concern. "It makes perfect sense." She paused, and then added, "You've been given many responsibilities in a very short amount of time, Zoey."

"I don't really mind," I assured her. "I mean, being leader of the Dark Daughters is an honor."

"Often things that bring us the most honor can also bring us the most problems." She paused again and maybe I was imagining it, but she seemed to be trying to decide whether to say more or not. Then she drew her already straight spine up even straighter and continued. "Neferet is your mentor, and it is only right that you go to her with your confidences, but sometimes High Priestesses can be difficult to talk with. I want you to know that you can come to me—about anything."

I blinked in surprise. "Thank you, Lenobia."

"I'll put these up for you. Run along. I'm sure your friends are wondering what has happened to you." She smiled and reached out to take the curry combs from me. "And feel free to come by the barn to visit Persephone anytime. I have often found that grooming a horse can somehow make the world seem less complex."

"Thank you," I said again.

As I left the barn I could swear that I heard her call softly after me something that sounded a lot like *May Nyx bless and watch over you.* But that was just too weird. Of course, it was also too weird that she had said I could talk to her. Fledglings formed special bonds with their mentors—and I had an extra-special mentor in the High Priestess of the school. Sure, we liked the other vamps, but if a kid had a problem she couldn't solve on her own, the kid took that problem to his or her mentor. Always.

The walk from the stables to the dorm wasn't a long one, but I took my time, trying to stretch out the sense of peace working with Persephone had given me. I meandered off the sidewalk a little, heading toward the old trees that lined the eastern side of the thick wall surrounding the school grounds. It was almost four o'clock (A.M., of course), and the deepness of the night was beautiful lit by the fat setting moon.

I'd forgotten how much I loved walking out here by the school wall. Actually, I'd avoided coming out here for the past month. Ever since I'd seen—or thought I'd seen—the two ghosts.

"Mee-uf-ow!"

"Crap, Nala! Don't scare me like that." My heart was beating like crazy as I lifted my cat into my arms and petted her while she complained at me. "Hello—you could have been a ghost." Nala peered at me and then sneezed right in my face, which I took as her comment on the possibility of her being a ghost.

Okay, the first "sighting" might have been a ghost. I'd been out here the day after Elizabeth had died last month. She'd been the first of two fledgling deaths to shake the school. Well, more accurately, to shake *me*. As fledglings who could—any of us—drop dead at any time during the four years it took the physiological Change from human to vampyre to happen within our bodies, the school expected us to deal with death as just another fact of fledgling life. Say a prayer or two for the dead kid. Light a candle. Whatever. Just get over it and go on with your business.

It still seemed wrong to me, but maybe that was because I was only a month into the Change and still more used to being human than vamp, or even fledgling.

I sighed and scratched Nala's ears. Anyway, the night after Elizabeth's death I'd caught a glimpse of something that I thought was Elizabeth. Or her ghost, 'cause she was definitely dead. So it was no more than a glimpse, and Stevie Rae and I had discussed it without really deciding what was up with it. The truth was that we knew all too well that ghosts existed—the ones Aphrodite had conjured a month ago had almost killed my human ex-boyfriend. So I might very well have seen Elizabeth's newly freed spirit. Of course I might also have caught a glimpse of a fledgling and, because it had been night and I'd only been here for a few days and had, in those few days, gone through all sorts of unbelievable crap, I might have imagined the whole thing.

I came to the wall and turned to my right, meandering along it in the direction that would eventually lead me near the rec hall, and then, in turn, the girls' dorm.

"But the second sighting definitely wasn't my imagination. Right, Nala?" The cat's answer was to burrow her face into the corner of my neck and purr like a lawn mower. I snuggled her, glad she'd followed me. Just thinking about the second ghost still freaked me out. Like now, Nala had been with me. (The similarity made me glance nervously around and step up my meandering.)

It had not been long after the second kid had drowned in his own lung tissue and bled out right in front of my Lit class. I shuddered, remembering how awful it had been—especially because of my gross attraction to his blood. Anyway, I'd watched Elliott die. Then later that day Nala and I had run into him (almost literally) not far from where we were right now. I'd thought he was another ghost. At first. Then he'd tried to attack me, and Nala (precious kitten) had launched herself at him, which had made him leap over the twenty-foot wall and disappear into the night, leaving Nala and me totally freaked out. Especially after I noticed that my cat had blood all over her paws. *The ghost's blood.* Which made no damn sense.

But I hadn't mentioned this second sighting to anyone. Not my best friend and roommate Stevie Rae, not my mentor and High Priestess Neferet, not my totally delicious new boyfriend, Erik. No one. I'd meant to. But then all the stuff had happened with Aphrodite . . . I'd taken over the Dark Daughters . . . started dating Erik . . . been extremely busy with school . . . blah, blah, one thing led to another and here I was a month later and I hadn't said anything to anyone. Just thinking about telling someone now sounded lame in my own mind. *Hey, Stevie Rae/Neferet/Damien/Twins/ Erik, I saw the specter of Elliott last month* after *he'd died and he'd been really scary and when he tried to attack me Nala made him bleed. Oh, and his blood smelled all wrong. Believe me. I'm way into good-smelling blood (just another freakish thing about me, most fledglings have no bloodlust). Just thought I'd mention it.*

Yeah, right. They'd probably want to send me to the vamp equivalent of a shrink, and oh, boy, wouldn't that help me to instill confidence in the masses as the new leader of the Dark Daughters? Not hardly.

Plus, the more time passed, the easier it was for me to convince myself that maybe I'd imagined some of the Elliott encounter.

Maybe it hadn't been Elliott (or his ghost or whatever). I didn't know every single one of the fledglings here. There could be another kid here who had ugly, bushy red hair and pudgy, too white skin. Sure, I hadn't seen that kid again, but still. And about the weird-smelling blood. Well, maybe some fledglings had weird-smelling blood. Like I could possibly be an expert in one month? Also both "ghosts" had glowing red eyes. What had that been about?

The whole thing was giving me a headache.

Ignoring the jumpy, spooky feeling this entire chain of thought was causing, I started to turn resolutely from the wall (and from the subject of ghosts and such) when a movement caught at the corner of my eye. I froze. It was a shape. A body. It was *some*body. The person was standing under the enormous old oak I'd found Nala in last month. His or her back was to me, and he or she was leaning against the tree, head bowed.

Good. It hasn't seen me. I didn't want to know who or what it was. The truth was that I already had enough stress in my life. I didn't need the addition of ghosts of any type. (And, I promised myself, this time I was going to tell Neferet about the weirdly bleeding ghosts that hung out by the school's wall. She was older. She could deal with the stress.) Heart pounding so loud that I swear the sound of it was drowning out Nala's purr, I slowly and quietly started backing away, telling myself firmly that I was never going to walk out here in the middle of the night alone again. Ever. What was I, mentally impaired? Why couldn't I learn the first, or even the second time?

Then my foot came down squarely in the middle of a dry branch. *Crack!* I gasped. Nala grumbled a very loud complaint (I was inadvertently squashing her to my bosom). The head of the figure under the tree snapped up and it turned around. I tensed to get ready to either scream and run from a red-eyed malevolent ghost, or to scream and fight a red-eyed malevolent ghost. Either way a scream would definitely be involved, so I sucked in air and—

"Zoey? Is that you?"

The voice was deep, sexy, and already familiar. "Loren?"

"What are you doing out here?"

He made no move to come closer to me, so out of pure awkward fidgeting I grinned as if I hadn't been scared poo-less just seconds ago, shrugged nonchalantly, and joined him under the tree. "Hi," I said, trying to sound grown. Then I remembered that he'd asked me a question and I was glad that it was dark enough that my blush wasn't totally obvious. "Oh, I was walking back from the stables and Nala and I decided to take a long-cut." A long-cut? Had I really said that?

I thought he'd looked tense when I'd walked up to him, but this made him laugh and his completely gorgeous face relaxed. "A long-cut, huh? Hello again, Nala." He scratched the top of her head and she rudely, but typically, grumbled at him and then leaped neatly from my arms to the ground, shook herself, and still grumbling, padded delicately away.

"Sorry. She's not very sociable."

He smiled. "Don't worry about it. My cat, Wolverine, reminds me of a grumpy old man."

"Wolverine?" I raised my eyebrows.

His gorgeous smile went all crooked and boylike and, unbelievably, it made him even more handsome. "Yeah, Wolverine. He chose me as his when I was a third former. That was the year I was completely into the *X-Men*."

"That name could account for why he's so grumpy."

"Well, it could have been worse. The year before I couldn't stop watching *Spider-Man*. He came within an inch of being Spidey or Peter Parker."

"Clearly, you're a great burden for your cat to bear."

"Wolverine would most definitely agree with you!" He laughed again and I tried hard not to let his overwhelming hotness make me giggle hysterically like a pre-teen at a boy band concert. I was, for the moment, actually *flirting with him! Remain calm. Don't say or do anything idiotic.*

"So, what are you doing way out here?" I asked, ignoring my mind babble.

"Writing haiku." He lifted his hand and I noticed for the first time that he was holding one of those cool, ultra-expensive leather-bound writer's journals. "I find inspiration being out here, alone, in the hours before dawn."

"Oh, gosh! I'm sorry. I didn't mean to interrupt you. I'll just say bye and leave you alone." I waved (like a dork) and started to turn away, but he caught my wrist with his free hand.

"You don't have to go. I find inspiration in more things than being out here alone."

His hand was warm against my wrist and I wondered if he could feel my pulse jump.

"Well, I don't want to bother you."

"Don't worry about that. You're not bothering me." He squeezed my wrist before (sadly) letting it go.

"Okay, so. Haiku." His touch had left me ridiculously flustered and I tried to regain my facade of good sense. "That's Asian poetry with a set meter count, right?"

His smile made me ever so glad I'd actually paid attention in Mrs. Wienecke's English class last year during the poetry unit.

"That's right. I prefer the five-seven-five format." He paused and his smile changed. Something about it made my stomach do a little fluttery thing, and his dark, beautiful eyes locked on mine. "Speaking of inspiration—you could help me out."

"Sure, I'd be happy to," I said, glad I didn't sound as breathless as I felt.

Still looking into my eyes, he lifted his hand so that it brushed my shoulder. "Nyx has Marked you there."

It didn't sound like a question, but I nodded. "Yes."

"I would like to see it. If it wouldn't make you too uncomfortable."

His voice shivered through me. Logic was telling me that he was only asking to see my tattoos because of how freakishly different they are, and that he was in no way coming on to me. To him I must seem nothing more than a child—a kid—a fledgling with weird Marks and unusual powers. That's what logic was telling me. But his eyes, his voice, the way his hand was still caressing my shoulder—those things were telling me something completely different.

"I'll show it to you."

I was wearing my favorite jacket—black suede and cut to fit me perfectly. Under it I had on a deep purple tank. (Yes, it's the end of November, but I don't feel the cold like I did before I was Marked. None of us do.) I started to shrug out of the jacket.

"Here, let me help you."

He was standing very close to me, in front and to the side. He reached up with his right hand, caught the collar of my jacket with his fingers, and slid it over and down my shoulder so that it pooled around my elbows.

Loren should be looking at my partially bare shoulder, gawking at the tattoos there that not one other fledgling or vampyre that I knew of had ever had. But he wasn't. He was still staring into my eyes. And suddenly something happened within me. I stopped feeling like a goofy, jittery, dorky teenage girl. The look in his eyes touched the woman inside me, awakening her, and as this new me stirred I found a calm confidence in myself that I had rarely known before. Slowly, I reached up and pushed the small strap of my ribbed cotton tank over my shoulder so that it joined my half-discarded jacket. Then, still meeting his eyes, I swept my long hair out of the way, lifted my chin, and turned my body slightly, giving him a clear view of the back of my shoulder, which was now completely bare except for the slim line of my black bra.

He continued to meet my gaze for several more seconds, and I could feel the cool breath of the night air and the caress of the nearly full moon on the exposed skin of my breast and shoulder and back. Very deliberately, Loren moved even closer to me, holding my upper arm while he looked at the back of my shoulder.

"It's incredible." His voice was so low it was almost a whisper. I felt his fingertip lightly trace the labyrinthlike spiral pattern that was, except for the exotic-looking runes interspersed around the spirals, much like my facial Mark. "I've never seen anything like this. It's as if you're an ancient priestess who has materialized in our time. How blessed we are to have you, Zoey Redbird."

He said my name like a prayer. His voice mixed with his touch made me shiver as goose bumps lifted on my skin.

"I'm sorry. You must be cold." Gently, but quickly, Loren pulled up my tank strap and my jacket.

"I wasn't shivering because I was cold." I heard myself say the words, and couldn't decide if I should be proud of myself or shocked at my boldness.

"Cream and silk as one
  How I long to taste and touch
  The moon watches us."

His eyes never left mine as he recited the poem. His voice, which was usually so practiced, so perfect, had gone all deep and rough, like he was having a hard time speaking. As if his voice had the ability to heat me, I was so flushed that I could feel my blood pounding fiery rivers through my body. My thighs tingled and it was hard to catch my breath. *If he kisses me I might explode.* The thought shocked me into speaking. "Did you write that just now?" This time my voice sounded as breathless as I felt.

He shook his head slightly, a smile barely touching his lips. "No. It was written centuries ago by an ancient Japanese poet about how his lover looked naked under the full moon."

"It's beautiful," I said.

"You're beautiful," he said, and cupped my cheek in his hand. "And tonight you have been my inspiration. Thank you."

I could feel myself leaning into him, and I swear his body responded. I may not be highly experienced. And, hell yes, I'm still a virgin. But I'm not an utter moron (most of the time). I know when a guy is into me. And this guy—for that moment—was definitely into me. I covered his hand with my own, and forgetting about everything, including Erik and the fact that Loren was an adult vamp and I was a fledgling, I willed him to kiss me, willed him to touch me more. We stared at each other. We were both breathing hard. Then, within the space of an instant, his eyes flickered and changed from dark and intimate to dark and distant. He dropped his hand from my face and moved a step back. I felt his withdrawal like an icy wind.

"It was nice to see you, Zoey. And thanks again for allowing me to look at your Mark." His smile was polite and proper. He gave me a little nod that was almost a formal bow, and then he walked away.

I didn't know whether I should scream in frustration, cry in embarrassment, or growl and be pissed. Frowning and muttering to myself, I ignored the fact that my hands were shaking and marched back to the dorm. This was definitely an I-need-my-best-friend emergency.

CHAPTER SIX

Still mumbling to myself about men and mixed messages, I entered the front room of the dorm and wasn't surprised to see Stevie Rae and the Twins clustered together watching one of the TVs. Clearly, they'd been waiting for me. I felt an incredible wash of relief. I didn't want the whole world (translation—the Twins and/or Damien) to know what had just happened, but I was going to tell Stevie Rae every single, tiny, juicy detail about Loren—and let her help me figure out what the hell all of it meant.

"Uh, Stevie Rae, I'm clueless about our, uh, Soc paper that's due Monday. Maybe you could help me with it. I mean, it won't take too long and—" I started, but Stevie Rae interrupted me without taking her eyes from the TV.

"Wait, Z, come here. You gotta see this." She motioned me over to the TV. The Twins' eyes were glued to the screen, too.

I frowned when I noticed how tense they all looked, causing the subject of Loren to (temporarily) slide from my mind. "What's going on?" They were watching a rebroadcast of the local Fox 23 evening news. Chera Kimiko, the anchor, was talking and some familiar pictures of Woodward Park were flashing on the screen. "It's hard to believe that Chera isn't a vamp. She is abnormally gorgeous," I said automatically.

"Shush and listen to what she's saying," Stevie Rae said.

Continuing to be surprised by how weird they were acting, I shushed and listened.

"So, to repeat our lead story tonight—the search continues for Union High School teenager Chris Ford. The seventeen-year-old disappeared yesterday after football practice." The picture on the screen was a shot of Chris in his football uniform. I let out a little yelp as the name and face registered.

"Hey—I know him!"

"That's why I called you over here," Stevie Rae said.

"Search parties are combing the area around Utica Square and Woodward Park, which is where he was last seen."

"That's really close to here," I said.

"Shush!" Shaunee said.

"We know!" Erin said.

"So far there are no leads as to why he was in the Woodward Park area. Chris's mother said she didn't even know her son knew the way to Woodward Park, she's never known him to go there before. Mrs. Ford also said that she expected him home right after football practice. He has now been missing for more than twenty-four hours. If anyone has any information that might help the police locate Chris, please call Crime Stoppers. You may remain anonymous."

Chera went on to another story and everyone unfroze.

"So, you know him?" Shaunee asked.

"Yeah, but not real well. I mean, he's one of Union's star running backs and when I was kinda sorta dating Heath—you guys know he's Broken Arrow's quarterback?"

They nodded impatiently.

"Well, he used to drag me to parties with him, and all the football jocks knew each other, so Chris and his cousin Jon were at a bunch of them. Rumor has it they've graduated from getting trashed on cheap beer to getting trashed on cheap beer while they pass around nasty joints." I looked at Shaunee, who had been showing an unusual amount of interest in the newscast. "And before you ask, yes, he is as cute in real life as he was in his picture."

"Damn shame when something bad happens to a cute brother," Shaunee said, shaking her head sadly.

"Damn shame when something happens to any cute guy—no matter what color, Twin," Erin said. "We shouldn't discriminate. Cuteness is cuteness."

"You're right, as usual, Twin."

"I don't like marijuana," Stevie Rae piped in. "It smells bad. I tried it once and it made me cough my head off and burned my throat. Plus I got some of the weed in my mouth. It was just nasty."

"We don't do ugly," Shaunee said.

"Yeah, and pot's ugly. Plus it makes you eat for no good reason. It's a shame the hottie football players are into that," Erin said.

"Makes them less hottie," Shaunee said.

"Okay, hottie-ness and pot are not really the point," I said. "I have a bad feeling about this whole disappearance thing."

"Oh, no," Stevie Rae said.

"Well shit," Shaunee said.

"I really hate it when she gets one of those feelings," Erin said.

All any of us could talk about was Chris's disappearance and how bizarre it was that he had last been seen so close to the House of Night. In comparison to a kid being missing, my little drama-trauma with Loren seemed insignificant. I mean, I still wanted to tell at least Stevie Rae about it, but I couldn't seem to concentrate enough on anything but the sucking black feeling that had filled me since I'd seen the news.

Chris is dead. I didn't want to believe it. I didn't want to know it. But everything inside me said that the kid would be found, but he'd be found dead.

We met Damien in the dining hall, and everyone's conversation was centered around Chris and theories about his disappearance, which ranged from the Twins' insistence that "the hottie probably had a fight with his parental units and he's off drinking cheap beer somewhere" to Damien's firm belief that he might have discovered homosexual tendencies and had taken off for New York City to fulfill his dream of being a gay model.

I didn't have a theory. All I had was a terrible feeling, which I wasn't willing to talk about.

Naturally, I couldn't eat. My stomach was killing me. Again.

"You're picking at your excellent food," Damien said.

"I'm just not hungry."

"That's what you said at lunch."

"Okay, well, I'm saying it again!" I snapped, and was instantly sorry when Damien looked hurt and frowned down at his yummy bowl of Vietnamese noodle salad called Bun Cha Gio. The Twins raised one eyebrow each at me, and then went back to focusing on using chopsticks correctly. Stevie Rae just stared at me, silent worry clear on her face.

"Here. I found this. I have a feeling it's yours."

Aphrodite dropped the silver hoop beside my plate. I looked up at her perfect face. It was weirdly expressionless, as was her voice.

"So, is it yours?"

I reached up automatically and touched its mate, which was still in my ear. I'd forgotten all about that I'd dropped the damn thing so that I could pretend to find it while I eavesdropped on Aphrodite and Neferet. Crap. "Yes. Thank you."

"Don't mention it. Guess you're not the only one who has *feelings* about things, huh?"

She turned and walked out of the dining hall through the glass doors and into the courtyard. Even though she was carrying a tray with her uneaten dinner on it, she didn't even pause to look at the table where her friends sat. I noticed that they glanced up as she passed, but then they looked hastily away. None of them met her eyes. Aphrodite ate outside in the dimly lit courtyard where she'd been eating for most of the past month. Alone.

"Okay, she is just weird," Shaunee said.

"Yeah, weird as in psycho bitch from hell," Erin said.

"Her own friends won't have anything to do with her," I said.

"Stop feeling sorry for her!" Stevie Rae said, sounding uncharacteristically pissed off. "She's trouble, can't you see that?"

"I didn't say she wasn't," I said. "I just commented that even her friends have turned their backs on her."

"Did we miss something?" Shaunee asked.

"What's going on with you and Aphrodite?" Damien asked me.

I opened my mouth to tell them about what I'd overheard earlier, and was silenced by Neferet's smooth, "Zoey, I hope you don't mind if I pull you away from your friends tonight."

I looked slowly up at her, almost scared about what I might see. I mean, last time I heard her voice she had sounded incredibly hateful and cold. My eyes lifted to hers. They were moss green and beautiful and her kind smile was just starting to look worried.

"Zoey? Is something wrong?"

"No! I'm sorry. My mind was wandering."

"I'd like you to have dinner with me tonight."

"Oh, sure. Of course. No problem; I'd like that." I realized I was babbling, but there didn't seem to be anything I could do about it. I hoped it would eventually stop. Kinda like how you can't have diarrhea forever—it eventually has to stop.

"Good." She smiled at my four friends. "I need to borrow Zoey, but I will return her soon."

The four of them gave her hero-worshiping grins and quick assurances that they were cool with whatever.

I know it's ridiculous, but their easy release of me made me feel abandoned and insecure. But that's stupid. Neferet is my mentor, and High Priestess of Nyx. She's one of the good guys.

So why was my stomach clenching as I followed her out of the dining hall?

I glanced over my shoulder at my group. They were already talking away. Damien was holding up his chopsticks, obviously giving the Twins another lesson in how to maneuver them. Stevie Rae was demonstrating for him. I felt eyes on me and looked from them to the wall of glass that separated the dining area and the courtyard. Sitting alone in the night, Aphrodite was watching me with an expression that might almost be pity.

CHAPTER SEVEN

The vamps' dining hall wasn't a cafeteria. It was a very cool room that was directly above the students' dining hall. It, too, had a wall of arched windows. Wrought-iron tables and chairs were set up on the balcony that overlooked the courtyard below. The rest of the room was tastefully and expensively decorated with a variety of different size tables and even a few booths made of dark cherry-wood. There were no trays here and no serve-yourself buffets. Linens, china, and crystal were set tastefully on the tables, and long, thin white tapers burned happily in crystal holders. There were a few professors eating in quiet couples or small groups. They nodded at Neferet respectfully and smiled quick welcomes to me before going back to their meals.

I tried to gawk at what they were eating without being too obvious, but all I saw was the same Vietnamese salad we'd been eating downstairs, and some fancy-looking spring rolls. There wasn't one sign of raw meat or anything that resembled blood (well, except for the red wine). And, of course, I really didn't need to bother about gawking. If they'd been feasting on bloody what-ever I would have smelled it. I was intimately familiar with the delicious scent of blood . . .

"Would the cool night bother you if we sat outside on the bal-cony?" Neferet asked.

"No, I don't think so. I don't feel the cold like I used to." I smiled brightly at her, reminding myself severely that she's an intuitive and she was probably "hearing" pieces of the stupid stuff cascading through my mind.

"Good, I prefer dining on the balcony in all seasons." She led me through the doors to a table already set for two. A server magically appeared—obviously a vampyre by her filled-in Mark and the series of slim tattoos that framed her heart-shaped face, but she looked really young. "Yes, bring me the Bun Cha Gio and a pitcher of the same red wine I had last night." She paused, and then with a secret smile to me added, "And please bring Zoey a glass of any brown pop we have, so long as it isn't diet."

"Thank you," I told her.

"Just try not to drink too much of that stuff. It's really not good for you." She winked at me, making her admonishment a little joke.

I grinned at her, happy that she remembered what I like, and I started to feel more relaxed. This was Neferet—our High Priestess. She was my mentor and my friend and in the month I'd been here she'd never been anything but kind to me. Yes, she'd sounded scary as hell when I overheard her with Aphrodite, but Neferet was a powerful Priestess, and as Stevie Rae kept reminding me, Aphrodite was a selfish bully who deserved to be in trouble. Hell! She'd probably been gossiping about me.

"Feeling better?" Neferet said.

I met her eyes. She was studying me carefully.

"Yeah, I am."

"When I heard about the missing human teenager I began to worry about you. This Chris Ford was a friend of yours, wasn't he?"

Nothing she said should surprise me. Neferet was incredibly smart and gifted by the Goddess. Add to that the weird sixth sense all the vamps had, and more than likely she knew literally everything (or at least everything important). It had probably been easy-peasy for her to know that I'd had my own intuitive feeling about Chris's disappearance.

"Well, he wasn't really a friend of mine. We've been at some of the same parties, but I don't really like to party, so I didn't know him that well."

"But something about his disappearance has upset you."

I nodded. "It's just a feeling I have. It's silly. He probably had a fight with his parents and his dad grounded him or something like that, so he took off. More than likely he's already home."

"If you really believed that you wouldn't still feel so worried." Neferet waited until the server finished giving us our drinks and food before she said more. "Humans believe that adult vampyres are all psychic. The truth is that though many of us do have a gift for precognition or clairvoyance, the vast majority of our people have simply learned to listen to their intuition—which is something most humans have been frightened out of doing." Her tone was much like it was in her classroom, and I listened to her eagerly while we ate. "Think about it, Zoey. You're a good student— I'm sure you remember from your history classes what has historically happened to humans, especially female humans, when they pay too much attention to their intuition and begin 'hearing voices in their head' or even foreseeing the future."

"They were usually thought of as in league with the devil, or whatnot, depending on what time it was in history. Bottom line was they caught hell for it." Then I blushed because I'd said the H word in front of a teacher, but she didn't seem to care, she was just nodding in agreement with me.

"Yes, exactly. They even attacked holy people, like their Joan of Arc. So you see that humans have learned to silence their instincts. Vampyres, on the other hand, have learned to listen and listen well to them. In the past, when humans attempted to hunt and destroy our kind, it was all that saved many of our foremothers and forefathers' lives."

I shivered, not liking to think about how tough it must have been to be a vampyre a hundred or so years ago.

"Oh, you don't need to worry, Zoeybird." Neferet smiled. Hearing my grandma's nickname for me made me smile, too. "The Burning Times will never come again. We may not be revered as we were in ancient days, but never again will humans be able to hunt and destroy us." For a moment her green eyes flashed dangerously. I took a big drink of my brown pop, not wanting to meet those scary eyes. When she continued, she sounded like herself again—all hint of danger was gone from her voice and she was just my mentor and friend. "So, what all this means is that I want you to be sure that you listen to your instincts. If you get bad feelings about a situation or about someone, pay attention to it. And, of course, if you need to talk with me, you may come to me at any time."

"Thanks, Neferet, that means a lot to me."

She waved away my thanks. "That's what it means to be a mentor and a High Priestess—two roles I fully expect you to take on someday."

When she talked about my future and me being a High Priestess, I always got a funny feeling. It was made up partially of hope and excitement, and partially of abject fear.

"Actually, I was surprised that you didn't come see me today after you finished in the library. Did you not decide on a new direction for the Dark Daughters?"

"Oh, uh, yeah. I did." I forced myself not to think about the library and my encounter with Loren, and the east wall and my encounter with Loren . . . No way did I want Neferet and her intuition picking up anything about . . . well . . . *him.*

"I sense your hesitation, Zoey. Would you rather not share what you've decided with me?"

"Oh, no! I mean, yes. Actually, I did come by your room, but you were . . ." I looked up quickly, remembering the scene I'd overheard. Her eyes seemed to see into my soul. I swallowed hard. "You were busy with Aphrodite. So I left."

"Oh, I see. Now your nervousness around me makes much more sense." Neferet sighed sadly. "Aphrodite . . . she has become a problem. It really is a pity. As I said on Samhain when I realized how far wrong she'd gone, I feel partially responsible for her behavior and her transformation into the dark creature she has become. I knew she was selfish, even when she first joined our school. I should have stepped in sooner and taken a firmer hand with her." Neferet's gaze caught mine. "How much did you overhear today?"

A warning skittered down my spine. "Not very much," I said quickly. "Aphrodite was crying really hard. I heard you tell her to look within. I knew you wouldn't want to be interrupted." I stopped, careful not to say specifically that that was *all* I had heard—careful not to lie outright. And I didn't look away from her sharp eyes.

Neferet sighed again and sipped her wine. "I would not normally talk about one fledging to another, but this is a unique case. You know that Aphrodite's Goddess-given affinity was to be able to foresee disastrous events?"

I nodded, noting the past tense she used when she mentioned Aphrodite's ability.

"Well, it seems that Aphrodite's behavior has caused Nyx to withdraw her gift. It's something that is highly unusual. Once the Goddess touches someone, she rarely revokes what she has given." Neferet shrugged sadly. "But who can know the mind of the Great Goddess of Night?"

"It must be awful for Aphrodite," I said, more thinking aloud than really meaning to comment.

"I appreciate your compassion, but I did not tell you this so that you would pity Aphrodite. Rather, I tell you so that you know to be on your guard. Aphrodite's visions are no longer valid. She might say or do things that are disturbing. As leader of the Dark Daughters, it will be your responsibility to be certain that she does not upset the delicate balance of harmony among the fledglings. Of course we encourage you to work out problems among yourselves. You are much more than human teenagers, and we expect more from you, but feel free to come to me if Aphrodite's behavior becomes too"—she paused, like she was considering the next word carefully—"erratic."

"I will," I said, my stomach beginning to hurt again.

"Good! Now, why don't you tell me the plans you've made for your reign as leader of the Dark Daughters."

I put Aphrodite out of my mind and outlined my new plans for the Prefect Council and the Dark Daughters. Neferet listened attentively and was openly impressed by my research and what she called a "logical reorganization."

"So, what you want from me is to lead the faculty in voting on the two new Prefects, because I agree with you that you and your four friends have more than proven your worth and are already an excellent working Council."

"Yes. The Council wants to nominate Erik Night for the first of the two open positions."

Neferet nodded her head. "Erik is a wise choice. He's popular with the fledglings, and he has an excellent future before him. Who did you have in mind for the last position?"

"Here's where my Council and I disagree. I think we need another upperclassman, and I also think that person should be one who belonged to Aphrodite's inner circle." Neferet raised her brows in surprise. "Well, including a friend of hers reinforces what I've said all along, that I didn't come into this because I'm power crazy and set out to steal what was Aphrodite's or anything stupid like that. I just wanted to do the right thing. I didn't want to start some kind of silly clique war. If one of her friends is on my Council, then the rest of them might understand that it's not about me getting over on her—it's about something more important than that."

Neferet considered for what seemed like forever. Finally she said, "You know that even her friends have turned from her."

"I realized that today in the dining hall."

"Then what is the point of putting an ex-friend of hers on your Council?"

"I'm not convinced they are ex-friends. People act different in private than they do in public."

"Again, I agree with you. I already made the announcement to the faculty that Sunday the Dark Daughters and Sons will convene a special Full Moon Ritual and meeting. I would expect that the vast majority of the old members will attend—if for no other reason than curiosity about your powers."

I gulped and nodded. I was already way too aware that I was the main attraction in a freak show.

"Sunday is the right time for you to tell the Dark Daughters about your new vision for it. Announce that there is one spot left on your Council, and that it must be filled by a sixth former. You and I will look over the applications and decide who is the best fit."

I frowned. "But I don't want it to just be our choice. I want the faculty to vote, as well as the student body."

"They will," she said smoothly. "Then we will decide."

I wanted to say more, but her green eyes had gone cold; I'm not ashamed to admit that that scared me. So instead of arguing with her (which was totally impossible) I went down a different road (as my grandma would say).

"I also want the Dark Daughters to get involved with a community charity."

This time Neferet's brows totally disappeared into her hairline.

"You mean community as in the human community?"

"I do."

"You think they will welcome your help? They shun us. They abhor us. They are afraid of us."

"Maybe that's because they don't know us," I said. "Maybe if we acted like part of Tulsa, we'd get treated like part of Tulsa."

"Have you read about the Greenwood riots in the 1920s? Those African-American humans were part of Tulsa, and Tulsa destroyed them."

"It's not 1920 anymore," I said. It was hard to meet her eyes, but I knew, deep inside, that I was doing the right thing. "Neferet, my intuition is telling me this is something I must do."

I watched her expression soften. "And I did tell you to follow your intuition, didn't I?"

I nodded.

"What charity will you choose to get involved with—providing they actually allow you to help them?"

"Oh, I think they'll let us help them. I've decided to contact Street Cats—the cat rescue charity."

Neferet threw back her head and laughed.

CHAPTER EIGHT

I was already out of the dining hall and heading to the dorm when I realized that I hadn't said anything to Neferet about the ghosts, but no way did I want to go back upstairs and start that subject. The conversation I'd already had with Neferet had completely exhausted me, and despite the beautiful dining room with its great view and its crystal and linen, I'd been eager to get out of there. I wanted to go back to the dorm and tell Stevie Rae about the whole Loren thing and then do nothing but veg out and watch bad reruns on TV and try to forget (at least for one night) that I had a terrible premonition about Chris's disappearance and that I was A Big Deal now and in charge of the most important student group at the school. Whatever. I just wanted to be me for a while. As I'd told Neferet, Chris was probably safely at home already. And there was plenty of time for everything else. Tomorrow I'd write down an outline of what I was going to say to the Dark Daughters on Sunday. I guess I'd also have to work on a Full Moon Ritual . . . my first real public circle casting and formal ritual. My stomach started to gurgle. I ignored it.

I was halfway to the dorm when I remembered that I also had an essay due Monday for Vamp Soc. Sure, Neferet had excused me from most of the third former work in that class so I could focus on reading ahead in the higher level Soc text, but I'd been trying really hard to be "normal" (Whatever that was—hello—I'm a teenager and a fledgling vampyre. How could any of that be normal?), which meant I made sure I turned in papers when the rest of the class did. So I hurriedly backtracked to my homeroom class, where my locker and all of my books were kept. It was also Neferet's room, but I'd just left her having wine with several of the other profs upstairs. For a change I didn't have any worries about overhearing something awful.

As usual, the door was unlocked. Why have locks when you had vamp intuition to scare the bejeezus out of kids instead? The room was dark, but that didn't matter. I'd only been Marked one month, but already I saw just as well with the lights off as with them on. Actually, better. Bright lights hurt my eyes—sunlight was almost unbearable.

I hesitated as I opened my locker, realizing that I hadn't seen the sun in almost a month. I hadn't even thought about it till now. Huh. Weird.

I was considering the bizarreness of my new life when I noticed the piece of paper that had been taped to the inside shelf of my locker. It fluttered in the temporary breeze I'd created by opening the door. My hand lifted to calm it, and I felt a jolt of shock when I realized what it was.

Poetry.

Or, more accurately, a poem. It was short and written in a bold, attractive cursive. I read it and reread it, registering specifically what it was. Haiku.

Ancient Queen awake
A chrysalis not yet formed
Will your wings unfold?

I let my fingers brush the words. I knew who had written it. There was only one logical answer. My heart squeezed as I whispered his name, "Loren . . ."

"I'm serious, Stevie Rae. If I tell you, you have to swear you won't say anything to anyone. And when I say *anyone* I especially mean Damien and the Twins."

"Dang, Zoey, you can trust me. I said I swear. What do you want me to do, open a vein?"

I didn't say anything.

"Zoey, you really can trust me. Promise."

I studied my best friend's face. I needed to talk to someone—someone who was not a vamp. I searched inside myself, to the core of what Neferet would call my intuition. It felt right to confide in Stevie Rae. It felt safe.

"Sorry. I know I can trust you. I'm just . . . I don't know." I shook my head, frustrated by my own confusion. "Okay, weird stuff has happened today."

"You mean more than the normal weirdness that goes on around here?"

"Yeah. Loren Blake came into the library today while I was there. He was the first person I talked to about the Prefect Council idea and my new ideas for the Dark Daughters."

"Loren Blake? As in the most gorgeous vamp any of us have ever seen? Ohmygoodness. I better sit down." Stevie Rae collapsed on her bed.

"That's who I mean."

"I can't believe you haven't said anything about this until now. You must have been dying."

"Well, that's not all. He . . . uh . . . touched me. And more than once. Okay, actually I saw him more than once today. Alone. And I think he wrote me a poem."

"What!"

"Yeah, at first I was sure it was perfectly innocent and I was imagining anything else. In the library we just talked about the ideas I had for the Dark Daughters. I didn't think it meant anything. But, well, he touched my Mark."

"Which one?" Stevie Rae asked. Her eyes were huge and round and she looked like she was going to explode.

"The one on my face. That time."

"What do you mean *that time!*"

"Well, after I got done with brushing Persephone I wasn't in any hurry to get back to the dorm. So I went for a walk over by the west wall. Loren was there."

"Ohmydearsweetlord. What happened?"

"I think we flirted."

"You think!"

"We were laughing and smiling at each other."

"Sounds like flirting to me. God, he is so totally gorgeous."

"Tell me about it. When he smiles at me I can hardly breathe. And get this—*he recited a poem to me,*" I said. "It was a haiku a man wrote about looking at his naked lover in the moonlight."

"You have got to be kidding!" Stevie Rae started fanning herself with her hand. "Get to the touching part."

I took a deep breath. "It was really confusing. Everything was going really well. Like I said, we were laughing and talking. Then he said he was out there by himself because that's how he gets inspired to write haiku—"

"Which is insanely romantic!"

I nodded and continued. "I know. Anyway, I told him I hadn't meant to mess up his inspiration and bother him, and he said that more things inspired him than just the night. And he asked me if *I'd* be his inspiration."

"Holy shit."

"Exactly what I thought."

"Naturally you said you'd be happy to inspire him."

"Naturally," I said.

"And . . ." Stevie Rae prompted eagerly.

"And he asked to see my Mark. The one on my shoulders and back."

"He did not."

"He did."

"Man, I would have peeled off my shirt faster than you can say Bubba loves trucks!"

I laughed. "Well, I didn't take my shirt off, but I slid my jacket down. Actually, he helped me."

"Are you telling me Loren Blake, Vampyre Poet Laureate and hottest f-ing male on two feet, helped you off with your jacket like an old-time gentleman?"

"Yeah. Like this." I demonstrated by pushing my jacket down around my elbows. "And then I don't exactly know what came over me, but all of a sudden I wasn't all nervous and stupid-acting. I took the strap of my tank off for him. Like this." I pushed my tank strap down, exposing my back and shoulder and a good part of my breast (relieved all over again that I had on my good black bra). "That's when he touched me. Again."

"Where?"

"He traced the pattern of my Mark on my back and shoulder. He told me that I look like an ancient vampyre queen and recited the poem to me."

"Holy shit," Stevie Rae said again.

I plopped down on my bed facing her and sighed, pulling the strap of my tank back up. "Yeah, it was amazing for a little while.

I was sure we connected. Really connected. I think he almost kissed me. Actually, I know he wanted to. And then, out of nowhere, he changed. He got all polite and formal and thanked me for showing him my Mark and then he walked away."

"Well, that's no big surprise."

"It sure as hell was to me. I mean, one second he was staring into my eyes and sending major signals that he wanted me and the next—nothing."

"Zoey, you're a student. He's a teacher. This is a vamp school and a whole different world from life at a normal high school, but some things don't change. Students are off-limits to teachers."

I chewed at my lip. "He's only a part-time, temporary teacher."

Stevie Rae rolled her eyes. "As if that matters."

"That's not all that happened. I just found this poem in my locker." I handed her the piece of paper with the haiku on it.

Stevie Rae sucked air. "Ohmygood*ness*. This is so romantic I could die. How? How did he touch the Mark on your back?"

"Jeesh, how do you think? With his finger. He traced the pattern." I swear I could still feel the heat of that touch.

"He recited a love poem to you, touched your Mark, and then wrote a poem for you . . ." She sighed dreamily. "It's like you're Romeo and Juliet with the whole forbidden lovers thing." In the middle of fanning herself dramatically she stopped and sat straight up again. "Ah oh, what about Erik?"

"What do you mean, what about Erik?"

"He's your boyfriend, Zoey."

"Not officially," I said sheepishly.

"Well, shoot, what does the kid have to do to make it 'official'? Get down on one knee? It's been pretty obvious this past month that y'all are dating."

"I know," I said miserably.

"So do you like Loren more than you like Erik?"

"No! Yes. Oh, hell, I don't know. It's like Loren's in a whole other world. And it's not like he and I can really date, or whatever." But I wasn't so sure about the whatever. Could Loren and I see each other secretly? Did I want to?

As if she could read my thoughts Stevie Rae said, "You could sneak around and see Loren."

"This is ridiculous. He probably doesn't even feel like that about me." But even as I said the words I remembered the heat of his body and the desire in his dark eyes.

"What if he does, Z?" Stevie Rae was studying me carefully. "You know, you're different than the rest of us. No one has ever been Marked like you before. No one has ever had an affinity for each of the five elements. Maybe the same rules don't apply to you."

My gut clenched. Since I'd arrived at the House of Night I had been struggling to fit in. All I really wanted was to make this new place my home—to have friends I considered family. I didn't want to be different and I didn't want to play by different rules. I shook my head and said through clenched teeth, "I don't want it to be like this, Stevie Rae. I just want to be normal."

"I know," Stevie Rae said softly. "But you *are* different. Everyone knows that. Plus, don't you want Loren to like you?"

I sighed. "I'm not sure what I want, except that I know I *don't* want anyone to find out about Loren and me."

"My lips are sealed." Stevie Rae, little Okie dork that she is, pantomimed zipping her lips closed and throwing the key away over her shoulder. "No one's gonna get a word from me," she mumbled through half-sealed lips.

"Hell! That reminds me, Aphrodite saw Loren touching me."

"That hag followed you out to the wall!" Stevie Rae squeaked.

"No no no. No one saw us out there. Aphrodite walked into the media center when he was touching my face."

"Ah, crap."

"Ah, crap, is right. And there's more. Remember when I missed part of Spanish 'cause I wanted to talk to Neferet? I didn't talk to her. I got to her class and the door was cracked, so I could overhear what was going on inside. Aphrodite was in there."

"That bitch was telling on you!"

"I'm not sure. I only heard a little of what they were saying."

"I'll bet you were totally freaked when Neferet pulled you out of the dining hall to eat with her."

"Totally," I agreed.

"No wonder you looked so sick. Jeesh, it all makes sense now." Then her eyes got even bigger. "Did Aphrodite get you in trouble with Neferet?"

"No. When Neferet talked to me tonight she said that Aphrodite's visions are false because Nyx has withdrawn her gift. So whatever Aphrodite told her, Neferet didn't believe."

"Good." Stevie Rae looked like she'd like to break Aphrodite in half.

"No, not good. Neferet's reaction was too harsh. She made Aphrodite sob. Seriously, Stevie Rae, Aphrodite was destroyed by what Neferet said to her. Plus, Neferet didn't even sound like herself."

"Zoey, I cannot believe we're going over this again. You've got to quit feeling sorry for Aphrodite."

"Stevie Rae, you're not getting the point. This isn't about Aphrodite, it's about Neferet. She was cruel. Even if Aphrodite was ratting me out and exaggerating what she saw, Neferet's response was wrong. And I'm getting a bad feeling about it."

"You're getting a bad feeling about Neferet?"

"Yes . . . no . . . I don't know. It's not just Neferet. It's like it's a mixture of stuff—everything coming down at once. Chris . . . Loren . . . Aphrodite . . . Neferet . . . something's off, Stevie Rae."

She looked confused, and I realized she needed an Okie analogy to get it. "You know how it feels right before a tornado hits? I mean when the sky's still clear, but the wind's starting to cool off and change direction. You know something's coming, but you don't always know what. That's how things feel to me right now."

"Like a storm's comin'?"

"Yep. A big one."

"So you want me to . . . ?"

"Help me be a storm watcher."

"I can do that."

"Thanks."

"But first can we be movie watchers? Damien just ordered *Moulin Rouge* from Netflix. He's bringing it over, and the Twins managed to get their hands on some honest-to-God real chips and non-fat-free dip." She glanced at her Elvis clock. "They're probably downstairs right now pissed because they've been waiting for us."

I loved the fact that I could unload what felt like earth-shattering stuff to Stevie Rae and one second she could be "ohmygoodness-ing" and the next talking about something as simple as movies and chips. She made me feel normal and grounded and like everything wasn't so overwhelming and confusing. I smiled at her. "*Moulin Rouge*? Doesn't that have Ewan McGregor in it?"

"Definitely. I hope we get to see his butt."

"You talked me into it. Let's go. And remember—"

"Jeesh! I know I know. Don't say anything about any of this to anyone." She paused and waggled her brows. "So just let me say it one more time. *Loren Blake has the hots for you!*"

"Are you done now?"

"Yeah." She grinned mischievously.

"I hope someone brought me some brown pop."

"You know, Z, you're weird about your brown pop."

"Whatever, Miss Lucky Charms," I said, pushing her out the door.

"Hey, Lucky Charms are good for you."

"Really? So, tell me, what are marshmallows—a fruit or a vegetable?"

"Both. They're unique—like me."

I was laughing at silly Stevie Rae and feeling better than I had all day when we trotted down the stairs and into the front area of the dorm. The Twins and Damien had staked out one of the big flat-screen TVs, and they waved us over. I could see Stevie Rae had been right, they were munching on real Doritos and dipping them in full-fatted green onion dip (it sounds gross, but it's really yummy). My good feeling got even better when Damien handed me a big glass of brown pop.

"Took you guys long enough," he said, scooting over so that we could sit by him on the couch. The Twins, naturally, had commandeered two identically big chairs they'd pulled over by the couch.

"Sorry," Stevie Rae said, and then added with a grin at Erin, "I had to have a bowel movement."

"Excellent use of proper descriptions, Stevie Rae," Erin said, looking pleased.

"Ugh, just put in the movie," Damien said.

"Hang on, I have the remote," Erin said.

"Wait!" I told her right before she clicked play. The volume had been turned down, but I could see Fox News 23's Chera Kimiko. Her face looked sad and serious as she talked earnestly into the camera. At the bottom of the screen ran the blurb *body of teenager found.* "Turn up the volume." Shaunee clicked off the mute.

"Repeating our lead story this morning: the body of the missing

Union running back, Chris Ford, was discovered by two kayakers late Friday afternoon. The body had become snagged in the rocks and sand barges used to dam the Twenty-first Street area of the Arkansas River to create the new recreational rapids. Sources tell us that the teenager died of loss of blood associated with multiple lacerations, and that he might have been mauled by a large animal. We'll have more on that for you after the official medical examiner's report is released."

My stomach, which had finally settled down and was acting normal, clenched. I felt my body go cold. But the bad news wasn't over. Chera's beautiful brown eyes looked earnestly into the camera as she continued.

"On the heels of this tragic news comes the report of another Union football player who has been listed as missing." The screen flashed a picture of another cute guy in Union's traditional red and white football uniform. *"Brad Higeons was last seen after school Friday at the Starbucks at Utica Square where he was posting pictures of Chris. Brad was not only Chris's teammate, he was also his cousin."*

"Ohmygoodness! The Union football team is dropping like flies," Stevie Rae said. She glanced at me and I saw her eyes widen. "Zoey, are you okay? You don't look so good."

"I knew him, too."

"That's weird," Damien said.

"The two of them were always at parties together. Everyone knew them because they're cousins, even though Chris is black and Brad is white."

"Makes perfect sense to me," Shaunee said.

"Ditto, Twin," Erin said.

I could barely hear them through the buzzing in my ears. "I . . . I need to go for a walk."

"I'll go with you," Stevie Rae said.

"No, you stay here and watch the movie. I just—I just need to get some air."

"Are you sure?"

"Positive. I won't be gone long. I'll be back in time to see Ewan's butt." Even though I could almost feel the worried look Stevie Rae was giving my back (and hear the Twins arguing with Damien about whether they would actually see Ewan's butt), I rushed out of the dorm and into the cool November night.

Blindly, I turned away from the main school building, instinctively moving in the opposite direction from anywhere I'd run into people. I forced myself to keep moving and to breathe. *What the hell was wrong with me?* My chest felt tight and my stomach was so sick I had to keep swallowing hard so I wouldn't puke. The buzzing in my ears seemed to be better, but there was no relief from the anxiety that had settled over me like a shroud. Everything inside me was screaming, *Something's not right! Something's not right! Something's not right!*

As I walked I gradually noticed that the night, which had been clear, with a sky full of stars helping the almost full moon to illuminate its thick darkness, suddenly had clouded up. The soft, cool breeze had turned cold, causing dry leaves to shower down around me, mixing the smells of earth and wind with the darkness . . . somehow this soothed me and the tumult of disjointed thoughts and anxiety lifted enough for me to actually think.

I headed to the stables. Lenobia had said that I could groom Persephone whenever I needed to think and be alone. I definitely needed that, and having a direction to go—an actual destination— was one small good thing in the midst of my internal chaos.

The stables were just ahead, sprawling long and low, and my breath had started to come a little easier when I heard the sound. At first I didn't know what it was. It was too muffled—too odd. Then I thought that it might be Nala. It was like her to follow me and complain at me in her weird old lady cat voice until I stopped and picked her up. I looked around and called "Kitty-kitty" softly.

The sound got more distinct, but it wasn't a cat, I could tell that. A movement close to the barn caught my eye, and I saw that a shape was slumped on the bench near the front doors. There was only one gaslight there, and it was right beside the doors. The bench was just outside the edge of the pool of flickering yellow light.

It moved again, and I could tell that the shape must be a person . . . or fledgling . . . or vampyre. It was sitting, but kinda hunched over, almost folded in on itself. The sound started again. This close I could hear that it was a weird wailing—like whoever was sitting there was in pain.

Naturally, I wanted to run in the opposite direction, but I couldn't. It wouldn't be right. Plus, I *felt* it—the knowledge within me that I could not leave. That whatever was happening on the bench was something I had to face.

I took a deep breath and approached the bench.

"Uh, are you okay?"

"*No!*" The word was an eerie, whispering explosion of sound.

"Can—can I help you?" I asked, trying to peer into the shadows and see who was sitting there. I thought I could see light-colored hair, and maybe hands covering a face . . .

"The water! The water is so cold and deep. Can't get out . . . can't get out."

She took her hands from her face then and looked up at me, but I already knew who it was. I'd recognized her voice. And I also recognized what was happening to her. I forced myself to approach her calmly. She stared up at me. Her face was covered with tears.

"Come on, Aphrodite. You're having a vision. I need to get you to Neferet."

"No!" she gasped. "No! Don't take me to her. She won't listen to me. She—she doesn't believe me anymore."

I remembered what Neferet had said earlier about Nyx withdrawing her gifts from Aphrodite. Why should I even mess with her at all? Who knew what was going on with Aphrodite? She was probably making some pathetic play for attention, and I didn't have time for this crap.

"Fine. Let's say I don't believe you either," I told her. "Stay here and have your vision or whatever. I have other things to worry about." I turned to head into the stable, and her hand snaked out, grabbing my wrist.

"You have to stay!" she said through chattering teeth. Obviously, she was having difficulty talking. "You have to hear the vision!"

"No, I do not." I pried her viselike fingers from my wrist. "Whatever's going on, it's about you—not me. You deal with it." This time when I turned I walked away more quickly.

But not quick enough. Her next words felt like she'd sliced them through me.

"You have to listen to me. If you don't your grandma will die."

CHAPTER NINE

"What in the hell are you talking about!" I rounded on her.

She was gasping in weird little panting breaths, and her eyes were starting to flutter. Even in the darkness I could see the whites in them beginning to show. I grabbed her shoulders and shook her.

"Tell me what you see!"

Clearly trying to control herself she nodded with a jerky little movement. "I will," she panted. "Just stay with me."

I sat beside her on the bench and let her grab my hand, not caring that she was squeezing so hard it felt like she was going to break something—not caring that she was my enemy and someone I'd never trust—not caring about anything except the fact that Grandma might be in trouble.

"I'm not going anywhere," I said grimly. Then I remembered how Neferet had prompted her. "Tell me what you see, Aphrodite."

"Water! It's awful . . . so brown and so cold. It's all confusion . . . can't—can't get the door of the Saturn open . . ."

I felt a horrible jolt. Grandma has a Saturn! She bought it because it was one of those ultra-safe cars that were supposed to be able to survive anything.

"But where's the car, Aphrodite? What water is it in?"

"Arkansas River," she panted. "The bridge—it collapsed."

Aphrodite sobbed, sounding terrified. "I saw the car in front of me fall and hit the barge. It's on fire! Those little boys . . . the ones who were trying to get truck drivers to honk as they passed . . . they're in the car."

I swallowed hard. "Okay, what bridge? When?"

Aphrodite's whole body suddenly tensed. "I can't get out! I can't get out! The water, it's . . ." She made a horrible noise that I swear sounded like she was being choked, and then she slumped back against the bench, her hand going limp in mine.

"Aphrodite!" I shook her. "You have to wake up. You have to tell me more about what you saw!"

Slowly, her eyelids moved. This time I didn't see the whites of her rolled back eyeballs, and when she opened them they looked like normal eyes. Aphrodite abruptly let go of my hand and shakily pushed her hair out of her face. I noticed it was damp, and that she was covered with sweat. She blinked a couple more times before meeting my eyes. Her gaze was steady, but I couldn't read anything except exhaustion in her expression or her voice.

"Good, you stayed," she said.

"Tell me what you saw. What happened to my grandma?"

"The bridge her car's on collapses and she crashes into the river and drowns," she said flatly.

"No. No, that won't happen. Tell me what bridge. When. How. I'll stop it."

Aphrodite's lips curled up in the hint of a smile. "Oh, you mean you suddenly believe my visions?"

Fear for Grandma was like a boiling pain inside me. I grabbed her arm and stood up, pulling her up with me. "Let's go."

She tried to jerk away from me, but she was too weak, I held on to her easily. "Where?"

"To Neferet, of course. She'll figure this crap out, and you'll damn sure talk to her."

"No!" she almost screamed. "I won't tell her. I swear I won't. No matter what, I'll say I don't remember anything except water and a bridge."

"Neferet will get this out of you."

"No she won't! She'll be able to tell that I'm lying, that I'm hiding something, but she won't be able to tell what. If you take me to her, your grandma will die."

I felt so sick I'd started to tremble. "What do you want, Aphrodite? Do you want to be leader of the Dark Daughters again? Fine. Take it back. Just tell me about my grandma."

A look of raw pain passed over Aphrodite's pale face. "You can't give it back to me, Neferet has to."

"Then what do you want?"

"I just want you to listen to me so that you know that Nyx hasn't abandoned me. I want you to believe that my visions are still real." She stared into my eyes. Her voice was low and strained. "And I want you to owe me. Someday you're going to be a powerful High Priestess, more powerful even than Neferet. Someday I may need protection, and that's when you owing me will come in handy."

I wanted to say that there was no way I could protect her from Neferet. Not now—maybe not ever. And I wouldn't want to. Aphrodite was messed up, and I'd already witnessed how selfish and hateful she could be. I didn't want to owe her; I didn't want anything to do with her.

I also didn't have any choice.

"Fine. I won't take you to Neferet. Now what did you see?"

"First give me your word that you owe me. And remember, this isn't an empty human promise. When vampyres give their word—be they fledgling or adult—it is binding."

"If you tell me how to save my grandma I give you my word that I will owe you a favor."

"Of my choice," she said slyly.

"Yeah, whatever."

"You have to say it to complete the oath."

"If you tell me how to save my grandma I give you my word that I will owe you a favor of your choice."

"So it is spoken; so it shall be done," she whispered. Her voice sent chills up my back, which I ignored.

"Tell me."

"I have to sit down first," she said. Suddenly shaky again, she collapsed onto the bench.

I sat beside her and waited impatiently while she collected herself. When she started to talk I felt the stark horror of what she was saying pass through me, and I knew deep within my soul that what she was telling was a true vision. If Nyx was pissed at Aphrodite, the Goddess wasn't showing it tonight.

"This afternoon your grandma will be on the Muskogee Turnpike on her way to Tulsa." She paused and cocked her head to the side, like she was listening in the wind for something. "Your birthday's next month. She's coming into town to get you a present."

I felt a jolt of surprise. Aphrodite was right. My birthday was in December—I had a sucky December twenty-fourth birthday, so I never got to really celebrate it. Everyone always wanted to mush it in with Christmas. Even last year, when I was turning sixteen and I should have had a big, cool party, I didn't get to do anything special. It was really annoying . . . I shook myself. Now was not the time to get lost in my lifelong birthday complaint.

"Okay, so she's coming into town this afternoon, and what happens?"

Aphrodite narrowed her eyes, like she was trying to see out into the darkness. "It's weird. I can usually tell exactly why these accidents happen—like a plane doesn't work or whatever, but this time I was so tuned in to your grandma, that I'm not sure why the bridge breaks." She glanced at me. "That might be because this is the first vision I've ever had where someone I recognize dies. It threw me off."

"She's not going to die," I said firmly.

"Then she can't be on that bridge. I remember the clock on her car's dashboard said three fifteen, so I'm sure it happens in the afternoon."

Automatically, I glanced at my watch—6:10 A.M. It'd be light in the next hour (and I should be going to bed), which meant that Grandma would be waking up. I knew her schedule. She woke up around dawn and went for a walk in the soft morning light. Then she came back to her cozy cabin and had a light breakfast before beginning whatever work needed to be seen to on her lavender farm. I'd call her and tell her to stay home, that she shouldn't even take a chance on driving anywhere today. She'd be safe; I'd make sure of it. Then another thought tickled at my mind. I looked at Aphrodite.

"But what about the other people? I remember you said something about some kids in the car in front of you, and that car crashed and caught on fire."

"Yeah."

I frowned at her. "Yeah, what?"

"Yeah, I was watching from your grandma's point of view and I saw a bunch of other cars crashing around me. It happened fast, though, so I couldn't really tell how many."

She didn't say anything else, and I shook my head in disgust. "What about saving them? You said little boys died!"

Aphrodite shrugged. "I told you my vision was confusing. I couldn't tell exactly where it was, and the only reason I knew when is because I saw the date and time on your grandma's dash."

"So you're just going to let the rest of those people die?"

"What do you care? Your grandma's going to be okay."

"You make me sick, Aphrodite. Do you care about anyone but yourself?"

"Whatever, Zoey. Like you're so perfect? I didn't hear you caring about anyone else except your grandma."

"Of course I was worried about her the most! I love her! But I don't want anyone else to die, either. And no one else is going to if I have anything to say about it. So, you need to figure out some way to let me know which bridge we're talking about."

"I already told you—it's on the Muskogee Turnpike. I can't tell which one."

"Think harder! What else did you see?"

She sighed and closed her eyes. I watched her face as her brow wrinkled and she seemed to cringe. With her eyes still closed she said, "Wait, no. It's not on the turnpike. I saw a sign. It's the I-40 bridge over the Arkansas River—the one that's right off the turnpike near Webber's Falls." Then she opened her eyes. "You know when and where. I can't tell you much more. I think some kind of flat boat, like a barge, hits the bridge, but that's all I know. I didn't see anything to identify the boat. So, how are you going to stop it?"

"I don't know, but I will," I muttered.

"Well, while you're thinking about how to save the world, I'm going to go back to the dorm and do my nails. Raggedy nails are something I consider tragic."

"You know, having crappy parents isn't an excuse to be heartless," I said. She'd turned away and I saw her pause. Her back got really straight and when she looked over her shoulder at me I could see that her eyes were narrowed in anger.

"What would you know about it?"

"About your parents? Not much except that they're controlling and your mom's a nightmare. About screwed-up parents in general? Plenty. I've been living with pain-in-the-ass parent issues since my mom remarried three years ago. It sucks, but it's not an excuse to be a bitch."

"Try eighteen years of a lot more than just 'pain-in-the-ass parent issues' and maybe you'll start to get something about it. Until then, you don't know shit." Then, like the old Aphrodite I knew and couldn't stand, she flipped her hair and stalked away, wiggling her narrow butt like I cared.

"Issues. The girl has major issues." I sat down on the bench and began rummaging through my purse for my cell phone, glad I carried it around with me even though I'd been forced to keep it on silent, without even vibrate on. The reason could be summed up in one word—Heath. He was my human almost-ex-boyfriend, and since he and my definitely ex-best friend, Kayla, had tried to "break me out" (that's actually what they'd said—morons) of the House of Night, Heath had been way over the top on his obsession level for me. Of course, that wasn't really his fault. I was the one who had tasted his blood and started the whole Imprint thing with him, but still. Anyway, even though his messages had dwindled down from like a zillion (meaning twenty or so) a day, to two or three, I still didn't feel like leaving my phone on and being bothered by him. And, sure enough, when I flipped it open there were two missed calls, both from Heath. No messages, though, so hopefully he's demonstrating the ability to learn.

Grandma sounded sleepy when she answered the phone, but as soon as she realized it was me she perked up.

"Oh, Zoeybird! It's so nice to wake up to your voice," she said.

I smiled into the phone. "I miss you, Grandma."

"I miss you, too, sweetheart."

"Grandma, the reason I called is kinda weird, but you're just going to have to trust me."

"Of course I trust you," she replied without hesitation. She's so different than my mom that sometimes I wonder how they could be related.

"Okay, later today you're planning on coming into Tulsa to do some shopping, right?"

There was a brief pause, and then she laughed. "I guess it's going to be hard to keep birthday surprises from my vampyre grand-daughter."

"I need you to promise me something, Grandma. Promise that you won't go anywhere today. Don't get in your car. Don't drive anywhere. Just stay home and relax."

"What's this about, Zoey?"

I hesitated, not sure how to tell her. Then with her lifelong ability to understand me, she said softly, "Remember, you can tell me anything, Zoeybird. I'll believe you."

I hadn't realized that I'd been holding my breath until that instant. On my let out breath I said, "The bridge on I-40 that goes over the Arkansas River by Webber's Falls is going to collapse. You were supposed to be on it, and you would have died." I said the last part softly, almost whispering.

"Oh! Oh, my! I'd better sit down."

"Grandma, are you okay?"

"I suppose I am now, but I wouldn't be if you hadn't warned me, which is why I'm feeling light-headed." She must have picked up a magazine or something because I could hear her fanning herself. "How did you find out about this? Are you having visions?"

"No, not me. It's Aphrodite."

"The girl who used to be leader of the Dark Daughters? I didn't think you two were friends."

I snorted. "We're not. Definitely not. But I found her having a vision and she told me what she saw."

"And you trust this girl?"

"No way, but I do trust her power, and I saw her, Grandma. It was like she was there, with you. It was awful. She saw you crash, and those little kids die . . ." I had to stop and breathe. The truth had suddenly caught up with me: my grandma could have died today.

"Wait, there were more people in the crash?"

"Yeah, when the bridge collapses a bunch of cars go into the river."

"But what about the other people?"

"I'm going to take care of that, too. You just stay home."

"Shouldn't I go to the bridge and try to stop them?"

"No! Stay away from there. I'll make sure no one gets hurt—I promise. But I have to know that you're safe," I said.

"Okay, sweetheart. I believe you. You don't have to worry about me. I'll be safe and sound at home. You take care of whatever you need to do, and if you need me, call. Anytime."

"Thanks, Grandma. I love you."

"I love you, too, *u-we-tsi a-ge-hu-tsa*."

After I hung up I spent a little while just sitting there, willing myself to stop shaking, but only a little while. A plan was already brewing in my head, and I didn't have time to freak out. I needed to get busy.

CHAPTER TEN

"So why can't we tell Neferet about this mess? All she'd have to do is make a few calls, like she did last month when Aphrodite had a vision about that plane going down at the Denver airport," Damien said, careful to keep his voice low. I'd hurried back to the dorm, huddled my group together, and given them the short version of Aphrodite's vision.

"She made me promise I wouldn't go to Neferet. The two of them are having some kind of weird fight."

"It's about time Neferet started seeing her as the bitch she is," Stevie Rae said.

"Hateful cow," Shaunee said.

"Hag from hell," Erin agreed.

"Yeah, well, what she is doesn't really matter. It's her visions and the people who are in danger of dying that matter," I said.

"I heard that her visions aren't really believable anymore because Nyx has withdrawn her favor from Aphrodite," Damien said. "Maybe that's why she made you promise not to go to Neferet, because this is all something she made up and she wants you to freak out and do something that will either embarrass you and make you look bad, or get you in trouble."

"I'd think that too if I hadn't watched her having the vision. She wasn't faking it, I'm sure of that."

"But is she telling you the whole truth?" Stevie Rae asked.

I thought about that for a second. Aphrodite had already admitted to me that she could withhold parts of her visions from Neferet. What made me think she wasn't doing that with me, too? Then I remembered the whiteness of her face, the way she had gripped my hand, and the fear in her voice as she joined my grandma in her death. I shivered.

"She was telling me the truth," I said. "You guys will just have to trust that my intuition is right." I looked at my four friends. None of them were happy about this, but I knew that each of them trusted me and that I could count on them. "So, here's the deal, I've already called my grandma. She won't be on that bridge, but a bunch of other people will. We need to figure out a way to save those other people."

"Aphrodite said that a bargelike boat hit the bridge causing it to collapse?" Damien asked.

I nodded.

"Well, you could pretend to be Neferet and do what she does, call whoever's in charge of the barge and tell them one of your students has had a vision of a tragedy. People listen to Neferet; they're scared not to. It's a well-known fact that her information has saved lots of human lives."

"I already thought about that, but it won't work because Aphrodite didn't see the boat clearly. She wasn't even sure it was a barge. So I have no way of knowing how to even begin contacting anyone about stopping it. And I can't pretend to be Neferet. It feels way wrong. I mean, talk about asking to get in trouble. You can't tell me that whoever I call won't call back with some kind of follow-up report to Neferet. Then all hell would break loose."

"Ugly scene," Shaunee said.

"Yeah, Neferet would find out that the hag had another vision, so your promise to keep it quiet would be broken," Erin said.

"Okay, so stopping the boat is out, and pretending to be Neferet is out. That leaves closing the bridge as our only option," Damien said.

"That's what I thought, too," I said.

"Bomb threat!" Stevie Rae said suddenly. We all looked at her.

"Huh?" Erin asked.

"Explain," Shaunee said.

"We call whoever those freaks who make bomb threats call."

"That could actually work," said Damien. "When there's a bomb threat in a building they always evacuate it. So it figures that if there's a bomb threat about a bridge, the bridge will be closed, at least until they find out the bomb threat is fake."

"If I call from my cell phone they won't be able to tell who I am, will they?" I asked.

"Oh, please," Damien said, shaking his head like I was a total moron. "Of course they can trace cell phones. This isn't the nineties."

"Then what do I do?"

"You can still use a cell. It just has to be a disposable one," Damien explained.

"You mean like a disposable camera?"

"Where have you been?" Shaunee asked.

"Who doesn't know about disposable cells?" Erin said.

"I don't," Stevie Rae said.

"Exactly," the Twins said together.

"Here"—Damien pulled a big dorky looking Nokia out of his pocket—"use mine."

"Why do you have a disposable?" I studied the phone. It looked fairly normal.

"I got it after my parents freaked about me being gay. Until I was Marked and came here it felt like they were grounding me for life from life. I mean, not that I really expected them to lock me in a closet somewhere, but it's good to be prepared. Since then I've made sure I always have one."

None of us knew what to say. It really sucked that Damien's parents were so psycho about him being gay.

"Thanks, Damien," I finally said.

"No problem. When you're done making the call be sure you turn it off and then give it back to me. I'll destroy it."

"Okay."

"And be sure you tell them that the bomb's planted under the waterline. That way they'll have to close the bridge long enough for them to send in divers to check it out."

I nodded. "Good idea. I'll tell them that the bomb's going to explode at three fifteen, which is the exact time Aphrodite saw on my grandma's dashboard clock when she crashed."

"I don't know how long these things take, but you should probably call about two thirty, that sounds like enough time for them to get out there and close the bridge, but not so much that they'll have time to figure out it's a fake threat, and let cars back on the bridge too soon," Stevie Rae said.

"Uh, guys," Shaunee said. "Who are you gonna call?"

"Hell, I don't know." I was feeling the stress settle around my shoulders and knew I was going to have a major headache very soon.

"Google it," Erin said.

"No," Damien said quickly. "We don't want any kind of computer trail. You just need to call the local branch of the FBI. That'll be in the phone book. They'll do whatever it is they do when freaks call."

"Like track them down and put them in jail for the rest of eternity," I muttered gloomily.

"No, they're not going to catch you. You're not leaving any

kind of a trail. They'll have no reason to think it's any of us. Call at about two thirty. Tell them you've planted a bomb under the bridge because . . ." Damien hesitated.

"Because of pollution!" Stevie Rae chirped.

"Pollution?" Shaunee said.

"I don't think it should be because of pollution. I think it should be because you're sick and tired of government interference in the private sector's lives," Erin said.

I just blinked at her. What the hell did she just say?

"Excellent point, Twin," Shaunee said.

Erin grinned. "I sounded just like my dad when I said that. He'd be proud. Well, not about the pretending to blow up a bridge part, but the other stuff, yeah."

"We understand, Twin," Shaunee said.

"I still like saying that it's because you're tired of pollution. Pollution's a real problem," Stevie Rae said stubbornly.

"Okay, how about I say it's because of government interference *and* pollution in our rivers? That'll be the reason the bomb's on a bridge." They looked at me with blank expressions. I sighed. "Because of pollution in the river."

"*Ohhh,*" they said.

"We'd make dorky terrorists," Stevie Rae said with a giggle.

"I think that's actually a good thing," Damien said.

"So we're in agreement? I call the FBI, and we all keep our mouths shut about Aphrodite's vision."

They nodded.

"Good. Okay. Guess I'll find a phone book and look up the number for the FBI, and then—"

A movement caught at the corner of my vision, and I glanced up to see Neferet escorting two men in suits into the dorm. Everyone went instantly silent, and I heard a whisper of *"They're human . . . "* begin to buzz through the room. Then I didn't have time to think or to listen, because it was obvious that Neferet and the two human men were walking directly over to me.

"Ah, Zoey, there you are." Neferet smiled at me with her usual warmth. "These gentlemen need to speak with you. I believe we can step into the library. This shouldn't take more than a moment." Neferet regally gestured for the suits and me to follow her as she swept from the big main room (with everyone gawking openmouthed at us) to the little side room we called the dorm library, but was actually more of a computer room with some comfortable chairs and a few shelves filled with paperbacks. There were only two girls at the row of computers, and with a quick command Neferet got rid of them. They scurried out and she closed the door behind them, then she turned to face us. I glanced at the clock over the computer. It was 7:06 A.M. on Saturday morning. What was going on?

"Zoey, this is Detective Marx"—she pointed at the taller of the two men—"and Detective Martin from the homicide division of the Tulsa Police Department. They wanted to ask you a few questions about the human boy who was killed."

"Okay," I said, wondering what kind of questions they could possibly want to ask me. Hell, I didn't know anything. I hadn't even known him that well.

"Miss Montgomery," Detective Marx began, but he was cut neatly off by Neferet.

"Redbird," she said.

"Ma'am?"

"Zoey legally changed her last name to Redbird when she became an emancipated minor upon entrance to our school last month. All of our students are legally emancipated. We find it helpful with the unique nature of our school."

The cop gave a short nod. I couldn't tell whether he was annoyed or not, but I guessed by the way he kept looking at Neferet the answer was not.

"Miss Redbird," he continued, "we have received information that you are acquainted with Chris Ford and Brad Higeons. Is this true?"

"Yeah, I mean yes," I hastily corrected. Clearly this wasn't a good time to sound like a silly teenager. "I know . . . well, *knew* both of them."

"What do you mean by *knew*?" Detective Martin, the shorter cop, said sharply.

"Well, I mean that I don't hang out with human teenagers anymore, but even before I was Marked I didn't see Chris or Brad much." I wondered what he was so uptight about, and then I realized that because Chris was dead and Brad was missing that my talking about them in the past tense probably sounded really bad.

"When was the last time you saw the two boys?" Marx asked.

I chewed my lip, trying to remember. "Not for months—since the beginning of football season, and then I just went to maybe two or three parties and they were there, too."

"So you weren't with either boy?"

I frowned. "No. I was kinda dating the Broken Arrow quarterback. That's the only reason I knew any of those Union guys." I smiled, trying to lighten things up. "People think Union players hate BA players. It's not really true. Most of them grew up together. A bunch of them are still friends."

"Miss Redbird, you've been at the House of Night for how long?" the short cop asked as if I hadn't tried to be pleasant.

"Zoey has been with us for almost exactly one month," Neferet answered for me.

"And in that month did either Chris or Brad visit you here?"

Totally surprised, I said, "No!"

"Are you saying no human teenagers have visited you here at all?" Martin fired the question quickly.

Caught off guard I sputtered like a moron and I'm sure looked completely guilty. Thankfully, Neferet saved me.

"Two friends of Zoey's did see her during her first week here, although I do not believe you'd call it an official visit," she said with a smooth, adult smile aimed at the detectives that clearly said *kids will be kids.* Then she nodded encouragement at me. "Go ahead and tell them about your two friends who thought it'd be fun to scale our walls."

Neferet's green eyes locked on mine. I'd told her all about Heath and Kayla climbing the wall with the ridiculous idea of busting me out. Or at least that had been Heath's idea. Kayla, my *ex*-best friend, had just wanted me to see that she'd staked a claim on Heath. I'd told Neferet all of that, and more. How I'd kinda accidentally tasted Heath's blood—until Kayla had caught me and totally lost her mind. Staring into Neferet's eyes I knew as sure as if she'd said the words aloud that I was to keep the little blood-tasting incident to myself, which was more than okay with me.

"There really wasn't much to it, and it was a whole month ago. Kayla and Heath thought they'd sneak in and bust me out." I paused to shake my head like I thought they were totally crazy, and the tall cop jumped in with, "Kayla and Heath who?"

"Kayla Robinson and Heath Luck," I said. (Yeah, Heath's last name really is Luck, but the only thing he was particularly lucky about is not getting picked up DUI.) "Anyway, Heath is kinda slow sometimes, and Kayla, well, Kayla's really good at shoes and hair, but not so good at common sense. So they hadn't really thought out the whole 'Hey, she's turning into a vampyre and if she leaves the House of Night she'll die' issue. So I explained to them that not only did I not want to leave, I *couldn't* leave. And that was about it."

"Nothing unusual happened when you saw your friends?"

"You mean when I went back to the dorm?"

"No. Let me rephrase the question. Nothing unusual happened when you saw Kayla and Heath?" Martin said.

I swallowed. "No." Which wasn't actually a lie. Apparently it's not unusual for fledglings to experience a vampyre's bloodlust. I shouldn't so early in my Change, but my Mark shouldn't be filled in and I shouldn't have the added decorative tattooing of an adult vamp either. Not to mention the fact that no other fledgling or vamp had ever been Marked on the shoulder and back like I had. Okay, I'm not exactly a normal fledgling.

"You didn't cut the boy and drink his blood?" The short cop's voice was like ice.

"No!" I cried.

"Are you accusing Zoey of something?" Neferet said, stepping closer to me.

"No, ma'am. We're simply questioning her to try and get a clearer idea of the dynamics of the friends of Chris Ford and Brad Higeons. There are several aspects of the case that are rather unusual and . . ." The short cop rambled on and on while my mind raced.

What was going on? I hadn't cut Heath; I'd scratched him. And I hadn't done it on purpose. And "drinking" his blood wasn't exactly what I'd done—it was more like I lapped it up. But how the hell did they know anything about it? Heath wasn't very bright, but I didn't think he'd run around telling people (especially not detective people) that the chick he had the hots for drank blood. No. Heath wouldn't have said anything, but—

And I knew why they were asking me questions.

"There's something you should know about Kayla Robinson," I

said suddenly, interrupting the short cop's boring tirade. "She saw me kiss Heath. Well, actually *Heath* kissed *me*. She likes Heath." I looked from one cop to the other. "You know, she really *likes* Heath, as in wants to date him now that I'm out of the way. So when she saw him kiss me she got pissed and started yelling at me. Okay, I admit I didn't act very mature. I got pissed back at her. I mean, it's just wrong when your best friend goes after your boyfriend. Anyway"—I fidgeted, like I was embarrassed to admit what I was telling them—"I said some mean stuff to Kayla that scared her. She freaked out and left."

"What kind of mean stuff?" Detective Marx asked.

I sighed. "Something like if she didn't go away I'd fly off the wall and suck her blood."

"Zoey!" Neferet's voice was sharp. "You know that's inappropriate. We have enough problems with image without you frightening human teenagers on purpose. Little wonder the poor child spoke to the police."

"I know. I'm really sorry." Even though I understood Neferet was playing along with me, I still had to work at not cringing away from the power in her voice. I glanced up at the detectives. Both of them were staring at Neferet with wide, startled eyes. Huh. So, up until then she'd only shown them her gorgeous public face. They had no idea what kind of power they were dealing with.

"And you haven't seen either teenager since then?" the tall cop asked after an uncomfortable pause.

"Only once more, and then it was just Heath alone, during our Samhain Ritual."

"Excuse me, your what?"

"Samhain is the ancient name for a night you would probably best know as Halloween," Neferet explained. She was back to stunningly beautiful and kind, and I could understand why the cops looked confused, but they returned her smile as if they had no choice. Knowing Neferet's powers—they might not. "Go on, Zoey," she told me.

"Well, there were a bunch of us and we were having a ritual. Kinda like a church service outside," I explained. Okay, it was *nothing* like a church service outside, but no way was I going to explain circle-casting and calling the spirits of carnivorous dead vamps to a couple human cops. I glanced at Neferet. She nodded encouragement. I drew a deep breath and mentally edited the past as I talked. I knew it really didn't matter what I said. Heath didn't remember anything about that night—the night he'd almost been killed by the ghosts of ancient vampyres. Neferet had made sure that his memory had been totally and permanently blocked. All he knew was that he'd found me with a bunch of other kids and then passed out. "Anyway, Heath snuck into the ritual. It was really embarrassing, especially since . . . well . . . he was totally wasted."

"Heath was drunk?" Marx asked.

I nodded. "Yes, he was drunk. I don't want to get him in any trouble, though." I'd already decided not to mention Heath's unfortunate, and hopefully temporary, experimentation with pot.

"He's not in trouble."

"Good. I mean, he's not my boyfriend but he's basically a good guy."

"Don't worry about it, Miss Redbird, just tell us what happened."

"Nothing really. He crashed our ritual, and it was embarrassing. I told him to go home and not come back, that we were through. He made a fool out of himself and then passed out. We left him there, and that was it."

"You haven't seen him since?"

"No."

"Have you heard from him in any way?"

"Yeah, he calls way too much and leaves annoying messages on my cell. But that's getting better," I added hastily. I really didn't want to get him into trouble. "I think he's finally getting it that we're through."

The tall cop finished taking some notes, and then he reached into his pocket and pulled out a plastic bag that had something in it.

"And how about this, Miss Redbird? Have you ever seen this before?"

He handed me the bag and I realized what was in it. It was a silver pendant on a long black velvet ribbon. The pendant was in the shape of two crescent moons back-to-back against a full moon encrusted with garnets. It was the symbol of the triple Goddess—mother, maiden, and crone. I had one just like it because it was the necklace that the leader of the Dark Daughters wore.

CHAPTER ELEVEN

"Where did you get this?" Neferet asked. I could tell she was trying to keep her voice under control, but there was a powerful, angry edge to it that was impossible to hide.

"This necklace was found near Chris Ford's body."

My mouth opened, but I couldn't seem to say anything. I knew my face had gone pale, and my stomach clenched painfully.

"Do you recognize the necklace, Miss Redbird?" Detective Marx repeated his question.

I swallowed and cleared my throat. "Yes. It's the leadership pendant of the Dark Daughters."

"Dark Daughters?"

"The Dark Daughters and Sons is an exclusive school organization, made up of our finest students," Neferet said.

"And you belong to this organization?" he asked.

"I'm its leader."

"So you wouldn't mind showing us your necklace?"

"I—I don't have it with me. It's in my room." Shock was making my head feel woozy.

"Gentlemen, are you accusing Zoey of something?" Neferet said. Her voice was quiet, but the thread of outraged anger that ran through it brushed against my skin, causing my flesh to prickle and rise. I could see from the nervous glance the detectives shared that they felt it, too.

"Ma'am, we're simply questioning her."

"How did he die?" My voice was faint, but it sounded abnormally loud in the tense silence that surrounded Neferet.

"From multiple lacerations and loss of blood," Marx said.

"Someone cut him with a switchblade or something?" On the news they'd said that Chris had been mauled by an animal, so I already knew the answer to the question, but I felt compelled to ask.

Marx shook his head. "The wounds were like nothing a knife would leave. They were more like animal scratches and bites."

"His body was almost entirely drained of blood," Martin added.

"And you're here because this appears to be a vampyre attack," Neferet said grimly.

"We're here looking for answers, ma'am," Marx said.

"Then I suggest you do a blood alcohol content test on the human boy. Just from the little I know about the group of teenagers the boy had as friends, they are habitual drunks. He probably got intoxicated and fell into the river. The lacerations were more than likely made by rocks, or perhaps even animals. It's not uncommon for coyotes to be found along the river, even within Tulsa city limits," Neferet said.

"Yes, ma'am. Tests are being performed on the body. Even drained of blood, it will still tell us many things."

"Good. I'm sure one of the many things it will tell you is that the human boy was drunk, perhaps even high. I think you should look to more reasonable causes for this death than a vampyre attack. Now, I assume you're done here?"

"One more question, Miss Redbird," Detective Marx asked me without looking at Neferet. "Where were you Thursday between eight and ten o'clock?"

"In the evening?" I asked.

"Yes."

"I was at school. Here. In class."

Martin gave me a blank look. "School? At that time?"

"Perhaps you should do your own homework before questioning my students. Classes at the House of Night begin at eight P.M. and go till three A.M. Vampyres have long preferred the night." The dangerous edge was still in Neferet's voice. "Zoey was in class when the boy died. *Now* are we finished?"

"For the time being we are finished with Miss Redbird." Marx flipped a couple pages back in the little notebook he'd been writing in before he added, "We do need to speak with Loren Blake."

I tried not to react to Loren's name, but I know my body jumped and I felt my face heat up.

"I'm sorry, Loren left yesterday before dawn on the school's private jet. He has gone to our East Coast school to support our students who are in the final round of our international Shakespearean monologue contest. But I can certainly give him a message to call you when he returns Sunday," Neferet said while she walked toward the door, clearly dismissing the two men.

But Marx hadn't moved. He was still watching me. Slowly he reached into his inside jacket pocket and pulled out a business card. Handing it to me he said, "If you think of anything—anything at all—that you believe might help us find who did this to Chris, call me." Then he nodded at Neferet. "Thank you for your time, ma'am. We'll be back Sunday to talk with Mr. Blake."

"I'll see you out," Neferet said. She squeezed my shoulder, and breezed by the two detectives, leading them from the room.

I sat there trying to collect my tumbling thoughts. Neferet had lied, and not just by omission about me drinking Heath's blood and Heath almost getting killed during the Samhain ritual. She'd lied about Loren. He hadn't left the school yesterday before dawn. At dawn he'd been at the east wall with me.

I clutched my hands together to try to keep them from shaking.

I didn't get to sleep until almost 10:00 (as in the A.M.). Damien, the Twins, and Stevie Rae wanted to know everything about the detectives' visit, and telling them was cool with me. I thought going back over the details might give me a clue about what the hell was going on. I was wrong. No one could figure out why a Dark Daughters' leadership necklace had been with a human kid's dead body. Yes, I checked and mine was still safely in my jewelry box. Erin, Shaunee, and Stevie Rae all thought that somehow Aphrodite was behind the cops getting the necklace and maybe even the killing. Damien and I weren't so sure. Aphrodite couldn't stand humans, but to me that didn't equate to kidnapping and killing a very built football player who couldn't exactly be hidden in her lovely Coach purse. She definitely didn't hang out with humans. And, yes, she used to have a Dark Daughters leadership necklace, but Neferet had taken it from her and given it to me the night I became the leader of the Dark Daughters and Sons.

Besides the mystery of the necklace, all we could figure was that "Stank Bitch Kayla" (as the Twins called her) had basically told the cops that I was the killer because she was jealous that Heath was still crazy about me. Obviously the cops didn't have any real suspects if they rushed over here on the word of a jealous teenager. Of course my friends didn't know anything about the blood-drinking issue. I still couldn't bring myself to tell them that I drank (lapped, whatever) Heath's blood. So I'd given them the same edited version I'd told the detectives. The only people who knew the real story about the blood thing (besides Heath and Stank Bitch Kayla) were Neferet and Erik. I'd told Neferet, and Erik had found me right after I'd had the big scene with Heath, so he knew the truth. Speaking of—I suddenly wanted Erik to hurry and get back to school. I'd been so busy lately that I hadn't actually had time to miss him, or at least I hadn't until today when I wished that there was someone who wasn't High Priestess I could talk to about what was going on.

Sunday, I reminded myself as I tried to fall asleep. Erik would be back Sunday. The same day Loren would be back. (No, I wouldn't think about the stuff that might be going on between Loren and me, and how that was part of the "busyness" that had kept me from missing Erik.) And why the hell did the detectives need to talk to Loren anyway? None of us could figure that out.

I sighed and tried to relax. I really hated needing to fall asleep and not being able to. But I couldn't shut off my mind. Not only was the Chris Ford/Brad Higeons mess going round and round in my head, but pretty soon I'd have to call the FBI and pretend to be a terrorist. Add to that the fact that I'd hardly thought about the circle I needed to cast and the Full Moon Ritual I was supposed to lead, and it was no wonder I had a horrible tension headache.

I glanced at the alarm clock. It was 10:30 A.M. Four more hours before I needed to get up and call the FBI, and then try to figure out how to get through the day while I waited to hear news about the bridge accident (hopefully that it was averted), and news about the Higeons kid being found (hopefully alive), and tried to figure out how I'd lead the Full Moon Ritual (hopefully without totally embarrassing myself).

Stevie Rae, who I swear could fall asleep standing on her head in the middle of a blizzard, snored softly across the room. Nala was curled up beside my head on my pillow. Even she'd stopped complaining at me and was breathing deeply with her weird cat snores. I worried briefly if I should have her checked out for allergies. She did sneeze an awful lot. But I decided I was just obsessively adding to my stress level. The cat was as fat as a Butterball turkey. I mean, her tummy looked like she had a pouch and could hide a herd of baby kangaroos in there. That's probably why she wheezed. Carrying around all that cat fat couldn't be easy.

I closed my eyes and started counting sheep. Literally. It was supposed to work. Right? So I made up a field in my head with a gate and had cute fuzzy white sheep start jumping over the gate. (I think that's the proper way to count sleep sheep. Sleep sheep . . . hee hee.) After sheep number 56 the numbers started to blur in my mind and I finally slipped into a fitful dream where I noticed the sheep were wearing Union's red and white football uniform. They had a shepherdess directing them over the gate they were jumping (which now looked like a mini-goalpost). My dreaming self was floating gently above the sheep scene like I was a superhero. I couldn't see the shepherdess's face, but even from the back I could tell she was tall and beautiful. Her auburn hair was waist length. As if she could feel me watching, she turned toward me and her moss green eyes looked up at me. I grinned. Of course Neferet was in charge, even if it was just a dream. I waved at her, but instead of responding, Neferet's eyes narrowed dangerously and she suddenly spun around. Snarling like a wild animal, she grabbed a football-playing sheep, lifted it, and in one practiced motion slashed its throat with her abnormally strong, talonlike fingernails, burying her face in the animal's bleeding throat. My dreaming self was horrified as well as freakishly drawn to what Neferet was doing. I wanted to look away, but I couldn't . . . wouldn't . . . then the sheep's body began to shimmer, like heat waves rising from a boiling pot. I blinked and it wasn't a sheep anymore. It was Chris Ford, and his dead eyes were wide open, set and staring at me accusingly.

I gasped in horror and tore my gaze from his blood, meaning to look away from the gory dream scene, but my vision got trapped because it was no longer Neferet who was feeding at Chris's throat. It was Loren Blake, and his eyes were smiling up at me over the river of red. I couldn't look away. I stared and stared and . . .

My dreaming body shivered as a familiar voice drifted in the air around me. At first the whisper was so soft I couldn't hear it, but as Loren drank the last drop of Chris's blood the words became audible as well as visible. They danced in the air around me with a silver light that was as familiar as the voice.

. . . *Remember, darkness does not always equate to evil, just as light does not always bring good.*

My eyelids jerked open and I sat up, breathing hard. Feeling shaky and slightly sick to my stomach, I looked at my clock: 12:30. I stifled a groan. I'd only slept for two hours. No wonder I felt so crappy. Quietly I went into the bathroom I shared with Stevie Rae to splash water on my face and try to wash away my grogginess. Too bad washing away the awful foreboding feeling the bizarre dream had given me wasn't as easy.

No way was I going to be able to sleep now. I walked listlessly over to our heavily curtained window and peeked out. It was a gray day. Low clouds obscured the sun and a light, constant drizzle made everything look blurred. It matched my mood perfectly, and it also made the daylight bearable. How long had it been since I'd gone outside during the day anyway? I thought about it and realized that I hadn't seen more than an occasional dawn in a good month. I shivered. And suddenly I couldn't stay inside for another instant. It felt claustrophobic, tomblike, *coffinlike.*

I went into the bathroom and opened the little glass jar that held the concealer that completely covered fledgling tattoos. When I'd first arrived at the House of Night I'd had a mini-panic attack when I'd realized that until I entered the school grounds, I'd never seen a fledgling. I mean ever. Naturally, I thought that meant that the vamps kept fledglings locked inside the walls of the school for four years. It didn't take long to find out the truth: fledglings had quite a bit of freedom, but if they chose to go outside the school walls they needed to follow two very important rules. First, they had to cover their Mark and not wear anything that bore any of the distinctive class insignias.

Second (and, to me, most important), once a fledgling entered the House of Night, he or she must stay in close proximity with adult vamps. The Change from human to vampyre was a bizarre and complex one—not even today's cutting-edge science completely understood it. But one thing was certain about the Change, if a fledgling was cut off from contact with adult vampyres, the process escalated and the teenager died. Every time. So, we could leave the school for shopping and whatnot, but if we stayed away from the vamps for more than a few hours our bodies would begin the rejection process and we'd die. It was no wonder that before I'd been Marked I thought I'd never seen a fledgling. I probably had, but (a) he/she/they had had all Marks covered, and (b) he/she/they understood that they couldn't just loiter about like typical teenagers. They'd been there, but they'd just been busy and disguised.

The reason for the disguise made sense, too. It wasn't about wanting to hide amid humans and spy or whatever ridiculous things humans would assume. The truth was that humans and vampyres coexisted in an uneasy state of peace. Broadcasting that fledglings actually left the school and went shopping and to the movies like normal kids was asking for trouble and exaggeration. I could just imagine what people like my horrid step-loser would say. Probably that vamp teenagers were hanging out in gangs, engaging in all sorts of sinful juvenile delinquent behavior. He was such an ass. But he wouldn't be the only human adult who freaked. Clearly the vamp rules made sense.

Resolutely, I stared, patting the concealer on the sapphire Marks that told the world what I was. It was amazing how well the stuff covered up Marks. As my darkened-in crescent moon disappeared, along with the small network of blue spirals that framed my eyes, I watched the old Zoey reappear and wasn't quite sure how I felt about her. Okay, I knew there'd been a lot more changed within me than a few tattoos could represent, but the absence of Nyx's Mark was shocking. It gave me a weird, unexpected sense of loss.

Looking back, I should have listened to my internal hesitation, scrubbed my face, grabbed a good book, and gone directly back to bed.

Instead, I whispered, "You look really young," to my reflection, and pulled on my jeans and a black sweater. Then I rummaged (quietly—if I woke up Stevie Rae or Nala no way would I get out of there alone) through my dresser drawers until I found my old *Borg Invasion 4D* hoodie and put it on, along with my comfy black Pumas, and with my OSU trucker's hat securely on my head and my cool Maui Jim sunglasses I was ready. Before I could (wisely) change my mind, I grabbed my purse and tiptoed out of the room.

No one was in the main room of the dorm. I opened the door and took a deep breath to steady myself before I walked outside. The whole vampyres-burst-into-flames-if-sun-touches-them thing was a ridiculous lie, but it is true that daylight causes adult vamps pain. As a fledgling who was weirdly "advanced" in the Change process, it's definitely uncomfortable for me, but I gritted my teeth and stepped out into the drizzle.

The campus looked totally deserted. It was weird not to pass one student or vamp all along the sidewalk that wound around behind the main building (which still reminded me of a castle) to the parking lot. My vintage 1966 VW Bug was easy to find amid the slick, expensive cars the vamps preferred. Its dependable engine sputtered for only a second, then it turned over and hummed like it was brand-new.

I tapped the garage door opener-like keypad that Neferet had given me after Grandma had brought my car to me. The wrought-iron gate to the school swung open silently.

Despite the fact that even the weak, foggy daylight bothered my eyes and made my skin feel twitchy, my mood lightened as soon as I was outside the school gates. It's not that I hated the House of Night or anything like that. Actually, the school and my friends there had become my home and family. It was just that today I needed something more. I needed to feel normal again—normal as in pre-Marked Zoey, when my biggest worry was geometry class and the only "power" I had was the eerie ability to find cute shoes on sale.

Actually, shopping sounded like a good idea. Utica Square was less than a mile down the street from the House of Night, and I loved the American Eagle store there. My wardrobe had, tragically, become overstocked in dark colors like purple, black, and navy since I'd been Marked. A bright red sweater was exactly what I needed.

I parked in the less used lot behind the row of stores that American Eagle sat in the middle of. The trees in this lot were bigger, so I liked the shade, along with the fact that there were fewer people in the back lot. I know my reflection showed a normal teenage kid, but inside I was still Marked, and more than a little nervous about my first daylight trip into my old world.

Not that I expected to run into anyone I knew. I was the one

my high school friends had called "weird" and "out there" because I liked to shop in the chic midtown stores versus the loud,
boring, food court–smelling mall. Grandma Redbird was responsible for my out-of-the-ordinary tastes. She used to call it "field-
tripping" when she'd take me all over Tulsa on fun day trips. No
way was I going to run into Kayla and the Broken Arrow crowd at
Utica, and pretty soon the familiar smells and sights of American
Eagle were working their retail magic on me. By the time I paid
for the totally cute red knit sweater my stomach had quit hurting,
and despite the fact that it was the middle of the day and I was
sleep-deprived, my headache was gone, too.

But I was starving. There was a Starbucks across the street
from American Eagle. It was on the corner that framed a pretty,
shady courtyard in the middle of the square. With the wet, dreary
day I would bet no one would be sitting at the little iron tables on
the wide, tree-lined sidewalk. I could get a yummy cappuccino,
one of their mega-big blueberry muffins, a copy of the *Tulsa
World*, and sit outside and pretend like I was a college kid.

It seemed like a seriously good plan. I was totally right—there
was no one sitting in the outside tables, and I snagged the one
closest to the big magnolia tree and set about putting the proper
amount of raw sugar in my cappuccino as I nibbled at my
mountain-sized muffin.

I don't remember when I first felt his presence. It started subtly,
like a weird itch under my skin. I moved restlessly in my chair,
trying to concentrate on the movie page and thinking that maybe
I could talk Erik into checking out the latest chick flick next
weekend . . . But I couldn't pay attention to the movie reviews.
The annoying, under-my-skin feeling wouldn't go away. Completely irritated I glanced up and froze.

Heath was standing under a streetlight not fifteen feet away
from me.

CHAPTER TWELVE

Heath was taping some kind of flyer to the light post. I could see his face clearly and it surprised me how handsome he looked. Okay, sure, I'd known him since third grade and watched him go from cute to gawky to cute to hot, but I'd never seen this look on him. His face was set in grim, nonsmiling lines that made him appear much older than eighteen. It was like I was catching a glimpse of the man he would turn into—and it was a nice glimpse. He was tall and blond, with high cheekbones and a really strong chin. Even from that distance I could see the thick eyelashes that were surprisingly dark, and knew the gentle brown eyes they framed.

And then, as if he could feel my gaze, his eyes slid from the light post and locked on me. I watched his body go completely still, and then a shudder ran through it, as if someone had blown freezing air across his skin.

I should have gotten up and retreated into Starbucks, where it was busy with clusters of people talking and laughing, and where it would be impossible for Heath and me to really be alone. But I didn't. I just sat there as he dropped the flyers. They fluttered around the sidewalk like dying birds as he walked quickly over to me. He stood across the little table without saying anything for what seemed like forever. I didn't know what to do, especially because I was unexpectedly nervous. Finally I couldn't stand the intense silence any longer.

"Hi, Heath."

His body jerked like someone had just jumped out from behind a door and scared the crap right outta him.

"Shit!" The word left his mouth in a rush of air. "You're really here!"

I frowned at him. He'd never been exactly brilliant, but even for him this sounded pretty dumb. "Of course I'm here. What did you think I was, a ghost?"

He dropped into the chair across from me as if his legs wouldn't hold him anymore. "Yes. No. I dunno. It's just that I see you a lot and you're never really there. I thought this was just another one of those times."

"Heath, what are you talking about?" I narrowed my eyes and sniffed in his direction. "Are you drunk?"

He shook his head.

"High?"

"No. I haven't had a drink in a month. I quit smoking then, too."

The words sounded simple, but I blinked and felt like I was trying to reason through mind mud. "You quit drinking?"

"And smoking. I quit it all. That's one of the reasons I've been calling you so much. I wanted you to know that I've changed."

I really didn't know what to say. "Oh, well. I'm, uh, glad." I know I sounded like a moron, but the way Heath's eyes were focused on me was almost a physical thing. And there was something else. I could smell him. It wasn't a cologne smell, or a sweaty guy smell. It was a deep, seductive scent that reminded me of heat and moonlight and sexy dreams. It was coming from his pores and it made me want to scoot my chair around the table so that I could be closer to him.

"Why didn't you return any of my calls? You didn't even text me back."

I blinked, trying to block the attraction I was feeling for him and think clearly. "Heath, there's no point. There can't be anything between you and me," I said reasonably.

"You know there's already something between us."

I shook my head and opened my mouth to explain to him how wrong he was, but he interrupted me.

"Your Mark! It's gone."

I hated his excited tone, and automatically snapped back, "You're wrong *again*. My Mark's not gone. It's just covered so the stupid humans around here won't freak out." I ignored the hurt look that seemed to take all the adultness out of his face and turn him back into that cute boy I used to be so crazy about. "Heath," I softened my voice. "My Mark will never go away. I'm either going to Change into a vampyre, or I'm going to die in the next three years. Those are my only two choices. I'll never be like I was. It can never be like it used to be between us." I paused, and then added gently, "I'm sorry."

"Zo, I get that. What I don't get is why any of that has to end things between us."

"Heath, things had ended between us before I was Marked, remember?" I said, exasperated.

Instead of his usual cocky comeback he kept looking into my eyes, and utterly sober and serious, said, "That's because I was acting like a jerk. You hated that I was getting drunk and high. And you were right. I was messing up. I've stopped that. Now I'm focusing on football and my grades so that I can get into OSU." He gave me the adorable, little-boy smile that's been melting my heart since third grade. "That's where my girlfriend will be going, too. She's gonna be a vet. A vampyre vet."

"Heath—I—" I hesitated, working hard to swallow back the

huge lump that was suddenly burning my throat and making me want to cry. "I don't know if being a vet is still what I want to do, and even if it is, that doesn't mean you and I can be together."

"You're seeing someone else." He didn't sound mad, he just sounded extremely sad. "I don't remember much from that night. I've tried, but whenever I think too hard about it, everything gets all jumbled up into one nightmare that doesn't make any sense and I get a really bad headache."

I sat very still. I knew he was talking about the Samhain Ritual he'd followed me to where Aphrodite had lost control of vampyre ghosts. Heath had almost been killed. Erik had been there, and as Neferet had said then, he had proven himself a warrior when he'd stayed by Heath's side and fought the specters, giving me time to cast my own circle and send the ghosts back to wherever it is they'd slithered away from. The last time I'd seen Heath he'd been unconscious and bleeding from multiple lacerations. Neferet had assured me that she would heal his wounds and fog his memory. Clearly, the fog had grown thin.

"Heath, don't think about that night. It's over and done with and better if—"

"You were there with someone," he interrupted me. "Are you going out with him?"

I sighed. "Yes."

"Give me a chance to get you back, Zo."

I shook my head, even though his words tugged at my heart. "No, Heath, it's impossible."

"Why?" He slid his hand across the table and put it on top of mine. "I don't care about the vampyre stuff. You're still Zoey. The same Zoey I've known forever. The Zoey who was the first girl I ever kissed. The Zoey who knows me better than anyone else on this earth. The Zoey I dream about every night."

His scent drifted up to me from his hand, hot and delicious, and I could feel his pulse thumping against my fingers. I didn't want to tell him, but I had to. I looked him straight in the eyes and said, "The reason you're not over me is because when I tasted your blood that time on the school wall I started to Imprint with you. So you want me because that's what happens when a vampyre, or apparently some fledglings, drink blood from a human victim. Neferet, our High Priestess, says that you haven't Imprinted all the way with me, and if I just stay away from you it'll fade and you'll be normal again and forget about me, so that's what I've been doing." I finished in a rush. I knew he'd probably freak out and call me a monster or something, but I really hadn't had a choice, and now that he knew he could put all of this in perspective and—

His laughter interrupted my mental tirade. He'd thrown back his head and was laughing with typical Heath exuberance, and the familiar, sweet, silly sound of it made it really hard for me not to smile at him.

"What?" I said, trying to frown.

"Oh, Zo, you crack me up." He squeezed my hand. "I've been crazy about you since I was eight. Like that had anything to do with you sucking my blood?"

"Heath, believe me, we've started to Imprint."

"I'm cool with that." He grinned at me.

"Will you also be cool with me outliving you by several hundred years?"

Dorklike, he wagged his eyebrows at me. "I can think of worse things than having a hot, young vampyre chic when I'm, like, fifty."

I rolled my eyes. He was such a guy. "Heath, it's not that simple. There're a lot of things to consider."

His thumb traced a circular pattern over the top of my hand. "You always did make things too complicated. There's you and me. That's all we need to consider."

"That's not all there is, Heath." A thought came to me and I lifted my brows and gave him a pretend-innocent smile. "Speaking of, how's my ex-best friend Kayla?"

Totally unaffected, he shrugged. "I dunno. I hardly ever see her anymore."

"Why not?" That was weird. Even if he wasn't dating Kayla, they'd hung out in the same group for years, we all had.

"It's not the same. I don't like the stuff she says." He wouldn't look at me.

"About me?"

He nodded.

"What has she been saying?" I couldn't decide if I was more hurt or pissed.

"Just stuff." He still wouldn't look at me.

I narrowed my eyes with realization. "She thinks I had something to do with Chris."

He moved his shoulders restlessly. "Not you, or at least she doesn't say you. She thinks it's vampyres, though, but so do a lot of people."

"Do you?" I asked softly.

His eyes shot back to mine. "No way! But something bad's happening. Someone's kidnapping football players. That's why I was here today. I'm taping up flyers with Brad's picture on them. Maybe someone will remember him being dragged away or something."

"I'm sorry about Chris." I laced my fingers through his. "I know you guys were friends."

"It sucks. I can't believe he's dead." He swallowed hard, and I knew he was trying not to cry. "I think Brad's dead, too."

I thought he was, too, but I couldn't say it out loud. "Maybe not. Maybe they'll find him."

"Yeah, maybe. Hey, Chris's funeral is Monday. Would you go with me?"

"I can't, Heath. Do you know what would happen if a fledgling showed up at the funeral of a kid people think was killed by a vampyre?"

"I guess it would be bad."

"Yes, it would be. And that's what I've been trying to make you see. You and me together—we'd have to deal with issues like that all the time."

"Not when we're out of school, Zo. Then you could wear that cover-up stuff you have on your face now, and no one would even know."

What he was saying probably should have pissed me off, but he was so serious, so sure that if I slapped a little concealer on my tattoos everything could go back to the way it was. And I couldn't be mad because I understood his wanting it. Wasn't that what I was doing there? Hadn't I been trying to relive part of my old life?

But this wasn't me anymore, and deep within me I didn't really want it to be. I liked the new Zoey, even if saying good-bye to the old Zoey wasn't only hard, it was a little sad, too.

"Heath, I don't want to cover my Mark. That wouldn't be who I am." I drew a deep breath and continued. "I've been Marked specially by our Goddess, and Nyx has given me some unusual powers. It would be impossible for me to pretend to be the human Zoey again, even if I wanted to. And, Heath, I don't want to."

His eyes searched my face. "Okay. We'll do it your way and say to hell with people who don't like it."

"That's not my way, Heath. I don't—"

"Wait, you don't have to say anything right now. Just think about it. We can meet here again in a few days." He grinned. "I'll even come at night."

It was a lot harder than I'd imagined to tell Heath that I'd never see him again. Actually, I hadn't imagined that I would have to have this talk with him. I'd thought we were over. Sitting here with him now felt weird—part normal, part impossible. Which actually described our relationship pretty well. I sighed and glanced down at our joined hands, and caught a look at my watch.

"Oh, shit!" I pulled my hand from his and grabbed my purse and my American Eagle bag. It was 2:15. I had to make that damn call to the FBI in fifteen minutes. "I gotta go, Heath. I'm really late for something at school. I'll—I'll call you later." I started to hurry away and wasn't really surprised that he came with me.

"No," he interrupted when I started to tell him to go away. "I'm walking you to your car."

I didn't argue with him. I knew that tone. As goofy and exasperating as Heath could be, his daddy had raised him right. Since third grade he'd been a gentleman, opening doors for me and carrying my schoolbooks, even when his friends called him a pussy-whipped dork. Walking me to my car was just part of what Heath did. Period.

My VW was sitting all alone under a big tree, just like when I'd parked it. As usual, he reached past me and opened my door. I couldn't help smiling at him. I mean, there was a reason I'd liked the kid for all these years—he really was sweet.

"Thanks, Heath," I said, and slid into the driver's seat. I was going to roll down the window and say bye to him, but he was already moving around the car and in about two seconds he was sitting in the passenger's seat grinning at me. "Uh, you can't come with me," I told him. "And I'm in a hurry, so I can't give you a ride anywhere."

"I know. I don't need a ride. I have my truck."

"Okay, well. Then bye. I'll call you later."

He didn't move.

"Heath, you have to—"

"I have to show you something, Zo."

"Can you show me quickly?" I didn't want to be mean to him,

but I really had to get back to the school and make that call. Why the hell hadn't I put Damien's disposable phone in my purse? I tapped the steering wheel impatiently while Heath put his hand in his jeans pocket and felt around for something.

"There it is. I started carrying this around a couple weeks ago, just in case." He pulled something that was about an inch long and flat out of his pocket. It was wrapped in what looked like folded cardboard.

"Heath, really. I gotta go and you . . ." My words faded as the breath left my body. He'd unwrapped the little thing. The blade caught the dim light and glittered seductively. I tried to speak, but my mouth had gone dry.

"I want you to drink my blood, Zoey," he said simply.

A shiver of terrible longing broke over my body. I was gripping the steering wheel with both hands to keep them from shaking . . . or reaching out and taking the razor blade and slicing it into his warm, sweet skin so that his delicious blood would drip and drip and . . .

"No!" I shouted, hating the way the power in my voice made him cringe. I swallowed and got control of myself. "Just put it away and get out of my car, Heath."

"I'm not scared, Zo."

"I am!" I almost sobbed.

"You don't have to be afraid. It's just you and me, like it's always been."

"You don't know what you're doing, Heath." I couldn't even look at him. I was scared if I did I wouldn't be able to keep saying no.

"Yes I do. You drank some of my blood that night. It was . . . it was incredible. I haven't been able to stop thinking about it."

I wanted to scream with frustration. I hadn't been able to stop thinking about it, either, no matter how hard I tried. But I couldn't tell him that. I wouldn't tell him that. Instead, I finally looked at him and forced my hands to relax. Just thinking about drinking his blood made my skin feel tight and hot. "I want you to go, Heath. This isn't right."

"I don't care about what people think is right, Zoey. I love you."

And before I could stop him, he lifted the razor blade and drew it down the side of his neck. Fascinated, I watched a thin line of scarlet spring up against the white of his skin.

Then the smell hit me—rich and dark and seductive. Like chocolate, only sweeter and wilder. In seconds the little car was thick with it. It drew me like nothing I'd ever experienced before. It wasn't just that I wanted to taste it. I needed to taste it. *I had to taste it.*

I hadn't even realized that I'd moved until Heath spoke, but suddenly I was leaning across the small space between our seats as his blood drew me to him.

"Yes. I want you to do it, Zoey." Heath's voice sounded deep and rough, like he was having a hard time controlling his breathing.

"I—I want to taste it, Heath."

"I know, baby. Go ahead," he whispered.

I couldn't stop myself. My tongue flicked out and licked the blood from his neck.

CHAPTER THIRTEEN

The taste exploded in my mouth. As my saliva touched the shallow wound his blood began to flow more quickly, and with a moan that I hardly recognized as my own, I opened my mouth and pressed my lips to his skin, licking up the delicious scarlet line. I felt Heath's arms go around me as mine wrapped around his shoulders so that I could hold him more firmly against my mouth. His head fell back and I heard him groan "yes." One of his hands cupped my butt and the other one went under my sweater to squeeze my breast.

His touch only made it better. Heat slammed through my body, setting me on fire. Like someone else was in control of my movements, my hand slid from Heath's shoulder, down his chest, to rub over the hard lump that was in the front of his jeans. I sucked on his neck. Rational thought flew from my mind. All I could do was feel and taste and touch. Somewhere in the depths of my mind I knew I was reacting on a level that was almost animalistic in its need and ferocity, but I didn't care. I wanted Heath. I wanted him like I'd never wanted anything in my life.

"Oh, God, Zo, *yes*," he gasped and his hips started to thrust in time with my hand.

Someone banged on the passenger's side window. "Hey! Y'all can't make-out here!"

The man's voice jolted through me, shattering the heat that had been building inside me. I caught a glimpse of a security guard's uniform, and started to lurch away from Heath, but he tucked my head down into the side of his neck and turned his body so that the guard, who was obviously standing right outside the passenger's door, couldn't see me very well, and so that the blood that was dripping steadily from Heath's neck was completely hidden.

"Did you kids hear me!" the guy bellowed. "Get out of here before I take your names and call your parents."

"No problem, sir," Heath yelled good-naturedly. Amazingly, he sounded perfectly normal, if a little breathless. "We're leaving."

"You better. I'm watching you two. Damn teenagers . . ." he grumbled as he stomped away.

"Okay, he's far enough away now that he can't see the blood," Heath said as he relaxed his hold on me.

Instantly I jerked back, pressing myself against the door, as far away from Heath as I could get. With shaking hands I zipped open my purse and fished out a Kleenex, handing it to him without touching him. "Press this against your neck so that it'll stop bleeding."

He did as I said.

I rolled down my window, clutched my hands together, and breathed deeply of the fresh air, trying to block the scent of Heath's body and Heath's blood from my mind.

"Zoey, look at me."

"I can't, Heath." I swallowed down the tears that burned in the back of my throat. "Please just leave."

"Not until you look at me and listen to what I have to tell you."

I turned my head and looked at him. "How the hell can you be so calm and normal-sounding?"

He was still pressing the Kleenex against his neck. His face was flushed and his hair was messed up. He smiled at me, and I didn't think I'd ever seen anyone look so absolutely adorable.

"Easy, Zo. Making-out with you is totally normal for me. You've been driving me crazy for years."

I'd had the whole I'm-not-ready-to-have-sex-with-you-yet conversation with him when I was fifteen and he was almost seventeen. He'd said then that he understood and was willing to wait—of course that didn't mean that we didn't do some heavy making-out—but what had just happened in the car had been different. It was hotter, rawer. I knew that if I allowed myself to continue seeing him I wouldn't be a virgin much longer, and not because Heath would pressure me into it. It would be because I couldn't control my bloodlust. The thought scared me almost as much as it fascinated me. I closed my eyes and rubbed my forehead. I was getting a headache. Again.

"Does your neck hurt?" I asked, peeking up at him through my fingers like I was watching a stupid slasher movie.

"Nope. I'm fine, Zo. You didn't hurt me at all." He reached over and pulled my hand from my face. "Everything'll be okay. Stop worrying so much."

I wanted to believe him. And, I suddenly realized, I also wanted to see him again. I sighed. "I'll try. But I really do have to go. I can't be late getting back to school."

He took my hand in his. I could feel the pulse of his blood, and knew it was beating in time with my own heart, like he and I had somehow become internally synchronized. "Promise me you'll call me," he said.

"I promise."

"And you'll meet me here again this week."

"I don't know when I can get away. During the week it's going to be hard for me."

I expected him to argue with me, but he just nodded and

squeezed my hand. "Okay, I get that. Living twenty-four seven at school is probably a pain in the ass. How about this: Friday we're playing Jenks at home. Could you meet me at Starbucks after the game?"

"Maybe."

"Will you try?"

"Yes."

He grinned and leaned over to give me a quick kiss. "That's my Zo! I'll see you Friday." He got out of the car and before he closed the door bent down and said, "I love ya, Zo."

As I drove away I could see him in my rearview mirror. He was standing in the middle of the parking lot, Kleenex still pressed to his neck, waving bye at me.

"You have no clue what you're doing, Zoey Redbird," I said aloud to myself as the gray sky opened and poured cold rain over everything.

It was 2:35 when I tiptoed back into our room. The fact that I was short on time was actually good. It didn't give me a chance to overthink what I had to do. Stevie Rae and Nala were still sound asleep. Actually, Nala had abandoned my empty bed and was curled up beside Stevie Rae's head on her pillow, which made me smile. (The cat was a notorious pillow hog.) Quietly I opened the top drawer on my computer desk and grabbed Damien's disposable phone, along with the slip of paper I'd scribbled the FBI's number on, and then went into the bathroom.

I took a couple deep, calming breaths, remembering Damien's advice: Keep it short. Sound a little angry, and kinda semi-crazy, but don't sound like a teenager. I dialed the number. When an official-sounding man answered, "Federal Bureau of Investigation. How may I help you?" I pitched my voice low and sharp, cutting off my words like I had to be careful to hold myself back because of the dam of hatred that was built up behind them (which is how Erin, with her suddenly and bizarrely unexpected political knowledge, described how I should pretend to feel). "I want to report a bomb." I kept talking, not giving him time to interrupt me, but speaking slowly and clearly because I knew I was being recorded. "My group, Nature's Jihad (Shaunee came up with our name), planted it just below the waterline on one of the pylons (a word Damien had come up with) of the bridge that crosses the Arkansas River on I-40 near Webber's Falls. It's set to go off at 1515 (using military time was another brilliant idea of Damien's). We're taking full responsibility for this act of civil disobedience (more Erin input, although she said terrorism is not actually civil disobedience, it's . . . well . . . terrorism, which is definitely different) protesting the U.S. government's interference in our lives and pollution in America's rivers. Be warned that this is only our first strike!" I hung up. Then I quickly flipped the scrap of paper over and punched in the phone number on the other side of it.

"Fox News Tulsa!" said the perky woman.

This part was actually my idea. I figured if I called a local news station we would have a better chance of having the threat reported quickly on the local news, and then we could keep an eye on the news and maybe even know when (or if) our attempt to get the bridge closed had been successful. I took another deep breath and then launched into the rest of the plan.

"A terrorist group known as Nature's Jihad has called the FBI with information that they've planted a bomb on the I-40 bridge over the Arkansas River by Webber's Falls. It's set to explode at three fifteen today." I made the mistake of pausing for a fraction of a second, and the woman, who was suddenly not so perky-sounding, said, "Who are you, ma'am, and where did you get this information?"

"Down with government intervention and pollution and up with the power of the people!" I yelled and then hung up. Immediately I pressed the power off button. Then my knees wouldn't hold me up any longer and I collapsed onto the closed toilet lid. I'd done it. I'd really done it.

Two soft knocks sounded against the bathroom door, followed by Stevie Rae's soft Oklahoma twang.

"Zoey? Are you okay?"

"Yeah," I said faintly. I forced myself to stand up and go to the door. I opened it to see Stevie Rae's rumpled face peering up at me like a sleepy, countrified rabbit.

"Did ya call 'em?" she whispered.

"Yeah, and you don't have to whisper. It's just you and me." Nala yawned and made a grumpy *mee-uf-ow* at me from the middle of Stevie Rae's pillow. "And Nala."

"What happened? Did they say anything?"

"Not after the 'hello FBI' part. Damien said I shouldn't give them a chance to talk, remember?"

"Did you tell them that we're Nature's Jihad?"

"Stevie Rae. We're *not* Nature's Jihad. We're just pretending to be."

"Well, I heard you yelling the down with the government and pollution thing, so I thought . . . maybe . . . actually I dunno what I thought. I guess I just got caught up in the moment."

I rolled my eyes. "Stevie Rae, I was just acting. The news lady asked me who I was and I guess I kinda freaked. And, yes, I told them everything we said I should. I just hope it works." I pulled off my hoodie and hung it on the back of a chair to dry.

Stevie Rae suddenly registered that my hair was wet and my Mark was covered, something I'd totally forgotten about in my hurry to make the phone calls. Hell.

"Did you go somewhere?"

"Yeah," I said reluctantly. "I couldn't sleep, so I went to the American Eagle at Utica and bought a new sweater." I pointed at the soggy American Eagle bag I'd tossed in the corner.

"You should have woken me up. I would have gone with you."

If she hadn't sounded so hurt I would have had more time to think about just exactly how much I was going to tell her about Heath before I blurted, "I ran into my ex-boyfriend."

"Ohmygood*ness*! Tell me everything." She plopped down on her bed, eyes shining. Nala grumbled and jumped from her pillow to mine. I got a towel and started to dry my hair.

"I was at Starbucks. He was taping up flyers with Brad's picture on them."

"And? What happened when he saw you?"

"We talked."

She rolled her eyes. "Come on—what else?"

"He's quit drinking and getting high."

"Wow, that's major. Isn't his drinking and smoking why you quit seeing him to begin with?"

"Yeah."

"Hey, what about Stank Kayla and him?"

"Heath says he's not seeing her because of the crap she's talking about vampyres."

"See! We were right about her being the reason those cops were here asking stuff about you," Stevie Rae said.

"Seems like it."

Stevie Rae was watching me way too closely. "You still like him, don't you?"

"It's not that simple."

"Well, actually, part of it is that simple. I mean, if you don't like him, that's pretty much it. You won't see him again. Simple," Stevie Rae said logically.

"I still like him," I admitted.

"I knew it!" She did a little bed bounce. "Man, you have like a zillion guys, Z. What are you gonna do?"

"I have not got one clue," I said miserably.

"Erik comes back from the Shakespeare competition tomorrow."

"I know. Neferet said that Loren went to support Erik and the rest of the kids from here, so that means he'll be back with them tomorrow, too. And I told Heath I'd go out with him Friday after the game."

"Are you going to tell Erik about him?"

"I dunno."

"Do you like Heath more than Erik?"

"I dunno."

"What about Loren?"

"Stevie Rae, I do not know." I rubbed at the headache that seemed to have firmly attached itself to me. "Can we just not talk about it for a while—at least until I get a little of this figured out."

"Okay. Let's go." She grabbed my arm.

"Where?" I blinked at her, totally confused. She'd gone from Heath to Erik to Loren and then to let's go way too fast.

"You need your Count Chocula fix, and I need my Lucky Charms. And we both need to watch CNN and the local news."

I started to shuffle to the door. Nala stretched, meowed grumpily, and then reluctantly followed me. Stevie Rae shook her head at both of us.

"Come on you two. Everything will seem better after you've had your Count Chocula."

"And brown pop," I said.

Stevie Rae screwed up her face like she just sucked a lemon. "For breakfast?"

"I have a feeling it's a brown-pop-for-breakfast kind of day."

CHAPTER FOURTEEN

Thankfully, we didn't have to wait long before we heard something. Stevie Rae, the Twins, and I were watching *The Dr. Phil Show* and at exactly 3:10 (Stevie Rae and I were on our second bowls of cereal and I was on my third brown pop) Fox News broke into the program with a Special Report.

"This is Chera Kimiko with breaking news. We have learned that shortly after two thirty this afternoon the Oklahoma branch of the FBI received a bomb threat from a terrorist group calling themselves Nature's Jihad. Fox News has discovered that the group claimed to have planted a bomb on the I-40 Arkansas River bridge not far from Webber's Falls. Let's go live to Hannah Downs for an update."

The four of us sat very still as we watched the camera shot take in the young reporter who was standing in front of a normal-looking highway bridge. Well, it was normal-looking except for the hordes of uniformed men who were swarming around it. I breathed a relieved sigh. The bridge was definitely closed.

"Thank you, Chera. As you can see the entire bridge has been closed by the FBI and local police, including Tulsa's ATF team. They're doing a thorough search for the alleged bomb."

"Hannah, have they found anything yet?" Chera asked.

"It's too early to tell, Chera. They just launched the FBI boats."

"Thank you, Hannah." The camera went back to the newsroom. "We'll keep you updated on this breaking story when we have more information on the alleged bomb, or on this new terrorist group. Until then, Fox returns you to . . ."

"A bomb threat. That was smart."

The words were spoken so softly and I was so focused on the TV that it took a second for Aphrodite's voice to register with me. When it did I looked up quickly. She was standing to my right, just a little behind the couch Stevie Rae and I were sitting on. I expected her face to be settled in its usual haughty sneer, so I was surprised when she nodded slightly, almost respectfully, at me.

"What do you want?" Stevie Rae's voice was uncharacteristically sharp, and I noticed that several girls who had been busy in their own little TV-watching groups up until then stopped what they were doing to look our way. By Aphrodite's instant change in expression, she noticed it, too.

"From an ex-refrigerator? Nothing!" she sneered.

I felt Stevie Rae stiffen beside me at the slur. I knew she hated the reminder that she had allowed Aphrodite and her inner group of Dark Daughters to use her blood in the ritual that had gone so totally wrong last month. Being used as a "refrigerator" was not a good thing—and being called one was an insult.

"Hey, hag bitch from hell," Shaunee said in a sweet, friendly tone. "That reminds us, seems the new Dark Daughters inner group—"

"Which would so be us and not you and your skanky friends," Erin inserted.

". . . Has an opening for a new refrigerator for the ritual tomorrow," Shaunee continued smoothly.

"Yeah, and since you're not shit anymore, the only way you'll get into the ritual is as that night's snack," Erin said. "Are you here to apply for the job?"

"If you are, sorry. There's no telling where you've been and we don't like nasty," Shaunee said.

"Bite me, bitch," Aphrodite snapped.

"Not even if you begged," Shaunee said.

"Ya ho," Erin finished.

Stevie Rae just sat there, looking pale and upset. I wanted to knock all their heads together.

"Okay, stop." They all shut up. I looked at Aphrodite. "Don't ever call Stevie Rae a refrigerator again." Then I turned to the Twins. "Fledglings being used during our rituals is one of the things I'm doing away with, so we won't need a kid to act as our sacrifice. Which means no one is going to be a snack." Okay, I hadn't actually yelled at the Twins, but they gave me identical looks of hurt and shock. I sighed. "We're all on the same side here," I said quietly, making sure my voice didn't carry to the obviously listening kids in the room. "So it would be nice if we could lose some of the bickering."

"Don't kid yourself. We're not on the same side—not even close." Then, with a laugh that was more like a snarl, she stalked off.

I watched her leave and just before she went out the front door she glanced back at me, met my eyes, and winked.

What was that about? She'd looked almost playful, like we were friends and just kidding around. But that wasn't possible. Was it?

"She gives me the creeps," Stevie Rae said.

"Aphrodite has issues," I said, and the three of them looked at me like I'd just said Hitler really hadn't been that bad. "You guys, I really want the new Dark Daughters to be a group that brings people together, not one that's stuck-up and so exclusive that only a few from a chosen clique can join." They just stared at me. "It was her warning that saved my grandma and several other people today."

"She only told you because she wants something from

you. She's hateful, Zoey. Don't ever think she's not," Erin said.

"Please do not tell me that you're thinking of letting her back into the Dark Daughters," Stevie Rae said.

I shook my head. "No. And even if I wanted to, which I *don't*," I added quickly, "according to my own new rules she doesn't qualify for membership. A Dark Daughter or Son has to uphold our ideals by her or his behavior."

Shaunee snorted. "No damn way that hag knows how to be authentic, faithful, wise, earnest, and sincere about anything except her own hateful plans."

"For world dominance," Erin added.

"And don't think they're exaggerating," Stevie Rae told me.

"Stevie Rae, she is not my friend. I just . . . I dunno . . ." I floundered, trying to put the instinct that so often whispered to me and goaded me to do, or not to do, things into words. "I guess I really do feel sorry for her sometimes. And I also think I understand her a little. Aphrodite just wants to be accepted, but she goes about it all wrong. She thinks manipulation and lies mixed with control can force people to like her. It's what she saw at home, and that's what made her like she is now."

"Sorry, Zoey, but that's bullshit," Shaunee said. "She's way too old to be acting a fool because she has a screwed-up mommy."

"Please. Just please with the blame-my-mommy-'cause-I'm-a-bitch crap," Erin said.

"Not to be mean or anything, but you have a screwed-up mama, too, Zoey, and you didn't let her, or your step-loser of a dad, mess you up," Stevie Rae said. "And Damien has a mama who doesn't like him anymore because he's gay."

"Yeah, and he didn't turn into a hateful slut hag," Shaunee said. "Actually, he's the opposite. He's like . . . he's like . . ." She paused, looking to Erin for help. "Twin, what's the Julie Andrews character's name in *The Sound of Music*?"

"Maria. And you're right, Twin. Damien is like that goody-goody nun. He needs to loosen up some or he's never gonna get any."

"I cannot believe you guys are discussing my love life," Damien said.

We all jumped guiltily and muttered, "*Sorry.*"

He shook his head while Stevie Rae and I scooted over so he could sit beside us. "And I'll have you know I don't just want to 'get some' as you guys so nastily put it. I want a lasting relationship with someone I really care about, and I'm willing to wait for that."

"Ja, fräulein," Shaunee whispered.

"Maria," Erin muttered.

Stevie Rae tried to hide her giggle in a cough.

Damien narrowed his eyes at the three of them. I decided that was my cue to talk.

"It worked," I said quietly. "They closed the bridge." I pulled his cell phone out of my pocket and gave it back to him. He checked to make sure it was off and nodded.

"I know, I saw the news and came right over." Damien glanced at the digital clock on the DVD player that sat in the entertainment center with the TV, then he grinned at me. "It's three twenty. We did it."

The five of us smiled at each other. It's true; I was relieved, but I still had a nagging worried feeling I couldn't seem to get rid of that was more than just the stress about Heath. Maybe I needed a fourth brown pop.

"Okay, well, that's taken care of. So why are we sitting around here talking about my love life?" Damien said.

"Or lack thereof," Shaunee whispered to Erin, who tried unsuccessfully (with Stevie Rae) not to laugh.

Ignoring them, Damien stood up and looked at me. "Well, let's go."

"Huh?"

He rolled his eyes heavenward and shook his head. "Must I do everything? You have a ritual to perform tomorrow, which means we have a rec hall to transform. Did you think Aphrodite was going to volunteer to get things set up for you?"

"I guess I hadn't thought about it." Like I'd had time?

"Well, think about it now." He yanked on my hand and pulled me to my feet. "We have work to do."

I grabbed my brown pop and we all followed the Damien whirlwind out into a very cold, cloudy Saturday afternoon. The rain had stopped, but the clouds were even darker.

"Looks like snow," I said, squinting up at the slate-colored sky.

"Oh, man, I wish. I'd love some snow!" Stevie Rae twirled around with her arms outstretched, looking like a little girl.

"Move to Connecticut. You'll have more snow than you can stand. It gets pretty damn tiresome after months and months of cold and wet. Please. It's why we northeasterners are so grumpy," Shaunee said pleasantly.

"I don't care what you say. You can't ruin it for me. Snow is magic. I think it makes the earth look like it has a fluffy white blanket pulled over it." She spread her arms wide and yelled, "I want it to snow!"

"Yeah, well, I want those four-hundred-fifty-dollar embroidered vintage jeans I saw in the new Victoria's Secret catalog," Erin said. "Which proves we can't always have what we want, snow or cool jeans."

"*Oooh*, Twin, maybe they'll go on sale. Those jeans are just too damn cute to give up on."

"So why don't you just take your favorite pair of jeans and see if you can reproduce the pattern yourself? I can't be that hard, you know," Damien said logically (and very gayly).

I was opening my mouth to agree with Damien when the first

snowflake plopped on my forehead. "Hey, Stevie Rae, your wish came true. It's snowing."

Stevie Rae squealed happily. "Yeah! Snow harder and harder!"

And she definitely got her wish. By the time we made it to the rec hall, fat, quarter-sized flakes of snow were covering everything. I had to admit that Stevie Rae was right. The snow was like a magic blanket on the earth. It turned everything soft and white, and even Shaunee (from grumpy, snowbound Connecticut) was laughing and trying to catch flakes with her tongue.

We were all giggling when we went into the rec hall. There were several kids inside. Some were playing pool, others were playing video games on the old-fashioned–looking arcade machines. Our laughing and brushing off snow made several of them stop what they were doing and pull back the thick black curtains that shielded the big room from daylight.

"Yep!" Stevie Rae yelled the obvious. "It's snowing!"

I just smiled and made my way toward the little kitchen area in the back of the building, with Damien, the Twins, and snow-crazed Stevie Rae following me. I knew there was a storage room off the kitchen, and inside was the stuff the Dark Daughters kept there for their rituals. Might as well get started setting things up, and I might as well pretend like I knew what the hell I was doing.

I heard the door open and then close behind me, and then was surprised by Neferet's voice.

"The snow is quite beautiful, isn't it?"

The kids standing around the windows answered Neferet with respectful yeses. I was surprised to feel a hint of annoyance, which I instantly squelched, as I stopped and turned to go back to greet my mentor. Like baby ducks, my gang followed me.

"Zoey, good. I'm glad I found you here." Neferet spoke with such obvious affection for me that the annoyance I'd felt at her interruption vanished. Neferet was more than my mentor. She was like a mother to me, and it was selfish of me to be irritated that she had come looking for me.

"Hi, Neferet," I said warmly. "We were just getting ready to set up the room for tomorrow night's ritual."

"Excellent! That's one thing I wanted to see you about. If you need anything for the ritual, please don't hesitate to ask. And I definitely will be here tomorrow night, but don't worry"—she smiled at me again—"I won't stay for the entire ritual—just long enough to show my support for your vision for the Dark Daughters. Then I'll leave the Daughters and Sons in your very capable hands."

"Thank you, Neferet," I said.

"Now, the second reason I wanted to find you and your friends"—she shared her brilliant smile with my group—"was that I wanted to introduce our newest student to you." She motioned, and a kid I hadn't noticed till then stepped slowly forward. He was cute, in a studious kind of a way, with tousled sandy blond hair and really pretty blue eyes. Clearly he was one of those geeky kids who is a dork, but a likable dork with potential (translation: he bathes and brushes his teeth, plus has good skin and hair and doesn't dress like a total loser). "I'd like all of you to meet Jack Twist. Jack, this is my fledgling, Zoey Redbird, leader of the Dark Daughters, and her friends and Prefect Council members, Erin Bates, Shaunee Cole, Stevie Rae Johnson, and Damien Maslin." Neferet gestured to each of them in turn, and there were "hi"s said all around. The new kid looked a little nervous and pale, but other than that he had a nice smile and didn't seem socially inept or anything like that. I was just wondering why Neferet had looked for me to introduce the kid to when she went on to explain.

"Jack is a poet and a writer, and Loren Blake is going to be his mentor, but Loren won't be back from his trip east until tomorrow. Jack is also going to be Erik Night's roommate. As you are all aware, Erik is away from school until tomorrow, too. So I thought it would be nice if the five of you would show Jack around and be sure he feels welcome and gets settled in today."

"Of course, we'd be happy to," I said without hesitation. It was never fun to be the new kid.

"Damien, you can show Jack to his and Erik's room, can't you?"

"Sure, no problem," Damien said.

"I knew I could count on Zoey's friends." Neferet's smile was incredible. It seemed to light the room by itself and it made me suddenly intensely proud that all of the other kids were standing around watching Neferet show such obvious favor for us. "Remember, if you need anything for tomorrow, just let me know. Oh, because it's your first ritual I asked the kitchen to prepare something special for you and the Dark Daughters and Sons as a treat afterward. It should be a lovely celebration for you, Zoey."

I was overwhelmed by her thoughtfulness, and couldn't help but compare it to the cold, unconcerned way my mom treated me. Hell, the truth was my mom didn't actually care enough to treat me like anything anymore. I'd only seen her that one time in a whole month, and after the stupid scene her loser husband had caused with Neferet, it looked like I wouldn't be seeing her again soon. Like I cared? No. Not when I had good friends and a mentor like Neferet to be there for me.

"I really appreciate this, Neferet," I said, swallowing hard around the lump of emotion that had built in my throat.

"It's my pleasure and the least I can do for my fledgling's first Full Moon Ritual as leader of the Dark Daughters." She gave me a quick hug, and then left the room, nodding kindly to the kids who spoke to her and saluted her respectfully.

"Wow," Jack said. "She's really amazing."

"She sure is," I said. Then I grinned at my friends (and the new kid). "So, ready to get to work now? We have lots of stuff to clear out of here." I saw poor Jack looking totally clueless. "Damien, you better give Jack a quick catch-up lesson in vamp rituals so he doesn't feel so lost." I started to walk back toward the kitchen (again), and heard Damien start his little professor act, beginning with the facts about the Full Moon Ritual.

"Uh, Zoey, can we help you?"

I glanced over my shoulder. Drew Partain, a short, athletic kid I recognized because he and I were in the same fencing class (he's an incredible fencer—as good as Damien, and that's saying something), was standing with a group of guys near the wall of black-shrouded windows. He smiled at me, but I noticed he kept checking out Stevie Rae. "There's a lot of stuff to be pulled around. I know because the guys and I used to help Aphrodite get the room ready."

"Huh," I heard Shaunee say under her breath. Before Erin could add to the sarcastic sound, I said, "Yeah, we could use your help." And then I tested them. "Except my ritual is going to be different. Damien can show you what I mean." I waited for the disdainful looks and the sarcasm that the jocklike guys tended to throw at Damien and the few other openly gay kids at the school, but Drew just shrugged and said, "Cool with me. Just tell us what to do." He grinned and winked at Stevie Rae, who giggled and blushed.

"Damien, they're all yours," I said.

"I'm sure hell is freezing over somewhere," Damien whispered, barely moving his lips. Then, in his regular voice he said, "Well, the first thing Zoey didn't like is that it looks like a morgue in here with all of the arcade machines pushed to the walls and covered with that black fabric. So let's see if we can move most of them into the kitchen and the hall." Drew's group started to work alongside Damien and the new kid, and Damien returned to his mini-lesson.

"We'll get the candles and pull the table out here," I told the guys, and motioned for the Twins and Stevie Rae to follow me.

"Damien has died and gone straight to gay boy heaven," Shaunee said as soon as we were out of earshot.

"Hey, it's about time those kids stopped acting like ignorant rednecks and behaved like they have some sense," I said.

"She doesn't mean that, even though we agree with you," Erin said. "She means little Mr. Jack the cute-gay-new-kid Twist."

"Now why in the world would you think he's gay?" Stevie Rae asked.

"Stevie Rae, I swear you have got to broaden your horizons, girl," Shaunee said.

"Okay, I'm lost, too. Why do you think Jack's gay?" I asked.

Shaunee and Erin shared a long-suffering look, then Erin explained. "Jack Twist is yummy Jake Gyllenhaal's totally gay cowboy character from *Brokeback Mountain*."

"And just please! Anyone who chooses that name and who looks all geeky cute like that is totally, completely playing for Damien's team."

"Huh," I said.

"Well, I'll be," Stevie Rae said. "You know, I never did see that movie. It didn't come to the Cinema 8 in Henrietta."

"You don't say?" Shaunee said.

"Please. I'm so shocked," Erin said.

"Well, Stevie Rae. I do believe it's time for a DVD showing of that excellent flick," Shaunee said.

"Do guys kiss in it?"

"Deliciously," Shaunee and Erin said together.

I tried, but failed miserably not to laugh at the look on Stevie Rae's face.

CHAPTER FIFTEEN

We were almost finished setting up the room when someone flipped on the nightly news on the big-screen TV we did have to leave in the main room. The five of us shared quick looks—what they were calling "the bomb hoax by Nature's Jihad" was the lead story. Even though I knew my call couldn't be traced, and I'd watched Damien "accidentally" drop and then totally step on and smash his disposable phone, I only breathed marginally easier when Chera Kimiko repeated that so far the police had no leads about the identity of the terrorist group.

In a related Arkansas River story Fox News reported that this evening Samuel Johnson, captain of a river transport barge, had a heart attack while piloting the barge. It was a "lucky coincidence" for him that river traffic had been halted and that police and paramedics were so close by. His life had been saved, and there had been no damage done to any other barges or bridges.

"That was it!" Damien said. "He had a heart attack and ran the barge into the bridge."

I nodded numbly. "And that proves that Aphrodite's vision was true."

"Not that that's good news," Stevie Rae said.

"I think it is," I said. "As long as Aphrodite lets us know about her visions, at least we can take them seriously."

Damien shook his head. "There has to be a reason Neferet believes Nyx has withdrawn her gift from Aphrodite. It's too bad we can't tell her about this, then maybe she'd explain what's going on, or maybe even change her mind about Aphrodite."

"No, I gave my word I wouldn't say anything."

"If Aphrodite was really changing from hag to nonhag, she'd go to Neferet herself," Shaunee said.

"Maybe you should talk to her about that," Erin said.

Stevie Rae made a rude noise.

I rolled my eyes at Stevie Rae, but she didn't notice because Drew had grinned his way up to us and she was too busy blushing to pay attention to me.

"How's it look, Zoey?" he asked without taking his eyes from Stevie Rae.

Like you've got a thing for my roommate, is what I wanted to say, but I thought he was kinda cute and Stevie Rae's blush clearly said she thought so, too, so I decided against mortifying her.

"Looks good," I said.

"Doesn't look too bad from here, either," Shaunee said, giving Drew a look up and down.

"Ditto, Twin," Erin said, waggling her eyebrows at Drew.

The boy didn't notice either of the Twins. Seems all he noticed was Stevie Rae.

"I'm starving," he said.

"Me, too," Stevie Rae said.

"So, how about getting something to eat?" Drew asked her.

"Okay," Stevie Rae said quickly, and then she seemed to remember we were all standing there watching her, and her face got even pinker. "Gosh, it is dinnertime. We better all go get something." With a nervous little gesture, she ran her fingers through her short curls and called across the room to Damien, who was thoroughly engrossed in a conversation with Jack. (From what I had overheard they were both into the same kind of books and were debating which of the Harry Potters was really the best. Clearly, they were dorkishly alike.) "Damien, we're gonna go eat. Are you and Jack hungry?"

Jack and Damien exchanged a look, and then Damien called back, "Yeah, we're coming."

"Okeydokey," Stevie Rae said, still grinning at Drew. "I guess we're all hungry."

Shaunee sighed, and started for the door. "Just please. The young love hormones in this room are enough to give me a headache."

"I feel like I'm stuck in a *Lifetime* movie. Wait for me, Twin," Erin said.

"Why are the Twins so cynical about love?" I asked Damien as he and Jack crossed the room to join us.

"They're not. They're just mad that the last few guys they've gone out with have bored them," Damien said.

As a group, we went outside into the magic of a snowy November evening. The flakes had changed and were smaller, but they were still coming down steadily, making the House of Night look even more mysterious and castlelike than usual.

"Yeah, the Twins are hard on guys. It's like they double-time them," Stevie Rae said. I noticed she was walking really close to Drew and that occasionally their arms brushed together.

I heard a bunch of muttered agreement noises from the guys who had been helping us drag furniture around the rec room. And I imagined it would be intimidating for any guy (vamp or human) to try to date one of the Twins.

"Do you remember when Thor asked Erin out?" said one of Drew's friends, whose name I think was Keith.

"Yeah, she called him a lemur. You know, like the moronic lemurs in that Disney movie," Stevie Rae said, laughing.

"And Walter went out with Shaunee a total of two and a half dates. Then, right in the middle of Starbucks, she called him a Pentium 3 processor," Damien said.

I gave him a totally clueless look.

"Z, we're up to Pentium 5 processors now."

"Oh."

"Erin still calls him Slowest McSlowenstein whenever she sees him," Stevie Rae said.

"Clearly it's going to take a couple of really special guys to date the Twins," I said.

"I think there's someone for everyone," Jack said suddenly. We all turned to him and he blushed. Before any of the kids could snicker at him I spoke up, "I agree with Jack." *But figuring out which someone is the one for you is the hard part*, I added silently to myself.

"Totally!" Stevie Rae said with her usual perky optimism.

"Absolutely," Damien said, winking at me. I grinned back at him.

"Hey!" Shaunee stepped out from behind a tree. "What are you guys talking about?"

"Your nonexistent love life!" Damien called cheerfully.

"Really?" she said.

"Really," Damien said.

"How about you talk about how cold and wet you are instead?" Shaunee said.

Damien frowned. "Huh? I'm not."

Erin popped out from around the other side of the tree, snowball in hand. "You will be!" she yelled, throwing it and hitting Damien smack in the middle of his chest.

Of course the snowball war was on. Kids squealed and ran for cover while they scooped up handfuls of new snow and took aim at Shaunee and Erin. I started to back away.

"I told you snow was great!" Stevie Rae said.

"Well, let's just hope for a blizzard then," Damien yelled, taking aim at Erin. "Lots of wind and snow. Totally the best for snowball fights!" He let fly, but Erin was too quick and jumped for cover just in time to miss being plastered right in the head.

"Where are you going, Z?" Stevie Rae called from behind an ornamental shrub. I noticed Drew was right beside her, firing cover shots at Shaunee.

"To the media center—have to work on the words for the ritual tomorrow, so I'll grab something to eat back at the dorm when I get done." I kept backing away more and more quickly. "Hate to miss all the fun, but . . ." and I retreated inside the closest door, slamming it behind me just in time for it to catch the *plop plop plop* of three snowballs against its ancient wood.

I hadn't just been making an excuse to get out of the snowball war. I actually had been planning to ditch dinner and spend a few hours in the media center. Tomorrow I'd have to cast a circle and lead a ritual that might be as ancient as the moon itself.

I didn't know what the hell I was doing.

Okay, sure. I'd cast one circle with my friends a month ago as a little experiment to see if I really had an affinity for the elements, or if I'd been delusional. Until I felt the power of wind, fire, water, earth, and spirit rush through me and my friends witnessed it, too, I would have bet on the side of delusional. Not that I'm totally cynical or anything, but please. Just please (as the Twins would say). Being able to tap into the power of the five elements was pretty bizarre. I mean, my life wasn't an X-Men movie (although I'd definitely like to spend some quality time with Wolverine).

The media center was predictably empty; it was, after all, Saturday night. Only total dorks spent Saturday night in the media center. Yes, I knew all too well what that made me. I'd already decided where to start my research. I pulled up the card catalogue on the computer and searched for old spell and ritual books, ignoring any that had recent publication dates. I was particularly drawn to one titled *Mystical Rites of the Crystal Moon* by Fiona. I vaguely recognized her name as one of the Vamp Poet Laureates from the early 1800s (there was a cool picture of her in our dorm). I scribbled down the Dewey Decimal Number for the book and found it up on an obscure shelf, dusty and lonely. I thought it was an excellent sign that it was one of those old leather-bound tomes. I wanted foundation and tradition so that under my leadership the Dark Daughters would know something more than Aphrodite's way too modern (and ho-ish) influence.

I opened my notebook and got out my favorite pen, which made me think about what Loren had said about preferring to write his poetry by hand rather than on a computer . . . and made me think about Loren touching my face . . . and my back . . . and the connection that had sizzled between us. I smiled and felt my cheeks get warm, and then realized I was sitting there grinning and blushing like a retard about a guy who was too old for me, *and* a vampyre. Both things made me really nervous (as well they should). I mean, he was totally gorgeous, but he was twenty-something. A real adult who knew all the vampyre secrets about bloodlust and, well, lust in general. Which, unfortunately, only made him more delicious, especially after my brief but very nasty bloodsucking make-out scene with Heath.

I tapped my pen against the blank notebook page. Okay, I'd been kissing and messing around a little with Erik some during the past month. Yes, I liked it. No, it hadn't gone very far. One reason was that despite recent evidence to the contrary, I didn't *usually* act like a slut. Another reason was that I was still way too aware that I'd accidentally watched Aphrodite, Erik's very ex-girlfriend, on her knees in front of him trying to give him a blowjob, and I didn't want there to be any confusion on Erik's part that I was definitely not a stank slut like Aphrodite the Ho. (I ignored the memory of my rubbing the bulge in Heath's pants.) So, I was definitely attracted to Erik, who everyone thought was my official boyfriend, even though we hadn't done much about that attraction.

My mind shifted to Loren. Outside in the moonlight with my skin bared to him Loren had made me feel like a woman—not an inexperienced, nervous girl, which is how I tended to feel around Erik. But when I'd seen the desire in Loren's eyes I'd felt beautiful and powerful and very, very sexy. And, yes, I had to admit to myself that I liked that feeling.

And how the hell did Heath fit into all of this? I felt different about Heath than I did about Erik or Loren. Heath and I had history. We'd known each other since we were kids, and we'd been dating, on and off, for the past couple years. I'd always been attracted to Heath, and we'd done some serious making-out, but he'd never turned me on before like he did when he cut his neck and I'd drunk his blood.

I shivered and automatically licked my lips. Just thinking about it made me feel hot and horrified at the same time. I definitely wanted to see him again. But was that because I still cared about him, or was it just because of the intense bloodlust I felt for him?

I had no idea.

True, I'd liked Heath for years. He was kinda dopey sometimes, but usually in a sweet way. He treated me right, and I liked to hang out with him—at least those things had been true before he'd started boozing it up and getting high. Then his dopiness had turned into stupidity, and I hadn't really trusted him anymore. But he said he'd quit all that, so did that mean he was back to the guy I used to like so much? And if so, what the hell was I supposed to do about (1) Erik, (2) Loren, (3) the fact that drinking Heath's blood was totally against the House of Night rules, and (4) I was definitely going to drink more of his blood.

My sigh sounded suspiciously like a sob. I really needed someone to talk to.

Neferet? No way. I wasn't about to tell an adult vamp about Loren. I knew I should admit that I'd been drinking Heath's blood (again—sigh) and had probably intensified the Imprint between us. But I couldn't. At least not yet. I know it was selfish, but I didn't want to be in trouble with her while I was still trying to settle into the Dark Daughters' leadership.

Stevie Rae? She was my best friend, and I wanted to tell her, but if I was going to *really* talk to her then that meant I'd have to admit to drinking Heath's blood. Twice. And how much I wanted to drink it again. How could that not freak her out? It freaked *me* out. I couldn't stand to think about my best friend looking at me like I was a monster. Plus, I didn't think she'd understand—not really.

I couldn't tell Grandma. She would definitely not like the fact that Loren was twenty-something. And I couldn't imagine talking to her about the lust part of bloodlust.

Ironically, I realized who the one person was who would not be freaked about the blood, and would definitely understand about the lust and such—Aphrodite. And, oddly enough, part of me wanted to talk to her, especially after discovering her visions were still true. I had a *feeling* about Aphrodite that was telling me there was a lot more to what was going on with her than the fact that she could definitely be a hateful bitch. She'd pissed off Neferet— that much was obvious. But Neferet had told Aphrodite, in cold, hateful words, that Nyx had withdrawn her favor from her, and she'd made it clear to me (and practically the entire school) that Aphrodite's visions were false. But I had proof that they weren't. It gave me a scared, skin-crawly feeling, but I was beginning to wonder how much I could actually trust Neferet.

Forcing my thoughts back to the media center and the research I had to do, I opened the old ritual book, and a slip of paper fluttered out of it. I picked up the paper, thinking some kid had left her notes in it, and froze. My name was printed at the top in elegant handwriting I definitely recognized.

For Zoey

Alluring Priestess.
Night can't cloak your scarlet dream.
Accept Desire's call.

The words of the poem sent a shiver through me. What the hell? How had anyone, let alone Loren who was supposed to be on the East Coast, known I'd look in that book!

My hand was shaking, so I put the paper down and slowly reread the poem. If I pushed aside the fact that it was incredibly romantic that the Vamp Poet Laureate was writing me poetry and read the poem without being totally blown away by how sexy it was I realized something as disturbing as the haiku being here in the first place. *Night can't cloak your scarlet dream.* Was I going absolutely crazy, or does that line sound like Loren knows I've been drinking blood? And suddenly the poem felt wrong . . . dangerous . . . like a warning that wasn't actually a warning, and I started to wonder about the poet. What if Loren hadn't written it? What if it was Aphrodite? I had overheard her talking to her parents. She was supposed to be getting me kicked out as the Dark Daughters' leader. Could this tie into her plan? (Jeesh, "her plan." I was starting to sound like a bad comic book.)

Okay, Aphrodite had seen me with Loren, but how could she

know about the haiku? Also, how would Aphrodite know that I'd be back in the media center looking at this particular old book? That sounded more like some weird piece of psychic info an adult vamp would have—although I didn't have a clue how. I mean, I hadn't even known I'd choose the book until a few minutes ago.

Nala jumped up on the computer desk, scaring the bejeezus out of me. She complained and rubbed against me.

"Okay, okay. I'll get to work." But as I searched through the old book for traditional rituals and spells my mind kept circling around and around the poem and the uneasy feeling that seemed to have permanently lodged itself beneath my breastbone.

CHAPTER SIXTEEN

I was carrying Nala out of the media center—the cat had been so sound asleep that she hadn't even bothered to complain at me when I picked her up. I checked the clock as I left the room, and couldn't believe that several hours had passed. No wonder my butt was asleep and my neck was so stiff. But being temporarily uncomfortable didn't really matter because I'd actually figured out what I was going to do for the Full Moon Ritual. It was a huge weight lifted from my mind. I was still nervous, and didn't spend too much time considering the fact that when I performed the ritual I'd be doing so in front of a bunch of kids, the majority of whom were probably not thrilled that I had taken over leadership from their buddy Aphrodite. I just needed to stay focused on the ritual itself, and remember the amazing feelings that filled me whenever I invoked the five elements. The rest would work itself out. Hopefully.

I pushed open the heavy front door of the school and walked out into a different world. It was snowing steadily, and must have been for the entire time I was in the media center. The school grounds were completely blanketed by a comforter of downy white. The wind had whipped up and visibility was terrible. The gaslights that marked the obscured path were not much more than glowing pinpoints of yellow against the white darkness. I probably should have gone back in the building and made my way along the school's hall toward the dorm, staying inside for as long as I could, and then making a quick run from the far side of the school to the girls' dorm, but I really didn't want to. I thought about how right Stevie Rae had been. Snow really was magical. It changed the world, made it quieter, softer, more mysterious. As a fledgling, I already had quite a bit of an adult vampyre's natural protection against the cold, which used to creep me out. I mean, it made me think of cold, dead creatures who existed by drinking the blood of the living—totally gruesome, even if I was bizarrely drawn to the thought. Now I knew more about what I was becoming, so I understood that my protection against the cold was more about a heightened metabolism than about being undead. Vampyres aren't dead. They're just Changed. It was humans who liked to fuel the scary myth of the walking dead, which I was beginning to find more than slightly annoying. Anyway, I really enjoyed being able to walk around in a blizzard without feeling like I was going to freeze. Nala burrowed herself against me, purring loudly when I wrapped my arms around her protectively. The snow muffled my steps and it seemed for that moment that I was alone in a world where black and white had mixed together to form a unique color just for me.

I'd only walked a few steps when I sighed and would have popped myself in the forehead if my arms hadn't been filled with my cat. I needed to go by the school spells and rituals store and get some eucalyptus. From what I'd read in the old ritual book, eucalyptus was associated with healing, protection, and purification—three things I thought were important to evoke during my first ritual as leader of the Dark Daughters. I supposed I could get the eucalyptus tomorrow, but I was going to need it knotted into a rope as part of the spell I planned to cast, and . . . well . . . it was probably smart that I practiced so I didn't drop

anything during the spell or, worse, suddenly discover that eucalyptus wasn't as flexible as I'd expected and it fell to pieces when
I tried to knot it and then I'd turn bright red and want to crawl
under the rec hall and curl up in a fetal position crying . . .

I shoved that lovely picture from my mind, turned around,
and began to trudge back to the main building. That's when I saw
the shape. It caught my eye because it didn't belong—and not
just because it was unusual that another fledgling was silly
enough to be out walking in the snowstorm. What struck me as
weird was that the person, because it definitely wasn't a cat or a
bush, wasn't walking on the sidewalk. He was heading in the general direction of the rec hall, but was cutting across the far lawn. I
stopped and squinted against the falling snow. The person was
wearing a long, dark cloak with a hood pulled up like a cowl.

An urge to follow him hit me with such strength that I gasped.
Almost as if I had no will of my own, I stepped off the sidewalk
and hurried after the mysterious person, who had just reached
the edge of the tree line that grew along the outside wall.

My eyes widened. The instant the figure entered the shadows,
whoever it was, he or she, began moving with inhuman speed,
cloak billowing behind them wildly in the snow-filled wind so
that the figure appeared to have wings. Red? Did I see scarlet
flashes against glimpses of white skin? Snow stung my eyes and
my vision blurred, but I held Nala tighter to me and kicked into a
fast jog, even though I could tell that I was being led to the area of
the east wall that held the trapdoor. The same place I'd seen the
other two ghosts or specters or whatever. The place that I'd told
myself I really didn't want to go again, at least not alone.

Yes, I should have turned to my left and marched directly to
the dorm. Naturally, I didn't.

My heart was thudding like crazy and Nala was grumbling in
my ear when I entered the tree line and continued to rush along

the wall, all the time thinking how absolutely insane it was for me to be out here chasing what was at best some kid who was trying to sneak away from the school, and at worst a seriously scary ghost.

I'd lost sight of the person, but I knew I was getting close to the trapdoor, so I slowed down, automatically staying within the deepest shadows and moving from tree to tree. It was snowing even harder now, and Nala and I were covered in white and I was actually starting to feel chilled. *What am I doing out here?* No matter what my gut was telling me, my mind was saying that I was acting crazy and that I needed to get myself (and my shivering cat) back to the dorm. This was really none of my business. Maybe one of the teachers was checking the . . . I dunno . . . the grounds to make sure some moronic fledgling (like me) wasn't wandering around out in the storm.

Or maybe someone had just snuck on the school grounds after brutally killing Chris Ford and abducting Brad Higeons, and now they were sneaking off again, and if I confronted him/her I'd be murdered, too.

Yeah, right. Talk about an overactive imagination.

Then I heard the voices.

I slowed way down, practically tiptoeing forward until I finally saw them. There were two figures standing by the open trapdoor. I blinked hard, trying to see more clearly through the curtain of falling white. The person closest to the door was the one I'd been following, and now that he wasn't running (at a ridiculous speed) I could see that he stood weirdly, crouched down with a hunched-back posture. I shifted my attention to the other figure, and I felt the chill that had been brushing my skin with the snow sink into my soul. It was Neferet.

She looked mysterious, and powerful with her auburn hair flying around her and the snow covering the long black dress she was wearing. She was facing me, so I could see that her expression was stern, almost angry, and she was speaking intently to the cloaked person, using her hands expressively. Silently, I moved closer, glad I had on a dark outfit so that I blended well with the shadows near the wall. From this new position pieces of what Neferet was saying drifted to me on the snow-filled wind.

". . . have more care with what you do! I will not . . ." I listened intently, trying to hear through the wailing wind, and realized that the breeze was bringing me more than just Neferet's words. I could smell something, even over the crisp scent of falling snow. It was a dry, moldy smell, weirdly out of place in this cold, wet night. ". . . much too dangerous," Neferet was saying. "Obey or . . ." I lost the rest of the sentence, and then she paused. The cloaked figure responded with a weird, grunting sound that was more animal than human.

Nala, who had been curled up under my chin and seemed to have fallen asleep, again, suddenly whipped her head around. I ducked even farther behind the trunk of the tree in whose shadow I was hiding as Nala began to growl.

"Shhh," I whispered to her and tried to pet her into being calm. She quieted, but I could feel that the fur on her back had lifted and her eyes were narrowed to angry slits as she stared at the cloaked person.

"You promised!"

The guttural sound of the mystery man's voice had my skin crawling. I peeked out from behind the tree in time to see Neferet raise her hand as if she was going to strike him. He cowered back against the wall, causing the hood to fall from his face, and my stomach clenched so hard I thought I might throw up.

It was Elliott. The dead kid whose "ghost" had attacked Nala and me last month.

Neferet didn't hit him. Instead she gestured violently at the open trapdoor. She'd raised her voice, so everything she said carried to me over the wind.

"You may not have any more! The time is not right. You cannot understand such things, and you may not question me. Now leave here. If you disobey me again you will feel my wrath, and the wrath of a goddess is terrible to behold."

Elliott cringed away from Neferet. "Yes, Goddess," he whimpered.

It was him; I knew it was. Even though his voice was rough I recognized it. Somehow Elliott had not died, and he had not Changed into an adult vampyre. He was something else. Something terrible.

Even as I thought how disgusting he was, Neferet's expression softened. "I do not wish to be angry with my children. You know that you are my greatest joys."

Revolted, I watched as Neferet moved forward and caressed Elliott's face. His eyes began to glow the color of old blood, and even from a distance I could see that his entire body was trembling. Elliott had been a short, pudgy, unattractive kid with too white skin and carrot red hair that was habitually frizzed out. He was still all those things, but now his pale cheeks were gaunt and his body was hunched, as if it had curled in on itself. So Neferet had to bend down to kiss his lips. Totally grossed out, I heard Elliott moan in pleasure. She straightened and laughed. It was a dark, seductive sound.

"Please, Goddess!" Elliott whimpered.

"You know you don't deserve it."

"Please, Goddess!" he repeated. His body was shivering violently.

"Very well, but remember. What a goddess gives, she can also take away."

Unable to stop watching, I saw Neferet lift her arm and brush back her sleeve. Then she ran her fingernail up her forearm, leaving a slender scarlet line that immediately began to bead with blood. I felt the draw of her blood. When she held out her arm, offering it to Elliott, I pressed against the rough bark of the tree, forcing myself to stay still and hidden as he fell to his knees before her and, while he made feral grunts and moans, began to suck Neferet's blood. I tore my eyes from him to look at Neferet. She'd thrown her head back and her lips were parted as if having the grotesque Elliott creature suck the blood from her arm was a sexual experience.

Deep within me I felt an answering desire. I wanted to slice open someone's skin and . . .

No! I ducked completely behind the tree. I would not become a monster. I would not be a freak. I couldn't let this thing control me. Slowly and silently I started back the way I'd come, refusing to look at the two of them again.

CHAPTER SEVENTEEN

I was still feeling shaky, confused, and more than a little sick to my stomach when I finally got to the dorm. Clusters of damp kids pooled around the main room watching TV and drinking hot chocolate. I grabbed a towel from a stack by the door and joined Stevie Rae, the Twins, and Damien sitting around our favorite TV watching *Project Runway*, and started drying a grumbling Nala. Stevie Rae didn't realize I was being uncharacteristically quiet. She was too busy gushing about how the snowball fight I'd avoided earlier had morphed into a major battle after dinner that had raged until someone had thrown a snowball that had hit one of the windows of Dragon's office. Dragon was what everyone called the fencing professor, and he was not a vamp any fledgling would want to piss off.

"Dragon ended the snow war." Stevie Rae giggled. "But it was real fun until then."

"Yeah, Z, you missed one hellacious wicked fight," Erin said.

"We knocked the crap outta Damien and his boyfriend," Shaunee said.

"He's not my boyfriend!" Damien said, but his little smile seemed to add an unspoken "yet" to the end of the sentence.

"What . . ."

". . . ever," said the Twins.

"I think he's cute," Stevie Rae said.

"Me, too," Damien said, turning adorably pink.

"What do you think of him, Zoey?" Stevie Rae asked.

I blinked at Stevie Rae. It was like I was inside a fishbowl in the middle of a typhoon, and everyone else was on the outside cluelessly enjoying lovely weather.

"Is everything okay, Zoey?" Damien said.

"Damien, can you get me some eucalyptus?" I said abruptly.

"Eucalyptus?"

I nodded. "Yeah, some strands of it, and some sage, too. I need both for the ritual tomorrow."

"Yeah, no problem," Damien said, watching me entirely too closely.

"Did you get the ritual all figured out, Z?" Stevie Rae asked.

"I think so." I paused and took a long breath. Then I met Damien's questioning gaze steadily. "Damien, has there ever been a case of a fledgling who seemed to have died, but later was found alive?"

To his credit, Damien didn't freak or ask me if I had gone insane. I could feel that the Twins and Stevie Rae were staring at me like I'd just announced I was going to be on *Girls Gone Wild: Vamp Edition*, but I ignored them and kept focused on Damien. We all knew he spent hours studying, and he remembered everything he read. If any of us would know the answer to my bizarre question, it would be him.

"When a fledgling's body starts rejecting the Change there is no stopping it. That's clear in all the books. It's also what Neferet has told us. Zoey," I'd never heard him sound so serious. "What is wrong?"

"Please, please, please tell me you're not feeling sick!" Stevie Rae practically sobbed.

"No! It's nothing like that," I said quickly. "I'm fine. I promise."

"What's going on?" Shaunee said.

"You're scaring us," Erin said.

"I don't mean to," I told them. "Okay, this is coming out all wrong, but I think I saw that Elliott kid."

"Huh!" "What!" the Twins said together.

"I don't understand," Damien said. "Elliott died last month."

Stevie Rae's eyes suddenly widened. "Like Elizabeth!" she said. Before I could say anything, she blurted, in one long, breathless sentence, "Last month Zoey thought she saw Elizabeth's ghost out by the east wall but we didn't say anything 'cause we didn't want to scare y'all."

I opened my mouth to explain about Elliott—and Neferet. And shut it again. I should have realized before I'd said one word to any of them that I absolutely could not tell them about Neferet. Vampyres were all intuitive to some degree. High Priestess Neferet was amazingly intuitive. So much so that she often seemed to be able to read actual thoughts. No way could my four friends walk around school knowing that I'd seen her letting some kind of disgusting undead Elliott creature suck her blood without Neferet knowing everything in their freaked-out minds.

What I'd witnessed tonight I would have to keep completely to myself.

"Zoey?" Stevie Rae put her hand on my arm. "You can tell us."

I smiled at her and wished with all my heart that I could.

"I did think I saw Elizabeth's ghost last month. And tonight I think I saw Elliott's," I finally said.

Damien frowned. "If you saw ghosts why did you ask me about fledglings recovering from rejecting the Change?"

I looked my friend in the eye and lied my ass off. "Because it seemed easier to believe than I was seeing ghosts—or at least it did until I said it. Then it sounded crazy."

"Seeing a ghost would have freaked me right out," Shaunee said.

Erin nodded enthusiastic agreement.

"Was it like with Elizabeth?" Stevie Rae asked.

At least this I didn't have to lie about. "No. He seemed more real, but I saw them both in the same place, over by the east wall, and both of their eyes glowed a weird red color."

Shaunee shivered.

"I'm sure as shit staying away from the spooky east wall," Erin said.

Damien, always the scholar, tapped his chin like a professor. "Zoey, maybe you have yet another affinity. Maybe you can see dead fledglings."

I would have thought this was a possibility, even though it was a gross one, if I hadn't seen the supposed ghost, solid and totally real, drinking my mentor's blood. Still, it was a good theory, and an excellent way to keep Damien busy. "You might be right," I said.

"Ugh," Stevie Rae said. "I hope not."

"Me, too. But could you do some research on it for me, Damien?"

"Of course. I'll also check out any references to hauntings by fledglings."

"Thanks, I appreciate that."

"You know, I do think I remember reading something in an old Greek history text about vampyre spirits that restlessly prowl the ancient tombs of . . ."

I shut out Damien's lecture, glad that Stevie Rae and the Twins were more involved with listening to his ghost stories than asking me more specific questions. I hated lying to them, especially since I really would have liked to have told them everything. What I saw had truly frightened me. How the hell was I going to face Neferet again?

Nala rubbed her face against mine and then settled down in

my lap. I stared at the TV and petted her while Damien droned on and on about old vamp ghosts. And then I realized what I was seeing and lunged across Stevie Rae for the remote that was sitting on the lamp table beside her, causing Nala to *mee-uf-ow* snort! in annoyance and jump from my lap. I didn't even take time to soothe her, but quickly turned up the volume.

It was Chera Kimiko again on a repeat of the evening news' lead story.

"The body of the second Union High School teenager, Brad Higeons, was found by museum security guards this evening in the stream that runs along the Philbrook Museum grounds. The cause of death is not being officially reported at this time, but sources have told Fox News that the boy died of blood loss through multiple lacerations."

"No . . ." I felt my head shaking back and forth. There was a terrible ringing in my ears.

"That's the stream we crossed over when we went to the yard of the Philbrook for the Samhain Ritual last month," Stevie Rae said.

"It's just down the street from here," Shaunee said.

"The Dark Daughters used to sneak out there all the time for rituals," Erin said.

Then Damien said what we were all thinking. "Someone is trying to make it look like vampyres are killing human kids."

"Maybe they are." I hadn't actually meant to speak my thought aloud, and pressed my lips closed, immediately sorry I'd let that slip.

"Why would you say that, Zoey?" Stevie Rae sounded utterly shocked.

"I—I don't know. I didn't really mean it," I stuttered, not sure what I really meant or why I'd said it.

"You're freaked, that's all," Erin said.

"Of course you are. You knew both those kids," Shaunee added. "And on top of all of this, you saw a damn ghost today."

Damien was studying me again. "Did you have a feeling about Brad before you heard he was dead, Zoey?" he asked quietly.

"Yes. No." I sighed. "I thought he was dead as soon as I heard he'd been taken," I admitted.

"Did any specifics come with the feeling? Do you know anything more?" Damien said.

As if Damien's questions had prodded them from my memory, the snatches of words that I'd heard Neferet speak replayed in my mind: . . . *much too dangerous . . . You may not have any more . . . You cannot understand . . . You may not question me . . .* I felt a terrible chill that had nothing to do with the snowstorm outside. "Nothing specific came with the feeling. I have to go to my room," I said, suddenly unable to look at any of them. I hated lying, and doubted I could keep it up if I stayed with them much longer. "I have to finish up the words for the ritual tomorrow," I said lamely. "And I didn't get much sleep last night. I'm really tired."

"Okay, no problem. We understand," Damien said.

They were all so obviously worried about me that I could barely meet their eyes. "Thanks, guys," I mumbled as I left the room. I was halfway up the stairs when Stevie Rae caught up with me.

"Do you mind if I come back to the room now, too? I have a really bad headache. I really just want to go to sleep. I won't bug you while you study or anything."

"No, I don't mind," I said quickly. I glanced at her. She did look kinda pale. Stevie Rae was so sensitive that even though she didn't know Chris or Brad, their deaths were clearly upsetting her. Add to that my announcement about ghosts, and the poor kid probably was scared to death. I put my arm around her and gave her a squeeze as we came to our door. "Hey, everything's gonna be okay."

"Yeah, I know. I'm just tired." She grinned up at me, but she didn't sound as perky as usual.

We didn't say much while we put on our pajamas. Nala scooted in through the cat door, jumped up on my bed, and was asleep almost as fast as Stevie Rae, which was a relief to me because I didn't have to pretend to be writing words to a ritual I'd already finished. There was something else I had to do, and I didn't want to explain any part of it to anyone, not even my best friend.

CHAPTER EIGHTEEN

My Vampyre Sociology 415 text was exactly where I left it in the bookshelf over my computer desk. It was a senior or, as they're called here, sixth former level book. Neferet had given it to me shortly after I'd arrived when it was obvious that the Change going on within my body was happening at a different rate than what went on with normal fledglings. She'd wanted to pull me out of my third former Soc class and move me into the upper level section of Soc, but I'd managed to talk her out of it, saying that I was already different enough, I didn't need anything else to make me more of a freak to the rest of the kids here. Our compromise was that I would go through the 415 level text, chapter by chapter, and ask her questions along the way.

Okay, well, I'd meant to do that, but what with one thing and another (taking over the Dark Daughters, dating Erik, regular schoolwork, and whatnot), I'd done little more than glance at the book on my shelf.

With a sigh that sounded almost as tired as I felt, I took the book to bed and propped myself up on a mound of pillows. Despite the horrible events of the day, I had to struggle to keep my eyes open as I turned to the index and found what I was looking for: bloodlust.

There were a whole string of page numbers after the word, so I marked the place in the index, wearily flipped to the first page listed, and started reading. At first it was stuff I'd already figured out for myself: as a fledgling gets farther into the Change, she develops a taste for blood. Blood drinking goes from being something abhorrent to something delicious. By the time a fledgling is well advanced in the Change process, she can detect the scent of blood from a distance. Because of changes in metabolism, drugs and alcohol have increasingly less effect on fledglings, and as this effect dissipates, they will find that the effects of drinking blood correspondingly increase.

"No kidding," I said under my breath. Even drinking fledgling blood mixed in wine had given me an incredible buzz. Drinking Heath's blood had been like fire exploding deliciously inside me. I flipped ahead in the reading. I already knew all the stuff about blood being yummy. Then my eye caught a new heading, and I stopped at that page.

SEXUALITY AND BLOODLUST

Though the frequency of need differs depending upon age, sex, and general strength of the vampyre, adults must periodically feed on human blood to remain healthy and sane. It is, therefore, logical that evolution, and our beloved Goddess, Nyx, have insured the blood drinking process is a pleasurable one, both for the vampyre and the human donor. As we have already learned, vampyre saliva acts as an anticoagulant for human blood. Vampyre saliva also secretes endorphins during blood drinking, which stimulate the pleasure zones of the brain, human and vampyre, and can actually simulate orgasm.

I blinked and rubbed a hand across my face. Well, hell! No wonder I'd had such a slutty reaction to Heath. Being turned on while I drank blood was programmed into my Changing genes. Fascinated, I kept reading.

The older the vampyre, the more endorphins are released during blood drinking, and the more intense the experience of pleasure for vampyre and human.

Vampyres have speculated for centuries that the ecstasy of blood drinking is the key reason humans have vilified our race. Humans feel threatened by our ability to bring them such intense pleasure during an act they consider dangerous and abhorrent, so they have labeled us as predators. The truth, of course, is that vampyres can control their bloodlust, so there is little physical danger to human donors. The danger lies in the Imprint that often occurs during the ritual of blood drinking.

Completely engrossed, I hurried on to the next section.

IMPRINTING

An Imprint between vampyre and human does not occur every time a vampyre feeds. Many studies have been performed to try to determine exactly why some humans Imprint and some do not, but though there are several determining factors, such as emotional attachment, relationship between the human and the vampyre pre-Change, age, sexual orientation, and frequency of blood drinking, there is no way to predict with certainty whether a human will Imprint with a vampyre.

The text went on to talk about how vampyres should take care when drinking from a live donor, versus getting blood from blood banks, which are highly secretive businesses very few humans are aware exist at all (apparently those few humans are extremely well paid for their silence). The Soc book definitely frowned on drinking blood from humans and there were lots of warnings about how dangerous it is to Imprint a human, how not only is the human now emotionally bound to the vampyre, but the vamp is tied to the human, too. This made me sit up straighter. With a sick feeling in my stomach I read about how once the Imprint is in place a vamp can feel the human's emotions, and in some cases can actually call and/or track the human. There the text went off on a tangent about how Bram Stoker had actually been Imprinted by a vamp High Priestess, but that he had not understood her commitment to Nyx had to come before their tie, and in a fit of jealous anger had betrayed her by exaggerating the negative aspects of an Imprint in his infamous book, *Dracula*.

"Huh. I had no idea," I said. Ironically, *Dracula* had been one of my favorite books since I read it when I was thirteen. I skimmed through the rest of the section until I came to a part that had me chewing my lip as I slowly read it.

FLEDGLING—VAMPYRE IMPRINTING

As discussed in the previous chapter, due to the possibility of Imprint, fledglings are prohibited from drinking the blood of human donors, but they may experiment with each other. It has been proven that fledglings cannot Imprint one another. However, it is possible for an adult vampyre to Imprint a fledgling. This leads to emotional and physical complications once the fledgling completes the Change that are often not beneficial for either vampyre; therefore, blood drinking between fledgling and adult vampyre is strictly prohibited.

I shook my head, appalled all over again by the blood drinking I'd witnessed between Neferet and Elliott. Setting aside the whole issue of Elliott being dead, which still confused the hell outta me, Neferet was a powerful High Priestess. No damn way should she be letting a fledgling drink from her (even a dead one).

There was a chapter about breaking Imprints, which I started reading, but it was just too depressing. Apparently it involved the aid of a powerful High Priestess, a lot of physical pain, especially on the part of the human, and even then the human and the vampyre had to be careful to stay away from each other or the Imprint could reestablish.

I suddenly felt overwhelmingly weary. How long had it been since I'd really slept? More than a day. I glanced at my alarm clock. It was 6:10 A.M. It would be getting light soon. Feeling stiff and old I got up and put the book back on the shelf. Then I pulled open one side of the heavy curtains that completely covered the one large window in our room and blocked out all light from the outside. It was still snowing, and in the hesitant light of predawn the world looked innocent and dreamy. It was hard to imagine that such horrible things as teenagers being killed and dead fledglings being reanimated could have happened out there. I closed my eyes and leaned my head against the cool windowpane. I didn't want to think of either of those things right now. I was too tired . . . too confused . . . too unable to come up with the answers that I needed.

My sleepy mind wandered. I wanted to lie down, but the cool window felt good against my forehead. Erik would be getting back later that day. The thought gave me equal pangs of pleasure and of guilt, which, of course, made me think of Heath.

I'd probably Imprinted him. The thought scared me, but it also drew me. Would it be so awful to be emotionally and physically tied to a sober Heath? Before I'd met Erik (or Loren) my answer would most definitely have been no, it wouldn't be awful. Now it wasn't the awfulness that I was worried about. It was the fact that I'd have to hide the relationship from everyone. *Of course I could lie . . .* the thought drifted like poison smoke through my overstressed mind. *Neferet and even Erik knew that I'd been put in a situation a month ago where I drank Heath's blood—before I knew anything about bloodlust and Imprinting. I could pretend like I'd Imprinted him then. I'd already mentioned the possibility to Neferet. Maybe I could figure out a way to keep seeing both Heath and Erik . . .*

I knew my thoughts were wrong. I knew that seeing both of them was dishonest to both Erik and Heath, but I was so torn! I was really starting to care about Erik, plus he lived in my world and understood issues like the Change and embracing a totally new way of life. Thinking about breaking up with him made my heart hurt.

But thinking about never seeing Heath again, never tasting his blood again . . . that made me feel like I was having a panic attack. I sighed again. If this was bad for me, it was probably a zillion times worse for Heath. After all, it'd been a month since I'd seen him, and all that time he'd been carrying around a razor blade in his pocket just on the outside chance he might run into me. He'd stopped drinking and smoking because of what had happened between us. And he'd been eager to cut himself and let me drink his blood. Remembering, I shivered, and not because of the coolness of the window I was still pressing my forehead against. Desire made me shiver. The Soc textbook had described the reasons behind bloodlust in logical, dispassionate words that didn't begin to represent the truth of it.

Drinking Heath's blood was an incredible turn on. Something I wanted to do again and again. Soon. Now, actually. I bit my lip to keep from moaning as I thought about Heath—the hardness of his body and the incredible taste of his blood.

And suddenly it was as if a part of my mind lifted, like a string thrown out of a big ball of yarn. I could feel that piece of me searching . . . hunting . . . tracking . . . until it burst into a dark room and hovered above a bed. I sucked in my breath. Heath!

He was lying flat on his back. His blond hair was tousled, making him look like a little boy. Okay, anyone would think the kid was totally cute. I mean, vamps were known for being stunningly beautiful and gorgeously handsome, and even a vamp would have to admit that Heath scored high on their own scale of good-looking.

As if he could sense my presence, he stirred in his sleep, turning his head and restlessly kicking off the sheet that covered him. He was naked except for a pair of blue boxers that had fat little green frogs all over them. The sight of them made me smile. But the smile froze on my face when I noticed that I could now see the thin pink line that ran down the side of his neck.

That was where he'd cut himself with the razor blade and where I'd sucked his blood. I could almost taste it again—the heat and the dark richness of it, like melted chocolate, only a zillion times better.

Unable to stop myself, I moaned, and at the same instant Heath moaned in his sleep.

"Zoey . . ." he muttered dreamily, and shifted restlessly again.

"Oh, Heath," I whispered. "I don't know what to do about us." I knew what I *wanted* to do all too well. I wanted to ignore my exhaustion, get in my car, drive directly to Heath's house, sneak in the window of his bedroom (it's not like I hadn't done that before), open the freshly closed cut in his neck, and let his sweet blood flood my mouth while I pressed my body against his and made love for the first time in my life.

"Zoey!" This time Heath's eyes were fluttering open. He moaned again and his hand moved down to the hard lump in his pants and he began to—

My eyes sprang open and I was back in my dorm room with my forehead pressed against the window, breathing entirely too heavily.

My cell phone bleeped with the tone that said I had a text message. My hands were shaking as I flipped it open and read: I felt u here. Promise you'll meet me Friday.

I took a deep breath and answered Heath with two words that made my stomach flutter with excitement. I promise.

I closed the phone and turned it off. Then, forcing away the image of Heath with the unhealed cut on his neck, warm and desirable, obviously wanting me as much as I wanted him, I moved from the window and climbed into bed. Incredibly, my clock told me it was now 8:27 A.M. I'd been standing by the window for more than two hours! No wonder my body felt so stiff and crappy. I made a mental note to look up more info about Imprinting and the connection between the human and the vamp next time I was in the media center (which had better be soon). Before I turned off the little table lamp I glanced over at Stevie Rae. She was curled up on her side and her back was to me, but her deep breathing told me that she was definitely still asleep. Well, at least my friends didn't know what a bloodlust-filled, hornie freak I was turning into.

I wanted Heath.

I needed Erik.

I was intrigued by Loren.

I had no damn idea what I was going to do about the mess that my life had become.

I smushed my pillow into a ball. I was so tired I felt like someone had drugged me, but my mind still wouldn't shut itself off. When I woke up I'd see Erik again and probably Loren. I'd have to face Neferet. I'd perform my first ritual in front of a group of kids who would probably be happy to see me fail, or at least embarrass myself miserably, and there was always the possibility that both would happen. Then there was the weirdness of knowing that I'd seen what could only be Elliott's ghost behaving in a very unghostlike way. Not to mention another human teenager was dead and it was looking more and more as if a vamp had something to do with it.

I closed my eyes and told my body to relax and my mind to concentrate on something pleasant, like . . . like . . . how pretty the snow was . . .

Slowly, exhaustion took over and I finally, gratefully, fell into a deep sleep.

CHAPTER NINETEEN

Someone banging on the door pulled me awake from a dream about cat-shaped snowflakes.

"Zoey! Stevie Rae! You're gonna be late!" Shaunee's voice sounded muffled but urgent through the door, like an annoying alarm covered up by a towel.

"Okay, okay, I'm coming," I called as I tried to struggle out of my covers while Nala complained loudly. I glanced at my alarm clock, which I hadn't bothered to set. I mean, it wasn't like it was a school day and I usually didn't sleep more than eight or nine hours at a time and—

"Hell!" I blinked. Sure enough, the time was 9:59 P.M. I'd slept more than twelve hours? I stumbled to the door, pausing to shake Stevie Rae's leg.

"Mumph," she muttered sleepily.

I cracked the door. Shaunee was glaring at me.

"Please with the sleeping all damn day! You two have got to stop staying up late if you can't get up. Erik's going to be performing in half an hour."

"Ah, hell!" I rubbed my face, trying to force myself awake. "I forgot all about that."

Shaunee rolled her eyes. "You better hurry up and get dressed. And slap some serious makeup on that pale face and do something about your nappy hair. Boyfriend's been looking all over for you."

"Okay, okay. Crap! I'm coming. Will you and Erin—"

Shaunee put up her hand, cutting me off. "Please. We've already got you covered. Erin's in the auditorium saving front row seats as we speak."

"Is that you, Mamma? I don't wanna go to school today . . ." Stevie Rae mumbled, clearly not awake.

Shaunee snorted.

"We'll hurry. You guys just save those seats for us." I slammed the door shut and hurried over to Stevie Rae. "Wake up!" I shook her shoulder. She squinted and frowned up at me.

"Huh?"

"Stevie Rae, it's ten o'clock. P.M. We slept forever and now we're so late it's ridiculous."

"Huh?"

"Just wake the hell up!" I snapped, taking out my frustration that I'd overslept on her.

"Wha—" She looked blearily at the clock, and that seemed to finally get through to her. "Ohmygood*ness*! We're late."

I rolled my eyes. "That's what I've been trying to tell you. I'm gonna throw on something and work on my hair and makeup. You better jump in the shower. You look terrible."

" 'Kay." She staggered into the bathroom.

I yanked on a pair of jeans and a black sweater, and then got to work on my hair and makeup. I could not believe I'd totally blown off the fact that Erik was performing the Shakespearian monologue he'd taken to the competition. Actually, I hadn't even worried about how he'd placed, which was definitely not good girlfriend etiquette. Of course it wasn't like I didn't have other things on my mind, but still. Everyone thought I was the lucky girl who had caught Erik after he'd escaped from Aphrodite's nasty spiderweb (and by web I mean crotch). Hell, *I* thought I was lucky to have him, something that had been hard to remember when I was sucking Heath's blood and flirting with Loren.

"Sorry about oversleeping, Z." Stevie Rae came out of the bathroom in a gush of steamy air, towel-drying her short, blond curls. She was dressed a lot like I was, and she must still be half asleep because she looked pale and tired. She gave a huge yawn and stretched like a cat.

"No, it's my fault." I felt bad for the way I'd jumped on her before. "I should have known with how little I've been sleeping that I needed to set my alarm." I guess it shouldn't have been a surprise that Stevie Rae hadn't gotten much sleep lately, either. We are best friends and she definitely knows when I'm overstressed. We probably both needed a good, long, comalike sleep.

"I'll be ready in just a sec. I'm just gonna put on some mascara and gloss. My hair will dry in like two minutes anyway," Stevie Rae said.

We were out of there in five minutes. No time for breakfast, we bolted out of the dorm and practically ran to the auditorium. We made it to seats Erin had saved for us just as the lights flicked on and off, announcing that there were two minutes before the program began, and for people to take their seats.

"Erik stayed out here waiting for you until just a second ago," Damien said. I was glad to see he was sitting beside Jack. The two really did make a cute couple.

"Is he mad?" I asked.

"I'd say confused is a better description," Shaunee said.

"Or worried. He looked worried, too," Erin added.

I sighed. "Did you not tell him that I'd overslept?"

"Hence the reason my Twin said he looked worried," Shaunee said.

"I filled him in on the deaths of the two friends of yours. Erik understands it's been hard on you, and that's why he looked worried," Damien said, frowning at Shaunee and Erin.

"I'm just sayin', Z, Erik is too hot to be stood up," Erin said.

"Ditto, Twin," Shaunee said.

"I did *not*—" I sputtered, but the lights going out cut me off.

The drama teacher, Professor Nolan, came out onstage and spent a while explaining the importance of actors being trained in the classics, and talking about how prestigious the Shakespeare monologue contest is for vamps around the world. She reminded us that each of the twenty-five House of Night campuses worldwide send their five strongest competitors, which meant there were a total of 125 talented fledglings who competed against one another.

"Jeesh, I had no idea Erik had to go up against so many kids," I whispered to Stevie Rae.

"Erik probably kicked butt. He's awesome," Stevie Rae whispered back. Then she yawned again and coughed.

I frowned at her. She looked like crap. How could she still be tired?

"Sorry." She smiled sheepishly. "I gotta frog in my throat."

"Shhh!" the Twins hissed together.

I turned my attention back to Prof Nolan.

"The results of the competition have been sealed until today, when all of the students have returned to their home schools. I will announce the placings of each of our five finalists as I introduce them. Each will perform their competition monologue. I cannot begin to tell you how proud we are of our team. Every one of them did an exceptional job." Prof Nolan beamed. Then she went on to introduce the first performer, who was a kid named Kaci Crump. She was a fourth former who I didn't know very well because around the dorm she was kinda shy and quiet, even though she seemed nice. I didn't think she was a member of the Dark Daughters, and I made a mental note to send her an invitation to join. Prof Nolan announced that Kaci had placed fifty-second in the competition with her rendition of Beatrice's monologue from *Much Ado About Nothing*.

I thought she was good, but was blown away by the next kid, Cassie Kramme, a fifth former who'd placed twenty-fifth overall. She performed Portia's famous speech from *The Merchant of Venice* that begins, "The quality of mercy is not strained . . ." I recognized it because I'd chosen it as the monologue I memorized my freshman year at SIHS. Uh, Cassie's acting definitely would have kicked my ass. I didn't think she was a member of the Dark Daughters, either. Huh. Seems Aphrodite hadn't wanted much competition in the way of other drama queens. Big surprise.

The next performer was a kid I knew because he was a friend of Erik's. Cole Clifton was tall, blond, and totally cute. He'd finished twenty-second with his rendition of Romeo's "But soft, what light through yonder window breaks . . ." speech. Okay, he was good. Really, really good. I heard Shaunee and Erin (especially Shaunee) making lots of appreciative noises, and the clapping was furious from them when he finished. Hum . . . I'd have to talk to Erik about fixing Shaunee up with Cole. In my opinion more white boys should date women of color. It was good for expanding their horizons (especially true in Oklahoma white boys).

Speaking of women of color—the next performer was Deino. She was a drop-dead mixed girl with to-die-for hair and skin the color of vanilla latte. She was also one of Aphrodite's inner circle, or she used to be. I'd been introduced to her at Aphrodite's Full Moon Ritual. Deino was one of Aphrodite's three best friends. They'd renamed themselves after the mythological sisters of the Gorgon and Scylla: Deino, Enyo, Pemphredo. Translated, the names mean Terrible, Warlike, and Wasp.

The names definitely fit. They were three hateful, selfish bitches who had run out on Aphrodite during the Samhain Ritual and, as far as I could tell, hadn't spoken to her since. Okay, Aphrodite had messed up, and she was definitely haggish, but I could mess up and be a total hag and I don't think Stevie Rae, the Twins, or Damien would turn their backs on me. Get pissed at me—yep, definitely. Tell me I'd lost my mind—of course. But run out on me—no way.

Professor Nolan introduced Deino, saying that she'd finished an amazing eleventh overall, and then Deino began Cleopatra's death scene monologue. I had to admit that she was good. Really good. Watching her I was so dazzled by her talent that I started to wonder how much of her hateful haggishness had been because of Aphrodite's influence. Since I'd taken over the Dark Daughters none of Aphrodite's close friends had caused any kind of problems. Actually, now that I thought about it, I realized that Terrible, Warlike, and Wasp had been keeping a pretty low profile. Huh. Well, I'd said that I wanted to include one of Aphrodite's old inner circle in my new Prefect Council. Maybe Deino would be the right choice. I could ask Erik about her. With Aphrodite out of power I could give Deino a chance (as well as sincerely wish her name wasn't so disturbing).

I was still considering how to go about telling my friends (who were also my fellow Prefects) that I was thinking about asking Terrible to join our Council when Professor Nolan returned to the stage and waited for the audience to quiet down. When she started speaking her eyes were shining with excitement and she seemed ready to burst. I felt a little thrill run through me. Erik had finished in the top ten!

"Erik Night is our final performer. He has been an incredible talent since the day he was Marked three years ago. I am proud to be his teacher and his mentor," she said, beaming. "Please give him the hero's welcome he deserves for placing *first* in the International Shakespearian Monologue Competition!"

The auditorium exploded as Erik strode, smiling, onto the stage. I could hardly breathe. How could I have forgotten how utterly gorgeous he is? Tall—taller than Cole even—he had black hair that did that adorable Superman curl thing, and eyes so brilliant blue they were like staring into the summer sky. Like the other performers, he was dressed all in black, with the fifth former insignia of Nyx's golden chariot pulling a trail of stars over his left breast as the only break in the dark color scheme. And, let me tell you, he made black look good.

He walked to center stage, stopped, smiled directly (and obviously) into my eyes, and winked at me. He was so damn hot I thought I would die. Then he bowed his head and when he raised it he wasn't eighteen-year-old Erik Night, vampyre fledgling, fifth former at the House of Night, anymore. Somehow, right in front of our eyes, he had become a Moorish warrior who was trying to explain to a room full of doubters how a Venetian princess had fallen in love with him, and he with her.

> *"Her father lov'd me; oft invited me;*
> *Still question'd me the story of my life*
> *From year to year, the battles, sieges, fortunes*
> *That I have pass'd."*

I couldn't take my eyes from him, and neither could anyone else in the room as he transformed into Othello. I also couldn't help but compare him to Heath. In his own way, Heath was as successful and talented as Erik. He was Broken Arrow's star quarterback, with a bright collegiate and maybe even pro football career in front of him. Heath was a leader. Erik was a leader. I'd grown up watching Heath play ball, had been proud of him, and had cheered for him. But I had never been awed by his talent like I was awed by Erik. And the only time Heath had ever made me feel like I couldn't breathe was when he sliced into his skin and offered his blood to me.

Erik paused in his monologue, and moved forward until he was standing at the edge of the stage, so close that if I stood I could reach up and touch him. Then he looked into my eyes and completed Othello's speech *to me*, as though I was the absent Desdemona he spoke of:

> *"She wish'd she had not heard it, yet she wish'd*
> *That heaven had made her such a man; she thank'd me,*
> *And bade me, if I had a friend that lov'd her,*
> *I should but teach him how to tell my story,*
> *And that would woo her. Upon this hint I spake:*
> *She lov'd me for the dangers I had pass'd,*
> *And I lov'd her that she did pity them."*

Erik touched his fingers to his lips, then held his hand out to me as if to offer me his formal kiss, and then pressed those fingers over his heart and bowed his head. The audience erupted into cheers and a standing ovation. Stevie Rae stood cheering next to me, wiping her eyes and laughing.

"That was so romantic I almost peed my pants," she yelled.

"Me, too!" I laughed.

And then Professor Nolan was back onstage, closing the performance and directing everyone to the wine and cheese reception set up in the lobby.

"Come on, Z," Erin said, grabbing one of my hands.

"Yeah, we're staying with you 'cause that friend of Erik's that played Romeo is insanely hot," Shaunee said as she grabbed my other hand. The Twins started hauling me through the crowd, shouldering us past the slow-moving kids like mini-tugboats. I looked helplessly back at Damien and Stevie Rae. Clearly they were going to have to catch up on their own. The Twins were a force beyond even my control.

We popped from the bottled-up crowd trying to exit the auditorium like three corks coming to the surface. And suddenly there Erik was, just entering the lobby from the side actors' entrance. Our eyes met and he instantly stopped talking to Cole and headed straight to me.

"Mmm, mmm, mmm. He is so totally *fiiiine*," Shaunee murmured.

"As usual, we're in complete agreement, Twin," Erin sighed dreamily.

I couldn't do anything but stand there and smile like a moron as Erik reached us. With a very naughty sparkle in his eyes he took my hand, kissed it, and then made a sweeping bow and proclaimed in his actor's voice that carried all around the room, "Hello, my sweet Desdemona."

I felt my cheeks getting really hot, and I actually giggled. He was just pulling me into a warm, but very proper-for-public-consumption hug when I heard a familiar hateful laugh. Aphrodite, looking amazing in a short black skirt, stiletto boots, and a slinky sweater, was laughing as she walked (actually, she twitched more than she walked—I mean, the girl could seriously shake her butt) past us. Over Erik's shoulder I met her eyes and, in a silky voice that would have sounded friendly had it not been coming from her mouth, said, "If he's calling you Desdemona, then I suggest you be careful. If it even looked like you're cheating on him he'll strangle you in your bed. But you'd never cheat on him, would you?" Then she flipped her long, blond, perfect hair and twitched away.

No one said anything for a second, then the Twins, at the same time, said, "Issues. She has issues," and everyone laughed.

Everyone but me. All I could think about was the fact that she'd seen Loren and me in the media center, and that it definitely could have looked like I was cheating on Erik. Was she warning me that she was going to tell Erik? Okay, I wasn't worried about him strangling me in my bed, but would he believe her? Also, Aphrodite's all-too-perfect appearance reminded me that I was wearing wrinkled jeans and a hastily thrown-on sweater. My hair and makeup had definitely looked better. Actually, I think I still might have pillow marks on my cheek.

"Don't let her get to you," Erik said gently.

I looked up at him. He was holding my hand and smiling down at me. I mentally shook myself. "Don't worry, she's not," I said brightly. "Anyway, who cares about her? You won the competition! That's amazing, Erik. I'm so proud of you!" I hugged him again, loving his clean smell and how his height made me feel small and delicate. Then our little pocket of privacy was gone as more and more people poured out of the auditorium.

"Erik, it's so cool you won!" Erin said. "But it's not like we're surprised. You definitely kick ass onstage."

"Totally. And so does boyfriend over there." Shaunee jerked her chin in Cole's direction. "He is one fine Romeo."

Erik grinned. "I'll tell him you said so."

"You can also tell him that if he wants a little brown sugar in his Juliet he need look no farther than right here." She pointed at herself and shimmied her hips.

"Twin, if Juliet had been black I do not believe things would have come to such a shitty end between her and Romeo. I mean, we would have shown more sense than drinking that sleeping potion crap and going through all that drama just because of some unfortunate parental issues."

"Exactly," Shaunee said.

None of us stated the obvious—that Erin, with her blond hair and blue eyes, was definitely NOT BLACK. We were too used to her and Shaunee being twinlike to question the weirdness of it.

"Erik, you were amazing!" Damien rushed up with Jack following close behind.

"Congratulations," Jack said shyly, but with definite enthusiasm.

Erik smiled at them. "Thanks, guys. Hey, Jack. I was too nervous before the performance to say that I'm glad you're here. It'll be nice to have a roommate."

Jack's cute face lit up, and I squeezed Erik's hand. This was one reason why I liked him so much. Besides being gorgeous and talented, Erik was an authentically nice guy. There were a lot of guys in his position (ridiculously popular) who would have either ignored this little third former roommate or, worse, been visibly pissed that they'd have to share a room with a "fag." Erik wasn't like that at all, and I couldn't help but compare him to Heath, who would probably have been freaked that he had to room with a gay kid. Not that Heath was hateful or anything like that, but he was a typical teenage Okie boy, which tended to mean narrowminded homophobe. Which made me realize that I'd never asked Erik where he was from. Jeesh, I was a crappy girlfriend.

"Did you hear me, Zoey?"

"Huh?" Damien's question shut off my inner babbling, but no, I hadn't heard him.

"Hello! Earth to Zoey! I asked if you realized what time it was. And are you remembering the Full Moon Ritual starts at midnight?"

I looked at the wall clock. "Ah, hell!" It was 11:05. I still needed to change my clothes and then get to the rec hall, light the circle candles, make sure the five candles for the elements were in place, and check on the Goddess's table. "Erik, I'm so sorry, but I have to leave. There are a million things to do before the ritual starts." I made eye contact with each of my four friends. "You guys have to come with me." They nodded like bobble-headed dolls. I turned back to Erik. "You're coming to the ritual, aren't you?"

"Yeah. And that reminds me. I got you something in New York. Hang on for just a sec, and I'll go get it."

He hurried back through the actors' entrance to the auditorium.

"I swear he is too damn good to be true," Erin said.

"Let's hope his friend is just like him," Shaunee said, sending Cole a flirty smile from across the room, which I noticed he returned.

"Damien, did you get the eucalyptus and sage for me?" I was already feeling nervous. Hell! I should have eaten. My stomach was an empty cavern just waiting to clench up on me.

"Don't worry, Z. I got the eucalyptus and I even braided it together with the sage for you," Damien said.

"Everything will be perfect, you'll see," Stevie Rae said.

"Yeah, you don't need to be nervous," Shaunee said.

"We'll be right there with you," Erin finished.

I smiled at them, incredibly glad they were my friends. And then Erik was back. He handed me the big white box he was carrying. I hesitated before tearing into it and Shaunee said, "Z, if you don't open it I will."

"Damn right," Erin said.

Eagerly, I slid off the decorative string that held it shut, opened the lid, and gasped (along with everyone else who was standing close enough to see). Inside the box pooled the most beautiful dress I'd ever seen. It was black, but woven into the material were metallic specks of silver, so that wherever the light touched, it glittered and sparkled like shooting stars against the night sky.

"Erik, this is beautiful." I sounded choked because I was trying really hard not to make a fool out of myself and burst into happy tears.

"I wanted you to have something special for your first ritual as leader of the Dark Daughters," he said.

We hugged again before my friends and I had to rush out and head to the rec hall. I clutched the dress to my chest and tried not to think about the fact that while Erik was buying me an amazingly cool present I had been either sucking Heath's blood or flirting with Loren. And while I tried not to think about that, I also tried to ignore the guilty voice inside my head that kept saying, over and over, *You don't deserve him . . . you don't deserve him . . . you don't deserve him . . .*

CHAPTER TWENTY

"Shaunee, Erin, and Stevie Rae—you guys start lighting the white candles. Damien, if you place the colored candles for the elements in their positions I'll be sure that everything's set for Nyx's table."

"Easy—" Shaunee said.

"Peasy," Erin chimed in.

"Japanesy," Stevie Rae added, making the Twins give her mirror eye rolls.

"Are the element candles still in the supply room?" Damien asked.

"Yep," I called as I headed to the kitchen. I was glad I'd already put together a big tray of fresh fruits, cheeses, and meats for Nyx's table. I just needed to retrieve it and the bottle of wine from the refrigerator, and arrange the bounty neatly on the table placed in the center of the large circle made of white candles. The table already had an ornate goblet on it, as well as a beautiful statue of the Goddess, a long, elegant lighter, and the purple candle that would represent spirit, the last element I would call to the circle. The table symbolized the richness of the blessings Nyx has given her children, vampyres and fledglings. I liked setting up the Goddess's table. It made me feel calm, something that I especially needed tonight. I arranged the food and wine, and went over and over in my mind the words of the ritual I was going to use in—I glanced at the clock and felt my stomach tighten—in fifteen minutes. Fledglings were already starting to come into the rec hall, but they were being pretty subdued and hanging out in the corners of the large room in clusters while they watched the Twins and Stevie Rae light the white candles that would form the circumference of the circle. Maybe I wasn't the only one nervous about tonight. It was a big change to have me lead the Dark Daughters. Aphrodite had been leader for the past two years, and in that time the group had become a cliquish, snobby club where fledglings who weren't part of the "in" crowd were used and made fun of.

Well, things were changing tonight.

I glanced at my friends. We'd all hurried to change our clothes before coming to the rec hall, and everyone had chosen to wear solid black to keep with the theme of the amazing dress Erik had given me. I glanced down at myself for the zillionth time. The dress was simple, but perfect. It had a round neckline that was low, but not as low as ho-ish Aphrodite's ritual dresses had been. It was long-sleeved and hugged my body to the waist, from there down it swirled gracefully to the floor. The silver specks that covered it glimmered in the candlelight whenever I moved. What also glittered whenever I moved was the necklace that dangled from the silver chain around my neck. Each Dark Daughter and Son had a similar necklace, with two exceptions—my triple moons were encrusted with garnets, and mine was the only necklace that had been found with the body of a dead human teenager. Okay, it wasn't exactly *my* necklace that had been found. It was one like mine. Just like mine.

No. I wouldn't think about negative things tonight. I would only concentrate on positives, and on preparing myself to lead my first public circle-casting and ritual. Damien returned to the main room with a big tray on which he balanced the four candles that represented each element: yellow for air, red for fire, blue for water, and green for earth. I already had my purple spirit candle on Nyx's table. I smiled and thought how great my friends looked, dressed chicly in black with their silver Dark Daughters' necklaces. Stevie Rae had already taken her place at the northernmost part of the circle where earth should be. Damien handed her the green candle. I just happened to be watching them, so there was no mistaking what I saw. As Stevie Rae touched the candle, her eyes widened and she let out a weird sound that was a cross between a scream and a gasp. Damien had taken such a hasty step back that he had to clutch at the other candles to keep them from tumbling off the tray.

"Did you feel it?" Stevie Rae's voice sounded weird, hushed yet amplified.

Damien looked shaky, but he nodded and said, "Yeah, and I smelled it, too."

Then they both turned to look at me.

"Uh, Zoey, could you come here for a second?" Damien asked. He sounded normal again, and had I not been watching what had happened between the two of them I would have thought nothing more was going on than maybe they needed help with the candles.

But I had been watching, which is why I didn't yell from the center of the circle and ask what they wanted. Instead I hurried over to them and kept my voice low. "What's going on?"

"Tell her," Damien said to Stevie Rae.

Still looking wide-eyed, startled, and more than a little pale, Stevie Rae said, "Can't you smell it?"

I frowned. "Smell it? What are—" And then I did smell it— freshly cut hay, honeysuckle, and something else that I swear reminded me of newly plowed dirt in my grandma's lavender fields.

"I do," I said hesitantly, feeling thoroughly confused. "But I didn't call earth into the circle." My affinity, or power, given to me by Nyx was the ability to materialize the five elements. Even after a month, I wasn't exactly sure what all that power encompassed, but one thing I did know was that when I cast a circle and called each element to it, all of them manifested very physically. The wind whipped around me when I called air. Fire made my skin glow with heat (and, quite frankly, made me sweat). I could feel the coolness of the sea when I evoked water. And when I called earth to the circle I smelled earthy things and even felt grass under my feet (even when I was wearing shoes, which was truly weird).

But, as I'd said, I hadn't begun casting the circle, so I hadn't called any of the elements, yet Stevie Rae, Damien, and I were clearly smelling earth smells.

Then Damien sucked air and his face split into a huge grin. "Stevie Rae has an affinity for earth!"

"Huh?" I said brilliantly.

"No way," Stevie Rae said.

"Try this," Damien went on, his excitement growing by the second. "Close your eyes, Stevie Rae, and think about the earth." He looked at me. "Don't *you* think about it."

" 'Kay," I said quickly. His excitement was contagious. It would be fantastic if Stevie Rae had an earth affinity. Having an elemental affinity was a powerful gift from Nyx, and I would definitely love it if my best friend had been blessed like that from our Goddess.

"Okay." Stevie Rae sounded breathless, but she closed her eyes.

"What's happening?" Erin said.

"Why's she have her eyes closed?" Shaunee said. Then she sniffed the air. "And why does it smell like hay over there? Stevie Rae, I swear if you're trying out some kind of bumpkin perfume I might have to smack you."

"Shhh!" Damien put his finger to his lips and shushed her. "We think Stevie Rae might have developed an earth affinity."

Shaunee blinked. "Nuh uh!"

"Huh," Erin said.

"I can *not* concentrate with y'all talking," Stevie Rae said, opening her eyes to glare at the Twins.

"Sorry," they muttered.

"Try again," I encouraged her.

She nodded. Then she closed her eyes and screwed her forehead up in concentration while she thought about the earth. I did *not* think about it, which was actually pretty hard because within a couple of seconds the air was filled with the smells of freshly mowed grass, and flowers, and I could even hear birds chirping like crazy and—

"Ohmygod! Stevie Rae has an affinity for earth!" I blurted.

Stevie Rae's eyes sprang open and she covered her mouth with both of her hands, looking shocked and thrilled.

"Stevie Rae, that's amazing!" Damien said, and in seconds all of us were congratulating and hugging her while she giggled through happy tears.

Then it happened. I had one of my *feelings*. And this time it was (thankfully) a good one.

"Damien, Shaunee, Erin—I want you guys to take your places in the circle." They gave me questioning looks, but must have recognized the tone of my voice because they instantly did what I told them to do. I wasn't exactly the boss of them, but my friends respected that I was in training to someday be their High Priestess, so they obediently walked to the place in the circle that I had assigned to each of them weeks ago when it had only been the five of us, and I was casting a circle to try to figure out if I really had a Goddess-given affinity, or if I just had very little sense and an overactive imagination.

As they took their places I looked around at the kids who were already in the rec hall. I definitely needed outside help. Then Erik walked into the room with Jack, and I grinned and motioned them over to me.

"What's up, Z? You look like you're going to explode," Erik said, and then he lowered his voice, and for my ears alone added, "And you look as hot in that dress as I thought you would."

"Thanks, I love it!" I did a quick little twirl that was partially flirting with Erik, and partially pure happiness at what I was almost sure was getting ready to happen. "Jack, would you please go over to Damien and get the tray of candles he's holding and bring them back here to the middle of the circle?"

"Yep," Jack said and scampered off to do as I asked. Okay, he didn't actually scamper, but he was very perky.

"What's going on?" Erik asked.

"You'll see." I grinned, barely able to suppress my excitement.

When Jack was back with the candles I put the tray on Nyx's table. I concentrated for a second, and decided my instincts were telling me fire would be the right choice. Then I picked up the red candle and handed it to Erik. "Okay, I need you to take this candle over to Shaunee."

Erik wrinkled his forehead. "Just take it over to her?"

"Yeah. Hand it to her and then pay attention."

"To what?"

"I'd rather not say."

He shrugged and gave me a look that said that even though he might think I was hot he also might think that I had lost my mind, but he did as I asked and walked over to where Shaunee was standing in the southernmost part of the circle—the area from which I called the element fire. He stopped in front of her. Shaunee looked around him at me.

"Take the candle from him," I called across the circle to her, concentrating on how cute Erik looked so that I wouldn't be thinking about fire at all.

Shaunee shrugged. "Okay," she said.

She took the red candle from Erik. I was watching her closely, but I hadn't needed to. What happened was so obvious that several of the kids standing around the outside of the circle gasped along with Shaunee. The instant her hand touched the candle there was a *whoosh* noise. Her long, black hair began to lift and crackle as if it was filled with static electricity, and her beautiful chocolate skin glowed as if she had been lit from within.

"I knew it!" I cried, practically jumping up and down with excitement.

Shaunee looked up from her glowing body to meet my eyes. "I'm doing this, aren't I?"

"You are!"

"I have an affinity for fire!"

"Yes, you do!" I yelled happily.

I heard lots of oohs and ahhs from the ever-increasing crowd, but I didn't have time for them right now. Following my gut feeling I motioned for Erik to come back to the center of the circle, which he did with a huge grin on his face.

"That may be the coolest thing I've ever seen," he said.

"Just wait. If I'm right, and I think I am, there's more." I gave him the blue candle. "Now take this one to Erin."

"Your wish is my command," he said with an old-time flourish. If anyone else bowed like that in public they would have looked like an utter dork. Erik looked like an utter hottie—part gentleman, part bad boy pirate. I was thinking about how yummy Erik was when Erin and Shaunee let out twin squeals of happiness at almost the same instant.

"Look at the floor!" Erin was pointing to the tile floor of the rec hall. In a circular area around her the tile floor was rippling and it appeared to be lapping against feet, even though nothing was actually getting wet, making it seem that Erin was standing in the middle of the ghost of an ocean shore. Then she looked up at me with shimmering blue eyes. "Oh, Z! Water is my affinity!"

I grinned at her. "Yes, it is!"

Erik hurried back to me. This time I didn't have to prompt him to pick up the yellow candle.

"Damien, right?" he said.

"Totally right."

He headed to Damien, who was fidgeting at the easternmost part of the circle where the element air should manifest. Erik offered the yellow candle to Damien. Damien didn't touch it. Instead, he peered around Erik to me. The boy looked scared to death.

"It's okay, go ahead and take it," I told him.

"Are you sure it's going to be okay?" He glanced nervously around at what was now a large crowd of fledglings watching him expectantly.

I knew what was wrong. Damien was afraid he would fail, that he would be left out of the magic that was happening to the girls. In Soc class I'd learned that it was unusual for a gift as strong as an affinity for an element to be given to a male. Nyx gifted men with exceptional strength, and their affinities usually had to do with the physical, like Dragon, our fencing instructor, had been gifted with exceptional quickness and visual accuracy. Air was definitely a female affinity, and it would be nothing short of incredible for Nyx to gift Damien with an air affinity. But I had a calm, happy feeling deep inside me. I nodded at Damien and tried to telegraph confidence to him. "I'm sure. Go on. I'll be busy thinking about how cute Erik is while you're calling air to you," I said.

As Erik grinned over his shoulder at me Damien drew a deep

breath, and looking a lot like he thought he was grabbing on to a live bomb, he took the candle from Erik.

"Superb! Glorious! Wondrous!" Damien made use of his large vocabulary while his brown hair lifted and his clothes flapped crazily in the sudden wind that surrounded him. When he looked at me again happy tears were running down his cheeks. "Nyx has given me a gift. *Me*," he enunciated carefully, and I knew what he was saying in that one word—that he realized Nyx found him worthy even though his parents didn't, and even though much of his life people had made fun of him because he liked guys. I had to blink hard to keep from bawling like a baby.

"Yes, you," I said firmly.

"Your friends are spectacular, Zoey." Neferet's voice carried above the excited noise of the kids who were now converging on the four newly discovered talents.

The High Priestess was standing just inside the entrance to the rec hall, and I wondered how long she'd been there. I could see that there were a few professors with her, but they were in the shadow of the doorway and it was difficult to make out exactly who they were. *Okay. You can do this. You can face her.* I swallowed hard and forced my thoughts to focus on my friends and the miracles that had just happened to them.

"Yes, my friends are spectacular!" I agreed enthusiastically.

Neferet nodded. "It is only right that Nyx, in her wisdom, has thought to gift you, a fledgling who has such unusual powers, with a group of friends who are also blessed with impressive powers of their own." She dramatically swept out her arms. "I prophesy that this group of fledglings will make history. Never before has so much been given to so many at the same time and place." Her smile included all of us and she truly looked like a loving mother. I would have been as taken in as everyone else by her warmth and beauty if it hadn't been for the glimpse I got of the thin red line of a newly healing cut that marred her forearm. I shivered and forced my eyes and my thoughts from the evidence that what I'd witnessed had definitely not been a figment of my imagination.

Good thing, too, because Neferet had turned her attention to me.

"Zoey, I believe this is the perfect time to announce your blue-print for the new Dark Daughters and Sons." I opened my mouth to start explaining what I had in mind (even though I hadn't planned on announcing the changes I wanted to make until *after* I'd cast the ritualistic circle and given the "old" membership some tangible proof that I actually had been gifted by Nyx), but no one paid any attention to me. Everyone's attention was riveted on Neferet as she strode out into the room and stood not far from Shaunee so that my friend's manifestation of fire lit up the High Priestess like a spotlight made of flame. In the same powerful, al-luring voice she used during rituals, Neferet spoke. Only this time she was using *my* words—*my* ideas.

"It is time the Dark Daughters had a foundation. It has been decided that Zoey Redbird will begin an era and a new tradition with her leadership. She will form a Prefect Council, made up of seven fledglings, of which she will be Head Prefect. The other members of the Council will be Shaunee Cole, Erin Bates, Stevie Rae Johnson, Damien Maslin, and Erik Night. There will be one more Prefect chosen from Aphrodite's old Inner Circle to repre-sent my wish for unity among the fledglings."

Her wish? I ground my teeth together and tried to find my happy place while Neferet paused to let the general sounds of cel-ebration die (which included the Twins, Stevie Rae, Damien, Erik, and Jack, cheering their brains out). Jeesh. She was making it seem like *she* was responsible for ideas I'd sweated over for weeks!

"The Prefect Council will be responsible for the workings of the new Dark Daughters and Sons, which includes being certain that from this day forth all members exemplify the following ideas: they should be authentic for air; they should be faithful for fire; they should be wise for water; they should be empathetic for earth; and they should be sincere for spirit. If a Dark Daughter or Son fails to uphold these new ideals, it will be the job of the Prefect Council to decide upon a penalty, which could include expulsion from the group." She paused again, and I observed how serious and attentive everyone was, which was the exact reaction I had hoped for when I made this announcement during the actual Full Moon Ritual. "I have also decided that it would behoove our fledglings to become more involved with the surrounding community. After all, ignorance breeds fear and hatred. So I want the Dark Daughters and Sons to begin working with a local charity. After much consideration I decided that the perfect organization would be Street Cats, the rescue charity for homeless cats."

There was good-humored laughter at this, which was the reaction Neferet had had when I'd told her *my* decision to have the Dark Daughters involved in that particular charity. I could not believe Neferet was taking credit for everything that I had told her that night at dinner.

"I will leave you now. This is Zoey's ritual, and I am simply here to show my heartfelt support for my talented fledgling." She gave me a kind smile, which I made myself return. "But first I have a gift for the new Prefect Council." She clapped her hands together and five male vampyres I'd never seen before emerged from the shadows of the entryway. They were each carrying what looked like thick, rectangular tiles that must have been about a foot square and a couple of inches thick. They placed them at the floor by her feet and they disappeared back out the door. I stared at the things. They were a creamy color and looked like they might be wet. I had no clue what they were. Neferet's laughter bubbled around us, making me grind my teeth together. Did no one else think she sounded totally patronizing?

"Zoey, I'm shocked you don't recognize your own idea!"

"I—no. I don't know what they are," I said.

"They're squares of wet cement. I remembered that you told me you wanted each of the members of the Prefect Council to have an imprint of his or her handprints made so that the fledgling's handprint will be preserved forever. Tonight six of the seven members of the new Council can do that."

I blinked at her. Great. She was finally giving me credit for something, and it was Damien's idea. "Thank you for the present," I said, and then added quickly, "And it was Damien's idea to make handprints, not mine."

Her smile was blinding, and when she turned it on Damien I didn't have to look at him to know that he practically wriggled with pleasure. "And what a lovely idea it was, too, Damien." Then she addressed the entire room again. "I am pleased that Nyx has gifted this group so fully. And I say blessed be to all of you, good night!" She dropped to the floor in a graceful curtsy. Then, to the cheers of the fledglings, she rose and made a skirt-flowing, magnificent exit.

Which left me standing in the middle of an un-cast circle feeling like I was all dressed up with nowhere to go.

CHAPTER TWENTY-ONE

It took forever to get everyone settled down and in place for the ritual to begin, especially because I couldn't show how I was really feeling—which was pissed. Not only would no one understand, but also no one would believe what I was beginning to see: that there was something dark and wrong about Neferet. And why should anyone understand or believe me? I was, after all, just a kid. No matter what powers Nyx had given me I was totally not in the same league with a High Priestess. Besides that, no one except me had witnessed the little puzzle pieces that were fitting together to create such a terrible picture.

Aphrodite would understand and believe me. I hated that the thought was true.

"Zoey, just let me know whenever you're ready and I'll start the music," Jack called from the back corner of the rec hall where all the audio equipment was kept. Apparently the new kid was a genius with electronics, so I'd instantly drafted him to run the music for the ritual.

"Okay, just a sec. How about I nod at you when I'm ready?"

"Fine with me!" he said with a grin.

I backed up a few feet, realizing that, ironically, I was now standing almost exactly where Neferet had stood not long before. I tried to clear my mind of all the confusion and negatives that were swirling in it. My eyes traveled around the circle. There was a fairly large group of kids present—actually more than I had expected to show. They had quieted down, though there was still a general air of excitement in the room. The white candles in their tall glass containers illuminated the circle in a clean, bright light. I could see my four friends standing in their positions, waiting expectantly for me to begin the ritual. I focused on them and the wonderful gifts they had been given, and got ready to nod at Jack.

"I thought I'd volunteer my services to you."

Loren's deep voice had me jumping and making an unattractive little squeaking noise. He was standing behind me in the entranceway.

"Crap, Loren! You scared me so bad I almost peed on myself!" I blurted before I had time to control my dorky mouth. But I was telling the truth, Loren had me clutching my pearls in a total freak-out.

Apparently he didn't mind my inability to control my mouth. He gave me a long, slow, sexy smile. "I thought you knew I was here."

"No. I was a little distracted."

"Stressed, I bet." He touched my arm in a gesture that probably looked innocent. You know, friendly and professorially supportive. But felt like a caress, a really warm caress. His widening smile made me wonder about his vamp intuitiveness. If he could read any part of my mind I would just die. "Well, I'm here to help you with that stress."

Was he kidding? Just the sight of him made me lose my mind. Stress-free around Loren Blake? Not hardly.

"Really? How are you going to do that?" I asked with just a hint of a flirty smile, very aware that the entire room was watching us and that the entire room included my boyfriend.

"I'll do for you what I do for Neferet."

The silence stretched between us as my mind wallowed around

in the gutter wondering just exactly what he did for Neferet. Thankfully, he didn't let me wallow too long.

"Every High Priestess has a poet who recites ancient verse to evoke the presence of the Muse as she enters into her rituals. Today, I'm offering to recite for a very special High Priestess in training. Plus I believe there are some misconceptions that need to be cleared up."

He crossed his fist over his heart in a gesture of respect people often used when they greeted Neferet. Unlike a cool, confident High Priestess, and very much like a dork, I just stood there staring at him. I mean, I didn't have a clue what he was talking about. Misconceptions? As in someone might believe I know what the hell I'm doing?

"But I will need your permission," he continued. "I wouldn't want to intrude upon your ritual."

"Oh, no!" Then I realized what he must think my silence and then my blurted *oh, no* meant, and I got hold of myself. "What I mean is that no, you definitely aren't intruding, and yes, I accept your offer. Graciously," I added, wondering how I had ever felt grown and sexy around this man.

His smile made me want to melt in a pool at his feet. "Excellent. Whenever you're ready, just give me the word and I'll begin your introduction." He glanced over to where Jack was gawking at us. "Mind if I have words with your assistant about the slight alteration in your plans?"

"No," I said, feeling utterly surreal. As Loren walked past me his arm brushed mine intimately. Was I imagining the flirting that was going on between us? I looked at the circle and saw that everyone was staring at me. Reluctantly, I found Erik where he was standing beside Stevie Rae. He smiled at me and winked. Okay, it didn't seem like Erik had noticed anything wrong in Loren's behavior toward me. I glanced at Shaunee and Erin. They were following Loren with hungry eyes. They must have felt me looking at them, because they both managed to pull their gazes from Loren's butt. They waggled their eyebrows at me and grinned. They, too, were acting completely normal.

It was just me who was being weird about Loren.

"Get yourself together!" I hissed at myself under my breath. *Concentrate . . . concentrate . . . concentrate . . .*

"Zoey, I'm ready when you are." Loren had moved back beside me.

I drew a deep, calming breath and lifted my head. "I'm ready."

His dark eyes held mine. "Remember, trust your instincts. Nyx speaks to the hearts of her priestesses." Then he walked a few paces into the room.

"It is a night for joy!" Loren's voice was not just deep and expressive, it was also commanding. He had the same ability Erik did to captivate a room using only his voice. Everyone instantly was silent, waiting eagerly for his next words. "But you should know that the joy of this night isn't found only in the gifts Nyx has so visibly allowed to manifest here. Some of tonight's joy was born two nights ago when your new leader was deciding upon the future she wanted for the Dark Daughters and Sons."

I felt a little start of surprise. I didn't know if anyone else really got what he was saying—that *I,* and not Neferet, had come up with the new standards for the Dark Daughters, but I appreciated his attempt to set things right.

"In celebration of Zoey Redbird, and her new vision for the Dark Daughters, I am honored to open her first ritual as your Head Prefect and High Priestess trainee with a classic poem about joy being newly born that was written by my namesake, the vampyre poet William Blake." Loren looked back at me and mouthed, *You're on!* then he nodded to Jack, who hurriedly turned to the audio equipment.

The magical sounds of Enya's orchestral song "Aldebaran" filled the room. I swallowed down the last of my nervousness, and began walking forward, tracing a path around the outside of the circle, like I'd watched both Neferet and Aphrodite do in the rituals they'd led. As they had, I moved in time with the music, making little impromptu turns and dance moves. I'd been really freaked out about this part of the ritual—I mean, I'm not clumsy, but I'm also not Ms. Cheerleader/Pom Squad. Thankfully, it was lots easier than I'd imagined it to be. I'd chosen this particular music because of its beautiful, lilting beat, and also because I'd Googled Aldebaran and found out it was a giant star—and I thought music that celebrated the night sky was appropriate for tonight. It was a good choice, because it seemed as if the music was carrying me, moving my body gracefully around the room and overcoming my initial nerves and awkwardness. When Loren's voice began reciting the poem, he, too, echoed the cadence of the music, just like my body was, and it felt like we were making magic together.

> " 'I have no name,
>   I am but two days old.'
>   What shall I call thee?
>   'I happy am,
>   Joy is my name.'
>   Sweet joy befall thee!"

The words of the poem thrilled me. And as I moved toward the center of the circle I felt like I was literally personifying the emotion.

> "Pretty joy!
>   Sweet joy but two days old,

Sweet joy I call thee;
Thou dost smile . . ."

Echoing the words of the poem, I smiled, loving the sense of magic and mystery that seemed to fill the room along with the music and Loren's voice.

"I sing the while—
Sweet joy befall thee."

Somehow Loren timed it perfectly, and his poem concluded as I reached Nyx's table at the middle of the circle. I was only a little breathless as I smiled around the circle and said, "Welcome to the first Full Moon Ritual for the new Dark Daughters and Sons!"

"Merry meet!" everyone responded automatically.

Without giving myself an opportunity to hesitate, I picked up the ornate ritualistic lighter and moved purposefully to stand before Damien. Air was the first element called when casting a circle, as well as the last to leave it when the circle was closed. I could feel Damien's excitement and expectation as if they were a physical force.

I smiled at him, swallowed hard to clear the dryness in my throat. When I spoke I tried to project my voice like Neferet. I'm not sure how good of a job I did at it. Let's just say I was glad that the circle was a relatively small one and the room was quiet.

"I call the element air first to our circle, and I ask that it guard us with winds of insight. Come to me, air!"

I touched the lighter to Damien's candle and it flared to life, even though he and I were suddenly standing in the middle of a very obvious whirlwind that lifted our hair and sang playfully within the full skirt of my beautiful dress. Damien laughed and whispered, "Sorry, it's all so new to me that it's hard for me not to be a little overexuberant."

"I understand completely," I whispered back to him. Then I turned to my right and continued around the circle to Shaunee, who was looking unusually serious, like she was getting ready to take a math test. "Relax," I whispered, trying not to move my lips.

She nodded jerkily, still looking scared to death.

"I call the element of fire to our circle and ask that it burn brilliantly here with the light of might and passion, bringing both to guard and aid us. Come to me, fire!"

I started to touch the end of my lighter to the red candle Shaunee held, but before I could get it there the wick burst into a flickering white light that lifted up well past the lip of the glass jar holding it.

"Oopsie," Shaunee mumbled.

I had to bite my cheek to keep from laughing, and I moved quickly on to my right to where Erin was waiting with the blue candle clutched before her like it was a bird that would fly away if she didn't keep hold of it.

"I call water to this circle and ask that you guard us with your oceans of mystery and majesty, and nurture us as your rain does the grass and trees. Come to me, water!"

I lit Erin's blue candle, and it was the weirdest thing. I swear it was like I was suddenly transported to the shores of a lake. I could smell the water and feel it cool against my skin, even though I knew I was standing in the middle of a room and absolutely could not be anywhere near water.

"Guess I should tone it down a little," Erin said softly.

"Nah," I whispered. Then I headed to Stevie Rae. I thought she looked kinda pale, but she had a big grin on her face when I moved into the space in front of her.

"I'm ready!" she said, so loud the kids standing around us laughed softly.

"Good," I said. "Then I call earth to the circle, and ask that you guard us with the strength of stone and the richness of wheat-filled fields. Come to me, earth!" I lit the green candle and was washed in the scents of a meadow—surrounded by birdsong and flowers.

"It's just so cool!" Stevie Rae said.

"So is that." Erik's voice surprised me and when I looked at him he pointed to the circle. Confused, I followed his hand to see a beautiful silver thread of light connecting each of my four friends—the four personifications of the elements—and making a boundary of power within the candles that had already lit the circumference.

"Like it was for us alone, only it's stronger now." Stevie Rae whispered the words, but I could tell by Erik's startled look that he'd heard her. Guess I'd have some explaining to do later, but now was definitely not the time to worry about that.

I moved quickly back to Nyx's table at the center of the circle to complete the casting. I faced the purple candle that sat on the table.

"Finally, I call spirit to our circle and ask that you join us bringing insight and truth with you, so that the Dark Daughters and Sons may be guarded by integrity. Come to me, spirit!" I lit the candle. It blazed even brighter than Shaunee's, and the space around me was filled with the scents and sounds of all of the other four elements. They filled me, too, making me feel strong, calming and steadying me, even as they energized me. With steady hands I took up the braided length of eucalyptus and sage. I lit it with the spirit candle, let it burn for a little while, and then blew it out so that the fragrant smoke billowed in waves around me. Then I faced the circle and began my speech. I had been worried about what I was going to say since Neferet had showed up and literally stolen the biggest part of what I'd planned to talk about. But now, in the middle of the circle I'd cast, filled with the power of all five of the elements, my confidence had been restored as I hastily reworded lines in my head.

I wafted the braided smudge stick around me as I walked the circle, meeting kids' eyes and trying to make everyone feel welcome.

"Tonight I wanted to change things from the type of incense burned, to the abuse of our classmates." I spoke slowly, letting my words and the smoke they mingled with soak into the listening group. They all knew that under the leadership of Aphrodite the incense used during Dark Daughters' rituals had been heavily laced with pot, just as well as they knew that Aphrodite had loved bleeding some poor kid they called "refrigerator" and "snack bar" and mixing his or her blood into the wine everyone sipped. Neither was going to happen again as long as I had anything to do with it. "I chose to burn eucalyptus and sage tonight for the properties the herbs contain. For centuries eucalyptus has been used by the American Indians for healing, protection, and purification, just as they used white sage to drive out negative spirits, energies, and influences. Tonight I ask the five elements to empower these herbs and magnify their energy."

Suddenly the air around me moved, drawing the smoke from the smudge braid with it in curls and wisps, carrying it throughout the circle as if a giant's hand was wafting through the air currents. The fledglings in the circle murmured in awe, and I sent a grateful, silent prayer to Nyx, thanking her for allowing my power over the elements to manifest so clearly.

When the circle quieted again I continued. "The full moon is a magical time when the veil between the known and the unknown is thin, and can even be lifted. That is mysterious and wonderful, but tonight I want to focus on another aspect of the full moon—that it is an excellent time to complete, or end, things. What I want to end tonight is the old negative reputation of the Dark Daughters and Sons. As of this full moon night that part of us has ended, and a new time has begun."

I kept walking, moving around the circle in a clockwise direction. Choosing my words carefully, I said, "From here on the Dark Daughters and Sons will be a group filled with integrity and purpose, and I believe the fledglings Nyx chose to gift with elemental affinities represent the ideals of our new group well." I smiled at Damien. "My friend Damien is the most authentic person I know, even when being true to himself has been a hard thing to be. He represents air well." The wind around Damien picked up as he smiled shyly at me.

I turned to Shaunee next. "My friend Shaunee is the most faithful person I know. If she's on your side, she's there whether you're right or wrong—and if you're wrong she'll tell you about yourself, but she won't desert you. She represents fire well." Shaunee's mocha skin glistened as her body glowed, unburned but alight with flame.

I went to Erin. "My friend Erin's beauty sometimes fools people into thinking she has great hair, but no brains. It's not true. She is one of the wisest people I know, and Nyx proved that she looks to the interior when she chose Erin. She represents water well." As I walked past her I could hear the sound of waves crashing on a shore.

I stopped in front of Stevie Rae. She was looking tired, with dark circles bruising the otherwise pale skin under her eyes, which made sense. Obviously, she'd been worrying too much about me—as usual. "My friend Stevie Rae always knows when I'm happy or sad, stressed or relaxed. She worries about me; she worries about all of her friends, sometimes she is too empathetic, and I'm glad that now she has the earth she can draw strength from. She represents earth well."

I grinned at Stevie Rae, and she smiled back at me, blinking fast so that she wouldn't cry. Then I walked to the center of the circle where I put down the smudge braid and picked up the purple candle. "I'm not perfect, and I'm not going to pretend to be. What I promise you is that I sincerely want what is best for the Dark Daughters and Sons, and for all of the fledglings at the House of Night." I was getting ready to say that I *hoped* I would represent spirit well when Erik's voice rang across the circle.

"She represents spirit well!" My four friends agreed loudly, and I was pleased (and more than a little surprised) to hear several other fledglings chime in with them.

CHAPTER TWENTY-TWO

When I started talking again everyone instantly quieted down. "Each of you who believes you can uphold the ideals of the Dark Daughters and Sons, and will try your best to be authentic, faithful, wise, empathetic, and sincere—you may continue your membership in this group. But I want you to know that there will be new fledglings joining us, and they won't be judged on the way they look or who their best friends are. Make your decision, and see me or any of the other Prefects and let us know if you want to stay with the group." I caught the eyes of some of Aphrodite's old buddies and added, "We won't hold the past against you. It's how you act from here on that counts." A couple of the girls looked guiltily away from me, and a few more looked like they were trying hard not to cry. I was especially glad to see Deino meet my gaze steadily and nod somberly—maybe she wasn't so "terrible" after all.

I put down the purple candle and picked up the big ceremonial goblet I'd filled earlier with sweet red wine. "And now let's drink in celebration of a full moon, and an end that leads to a new beginning." As I worked my way around the circle offering the wine to each fledgling, I recited a Full Moon Ritual prayer I'd found in the old *Mystical Rites of the Crystal Moon* by Fiona, the Vampyre Poet Laureate of the early 1800s.

"Airy light of the moon
  Mystery of the deep earth
  Power of the flowing water
  Warmth of the burning flame
  In Nyx's name we call to thee!"

I focused on the words to the beautiful old poem, and sincerely hoped that tonight actually would be the beginning of something special.

"Healing of ills
  Righting of wrongs
  Cleansing of impurity
  Desiring of truths
  In Nyx's name we call to thee!"

I moved quickly around the circle, and was happy that the majority of the kids smiled at me and murmured "Blessed be" after they sipped from the goblet. Guess no one minded that tonight's wine was absent the blood of a bullied fledgling. (I refused to think about how much I would have loved the taste of fledgling blood mixed with the wine.)

"Sight of the cat
  Hearing of the dolphin
  Speed of the snake
  Mystery of the phoenix
  In Nyx's name we call to thee
  and ask that with us you will blessed be!"

I drank the last of the wine and put the goblet back on the table. In reverse order, I thanked each element and sent them away as in turn Stevie Rae, Erin, Shaunee, and finally Damien blew out their candles. Then I completed the ritual by saying, "This Full Moon Rite is ended. Merry meet and merry part and merry meet again!"

The fledglings echoed, "Merry meet and merry part and merry meet again!"

And that was it. My first ritual as leader of the Dark Daughters was over.

I was actually feeling a little empty and almost sad—you know, kinda like the letdown you have after you've waited and waited for spring break, and then it comes and you realize you don't have anything to do now that there's no school. Well, honestly I only had about a second to feel like that before my friends converged on me, all talking at once about handprints and cement drying too soon.

"Please. Like my Twin can't call in a little water to soup that cement right up if it has the nerve to dry before we can make our handprints," Shaunee said.

Erin nodded. "That's what I'm here for, Twin. That and being an example of incredibly good fashion sense."

"Both are very important, Twin."

Damien gave a big, exaggerated eye roll.

"Y'all, let's just make the handprints and get out of here. My stomach kinda hurts and I got a killer headache," Stevie Rae said.

I nodded in complete understanding with Stevie Rae. We'd slept so late we hadn't had time to eat anything. I was starved, too. And I'd probably get a caffeine-deprived headache myself if I didn't eat and drink something pretty soon.

"I agree with Stevie Rae. Let's hurry and make the handprints, and then we can join everyone else in the other room with the food."

"Neferet had the cooks make a special taco bar. I stuck my head in there earlier and it really looked yummy," Damien said.

"Well, come on then. Stop dillydallying," Stevie Rae grumped while she practically stomped over to one of the cement squares.

"What's wrong with her?" Damien whispered.

"Clearly she's having PMS issues," Shaunee said.

"Yeah, I noticed earlier she was looking kinda pale and bloated, but I didn't want to be mean and say anything," Erin said.

"Let's just make the prints and eat," I said, picking my own cement square, pleased that Erik chose the one right beside me.

"Um, I wetted some towels in the kitchen so you guys could wipe your hands when you're done," said Jack, who was looking very cute and nervous holding an armload of damp white towels.

I smiled at him. "That's really nice of you, Jack. Okay, let's do it!"

Close up I could tell that the cement had been poured into what looked like cardboard molds, and I figured it would be easy to tear off the cardboard once the cement had dried. I still liked Damien's idea of putting the handprints in the courtyard outside the dining hall—kinda like weird stepping stones.

The cement was definitely still wet, and there was a lot of laughing going on as we made our prints and then used twigs Jack ran out to collect (the kid was certainly handy to have around) to write our names.

While we were wiping our hands with the towels and studying our work, Erik leaned close to say, "I'm really glad Neferet chose me for the Prefect Council."

I kept my mouth shut and nodded. If I told him that actually I had chosen him, with Damien, Stevie Rae, and the Twins agreeing, I would probably let the air right out of his sails. Neferet was a big deal. And it really wouldn't hurt anything (except my ego) to let him think that she was the one who picked him. I was just getting ready to change the subject and call everyone into the room with the food when I heard some weird sounds to my right. When I realized what the weird sounds were I felt my heart clench.

Stevie Rae was coughing.

Damien was directly to my right. Then came the Twins. Stevie Rae had chosen the block of cement farthest to the right, and closest to the entrance to the room with the food. A bunch of the kids were already eating, but about half of the group had stayed to watch us make the handprints and talk, so there were several more people between Stevie Rae and me, but I could see that she was still on her knees in front of her cement block. She must have felt my eyes on her because she sat back on her heels and looked over at me. I could hear her clear her throat. She gave me a tired smile and I saw her shrug and then mouth the words, *Frog in my throat.* And I remembered that's what she'd said during the monologue performance. She'd been coughing then, too.

Without looking at him I told Erik, "Get Neferet. Fast!"

I stood up and started moving toward her. Stevie Rae had already made her handprint and signed it, and she was wiping her hands on a towel. Before I could get to her a wrenching cough claimed her. Her shoulders shook with it. She had the towel pressed to her mouth.

Then I smelled it, and it was like I'd slammed into an invisible wall. The scent of blood washed over me, seductive, alluring, and horrible. I stopped and closed my eyes. Maybe if I stayed very still and didn't open them I could convince myself that this was all just a bad dream, that I would wake up in a few hours, still nervous about the Full Moon Ritual, with Nala snoring peacefully on my pillow and Stevie Rae snoring just as peacefully in the bed beside me.

I felt an arm go around me, and still I didn't move.

"She needs you, Zoey." Damien's voice was shaking only a little.

I opened my eyes then and stared at him. He was already crying. "I don't think I can do this."

His grip on my shoulders tightened. "Yes, you can. You have to."

"Zoey!" Stevie Rae sobbed.

Without another thought, I wrenched myself from Damien's arm and ran to my best friend. She was on her knees clutching the blood-soaked towel to her chest. She coughed and gagged again, and more blood sprayed from her mouth and nose.

"Get me more towels!" I snapped to Erin, who was sitting white-faced and silent beside Stevie Rae. Then I crouched in front of Stevie Rae. "It's going to be okay. I promise. It's going to be okay."

Stevie Rae was crying, and her tears were tinged red. She shook her head. "It's not. It can't be. I'm dying." Her voice was weak and gurgled as she tried to speak through the blood hemorrhaging in her lungs and throat.

"I'm staying with you. I won't let you be alone," I said.

She grasped my hand and I was shocked by how cold hers was. "I'm scared, Z."

"I know, I'm scared, too. But we'll get through this together. I promise."

Erin handed me a pile of towels. I took the blood-soaked towel from Stevie Rae's hands, then I started wiping her face and mouth with a clean one, but she started coughing again and I couldn't keep up. There was just too much blood. And now Stevie Rae was shaking so hard that she couldn't hold a towel herself. With a cry, I pulled her onto my lap and wrapped my arms around her, and like she was a child again, I began rocking her, telling her over and over that it would be all right, that I wouldn't leave her.

"Zoey, this might help." I'd forgotten that there were other people in the room, so Damien's voice surprised me. I looked up to see that he was holding the relit green candle that represented earth. Then somehow, in the midst of my fear and despair, my instinct kicked in and I suddenly felt very calm.

"Come down here, Damien. Hold the candle close to her."

Damien dropped to his knees, and oblivious to the growing pool of blood that surrounded us and soaked us, he pressed close to Stevie Rae, holding the candle in front of her face. I felt more than I saw Erin and Shaunee kneel on either side of me, and I drew strength from their presence.

"Stevie Rae, open your eyes, honey," I said softly.

With a nasty, gurgling breath, Stevie Rae's eyelids fluttered open. The whites of her eyes were totally red and more pink tears leaked down her colorless cheeks, but her eyes caught on the candle, and they held.

"I call the element earth to us now." My voice strengthened and got louder as I spoke. "And I ask that earth be with this very special fledgling, Stevie Rae Johnson, who has been so newly gifted with an affinity for the element. Earth is our home—our provider—and earth is where we will all someday return. Tonight I ask that earth hold and comfort Stevie Rae, and make her journey home a peaceful one."

With a rush of fragrant air we were suddenly enveloped in the scents and sounds of an orchard. I smelled apples and hay, and heard birds chirping and bees buzzing.

Stevie Rae's reddened lips tilted up. Her eyes never left the green candle, but she whispered, "I'm not scared anymore, Z."

Then I heard the front door burst open and Neferet was there crouched beside me. She started to move Damien and the Twins out of the way and take Stevie Rae from my arms.

My voice blasted the room with its power, and I saw even Neferet jerk back with surprise. "No! We stay with her. She needs her element and she needs us."

"Very well," Neferet said. "It's very nearly over anyway. Help me get her to drink this so that her passing will be painless."

I was going to take the vial filled with milky liquid from her when Stevie Rae spoke with surprising clearness. "I don't need it. Since earth came there hasn't been any pain."

"Of course there hasn't been, child." Neferet touched Stevie Rae's blood-smeared cheek and I felt her body relax and stop trembling completely. Then the High Priestess looked up. "Help Zoey lift her onto the stretcher. Keep them together. Let's get her to the infirmary," Neferet told me.

I nodded. Strong hands gripped Stevie Rae and me, and in moments I was placed on the stretcher with Stevie Rae still in my arms. Surrounded by Damien, Shaunee, Erin, and Erik, we were carried swiftly out into the night. Later, I remembered so many weird things about the short trip from the rec hall to the infirmary—how it was snowing heavily, but that it seemed none of the flakes touched us. And it seemed abnormally quiet, as if the earth were holding itself still because it was already mourning. I kept whispering to Stevie Rae, telling her that everything was okay, and that there was nothing to be scared of. I remember her leaning forward and vomiting blood over the side of the stretcher and how the scarlet drops looked against the clean white of the new-fallen snow.

Then we were inside the infirmary, and lifted off the stretcher onto a bed. Neferet gestured for my friends to move close to us. Damien crawled up beside Stevie Rae. He was still holding the lit green candle, and he lifted it so that if she opened her eyes again, Stevie Rae would see it. I drew a deep breath. The air around us was still filled with apple blossoms and birdsong.

Then Stevie Rae opened her eyes. She blinked a couple times, looking confused, then she looked up at me and smiled.

"Would you tell my mamma and daddy that I love them?" I could understand her, but she sounded weak, and her voice was filled with a terrible wetness.

"Of course I will," I said quickly.

"And do something else for me?"

"Anything."

"You don't really have a mamma or a daddy, so would you tell my mamma that you're their daughter now? I think I'd worry about them less if I know y'all have each other."

Tears were pouring down my cheeks and I had to take several sobbing breaths before I could answer her. "Don't worry about anything. I'll tell them."

Her eyes fluttered and she smiled again. "Good. Mamma will make chocolate chip cookies for you." With obvious effort, she opened her eyes again and looked around at Damien, Shaunee, and Erin. "Y'all stick with Zoey. Don't let anything pull you apart."

"Don't worry," Damien whispered through his tears.

"We'll take care of her for you," Shaunee managed to say. Erin was clutching Shaunee's hand and crying hard, but she nodded in agreement and smiled at Stevie Rae.

"Good," Stevie Rae said. Then she closed her eyes. "Z, I think I'm gonna sleep for a while now, 'kay?"

"Okay, honey," I said.

Her eyelids lifted once more and she looked up at me. "Will you stay with me?"

I hugged her closer. "I'm not going anywhere. You just rest. We'll all be right here with you."

" 'Kay . . ." she said softly.

Stevie Rae shut her eyes. She took a few more gurgling breaths.

Then I felt her go completely limp in my arms and she didn't breathe again. Her lips opened just a little, as if she was smiling. Blood trickled from her mouth, her eyes, nose, and ears, but I couldn't smell it. All I could smell were the scents of the earth. Then, with an enormous rush of meadow-filled wind, the green candle went out, and my best friend died.

CHAPTER TWENTY-THREE

"Zoey, sweetheart, you have to let her go."

Damien's voice didn't really register in my mind. I mean, I could hear his words, but it was like he was speaking a weird foreign language. I couldn't make any sense of them.

"Zoey, why don't you come with us, now?"

That was Shaunee. *Shouldn't Erin chime in?* I'd barely formed the thought when I heard, "Yeah, Zoey, we need you to come with us." *Oh, there's Erin.*

"She's in shock. Speak calmly to her and try to get her to release Stevie Rae's body," Neferet said.

Stevie Rae's body. The words echoed weirdly through my mind. I was holding on to something. I could tell that much. But my eyes were closed and I was really, really cold. I didn't want to open them, and I didn't think I'd ever get warm again.

"I have an idea." Damien's voice bounced around inside my mind like a pinball machine. "We don't have candles and we don't have a sacred circle, but it's not like Nyx isn't here. Let's use our elements to help her. I'll go first."

I felt a hand grasp my upper arm, and then I heard Damien muttering something about calling air to blow about the scent of death and despair. A big wind whooshed around me, and I shivered.

"I better go next. She looks cold." That was Shaunee. Someone else touched my arm and after some words I didn't quite catch, I felt surrounded by warmth, like I was standing very close to an open fireplace.

"My turn," Erin said. "I call water and ask that you wash from my friend and future High Priestess the sadness and pain she's feeling. I know all of it can't go away, but could you please take just enough from her that she can bear to go on?" Her words registered more clearly on my mind, but I still didn't want to open my eyes.

"There's still one more element in the circle."

I was surprised to hear Erik. Part of me wanted to open my eyes so that I could look at him, but the rest of me, too much of me, refused to move.

"But Zoey always manifests spirit," Damien said.

"Right now Zoey can't manifest anything by herself. Let's give her some help." Two strong hands gripped my shoulders, along with the other hands that grasped places on my arms. "I have no affinity for these things, but I do care about what happens to Zoey, and she has been gifted with an affinity for all five elements," Erik said. "So I, along with all of her friends, ask that the element spirit help her wake up so that she can get over the death of her best friend."

Like an electric shock, my body was suddenly zapped, filled with an incredible sense of awareness. Against my closed eyelids I saw Stevie Rae's smiling face. It wasn't bloodstained and pale, like it had been the last time she'd smiled at me. The image I saw was a healthy, happy Stevie Rae, and she was walking into a beautifully familiar woman's arms while she laughed joyfully.

Nyx, I thought, *Stevie Rae is being embraced by the Goddess.*

And my eyes opened.

"Zoey! You're back with us!" Damien cried.

"Z, you're going to need to let go of Stevie Rae now," Erik said somberly.

I looked from Damien to Erik. Then my eyes went to Shaunee and Erin. All four of my friends had their hands on me, and they were all crying. Then I realized what it was I was clutching in my arms. Slowly, I looked down.

Stevie Rae looked peaceful. She was too pale, and her lips were turning blue, but her eyes were closed and her face was relaxed, even though it was covered with blood. Her blood wasn't dripping from her orifices anymore, and part of my mind realized that it smelled wrong—stale, old, dead. Almost like mold.

"Z," Erik said. "You have to let her go."

I met his eyes. "But I told her I'd stay with her." My voice sounded strange and scratchy.

"You did. You stayed with her the whole time. She's gone now, so there's nothing else you can do."

"Please, Zoey," Damien said.

"Neferet needs to clean her up so it's okay for her mom to see her," Shaunee said.

"You know she wouldn't want her mom and dad to see her all covered with blood," Erin said.

"Okay, but . . . but I don't know how to let her go." My voice cracked and I felt fresh tears leak down my cheeks.

"I'll take her from you, Zoeybird." Neferet held her arms out, like she was ready to receive a baby I'd been holding. She looked so sad and beautiful and strong—so familiar—that I forgot all the questions I had about her and simply nodded and slowly leaned forward. Neferet slid her arms under Stevie Rae's body and lifted her away from me. She shifted her hold on Stevie Rae, and then turned and laid her gently on the empty bed beside mine.

I looked down at myself. My new black dress was soaked with

blood that was already stiffening and drying. The silver threads still tried to glitter in the gaslights of the room, but instead of the pure light they gave off before, they now sparkled with a copper hue. I couldn't keep looking at them. I had to move. I had to get out of there and get this dress off. I swung my feet over the side of the bed and tried to stand up, but the room pitched and rolled around me. Then the strong hands of my friends were back on my arms, and I felt anchored to the earth through their warmth.

"Take her back to her room. Get her out of that dress and cleaned up. Then be sure she goes to bed and is kept warm and quiet." Neferet was talking about me like I wasn't there, but I didn't care. I didn't want to be there. I didn't want any of this. "Give her this to drink before you put her to bed. It will help her sleep without nightmares." I felt Neferet's soft hand on my cheek. The warmth that passed from her body to mine was a shock, and I instinctively jerked away. "Be well, Zoeybird," Neferet said kindly. "I give you my word that you will recover from this." I didn't look at her, but I knew she shifted her attention back to my friends. "Take her to the dorm now."

I was moving forward. Erik was on one side of me with his hand securely under my right elbow, Damien was on my left, holding me tightly, too. The Twins were close behind us. No one spoke as they led me from the room. I glanced back over my shoulder to see Stevie Rae's lifeless body on the bed. It almost looked like she was sleeping, but I knew better. I knew she was dead.

The five of us left the infirmary and walked into the snowy night. I shivered, and we paused long enough for Erik to take off his jacket and drape it around my shoulders. I liked the way it smelled, and tried to think of it and not the hushed fledglings we were passing and how as we approached each of them, whether they were alone or in groups, the kids moved off the sidewalk, bowed their heads, and silently crossed their right fists over their hearts.

We got to the dorm in what seemed like seconds. As we entered the main room the girls who were watching TV and sitting around in groups all fell totally silent. I didn't look at any of them. I just let Erik and Damien lead me to the stairs, but before we got there Aphrodite was blocking our way. I blinked hard to focus on her face. She looked tired.

"I'm sorry Stevie Rae died. I didn't want her to," Aphrodite said.

"Don't say shit to us, you fucking hag!" Shaunee snarled. She and Erin stepped forward, looking like they wanted to beat the crap out of Aphrodite.

"No, wait," I made myself say, and they hesitated. "I need to talk to Aphrodite."

My friends looked at me like I'd lost every bit of my mind, but I stepped out of the nest of arms that were holding me up and walked unsteadily a few paces away from the group. Aphrodite hesitated, and then she followed me.

"Did you know about what was going to happen to Stevie Rae?" I asked, keeping my voice low. "Did you have a vision about her?"

Aphrodite shook her head slowly. "No. I just had a *feeling*. I knew something terrible was going to happen tonight."

"I get them, too," I said softly.

"Feelings about things or people?"

I nodded.

"They're harder than my visions—not as specific. Did you have a feeling about Stevie Rae?" she asked.

"No. I was clueless, even though now I can look back and see signs that something was wrong with her."

Aphrodite met my eyes. "You couldn't have stopped it. You

couldn't have saved her. Nyx didn't let you know it was going to happen because there was nothing you could have done."

"How do you know? Neferet says Nyx has deserted you," I said bluntly. I knew I was purposefully being cruel. I didn't care. I wanted everyone to hurt as much as I did.

Still looking me straight in the eyes, Aphrodite said, "Neferet lies." She started to walk away, but changed her mind and came back. "And don't drink whatever she gave you," she said. Then she left the room.

Erik, Damien, and the Twins were at my side in a blink.

"Don't listen to whatever that hag had to say," Shaunee huffed.

"If she said something nasty about Stevie Rae, we're gonna kick her ass," Erin said.

"No. It wasn't anything like that. She just said she was sorry, that's all."

"Why did you want to talk to her?" Erik asked. He and Damien had ahold of me again, and now they were leading me up the stairs.

"I wanted to know if she had a vision about Stevie Rae's death," I said.

"But Neferet has made it clear that Nyx has turned her back on Aphrodite," Damien said.

"I wanted to ask anyway." I was going to add that Aphrodite had been right about the accident that almost happened to my grandma, but I couldn't say anything in front of Erik. We came to the door to my room—*our* room—Stevie Rae's and mine, and I stopped. Erik opened it for me and we stepped in.

"No!" I gasped. "They've taken her stuff! They can't do that!" Everything that was Stevie Rae was gone—from the cowboy boot lamp and the Kenny Chesney poster, to the gyrating Elvis clock. The shelves over her computer desk were empty. Her computer was gone. I knew if I looked in her closet, all of her clothes would be gone, too.

Erik put his arm around me. "It's what they always do. Don't worry, they didn't throw away her stuff. They just moved it so that it wouldn't make you sad. If there's something of hers you want, and her family doesn't mind, they'll give it to you."

I didn't know what to say. I didn't want Stevie Rae's *stuff*. I wanted Stevie Rae.

"Zoey, you really need to get out of those clothes and take a hot shower," Damien said gently.

"Okay," I said.

"While you're in the shower we'll get you something to eat," Shaunee said.

"I'm not hungry."

"You need to eat. We'll get you something simple, like soup. Okay?" Erin said. She looked so upset, and was so obviously trying to do something, anything, to make me feel better that I nodded. Plus, I was too tired to argue with anyone. "Okay."

"I'd stay, but it's past curfew and I can't be in the girls' dorm," Erik said.

"That's okay. I understand."

"I want to stay, too, but well, I'm not actually a girl," Damien said. I knew he was trying to make me smile, so I made my lips move up. I imagined I looked like one of those scary, sad clowns who had a smile painted on his face along with a teardrop.

Erik hugged me, and so did Damien. Then they left.

"Do you need one of us to stay while you take a shower?" Shaunee asked.

"No, I'm fine."

"Okay. Well . . ." Shaunee looked like she was going to cry again.

"We'll be right back." Erin took Shaunee's hand and they left the room, closing it with a soft, final click.

I moved carefully, like someone had switched me "on," but had set my speed at slow. I took off my dress, bra, and panties and put them in the plastic-lined wastepaper basket that sat in the corner of our—I mean *my*—room. I closed up the plastic bag and put it by the door. I knew one of the Twins would throw it away for me. I went into the bathroom and meant to get straight into the shower, but my reflection caught me, and I stopped, staring. I had turned into a familiar stranger again. I looked horrible. I was pale, but I had bruised-looking circles under my eyes. The tattoos on my face, back, and shoulders stood out in stark, sapphire contrast to the white of my skin and the rust-colored smears of blood that covered my body. My eyes looked huge and unusually dark. I hadn't taken off my Dark Daughters necklace. The silver of the chain and the copper of the garnets caught the light and gleamed.

"Why?" I whispered. "Why did you let Stevie Rae die?"

I didn't really expect an answer, and none came. So I got in the shower and stood there for a very long time, letting my tears mix with the water and the blood and wash down the drain.

CHAPTER TWENTY-FOUR

When I came out of the bathroom Shaunee and Erin were sitting on Stevie Rae's bed. They had a tray between them that held a bowl of soup, some crackers, and a can of brown pop, nondiet. They had been talking in low voices, but as soon as I entered the room they stopped.

I sighed and sat on my bed. "If you guys start acting all abnormal around me I'm not going to be able to handle it."

"Sorry," they muttered together, looking sheepishly at each other. Then Shaunee handed me the tray. I looked at the food like I couldn't remember what to do with it.

"You need to eat so that you can take the stuff Neferet gave us to give you," Erin said.

"Plus, it might make you feel better," Shaunee said.

"I don't think I'll ever feel better."

Erin's eyes filled with tears that spilled over and dripped down her cheeks. "Don't say that, Zoey. If you never feel better that means none of us will, either."

"You have to try, Zoey. Stevie Rae would be pissed if you didn't," Shaunee said, sniffing through her tears.

"You're right. She would be." I picked up the spoon and started sipping at the soup. It was chicken noodle, and it made a familiar, warm path down my throat, expanding into my body and chasing away some of the terrible chill I'd been feeling.

"And when she got pissed that accent of hers went out of control," Shaunee said.

That made Erin and me smile.

"*Y'all be niiice,*" Erin twanged, repeating the words Stevie Rae had said to the Twins a gazillion times.

We smiled at that, and the soup began to seem easier to swallow. About halfway through the bowl, I had a sudden thought. "They're not going to have a funeral or anything like that for her, are they?"

The Twins shook their heads. "Nope," Shaunee said.

"They never do," Erin said.

"Well, Twin, I think some of the kids' parents do, but that'd be back in their hometown."

"True, Twin," Erin said. "But I don't think anyone from here is going to travel to . . ." she trailed off, thinking. "What was the name of that little bumpkin town Stevie Rae was from?"

"Henrietta," I said. "Home of the Fighting Hens."

"Fighting Hens?" the Twins said together.

I nodded. "It drove Stevie Rae crazy. Even in her bumpkinness she wasn't okay with being a Fighting Hen."

"Hens fight?" Shaunee asked.

Erin shrugged. "How should I know, Twin?"

"I thought only cocks fought," I said. We all looked at each other and said, "Cocks!" and then burst out into laughter, which pretty soon was mixed with tears. "Stevie Rae would have thought that was hilarious," I said when I could catch my breath again.

"Is it really going to be okay, Zoey?" Shaunee asked.

"Is it?" Erin echoed.

"I think so," I said.

"How?" Shaunee asked.

"I don't really know. I think all we can do is take one day at a time."

Surprisingly, I'd finished all my soup. I did feel better—warmer, more normal. I was also unbelievably tired. The Twins must have noticed my eyelids getting heavy, because Erin took my tray. Shaunee handed me a little vial of milky liquid.

"Neferet said you should drink this, that it'll help you sleep without nightmares," she said.

"Thanks." I took it from her, but I didn't drink it. She and Erin just stood there looking at me. "I'll take it in a minute. After I go to the bathroom. Just leave my pop in case it tastes nasty."

That seemed to satisfy them. Before they left Shaunee said, "Zoey, can we get you anything else?"

"No, thanks though."

"You'll call us if you need anything, right?" Erin said. "We promised Stevie Rae . . ." Her voice broke and Shaunee finished for her, "We promised her we'd take care of you, and we live up to our promises."

"I'll call you," I said.

" 'Kay," they said. "Night . . ."

"Night," I called to the closing door.

As soon as they were gone I poured the creamy white liquid down the sink and threw away the vial.

Then I was alone. I glanced at my alarm clock, 6:00 A.M. It was amazing how much things could change in just a few hours. I tried not to, but flashes of Stevie Rae's death kept playing across my mind, like there was a horrible movie screen stuck inside my eyes. I jumped when my cell phone rang, and checked the caller ID. It was my grandma's number! Relief surged through me. I flipped the phone open and struggled not to burst into tears.

"I'm so glad you called, Grandma!"

"Little Bird, I woke from a dream about you. Is everything all right?" Her worried tone said she already knew it wasn't, which didn't surprise me. For my whole life my grandma and I had been linked.

"No. Nothing is right," I whispered as I began to cry again. "Grandma, Stevie Rae died tonight."

"Oh, Zoey! I'm so terribly sorry!"

"She died in my arms, Grandma, just minutes after Nyx gifted her with an affinity for the element earth."

"It must have been a great comfort for her that you were with her at the end." I could hear that Grandma was crying now, too.

"We were all with her, all of my friends."

"And Nyx must have been with her, too."

"Yes," my voice caught on a sob. "I think the Goddess was, but I don't understand it, Grandma. It doesn't make any sense that Nyx would gift Stevie Rae, and then let her die."

"Death never makes sense when it happens to the young. But I believe that your Goddess was close to Stevie Rae, even though her death happened too soon, and now she is resting peacefully with Nyx."

"I hope so."

"I wish I could come visit you, but with all this snow the roads out here are impossible. How about I fast and pray for Stevie Rae today?"

"Thank you, Grandma. I know she'd appreciate that."

"And, honey, you have to move past this."

"How, Grandma?"

"By honoring her memory by living a life she'd be proud of you for living. Live for her, too."

"It's hard, Grandma, especially when the vamps want us to just forget about the kids who die. They're treated like speed bumps, just something to pause a little about, and then go on."

"I don't mean to second-guess your High Priestess, or any of the other adult vampyres, but that seems shortsighted. Death is more difficult if it goes unacknowledged."

"That's what I think. Actually, that's what Stevie Rae thought, too." Then an idea came to me, along with a *feeling* that it was the right thing to do. "I can change that. With or without permission, I'm going to be sure Stevie Rae's death is honored. She's going to be more than a speed bump."

"Don't get in trouble, honey."

"Grandma, I am the most powerful fledgling in the history of vampyres. I think I should be willing to get in a little trouble for something I feel strongly about."

Grandma paused, then she said, "I think you might be right about that, Zoeybird."

"I love you, Grandma."

"I love you, too, *u-we-tsi a-ge-hu-tsa.*" The Cherokee word for daughter made me feel loved and safe. "And now I want you to try to sleep. Know that I'll be praying for you, and asking the spirits of our grandmothers to watch over and comfort you."

"Thanks, Grandma. Bye."

"Good-bye, Zoeybird."

I closed the phone softly. I felt better now that I'd talked to Grandma. Before it had been like there was a huge, invisible weight pressing down on my chest. Now that it had shifted some it was easier for me to breathe. I started to lie down, and Nala popped in through the kitty door, leaped up on my bed, and instantly began *me-uf-ow*-ing at me. I petted her and told her how glad I was to see her, and then glanced over at Stevie Rae's empty bed. She always laughed at Nala's grumpiness, and said she sounded like an old woman, but she had loved the cat as much as me. Tears stung my eyes and I wondered if there was a limit to how much someone could cry. Just then my cell phone chimed that I had a new text message. I rubbed my eyes clear and flipped my phone back open.

R U OK? Somethings wrong.

It was Heath. Well, at least now there could be no doubt at all that he and I were linked through an Imprint. And what the hell I was going to do about that, I didn't know.

Bad day. My best friend died. I text messaged him back.

It was so long that I didn't think he was going to respond. Then finally my phone chimed again.

My friends have died 2.

I closed my eyes. How could I have forgotten that two of Heath's friends had just recently been killed?

I'm sorry, I typed back.

Me 2. Do u want me to come see u?

The instant, powerful *yes!* that burst through my body surprised me, but I suppose it shouldn't have. It would be wonderful to find oblivion in Heath's arms ... in the scarlet seduction of Heath's blood ...

No, I typed hastily, my hands shaking. You have school.

Nuh uh SNOW DAY!

I smiled, and spent a sweet second or two wishing that I could return to the time when a snow day meant a mini-holiday of tramping through snow with my friends and then curling up to watch rented movies and eat delivery pizza. My phone chimed again, breaking into my past-life fantasy.

I'll make u feel btr fri

I sighed. I'd totally forgotten about promising Heath I'd meet him after the game Friday. I shouldn't meet him. I knew it. Actually, I should go to Neferet and confess everything about Heath and have her help me fix it.

Neferet lies. Aphrodite's voice whispered through my mind. No. I couldn't go to Neferet, and for more reasons than just

Aphrodite's warning. Something felt wrong about Neferet. I couldn't confide in her. My phone chimed.

Zo?

I sighed. I was so tired that it was getting hard to concentrate. I started to text back no and tell Heath that I just couldn't meet him, no matter how much I'd like to. I even hit the N and the O keys. Then I stopped, back-spaced over them, and resolutely typed: OK.

What the hell. It felt as if my life was unraveling like the hem of an old skirt. I didn't want to tell Heath no, and worrying about our Imprint was just one thing too many to worry about right now.

OK! Came his quick reply.

I sighed again, shut off my phone, and sat heavily on my bed, petting Nala, staring at nothing in particular, and wishing desperately that I could turn the clock back a day . . . or maybe even a year . . . Eventually I noticed that, for whatever reason, the vamps who had cleared out Stevie Rae's stuff had forgotten the old, handmade quilt that she kept folded on the end of her bed. I put Nala on my pillow and got up, pulling the quilt from Stevie Rae's bed. Then Nala and I curled up under it.

It felt like every molecule of my body was tired, but I couldn't sleep. I guess I missed Stevie Rae's soft snores and the sense that I wasn't alone. A sadness washed over me that was so deep I thought I might drown in it.

Two soft knocks came on the door. Then it opened slowly. I half sat up to see Shaunee and Erin, both in their pajamas and slippers, clutching pillows and blankets.

"Can we sleep with you?" Erin asked.

"We didn't want to be alone," Shaunee said.

"Yeah, and we thought you might not want to be alone, either," Erin finished.

"You're right. I don't." I swallowed back more tears. "Come on in."

They shuffled in and, with only a little hesitation, piled onto Stevie Rae's bed. Their long-haired silver-gray cat, Beelzebub, hopped up between them. Nala raised her head from my pillow to glance at him, and then, as if he were beneath her queenly notice, she curled back up and went promptly to sleep.

I was just drifting off to sleep when another soft knock came on the door. This time it didn't open, so I called, "Who is it?"

"Me."

Shaunee, Erin, and I blinked at each other. Then I hurried over to the door and opened it to find Damien standing in the hall wearing flannel pj's with pink bow-tied bears all over them. He looked kinda damp, and unmelted snowflakes were caught in his hair. He was carrying a sleeping bag and a pillow. I grabbed his arm and pulled him quickly into the room. His chubby tabby cat, Cameron, padded in with him.

"What are you doing, Damien? You know you're gonna get in a buttload of trouble if you get caught in here."

"Yeah, it's way past curfew," Erin said.

"You might be here getting ready to defile us virgins," Shaunee said. Then she and Erin looked at each other and burst out laughing, which made me smile. It was weird to have a happy feeling in the middle of such sadness, which is probably why the Twins' laughter and my smile faded quickly.

"Stevie Rae wouldn't want us to quit being happy," Damien said into the uncomfortable silence. Then he walked to the middle of the room and spread out his sleeping bag on the floor between the two beds. "And I'm here because we need to stick together. *Not* because I want to defile any of you, even if all of you were still virgins, although I do appreciate your use of vocabulary."

Erin and Shaunee snorted, but looked more amused than offended, and I made a mental note to ask them sex questions later.

"Well, I'm glad you came, but we're gonna have one heck of a time sneaking you out of here when everyone's eating breakfast and rushing around before school," I said, trying out escape plans in my head.

"Oh, you don't have to worry about that. The vamps are posting that the school's closed today due to snow. No one'll be rushing anywhere. I'll just walk out with y'all whenever."

"Posting? You mean we'd have to wake up, get dressed, and go downstairs before we found out there wasn't any school? That sucks," I said.

I could hear the smile in Damien's voice. "They announce it on the local radio stations like normal schools do. But do you and Stevie Rae listen to the news while you get . . ." Damien trailed off, and I realized that he'd started phrasing the question as if Stevie Rae were still alive.

"No," I said quickly, trying to cover his awkwardness. "We used to listen to country music. It always made me hurry up and get ready quicker so I could escape from it." My friends laughed softly. I waited until everyone was quiet again, and then I said, "I'm not going to forget her, and I'm not going to pretend like her death doesn't mean anything to me."

"Neither am I," Damien said.

"Me either," Shaunee said.

"Ditto, Twin," Erin said.

After a while I said, "I didn't think it could happen to a fledgling who had been given an affinity by Nyx. I—I just didn't think it could happen."

"No one's guaranteed to make it through the Change, not even those gifted by the Goddess," Damien said quietly.

"That just means we have to stick together," Erin said.

"It's the only way we can get through this," Shaunee said.

"That's what we'll do then—stick together," I said with finality. "And promise that if the worst happens, and some of the rest of us don't make it through, the others won't let them be forgotten."

"Promise," my three friends said solemnly.

We all settled down then. The room didn't feel so lonely anymore, and just before I drifted off to sleep I whispered, "Thanks for not letting me be alone . . ." and wasn't sure if I was thanking my friends, my Goddess, or Stevie Rae.

CHAPTER TWENTY-FIVE

It was snowing in my dream. At first I thought that was cool. I mean, it really was beautiful . . . it made the world look Disney-like and perfect, as if nothing bad could happen, or if it did it was only temporary, because everyone knows Disney is all about happily ever after . . .

I walked slowly, not feeling the cold. It seemed to be just before sunrise, but it was hard to tell with the sky all snowy and gray. I tilted my head back and looked at how the snow clung to the thick branches of the old oaks, and made the east wall look soft, and less imposing.

The east wall.

In my dream I hesitated when I realized where I was. Then I saw the figures, hooded and cloaked, standing in a group of four in front of the open trapdoor in the wall.

No! I told my dreaming self. *I don't want to be over here. Not so soon after Stevie Rae died. After the last two times fledglings died I saw their ghosts or spirits or undead walking bodies or whatever here. Even if I had been gifted with a weird ability to see the dead by Nyx. Enough was enough! I didn't want—*

The smallest of the cloaked figures turned around and my internal argument scattered from my mind. It was Stevie Rae! Only it wasn't. She looked too pale and thin. And there was something else about her. I stared, and my initial hesitation was overcome by a terrible need within me to understand. I mean, if it really was Stevie Rae, then I didn't need to be afraid of her. Even weirdly changed by death, she was still my best friend. Wasn't she? I couldn't help moving forward until I was standing only a few feet from the group. I held my breath, waiting for them to turn on me, but no one noticed me. In my dream world it was as though I was invisible to them. So I moved even closer, unable to take my eyes from Stevie Rae. She looked terrible—frantic—and she kept moving restlessly, shifting her eyes around her like she was extremely nervous or extremely afraid.

"We shouldn't be here. We need to leave."

I jumped at the sound of Stevie Rae's voice. She still had her Okie accent, but nothing else was recognizable. Her tone was hard and flat, lacking all emotions except a kind of animallike nervousness.

"You're not in charge of usssss," one of the other cloaked figures hissed, baring his teeth at Stevie Rae. Oh, ugh! It was that Elliott creature. Even though his body was weirdly hunched, he stood over her aggressively. His eyes had begun to glow a dirty red. I was afraid for her, but she didn't let him intimidate her, instead Stevie Rae bared her own teeth, her eyes blazed scarlet, and she gave an ugly snarl. Then she spat the words at him, "Does the earth answer you? No!" She walked forward, and Elliott automatically took several steps backward. "And until it does, you will obey me! That's what *she* said."

The Elliott thing made an awkward, subservient bow that the two other cloaked figures mimicked. Then Stevie Rae pointed toward the open trapdoor. "Now, we go *quickly*." But before any of them moved I heard a familiar voice from the other side of the wall.

"Hey, do y'all know Zoey Redbird? I need to tell her I'm here and—"

Heath's voice broke off when the four creatures, with blurring speed, rushed through the door after him.

"No! Stop! What the hell are you doing?" I yelled. My heart was beating so hard that it hurt as I ran to the closing door in time to see the three of them grabbing Heath. I heard Stevie Rae say, "He's seen us. Now he comes with us."

"But she said no more!" Elliott yelled as he kept an iron grip on the struggling Heath.

"He's seen us!" Stevie Rae repeated. "So he comes with us until she tells us what to do with him!"

They didn't argue with her, and with inhuman strength they dragged him away. The snow seemed to swallow his screams.

I sat bolt upright in bed, breathing hard, sweating and trembling. Nala grumbled. I looked around the room and felt momentarily panicked. I was alone! Had I just dreamed everything that had happened yesterday? I looked at Stevie Rae's empty bed, and at the lack of any of her stuff around the room. No. I hadn't dreamed it. My best friend was dead. I let the weight of the sadness settle into me, and knew I'd be carrying it around for a very long time.

But hadn't the Twins and Damien slept here? Still groggy, I rubbed my eyes and looked at my clock. It was 5:00 P.M. I must have fallen asleep some time between 6:30 and 7:00 A.M. Sheesh, I'd definitely gotten enough sleep. I got up, went to the heavily draped window, and peered out. Unbelievably, it was still snowing, and even though it was early, the gaslights were illuminating a slate-colored night and glistening with little snow haloes. Fledglings were doing typical kid stuff—building snowmen and having snow fights. I saw someone I thought was that Cassie Kramme girl who'd done so well in the monologue competition making snow angels with a couple other girls. Stevie Rae would have loved it. She would have made me wake up hours ago and had me out there with her in the thick of all of the fun (whether I wanted to be or not). Thinking about it, I didn't know whether I wanted to cry or smile.

"Z? Are you awake?" Shaunee called tentatively from the cracked door.

I motioned for her to come in. "Where'd you guys go?"

"We've been up a couple hours. We've been watching movies. Wanta come down with us? Erik and Cole, that totally *fiiiine* friend of his, are gonna come over." Then she looked around guiltily, as if remembering that Stevie Rae was gone and sorry she'd been acting normal. Something inside me made me speak.

"Shaunee, we have to go on. We have to date and be happy and live our lives. Nothing's guaranteed, Stevie Rae's death proved that. We can't waste the time we've been given. When I said I'd make sure she was remembered, I didn't mean that we were going to be sad forever. It meant I'd remember the happiness she brought to us, and keep her smile close to my heart. Always."

"Always," Shaunee agreed.

"If you give me a second I'll put on some jeans and meet you guys downstairs."

" 'Kay," she said with a grin.

When Shaunee was gone, some of my happy facade faded. I'd meant what I said to her, it was just the acting out of it that was going to be hard. Plus, I was having a hard time shaking the bad dream. I knew it was just a dream, but it still bothered me. It was like I could hear the echoes of Heath's screams in the oppressive silence of my room. Moving automatically, I got dressed in my most comfortable jeans and a ginormic sweatshirt I'd bought from the school store a couple of weeks ago. Over my heart it had the silver embroidered insignia of Nyx standing with upraised hands cupping a full moon, and somehow it made me feel better. I brushed my hair and sighed at my reflection in the mirror. I looked like poo. So I spackled some concealer on the dark smudges under my eyes, added mascara and my shiny lip gloss that smelled like strawberries. Feeling more ready to face the world, I headed downstairs.

And paused at the end of the staircase. The scene was familiar, yet completely changed. Kids clustered around the flat-screen TVs. There should be talking, and there was, but it was definitely subdued. My group of friends were sitting around the TV we liked best: the Twins in their matching poofy chairs, Damien and Jack (looking very cozy) were sitting on the floor by the love seat, Erik was on the love seat, and I was surprised to see that his *fiiiine* friend, Cole, had pulled up a chair and was actually sitting between the Twins. I felt my lips twitch up. He was either very brave or very moronic. They were all chattering softly, and definitely not paying attention to *The Mummy Returns*, which was playing on TV. So, except for two things, it was a perfectly familiar scene. First, they were being way too quiet. Second, Stevie Rae should have been sitting on the love seat with her feet folded under her telling everyone to be quiet so she could hear the movie.

I swallowed back the teary, burning feeling in the back of my throat. I had to go on. *We* had to go on.

"Hi, guys," I said, trying to sound normal.

This time there wasn't an awkward silence at my presence. Instead there was an equally awkward everyone-talking-perkily-all-at-once.

"Hi, Z!"

"Zoey!"

"Hey there, Z!"

I managed not to sigh or roll my eyes as I took my place beside Erik. He put his arm around me and squeezed, which made me feel weirdly better but guilty. Better—because he was totally sweet and hot and I was still a little amazed that he seemed to like me so much. Guilty—well, that could be summed up in one word: Heath.

"Good! Now that Z's here we can start the marathon," Erik said.

"You mean the dorkathon," Shaunee said with a snort.

"If it was the weekend we could call it the geekend," Erin said.

"Let me guess." I looked up at Erik. "You brought the DVDs."

"Yep I did!"

The rest of the group groaned in exaggerated pain.

"Which means we're watching *Star Wars*," I said.

"Again," his friend Cole muttered.

Shaunee arched one perfectly waxed brow at Cole. "Are you saying that you're not a big *Star Wars* fan?"

He smiled at Shaunee, and even from where I was sitting I could see the flirty glimmer in his eyes. "Watching Erik's long extended director's cut of *Star Wars* for the millionth time is not why I came over here. I am a fan, but it's not of Darth and Chewbacca."

"Are you saying Princess Leia does it for you?" Shaunee quipped.

"No, I'm more *colorful* than that," he said, leaning toward her.

"I'm not here because I'm a fan of *Star Wars* either," Jack piped in, giving Damien an adoring look.

Erin giggled. "Well, we know Princess Leia doesn't do it for you."

"Thankfully," Damien said.

"I wish Stevie Rae was here," Erik said. "She'd be all, *Y'all, you're not bein' very niiiice*."

Erik's words made everyone shut up. I glanced at him and saw that his cheeks were getting red, like he hadn't realized exactly what he'd said till after he said it. I smiled and rested my head on his shoulder.

"You're right. Stevie Rae would be scolding us like a mamma."

"And then she'd make everyone some popcorn and tell us to share nice," Damien said. "Even though she should say share *nicely*."

"I liked the way Stevie Rae messed up the English language," Shaunee said.

"Yeah, she Okie-fied it," Erin said.

We all smiled at each other, and I felt a small warmth begin in my chest. This is how it started—this is how we would remember Stevie Rae—with smiles and love.

"Uh, can I sit with you guys?"

I looked up to see that cute Drew Partain kid standing nervously at the edge of our group. He looked pale and sad, and his eyes were red as if he'd been crying. I remembered how he had looked at Stevie Rae, and felt a stab of sympathy for him.

"Sure!" I said warmly. "Pull up a chair." Then an inner prompting made me add, "There's room over there by Erin."

Erin's blue eyes widened a little, but she recovered quickly. "Yeah, pull up a chair, Drew. But be warned, we're watching *Star Wars*."

"Cool with me," Drew said, giving Erin a hesitant smile.

"Short, but cute," I heard Shaunee whisper to Erin, and I do believe I saw Erin's cheeks get a little pink.

"Hey, I'm going to make us some popcorn. Plus, I need my—"

"Brown pop!" Damien, the Twins, and Erik said together.

I disentangled myself from Erik's arm and went to the kitchen, feeling more lighthearted than I had since Stevie Rae began coughing. Everything would be okay. The House of Night was my home. My friends were my family. I'd follow my own advice and take one day at a time—one issue at a time. I'd figure out a way to wade through my boyfriend issues. I'd do my best to avoid Neferet (without being too obvious that I was avoiding her) until I could figure out what was going on with her and the weird nondead Elliott (who was enough to give anyone nightmares—no wonder I'd had such a terrible dream about Stevie Rae and Heath).

I put one bag of extra-butter, super-pop popcorn in each of the four microwaves and grabbed big bowls as they started popping. Maybe I should cast another private circle and ask Nyx for help understanding the gross Elliott issue. My stomach clenched as I realized that I would be minus Stevie Rae. How was I going to deal with replacing her? It made me feel sick, but it had to be done. If not now, for my private ritual, I'd have to find someone before the next Full Moon Ritual. I closed my eyes against the pain of missing Stevie Rae and the reality of going on without her. *Please show me what to do,* I prayed silently to Nyx.

"Zoey, you need to come into the living room."

My eyes sprang open as Erik's voice startled me. The look on his face had my adrenaline surging through my body. "What's going on?"

"Just come on." He took my hand and we hurried out of the kitchen. "It's the news."

Even though the big living room was full of kids, it had gone completely silent. They were all staring at our big-screen TV, where Chera Kimiko was looking into the camera and speaking solemnly.

"*. . . police are warning the public not to panic, even though this is the third teenager to have disappeared. They are investigating, and assure Fox News that they have several viable leads.*

"*To repeat this special bulletin, a Broken Arrow teenager, another high school football player, has been reported as missing. His name is Heath Luck.*"

My knees no longer held me, and I would have fallen if Erik hadn't put his arm around my waist and helped me to the love seat. It felt like I couldn't catch my breath as I listened to Chera continue:

"Heath's truck was found outside the House of Night, but the High Priestess there, Neferet, assures police that he did not enter the school grounds, and that he has not been seen by anyone there. Of course there is much speculation about these disappearances, especially since the medical examiner's report states that the cause of death of the other two abducted boys was blood loss from multiple bites and lacerations. And while it is true that vampyres do not bite when they take blood from humans, the lacerations do follow a pattern that is consistent with vampyric feeding. It is important that we remind the public that vampyres have a binding legal agreement with humans to not feed on any human being against his or her will. We'll have more on this story at ten o'clock, and of course will break as news becomes available . . ."

"Someone get me a bowl, I'm gonna be sick!" I managed to yell over the humming in my head. A bowl was thrust into my hands and I promptly puked my guts into it.

CHAPTER TWENTY-SIX

"Here, Zoey, it'll help if you swish this around in your mouth." Blindly I took whatever Erin handed me, relieved when it was just cold water. I spit it into the nasty bowl of puke.

"Ugh, take it away," I said, suppressing my gag reflex as I got a whiff of puke. I wanted to cover my face with my hands and burst into tears, but I knew that the entire room was looking at me, so I slowly straightened my shoulders and pushed my damp hair back behind my ears. I didn't have the luxury of dissolving into a panicked heap. My mind was already processing the things I needed to do—had to do. For Heath. He was what was important right now, not me, and not my need for hysteria. "I have to see Neferet," I said resolutely and stood up, surprised at how steady my knees had become.

"I'll go with you," Erik said.

"Thanks, but first I need to brush my teeth and put on some shoes." (I'd just stuck on a pair of thick socks to come down and watch TV.) I smiled my thanks to Erik. "I'll run up to my room and be right back." I could feel the Twins getting ready to follow me. "I'll be fine. Just give me a sec." Then I turned and hurried up the stairs.

I didn't pause at my room, but kept going down the hall,

turned right, and stopped before room number 124. I'd raised my fist, but hadn't knocked when the door opened.

"I thought it would be you." Aphrodite gave me a cold look, but she stepped to the side. "Come on in."

I walked in, surprised by the pretty pastel interior of the room. I guess I'd expected it to be dark and scary, like a black widow's web.

"Do you have any mouthwash? I just puked and I've seriously grossed myself out."

She pointed her chin at the medicine cabinet over the sink. "In there. The glass on the sink is clean."

I washed out my mouth, taking the opportunity to try to collect my thoughts. When I was done I turned to face her. Deciding not to waste time on bullshit, I got straight to the point. "How can you tell if a vision is real or just a dream?"

She sat down on one of the beds and shook back her long, perfect blond hair. "It's a feeling in your gut. Visions are never easy or comfortable or fucking flower-draped like they are in the movies. Visions suck. At least real ones do. Basically, if it makes you feel like shit, it's probably real and not just a dream." Her blue eyes looked me over carefully. "So, you've been having visions?"

"I thought I had a dream last night, a nightmare actually. Today I think it was a vision."

Aphrodite's lips turned up only slightly. "Well, that sucks for you."

I changed the subject. "What's going on with Neferet?"

Aphrodite's face went carefully blank. "What do you mean?"

"I think you know exactly what I mean. Something's off about her. I want to know what."

"You're her fledgling. Her favorite. Her new golden girl. Do you think I'm actually going to say shit to you? I may be blond, but I'm definitely not stupid."

"If that's the way you really feel, why did you warn me against taking the medicine she gave me?"

Aphrodite looked away. "My first roommate died six months after she got here. I took the medicine. It—it affected me. For a long time."

"What do you mean? How did it affect you?"

"It made me feel funny, detached. And it stopped my visions. Not permanently, just for a couple of weeks. And then it was hard for me to even remember what she looked like." Aphrodite paused. "Venus. Her name was Venus Davis." Her eyes met mine again. "She was the reason I chose Aphrodite as my new name. We were best friends and we thought it was cool." Her eyes were filled with sadness. "I've made myself remember Venus, and I figured you'd want to remember Stevie Rae."

"I do. I will. Thanks."

"You should go. It won't be good for either of us if anyone knows you've been here talking to me," Aphrodite said.

I realized that she was probably right, and turned for the door. Her voice stopped me.

"She makes you think she's good, but she's not. Everything that's light isn't good, and everything that's darkness isn't always bad."

Darkness does not always equate to evil, just as light does not always bring good. The words that Nyx had said to me the day I was Marked were mirrored in Aphrodite's warning.

"In other words, be careful around Neferet and don't trust her," I said.

"Yeah, but I never said that."

"Said what? We're not even having this conversation." I shut the door behind me and hurried to my room where I washed my face and brushed my teeth, pulled on some shoes, and then returned to the living room.

"Ready?" Erik asked.

"We'll come, too," Damien said, motioning to include the Twins, Jack, and Drew.

I started to tell them no, but I couldn't make the word come out. The truth was that I was glad they were here, glad they obviously felt the need to join forces around me and protect me. I'd worried for a really long time that my extra powers and my weird Goddess-chosen Mark would brand me such a freak that I wouldn't fit in, wouldn't have any friends. But the opposite seemed to be happening.

"Okay, let's go." We headed for the door. I wasn't entirely sure what I was going to say to Neferet. All I knew was that I couldn't continue to keep my mouth shut, and that I had a terrible feeling my "dream" had really been a vision, and that there was more to the "spirits" I'd been seeing than ghosts. Most of all, I was afraid they'd taken Heath. What that said about what Stevie Rae had become chilled me to my core, but it didn't change the fact that Heath was missing, and that I think I knew who had taken him (if not what).

We hadn't quite made it to the door when it opened and Neferet glided into the room on a tide of snow-scented air. She was followed by Detective Marx and Detective Martin. They had blue down jackets on that were zipped to their chins. Their hats were covered with snow and their noses were red. Neferet, as usual, looked perfectly poised, perfectly groomed, perfectly in control.

"Ah, Zoey, good. This saves me from having to look for you. The two detectives have some rather bad news, and they'd also like to speak with you for a moment."

I didn't spare a glance for Neferet, and I could feel her stiffening as I responded directly to the detectives. "I already heard on the news that Heath's missing. If there's any way I can help, I will."

"Could we use the library again?" Detective Marx asked.

"Of course," Neferet said smoothly.

I started to follow Neferet and the detectives from the room, but paused to look back at Erik.

"We'll be here," he said.

"All of us," Damien said.

I nodded. Feeling better, I went to the library. I'd hardly entered the room when Detective Martin started questioning me.

"Zoey, can you account for your whereabouts between six thirty and eight thirty this morning?"

I nodded. "I was upstairs in my room. Around that time I was talking on the phone to my grandma, and then Heath and I text messaged each other back and forth a few times." I reached into my jeans pocket and pulled out my cell phone. "I haven't even deleted the messages. You can see them if you want."

"You don't have to give him your phone, Zoey," Neferet said.

I made myself smile at her. "That's okay. I don't mind."

Detective Martin took my phone and started going through the text message files, copying onto a little pad the messages.

"Did you see Heath this morning?" Detective Marx asked.

"No. He asked if he could come see me, but I told him no."

"This says that you were planning on seeing him Friday," Detective Martin said.

I could feel Neferet's sharp eyes on me. I drew a deep breath. The only way I could do this would be to stick as close to the truth as I was able.

"Yeah, I was going to go out with him after the game Friday."

"Zoey, you know it is strictly against school rules to continue to date humans from your old life." I noticed, as if for the first time, the disgust that filled her voice when she said *humans*.

"I know. I'm sorry." Again, I told the truth, only omitting a bloodsucking, Imprinting detail here and an I-don't-trust-you-anymore detail there. "It's just that Heath and I had so much history between us that it was really hard to totally stop talking to him, even though I knew I had to. I thought it would be easier if we met and I told him to his face, once and for all, why we couldn't see each other. I would have told you, but I wanted to handle it on my own."

"So, you didn't see him this morning?" Detective Marx repeated.

"No. After we were done text messaging I went to bed."

"Can anyone substantiate that you were in your room sleeping at that time?" Detective Martin asked, handing me back my phone.

Neferet's voice was ice. "Gentlemen, I already explained to you the terrible loss Zoey experienced just yesterday. Her roommate died. So, how she could have anyone substantiate her whereabouts at—"

"Um, excuse me, Neferet, but actually I wasn't sleeping alone. My friends Shaunee and Erin didn't want me to be by myself, so they came to my room and slept with me." I left Damien out. No point getting the kid in trouble.

"Oh, that was very kind of them," Neferet said gently, switching in one breath from scary vampyre to concerned mother. I tried not to think of how *not* fooled I was by her.

"Do you have any idea where Heath might be?" I asked Detective Marx (I still liked him better of the two).

"No. His truck was found not far from the school wall, but the snow is falling so fast that any tracks he might have made have been completely covered."

"Well, I should think that instead of wasting your time questioning my fledgling, the police would be spending time searching the gutters for the teenager," Neferet said in an offhand tone that made me want to scream.

"Ma'am?" Marx said.

"It seems clear to me what happened. The boy was trying to see Zoey, again. It was only last month that he and that girlfriend of his climbed our wall saying they were going to break her out of the school." Neferet waved her hand dismissively. "He was drunk and high then, he was probably drunk and high this morning, too. The snow was too much for him and he's probably fallen into a gutter somewhere. Isn't that where drunks usually end up?"

"Ma'am, he's a teenager, not a drunk. And his parents and friends say he hasn't had a drink in a month."

Neferet's soft laugh made it obvious how much she didn't believe him. Surprising me, Marx ignored her and studied me carefully. "How about it, Zoey? You two dated for a couple of years, right? Can you think of where he might have gone?"

"Not out this way. If his truck was missing off Oak Grove Road in BA I could tell you where the keg party might be." I didn't mean it as a joke, especially after Neferet's mean cracks about Heath, but the detective seemed to be trying not to smile, which suddenly made him appear kind, and even approachable. Before I could change my mind, I blurted, "But I had a weird dream this morning that might not actually have been a dream but could have been some kind of vision about Heath."

Into the stunned silence Neferet's voice sounded clipped and harsh. "Zoey, you have never before manifested an affinity for prophecy or visions."

"I know." Purposefully I made myself sound unsure and even a little scared (the scared part wasn't exactly pretense). "But it's just too weird that I dreamed that Heath was over by the east wall, and that he was grabbed there."

"What grabbed him, Zoey?" Detective Marx's voice was urgent. He was definitely taking me seriously.

"I don't know." Which definitely wasn't a lie. "I do know they weren't fledglings or vampyres. In my dream four cloaked figures dragged him away."

"Did you see where they went?"

"No, I woke up screaming for Heath." I didn't have to fake the tears that filled my eyes. "Maybe you should search everything around the school. Something's out there, and something's taking kids, but it's not us."

"Of course it's not us." Neferet came over to me and put her arm around me, patting my shoulder and making soft mom sounds. "Gentlemen, I think Zoey's had more than enough upsetting for one day. Why don't I introduce you to Shaunee and Erin, who, I'm sure, will collaborate her alibi."

Alibi. The word sounded chilling.

"If you remember anything else, or have any other odd dreams, please don't hesitate to contact me, anytime day or night," Detective Marx said.

This was the second time he'd given me his card—he certainly was persistent. I took his card from him and thanked him. Then as Neferet led him from the room Detective Marx hesitated and walked back to me.

"My twin sister was Marked and Changed fifteen years ago," he said softly. "She and I are still close, even though she was supposed to forget her human family. So when I say you can call me anytime, and tell me anything, you can believe me. You can also trust me."

"Detective Marx?" Neferet stood in the doorway.

"Just thanking Zoey again, and telling her how sorry I am about her roommate," he said smoothly as he strode from the room.

I stayed where I was, trying to collect my thoughts. Marx's sister was a vampyre? Well, that really wasn't so bizarre. What was bizarre is that he still loved her. Maybe I could trust him.

The door clicked shut and I jerked in surprise. Neferet was standing with her back to it, watching me carefully.

"Did you Imprint with Heath?"

I had an instant of cold, white panic. She was going to be able to read me. I'd been fooling myself. There was no way I was any kind of a match for this High Priestess. Then I felt the brush of a gentle, impossible breeze . . . the warmth of an invisible fire . . . the freshness of a spring rain . . . the green sweetness of a fertile meadow . . . and the powerful infilling of elemental strength flowing into my spirit. With new confidence I met Neferet's eyes.

"But you said I didn't. You told me before that what happened between him and me on the wall wasn't enough to Imprint." I made sure my voice sounded confused and upset.

Her shoulders relaxed almost imperceptibly. "I don't think you Imprinted with him then. So, you're saying you haven't been with him since? You haven't fed from him again?"

"Again!" I let myself sound as shocked as I always felt at the disturbing, yet seductive thought of feeding on Heath. "But I didn't really *feed* on him then, did I?"

"No, no, of course not," Neferet reassured me. "What you did was very minor, very minor indeed. It's just that your dream made me wonder if you'd been with your boyfriend again."

"Ex-boyfriend," I said almost automatically. "No. But he's been texting and calling me a bunch lately, so I thought it would be best if I met him and tried to make him understand, once and for all, that we can't see each other anymore. I'm sorry. I should have told you, but I really did want to solve it myself. I mean, I got myself into the mess. I should be able to handle getting myself out of it."

"Well, I do commend your sense of responsibility, but I don't think it was wise to make the detectives believe your dream might have been a vision."

"It just seemed so real," I said.

"I'm sure it did. Zoey, did you take the medicine I asked you to drink last night?"

"You mean that milky stuff? Yeah, Shaunee gave it to me." And she had, but I'd poured the crap down the sink.

Neferet looked even more relaxed. "Good. If you keep having disturbing dreams, come to me and I'll give you a stronger mixture. That should have kept the nightmares from you, but clearly I underestimated the dosage you required."

The dosage wasn't all she'd underestimated.

I smiled. "Thanks, Neferet. I appreciate that."

"Well, you should return to your friends, now. They are quite protective of you, and I'm sure they're worried."

I nodded and walked with her back to the living room, careful not to show my disgust when she hugged me in front of everyone and said good-bye with the warmth of a mom. Actually, she was exactly like a mom, specifically *my* mom, Linda Heffer. The woman who had betrayed me for a man and cared more about herself and appearances than she cared about me. The similarities between Neferet and Linda were becoming clearer and clearer.

CHAPTER TWENTY-SEVEN

We resettled in our little group after they left, and didn't say much as the room got back to normal. I noticed no one changed the local station. The *Star Wars* DVD was forgotten, at least for tonight.

"Are you okay?" Erik finally asked softly. He put his arm back around me and I snuggled against him.

"Yeah, I think so."

"Did the cops have any news about Heath?" Damien asked.

"Nothing more than what we already heard," I said. "Or if they do, they weren't telling me."

"Is there anything we can do?" Shaunee asked.

I shook my head. "Let's just watch local TV and see what the ten o'clock news says."

They mumbled okays and everyone settled in to watch the *Will and Grace* rerun marathon while we waited for the news. I stared at the TV, and thought about Heath. Did I have a bad feeling about him? Definitely. But was it the same bad feeling I'd had about Chris Ford and Brad Higeons? No, I didn't think so. I didn't know how to explain it. My gut said Heath was in danger, but it wasn't saying that he was dead. Yet.

The more I thought about Heath, the more restless I became. By the time the late news came on I could hardly sit through the stories on the unexpected blizzard that had caused a white-out in Tulsa and the surrounding area. I fidgeted while we watched the shots of downtown and the expressways, eerily empty and looking post-meteor-hit-or-nuclear-war-like.

There was nothing new on Heath except a grim report about how the weather was hampering search efforts.

"I have to go." The words were out of my mouth and I was standing before my mind could remind me that I didn't have a clue where I was going or how I was going to get there.

"Go where, Z?" Erik asked.

My mind flailed around and landed on one thing—one little island of contentment in a world that had turned into stress and confusion and madness.

"I'm going to the stables." Erik's look was as blank as everyone else's. "Lenobia said that I could brush Persephone anytime I wanted to." I moved my shoulders. "Brushing her makes me feel calm, and right now I could use some calm."

"Well, okay. I like horses. Let's go groom Persephone," Erik said.

"I need to be alone." The words sounded so much harsher than I'd meant them that I sat back down next to him and slid my hand in his. "I'm sorry. It's just that I need time to think, and that's something I have to do alone."

His blue eyes looked sad, but he gave me a little smile. "How about I walk you to the stable, and then come back here and keep an eye on the news for you till you get through thinking?"

"I'd like that."

I hated the worried looks on my friends' faces, but I couldn't do much to reassure them. Erik and I didn't bother with coats. The stable wasn't far. The cold wouldn't get a chance to bother us.

"This snow is awesome," Erik said after we'd walked a little way down the sidewalk. Someone had attempted to plow it because it was way less deep on the sidewalk than the surrounding grounds, but the snow was coming down so steadily that the plows couldn't keep up with it and it was already up to midcalf on us.

"I kinda remember it snowing like this when I was six or seven. It was during Christmas break and it sucked that we didn't miss any school."

Erik grunted a vague, guylike response, and then we walked on in silence. Usually, our silences weren't awkward, but this one felt weird. I didn't know what to say—how to make it better.

Erik cleared his throat. "You still care about him, don't you? I mean, as more than just an ex-boyfriend."

"Yes." Erik deserved the truth, and I was totally sick of lies.

We'd come to the stable door, and stopped in the halo of a yellow gaslight. The entryway shielded us from the worst of the snow, so it seemed like we were standing in a bubble inside a snow globe.

"And what about me?" Erik asked.

I looked up at him. "I care about you, too. Erik, I wish I could fix this, make all of the bad stuff go away, but I can't. And I'm not going to lie to you about Heath. I think I've Imprinted him."

I saw the surprise in Erik's eyes. "From just that one time on the wall? Z, I was there, and you hardly tasted any of his blood at all. He just doesn't want to lose you, that's why he's so obsessed. Not that I blame him," he added with a wry smile.

"I saw him again."

"Huh?"

"It was just a couple days ago. I couldn't sleep, so I went to the Starbucks at Utica Square by myself. He was there putting up posters about Brad. I hadn't meant to see him, and if I'd known he was going to be there I wouldn't have gone. I promise you that, Erik."

"But you did see him."

I nodded.

"And you fed from him?"

"It—it just kinda happened. I tried not to, but he cut himself. On purpose. And I couldn't stop myself." I kept my gaze squarely on his, asking him with my eyes to understand. Now that I was actually confronted with the very likely possibility that Erik and I were going to break up, I realized how much I didn't want that to happen, which definitely didn't help my confusion or my stress level because I did still care about Heath. "I'm sorry, Erik. I didn't ask for it to happen, but it did, and now there's this thing between Heath and me, and I'm not sure what I'm going to do about it."

He sighed deeply and brushed some snow off my hair. "Okay, well, there's a *thing* between you and me, too. And someday, if we make it through this damn Change, we'll be alike. I won't turn into a wrinkled old man and die decades before you will. Being with me won't be something other vampyres will whisper about, and humans will hate you for. It'll be normal. It'll be right." Then his hand was behind my neck and he was pulling me to him. He kissed me hard. He tasted cold and sweet. My arms went up around his shoulders and I kissed him back. At first I just wanted to make the hurt I was causing him go away. Then our kiss deepened, and we pressed our bodies together. I wasn't overwhelmed with blinding bloodlust for him, like what happened when I was with Heath, but I liked the way kissing Erik made me feel, all kinda warm and light-headed. Hell, the bottom line was that I liked *him*. A lot. Plus, he had a point. He and I would be right together. Heath and I would not.

The kiss ended with both of us breathing hard. I cupped Erik's cheek in my hand. "I really am sorry."

Erik turned his head and kissed my palm. "We'll figure this out."

"I hope so," I whispered, more to myself than him. Then I stepped away from him and put my hand on the old iron doorknob. "Thanks for walking me here. I don't know when I'll be back. You shouldn't wait for me." I started to open the door.

"Z, if you really did Imprint with Heath you might be able to find him," Erik said. I paused and turned back to Erik. He looked strained and unhappy, but he didn't hesitate to explain. "While you're brushing the mare, think about Heath. Call to him. If he's able to, he'll come to you. If he's not and your Imprint is strong enough, you may be able to get an idea of where he is."

"Thank you, Erik."

He smiled, but he didn't look happy. "Later, Z." He walked away and the snow swallowed him.

The warm hay smell mixed with clean, dry horse contrasted dramatically with the cold, snowy outside. The stables were dimly lit by only a couple of soft gaslights. The horses were making sleepy, chewing noises. Some of them were blowing through their noses, which sounded a little like snoring. I looked around for Lenobia while I brushed the snow from my shirt and hair and started toward the tack room, but it was pretty obvious that except for the horses I was alone.

Good. I needed to think, and not explain what I was doing here in the middle of a snowstorm in the middle of the night.

Okay, I'd told Erik the truth about Heath and he hadn't broken up with me. Of course, depending on what happened with Heath, he might still dump me. How did those ho-ish girls go out with a dozen or so guys at the same time? Two was exhausting. Memory of Loren's sexy smile and incredible voice flashed through my guilt-filled mind. I chewed my lip as I grabbed a curry brush and a mane comb. Actually, I'd been kinda sorta seeing three guys, which was utterly insane. I decided then and there that I had enough problems without adding the weird flirting that may or may not be going on between Loren and me into the mix. Just thinking about Erik finding out that I'd shown all that skin to

Loren . . . I shuddered. It made me want to dump myself. From now on I'd avoid Loren, and if I couldn't avoid him I'd treat him like any other teacher, which meant *no flirting*. Now if I could just figure out what to do with Erik and Heath.

I opened Persephone's stall and told her what a pretty, sweet girl she was as she gave me a sleepily surprised snort and lipped my face after I kissed her soft nose. She sighed and rested on three feet when I started brushing her.

Okay, no way I could figure out anything about dating Erik and Heath until Heath was safe. (I refused to consider that he might never be safe—might never be found alive.) I began to quiet the babble and clutter and confusion that was my mind. Truthfully, I hadn't needed Erik to tell me that I might be able to find Heath. That possibility was one of the many things that had been making me so restless all night. The cowardly truth was that I was afraid—afraid of what I might find and what I might not find, and afraid I wouldn't be strong enough to deal with either. Stevie Rae's death had left me broken, and I wasn't sure I was up to saving anybody.

But it wasn't like I had any choice.

So . . . thinking of Heath . . . I started by remembering what a cute kid he'd been in grade school. In third grade his hair had been lots blonder than it was now, and he'd had like a zillion cowlicks. It used to stand up all over his head like duck fluff. Third grade was when he'd first told me that he loved me and was gonna someday marry me. I'd been in second grade, and I so didn't take him seriously. I mean, even though I was almost two years younger I'd been a foot taller. He was cute, but he was also a boy, which meant he was annoying.

Okay, so he could still be annoying, but he'd grown up and filled out. Somewhere between third and eleventh grade I'd started taking him seriously. I remembered back to the first time he'd *really* kissed me, and the fluttery, excited way it made me feel. I remembered how sweet he was, and how he could make me feel beautiful, even when I had a terrible cold and my nose was bright red. And how he was an old-fashioned gentleman. Heath had been opening doors and carrying books for me since he was nine.

Then I thought about the last time I'd seen him. He'd been so sure that we belonged together and so unafraid of me that he'd cut himself and offered his blood to me. I closed my eyes and leaned against Persephone's soft flank, thinking of Heath and letting the memories of him drift past my closed lids like a movie screen. Then the images of our past changed and I got a vague sense of darkness and dampness and cold—and fear slammed into my gut. I gasped, keeping my eyes tightly closed. I wanted to focus in on him, like I had that one other time when somehow I'd seen him in his bedroom, but this connection between us was different. It was less clear, more filled with dark emotions than playful desire. I concentrated harder, and did what Erik had said to do. I called Heath.

Aloud, as well as with everything inside of me, I said, "Heath, come to me. I'm calling you, Heath. I want you to come to me now. Wherever you are, get out of there and come to me!"

Nothing. There was no answer. No response. No sense of anything more than damp, cold fear. I called again. "Heath! Come to me!" This time I felt a surge of frustration, followed by despair. But I didn't get an image of him. I knew he couldn't come to me, but I didn't know where he was.

Why had I been able to see him so much more easily before? How had I done it? I'd been thinking about Heath then, just like I had been now. I'd been thinking about . . .

What had I been thinking about? Then I felt my cheeks get hot as I realized what had drawn me to him before. I hadn't been thinking about how cute a kid he'd been or how pretty he made me feel. I'd been thinking about drinking his blood . . . feeding from him . . . and the red-hot bloodlust that caused.

Okay, well then . . .

I drew a deep breath and thought about Heath's blood. It tasted like liquid desire, hot and thick and electric. It made my body burst alive in places that had only begun to rouse before. And those places were starving. I wanted to drink Heath's sweet blood while he satisfied my yearning for his touch, his body, his taste—

The disjointed image I had of darkness cleared with an abruptness that was shocking. It was still dark, but that was no problem for my night vision. At first I didn't understand what I was seeing. The room was weird. It was more like a little alcove in a cave or a tunnel than a room. The walls were round and damp. There was some light, but it was coming from a dim, smoky lantern that hung from a rusted hook. Everything else was complete darkness. What I thought at first was a pile of dirty clothes moved and moaned. This time it wasn't just a threadlike feeler I was looking through. It was actually as if I was floating, and when I recognized the moan my hovering body drifted over to him.

He was curled up on a stained mattress. His hands and ankles were duct taped together and he was bleeding from several slashes on his neck and arms.

"Heath!" My voice wasn't audible, but his head snapped up as if I'd just yelled at him.

"Zoey? Is that you?" And then his eyes widened and he sat straight up, looking wildly around. "Get out of here, Zoey! They're crazy. They'll kill you like they did Chris and Brad." And he started to struggle, trying desperately to break the tape, even though all that was happening was he was making his already raw wrists bleed.

"Heath, stop! It's okay—I'm okay. I'm not here, not really." He stopped struggling and squinted around him like he was trying to see me.

"But I can hear you."

"Inside your head. That's where you hear me, Heath. It's because we've Imprinted and now we're linked."

Unexpectedly, Heath grinned. "That's cool, Zo."

I gave a mental eye roll. "Okay, Heath, focus. Where are you?"

"You won't believe this, Zo, but I'm under Tulsa."

"What does that mean, Heath?"

"Remember in Shaddox's History class? He told us about the tunnels that were dug under Tulsa in the twenties because of the un-alcohol thing."

"Prohibition," I said.

"Yeah, that. I'm in one of them."

I didn't know what to say for a second. I vaguely remembered learning about the tunnels in History class, and was astounded that Heath—not exactly an excellent student—would remember at all.

As if he understood my hesitation he grinned and said, "It was about sneaking booze. I thought it was cool."

After another mental eye roll I said, "Just tell me how to get there, Heath."

He shook his head and a way too familiar stubborn look settled over his face. "No way. They'll kill you. Go tell the cops and have them send a SWAT team or something."

That was exactly what I wanted to do. I wanted to get Detective Marx's card out of my pocket, call him, and have him save the day.

Unfortunately, I was afraid I couldn't.

"Who is the 'they'?" I asked.

"Huh?"

"The people who took you? Who are they?"

"They're not people, and they're not vampyres even though they drink blood, but they're not like you, Zo. They're—" he broke off, shuddering. "They're something else. Something wrong."

"Have they been drinking your blood?" The thought made me furious with such an intensity that I was having a hard time controlling my emotions. I wanted to rage at someone and shriek, *He belongs to me!* I forced myself to take several deep breaths while he answered me.

"Yeah, they have." Heath grimaced. "But they complain a lot about it. They say my blood doesn't taste right. I think that's the main reason I'm still alive." Then he swallowed hard and his face got a shade paler. "It's not like when you drink my blood, Zo. That feels good. What they do is—is disgusting. *They're* disgusting."

"How many of them are there?" I said through gritted teeth.

"I'm not really sure. It's so dark down here and they always come in weird groups, all smushed together like they're scared of being alone. Well, except for three of them. One's named Elliott, one's called Venus—how weird is that—and the other one is called Stevie Rae."

My stomach knotted. "Does Stevie Rae have short, curly blond hair?"

"Yeah. She's the one that's in charge."

Heath had just substantiated my fears. I couldn't call in the police.

"Okay, Heath. I'm going to get you out of there. Tell me how to find your tunnel."

"Are you going to get the cops?"

"Yes," I lied.

"Nope. You're lying."

"I am not!"

"Zo, I can tell you're lying. I can feel it. It's that link thing." He grinned.

"Heath. I can't get the police."

"Then I'm not telling you where I am."

Echoing from down one end of the tunnel came a skittering that reminded me of the sound the science experiment rats made as they scurried through the mazes we made in AP Bio. Heath's grin was gone, as was the color that had returned to his cheeks while we talked.

"Heath, we don't have time for this." He started to shake his head no. "Listen to me! I have special powers. Those—" I hesitated, not sure what to call the group of creatures that somehow included my dead best friend. "Those *things* aren't going to be able to hurt me."

Heath didn't say anything, but he didn't look convinced and the ratlike sounds were getting louder.

"You said you can tell I'm lying because of our link. It has to go both ways. You've got to be able to tell when what I say is the truth." He looked like he was waffling, so I added, "Think hard. You said you remembered some of that night you found me at Philbrook. I saved you that night, Heath. Not the cops. Not an adult vamp. I saved you, and I can do it again." I was glad I sounded a lot more certain than I felt. "Tell me where you are."

He thought for a while, and I was getting ready to yell at him (again) when he finally said, "You know where the old depot is downtown?"

"Yeah, you can see it from the Performing Arts Center where we went to see *Phantom* for my birthday last year, right?"

"Yeah. They took me to the basement of it. They got in through something that looks like a barred door. It's old and rusted, but it lifts right up. The tunnel starts from the drainage grates down there."

"Good, I'll—"

"Wait, that's not all. There are lots of tunnels. They're more like caves. It's not cool like I thought they'd be from History class. They're dark and wet and disgusting. Pick the one on your right, and then keep turning to your right. I'm at the end of one of those."

"Okay. I'll be there as soon as I can."

"Be careful, Zo."

"I will. You be safe."

"I'll try." Hissing was added to the scurrying noises. "But you should probably hurry up."

CHAPTER TWENTY-EIGHT

I opened up my eyes and I was back in the stall with Persephone. I was breathing hard and sweating, and the mare was nuzzling me and making soft, worried, nickering noises. My hands were shaking as I caressed her head and rubbed her jaw, telling her that it was going to be okay, even though I was pretty sure it wasn't.

The old downtown depot was six or seven miles away in a dark, unused part of town under a big, scary bridge that linked one part of the city to the other. It used to be majorly busy, with freight and passenger trains coming and going almost nonstop. But in the past couple decades all of the passenger traffic had stopped (I knew because my grandma had wanted to take me on a train trip for my thirteenth birthday, and we'd had to drive to Oklahoma City to catch the train there) and the freight train business had definitely dwindled. Under normal circumstances, it would only take a few minutes to zip from the House of Night to the depot.

Tonight I was not dealing with normal circumstances.

The ten o'clock news had said the roads were impassable, and that had been—I checked my watch and blinked in surprise—a couple hours ago. I couldn't drive there. I suppose I could walk, but the urgency I felt was telling me that wasn't good enough.

"Take the horse."

Persephone and I both shied at the sound of Aphrodite's voice. She was leaning against the stall door looking pale and grim.

"You look like crap," I said.

She almost smiled. "Visions suck."

"Did you see Heath?" My stomach clenched again. Aphrodite didn't have visions of happiness and light. She saw death and destruction. Always.

"Yeah."

"And?"

"And if you don't get on that horse and get your ass to wherever he is, Heath is going to die." She paused, meeting my eyes. "That is, unless you don't believe me."

"I believe you," I said without hesitation.

"Then get the hell out of here."

She came into the stall and handed me a bridle I hadn't noticed she'd been holding. While I put it on Persephone, Aphrodite disappeared to come back with a saddle and saddle blanket. Silently, we put the tack on Persephone, who seemed to sense our intensity because she held completely still. When she was ready I led her from the stall.

"Call your friends first," Aphrodite said.

"Huh?"

"You can't beat those things on your own."

"But how are they going to go with me?" My stomach hurt, I was so scared my hands were shaking, and I was having trouble understanding what the hell Aphrodite was saying.

"They can't go with you, but they can still help you."

"Aphrodite, I don't have time for riddles. What the hell do you mean?"

"Shit, I don't know!" She looked as frustrated as I felt. "I just know that they can help you."

I flipped open my cell phone and, following my gut and

breathing a silent prayer for guidance from Nyx, punched Shaunee's number. She answered on the first ring.

"What's up, Zoey?"

"I need you and Erin and Damien to go somewhere together and call to your elements, like you did for Stevie Rae."

"No problem. Are you gonna meet us?"

"No. I'm going to get Heath." To her credit, Shaunee hesitated for only a second or two, then said, "Okay. What can we do?"

"Just be together, manifest your elements, and think about me." I was getting really good at sounding calm even when I thought my head might explode.

"Zoey, be careful."

"I will. Don't worry." Yeah, I'd worry enough for both of us.

"Erik isn't going to like this."

"I know. Tell him . . . tell him . . . that I'll, uh, talk to him when I get back." I had not a clue about what else to say.

"Okay, I'll tell him."

"Thanks, Shaunee. I'll see ya," I said and closed the phone. Then I faced Aphrodite. "What are those creatures?"

"I don't know."

"But you saw them in your vision?"

"Today was the second vision I had about them, though. The first time I saw the other two guys being killed by them." Aphrodite brushed a thick strand of blond hair from her face.

Instantly I was pissed. "And you didn't say anything about it because they're *just* human teenagers and not worth your time to save?"

Aphrodite's eyes blazed with anger. "I told Neferet. I told her everything—about the human kids—about those *things*—everything. That's when she started saying my visions were false."

I knew she was telling the truth, just as surely as I had begun to know that there was something dark about Neferet.

"Sorry," I said shortly. "I didn't know."

"Whatever," she said. "You need to get out of here or your boyfriend is going to die."

"Ex-boyfriend," I said.

"Again I say whatever. Here, I'll give you a leg up."

I let her hoist me into the saddle.

"Take this with you." Aphrodite handed me a thick, plaid horse blanket. Before I could protest she said, "It's not for you. He'll need it."

I wrapped the blanket around me, taking comfort in its earthy, horsey smell. I followed as Aphrodite went to the rear doors of the stable and slid them apart. Frigid air and snow swirled in little mini-tornadoes into the barn, making me shiver, although it was more from nerves and apprehension than from the cold.

"Stevie Rae's one of them," Aphrodite said.

I looked down at her, but she was staring out into the night.

"I know," I said.

"She's not who she used to be."

"I know," I repeated, even though saying the words aloud hurt my heart. "Thanks for this, Aphrodite."

She did look up at me then and her expression was flat and un-readable. "Don't start acting like we're friends or anything," she said.

"Wouldn't think of it," I said.

"I mean, we're not friends."

"Nope, definitely not." I was pretty sure I saw her trying not to smile.

"As long as we have that straight," Aphrodite said. "Oh," she added. "Remember to pull silence and darkness around yourself so humans will have a hard time seeing you on the way there. You don't have time to be stopped."

"Will do. Thanks for reminding me," I said.

"Okay, well, good luck," Aphrodite said.

I gripped the reins, took a deep breath, and then squeezed my thighs together, clucking at Persephone to go.

I entered a world that was weirdly made of white darkness. Whiteout was definitely the right description of it. The snow had changed from big, friendly flakes to sharp little razorlike pieces of snow-ice. The wind was steady, making the snow slant sideways. I pulled the blanket over my head so that I was partially protected from the snow and leaned forward, kicking Persephone into a quick trot. *Hurry!* My mind was yelling at me. *Heath needs you!*

I cut across the parking lot and rear part of the school grounds. The few cars still at school were covered with snow, and the flickering gaslights that shined crazily off of their backs made them look like june bugs on a screen door. I pressed the inside button for the gate to open. It tried to swing wide, but a snowdrift caught it and Persephone and I had barely enough room to squeeze through. I turned her to the right and stood for a moment under the cover of the oaks that framed the school grounds.

"We're silent . . . ghosts . . . no one can see us. No one can hear us." I murmured against the whining wind, and was shocked when the area around me stilled. With a sudden thought I continued. "Wind, be calm near me. Fire, warm my way. Water, still the snow in my path. Earth, shelter me when you can. And spirit, help me not to give in to my fear." The words were barely out of my mouth when I saw a little flash of energy around me. Persephone snorted and she skittered a little to the side. And as she moved it was like a little bubble of serenity moved with her. Yes, it was still blizzarding and the night was still cold and frighteningly alien, but I was filled with calm and surrounded by the protection of the elements. I bowed my head and whispered, "Thank you, Nyx, for the great gifts you have given me." Silently I added that I hoped I deserved them.

"Let's get Heath," I told Persephone. She swung into her ground-eating canter easily and I was amazed to see that the snow and ice seemed to fly back from her hooves as we magically blasted through the night under the watchful eye of the Goddess who was, herself, Night personified.

My journey was surprisingly fast. We cantered down Utica Street until we came to the exit to the Broken Arrow Expressway. Barricades were up with flashing lights warning that the expressway was closed. I felt myself smiling as I guided Persephone neatly around the barricades onto the utterly deserted highway. Then I gave the mare her head and she galloped downtown. I clung to her, leaning low over her neck. With the blanket streaming out behind us I imagined that I looked like the heroine in an old historical romance novel, and wished I was galloping to a naughty keg party with someone my kingly father had decided was inappropriate instead of heading into hell.

I steered Persephone to the exit that would take us to the Performing Arts Center and the old depot beyond it. I hadn't seen anyone between midtown and the highway, but now I saw occasional shufflings of street people around the bus station and noticed an occasional cop car here and there. *We're silent... ghosts... no one can see us. No one can hear us.* I kept the prayer going in my mind. No one so much as glanced in our direction. It really was as if I'd turned into a ghost, which wasn't a thought I found very comforting.

I slowed Persephone as we passed the Performing Arts Center and trotted over the wide bridge that spanned the confusing side-by-side meshing of old railroad tracks. When we reached the center of the bridge I stopped Persephone and stared down at the abandoned depot building that sat below us dark and silent. Thanks to Mrs. Brown, my ex-art teacher at South Intermediate High School, I knew it used to be a beautiful art deco building that had been abandoned and eventually looted when the trains stopped running. Now it looked like something that should be in the Gotham City of the Batman Dark Night comics. (Yes, I know. I'm a dork.) It had those huge arched windows that reminded me of teeth between two towers that looked like perfectly creepy haunted castles.

"And we have to go down there," I told Persephone. She was breathing hard from our ride, but she didn't seem particularly worried, which I hoped was a good sign. You know, animals being able to sense bad stuff and all.

We finished crossing the bridge and I found the broken little side road that led down to the depot. The track level was dark. Really dark. That shouldn't have bothered me, what with my excellent fledgling night vision, but it did. The truth was that I was totally creeped out as Persephone walked to the building and I began slowly circling it, looking for the basement entrance Heath had described.

It didn't take long to find the rusted iron grill that appeared to be an impassable barrier. I didn't let myself hesitate and think about how completely afraid I was. I got off Persephone and led her over to the covered entryway so she'd be out of the wind and protected from most of the snow. I looped her reins around a metal thingie, laid the extra blanket over her back, and spent as long as I could patting her and telling her what a brave, sweet girl she was and that I'd be back real soon. I was working toward that self-fulfilling prophecy thing, and hoped if I kept saying it, it would be true. Walking away from Persephone was hard. I guess I hadn't realized how comforting her presence had been. I could have used some of that comfort as I stood in front of the iron grill and tried to squint into the darkness beyond.

I couldn't see anything except the indistinct shape of a huge dark room. The basement of the creepy unfortunately-not-abandoned building. Great. *Heath is down there*, I reminded myself, grabbed the edge of the grill, and pulled. It opened easily, which I took to be evidence of how often it must be used. Again, great.

The basement was not as awful as I'd imagined it would be. Stripes of weak light filtered between the barred, ground-level windows and I could clearly see that homeless people must have been using the room. Actually, there was a lot of stuff left from them: big boxes, dirty blankets, even a shopping cart (Who knows how they managed to get that down there?). But, weirdly, not one homeless person was present. It was like a homeless ghost town, which was doubly weird when I considered the weather. Wouldn't tonight be the perfect night to retreat to the comparative warmth and shelter of this basement, versus trying to find someplace warm and dry on the streets or smush into the Y? And it had been snowing for days. So, realistically, this room should be packed with the people who had brought the boxes and stuff down here to begin with.

Of course if scary undead creatures had been using the basement the desertion of the homeless folks made much more sense.

Don't think about it. Find the drainage grate and then find Heath.

The grate wasn't hard to find. I just headed for the darkest, nastiest corner of the room, and there was a metal grate on the floor. Yep. Right in the corner. On the floor. Never, in a gazillion years would I have ever even considered touching the disgusting thing, let along lifting it and going down there.

Naturally, that's what I had to do.

The grate lifted as easily as the outside "barrier" had opened, telling me (again) that I wasn't the only person/fledgling/human/creature who had come this way recently. There was an iron ladder thing that I had to climb down, probably about ten feet. Then I dropped to the floor of the tunnel. And that's exactly what it was—a big, damp sewer tunnel. Oh, and it was dark, too. Really dark. I stood there for a while letting my night vision accustom itself to the dense darkness, but I couldn't just stand there for very long. The need to find Heath was like an itch beneath my skin. It goaded me on.

"Keep to the right," I whispered. Then I shut up because even that little sound echoed around me. I turned to the right and started to walk as quickly as I was able.

Heath had been telling the truth. There were lots of tunnels. They split off over and over again, reminding me of worm holes burrowed into the ground. At first I saw more evidence that homeless people had been down here, too. But after a few right-hand turns, the boxes and scattered trash and blankets stopped. There was nothing but damp and dark. The tunnels had gone from being smooth and round and as civilized as I imagined well-made tunnels could be to absolute crap. The sides of the walls looked like they had been gouged out by very drunk Tolkien dwarfs (again, I am aware that I'm a dork). It was cold, too, but I didn't really feel it.

I kept to the right, hoping that Heath had known what he was talking about. I thought about stopping long enough to concentrate on his blood so that I could hook into our Imprint again, but the urgency I felt wouldn't let me stop. I. Had. To. Find. Heath.

I smelled them before I heard the hissing and rustling and actually saw them. It was that musty, old, wrong scent I'd noticed every time I'd seen one of them at the wall. I realized it was the smell of death, and then wondered how I didn't recognize it earlier.

Then the darkness that I'd become so accustomed to gave way to a faint, flickering light. I stopped to focus myself. *You can do this, Z. You've been Chosen by your Goddess. You kicked vampyre ghost ass. This is something you can definitely handle.*

I was still trying to "focus" (aka, talk myself into being brave) when Heath screamed. Then there was no more time for focusing or internal pep talks. I ran forward toward Heath's scream. Okay, I probably should explain that vampyres are stronger and faster than humans, and even though I'm still just a fledgling, I'm a very weird fledgling. So when I say I ran—I mean I seriously moved fast—fast and silent. I found them in what must have been seconds, but felt like hours. They were in the little alcove at the end of the crude tunnel. The lantern I'd noticed before was hanging from a rusty nail, throwing their shadows grotesquely against the crudely curved walls. They had formed a half circle around Heath. He was standing on the dirty mattress and his back was pressed to the wall. Somehow he'd gotten the duct tape off his ankles, but his wrists were still securely bound together. He had a new cut on his right arm and the scent of his blood was thick and seductive.

And that was my last goad. Heath belonged to me—despite my confusion about the whole blood issue, and despite my feelings for Erik. Heath was mine and no one else was ever, *ever* going to feed from what was mine.

I burst through the circle of hissing creatures like I was a bowling ball and they were brainless pins, and moved to his side.

"Zo!" He looked deliriously happy for a split second, and then, just like a guy, he tried to push me behind him. "Watch out! Their teeth and claws are really sharp." He added in a whisper, "You really didn't bring the SWAT team?"

It was easy to keep him from pushing me anywhere. I mean, he's cute and all, but he is just a human. I patted his bound hands where he clutched my arm and smiled at him, and with one slash of my thumbnail I cut through the gray tape that held his wrists. His eyes widened as he pulled his hands apart.

I grinned at him. My fear was gone. Now I was just incredibly pissed. "What I brought is better than a SWAT team. Just stay behind me and watch."

I pushed *Heath* to the wall and stepped in front of him as I turned to face the closing circle of . . .

Eesh! They were the most disgusting things I'd ever seen. There were probably a dozen or so of them. Their faces were white and gaunt. Their eyes glowed a dirty red. They snarled and hissed at me and I saw that their teeth were pointed and their fingernails! Ugh! Their fingernails were long and yellow and dangerous-looking.

"It'sss just a fledgling," hissed one of them. "The Mark doesn't make her a vampyre. It makesssss her a freak."

I looked at the speaker. "Elliott!"

"I wasss. I'm not the Elliott you knew anymore." Snakelike his head wove back and forth as he spoke. Then his glowing eyes flattened and he curled his lip. "I'll ssshow you what I mean . . ."

He started to move toward me with a feral, crouching stride. The other creatures stirred, gaining bravery from him.

"Watch out, Zo, they're coming for us," Heath said, trying to step around in front of me.

"No they're not," I said. I closed my eyes for just a second and centered myself, thinking of the power and warmth of flame—the way it can cleanse as well as destroy—and I thought of Shaunee. "Come to me, flame!" My palms started to feel hot. I opened my eyes and raised my hands, which were now glowing with a brilliant yellow flame.

"Stay back, Elliott! You were a pain in the ass when you were alive, and death hasn't changed anything." Elliott cringed back from the light I was producing. I took a step forward, ready to tell Heath to follow me so we could get the hell outta there, but her voice made me freeze.

"You're wrong, Zoey. Death has changed some things."

The crowd of creatures parted to let Stevie Rae through.

CHAPTER TWENTY-NINE

The flame in my palms sputtered and faded as shock broke my concentration. "Stevie Rae!" I started to take a step toward her, but the truth of her appearance hit me and I felt my body go cold and still. She looked terrible—worse than she had in the dream vision I'd had. It wasn't so much her pale thinness and the awful wrongness of the smell that clung to her that made her appear so changed. It was her expression. In life, Stevie Rae had been the kindest person I'd ever known. But now, whatever she was— dead, undead, bizarrely resurrected—she was different. Her eyes were cruel and flat. Her face devoid of any emotion except one, and that one emotion was hatred.

"Stevie Rae, what happened to you?"

"I died." Her voice was only a twisted, malformed shadow of what it had once been. She still had her Okie twang, but the soft sweetness that had filled it was totally gone. She sounded like mean trailer trash.

"Are you a ghost?"

"A ghost?" Her laugh was a sneer. "No, I ain't no damn ghost."

I swallowed and felt a dizzy wash of hope. "So you're alive?"

She curled her lip in a sarcastic sneer that looked so wrong on her face it made me physically sick. "You'd say I'm alive, but I'd say it's not that simple. Then again I'm not as *simple* as I used to be."

Well, at least she hadn't hissed at me like that Elliott thing had. *Stevie Rae is alive.* I held tightly to that miracle, swallowed my fear and revulsion, and moving so quickly that she didn't have time to jerk away (or bite me or whatever), I grabbed her and, ignoring the horrid way she smelled, hugged her hard. "I'm so glad you're not dead!" I whispered to her.

It was like hugging a smelly piece of stone. She didn't jerk away from me. She didn't bite me. She didn't react at all, but the creatures surrounding us did. I could hear them hissing and muttering. I let go of her and stepped back.

"Don't touch me again," she said.

"Stevie Rae, is there someplace we can go so we can talk? I need to get Heath home, but I can come back and meet you. Or maybe you could come back to the school with me?"

"You don't understand anything, do you?"

"I understand that something bad has happened to you, but you're still my best friend, so we can figure this out."

"Zoey, you're not going anywhere."

"Fine," I purposefully pretended to misunderstand her threat. "I guess we could talk here, but, well . . ." I looked around at the grossly hissing creatures. "It's not very private, and it's also disgusting down here."

"Jusssst kill them!" Elliott snarled from behind Stevie Rae.

"Shut up, Elliott!" Stevie Rae and I snapped at him together. Her eyes met mine and I swear I saw a flash of something in them that was more than anger and cruelty.

"You know they can't live now that they've sssseen us," Elliott said. The other creatures stirred restlessly, making evil little noises of agreement.

Then a girl stepped out of the pack of creatures. She obviously used to be beautiful. Even now there was an eerie, surreal allure about her. She was tall and blond, and she moved more gracefully than the others. But when I looked into her red eyes I saw only meanness.

"If you can't do it, I will. I'll take the male first. I don't mind that his blood has been tainted by Imprint. It's still warm and alive," she said, and she seemed to dance toward Heath.

I stepped in front of him, blocking her path. "Touch him and you die. Again," I said.

Stevie Rae interrupted her hissing laughter.

"Get back with the others, Venus. You don't strike until I tell you to."

Venus. The name triggered my memory. "Venus Davis?" I said.

The pretty blonde narrowed her eyes at me. "How do you know me, fledgling?"

"She knows a lot of stuff," Heath said, stepping around me. He was using what I used to call his football player voice. He sounded tough and pissed and totally ready for a fight. "And I'm about sick of all of you fucked-up creatures."

"Why is *that* speaking?" Stevie Rae spat.

I sighed and rolled my eyes. I agreed with Heath—I was totally sick of all of this scary weirdness. It was time we got out of there, and it was also time my best friend started acting like the person I'd glimpsed hiding in her eyes. "He isn't a *that.* He's Heath. Remember, Stevie Rae? My ex-boyfriend?"

"Zo. I am *not* your ex-boyfriend. I'm your boyfriend."

"Heath. I told you before that this can't possibly work out between us."

"Come on, Zo, we're Imprinted. That means it's you and me, baby!" He grinned at me as if we were in the middle of a prom instead of in the middle of a group of undead creatures that wanted to eat us.

"That was an accident, and we're gonna have to talk about it, but this is definitely not the time."

"Oh, Zo, you know you love me." Heath's grin didn't fade one bit.

"Heath, you are the most stubborn kid I've ever known." He winked at me and I couldn't help smiling back at him. "Fine. I love you."

"What'sss happening . . ." the gross Elliott creature hissed. The rest of the horrid things that surrounded us moved restlessly, and Venus glided one step closer to Heath. I forced myself not to shiver or scream or whatever. Instead, a weird calm came over me. I looked at Stevie Rae, and suddenly knew what I needed to say. I put my hands on my hips and faced her.

"Tell him," I said. "Tell all of them."

"Tell them what?" She narrowed her garnet eyes dangerously.

"Tell them what's happening here. You know. I know you do."

Stevie Rae's face contorted, and the words sounded like they were being wrenched from her throat. "*Humanity!* They're showing their humanity." The creatures snarled like she'd just thrown holy water on them (and please, that's such an untrue cliché about vampyres).

"Weakness! It's why we're stronger than they are." Venus curled her lip. "Because it's a weakness we don't have anymore."

I ignored Venus. I ignored Elliott. Hell, I ignored them all and stared at Stevie Rae, forcing her to meet my eyes, and forcing myself not to look away or flinch as hers glowed hot and red.

"Bullshit," I said.

"She's right," Stevie Rae said. Her voice was cold and mean. "When we died, so did our humanity."

"That might be true with them, but I don't believe it's true with you," I said.

"You don't know anything about this, Zoey," Stevie Rae said.

"I don't have to. I know you, and I know our Goddess, and that's all I need to know."

"She's not my Goddess anymore."

"Really, just like your mamma's not your mamma anymore?" I knew I'd hit a nerve when I saw her jerk as if she were in physical pain.

"I don't have a mamma. I'm not a human anymore."

"Big f-ing deal. Technically, I'm not a human anymore, either. I'm somewhere in the middle of the Change, which makes me a little of this and a lot of that. Hell, the only one here who's still human is Heath."

"Not that I hold your un-human-ness against you guys," Heath said.

I sighed. "Heath, un-human-ness isn't a word. It's inhumanity."

"Zo, I'm not stupid. I know that. I was just coining a word."

"Coining?" Had he really said that?

He nodded. "I learned about it in Dickson's English class. It has to do with . . ." He paused, and I swear the creatures were even listening expectantly. *"Poetry."*

Despite our awful situation I laughed. "Heath, you really have been studying!"

"Told you so." He grinned, looking completely adorable.

"Enough!" Stevie Rae's voice echoed off the round walls of the tunnel. "I'm done with this." She turned her back to Heath and me, ignoring us completely. "They've seen us. They know too much. They have to die. Kill them." And she walked away.

This time Heath didn't mess with trying to pull me behind him. Instead he whirled around and, completely catching me off guard, tackled me so that I landed on my butt on the disgusting mattress with an *oofh*. Then he turned to the closing circle of snarling undead creatures with his legs planted a hip's width apart and his hands balled into fists and he gave his Broken Arrow Tiger football growl.

"Bring it, freaks!"

Okay, it wasn't that I didn't appreciate Heath's machoness. But the boy was in over his cute blond head. I stood up and centered myself.

"Fire, I need you again!" This time I yelled the words with the command of a High Priestess. Flames burst into life from the palms of my hands all up and down my arms. I would have liked to have taken time to study the fire I'd called into being—it was cool that it could burn on me, and not actually burn me, but there was no time for that. "Move, Heath."

He looked over his shoulder at me, and his eyes got huge and round. "Zo?"

"I'm fine. Just move!"

He jumped out of my way as, burning, I walked forward. The creatures cringed back from me, even as their hands tried to reach around me to get to Heath.

"Stop it!" I yelled. "Back off and leave him alone. Heath and I are going to walk out of here. Now. If you try to stop us, I'm going to kill you, and I have a feeling that this time you're going to die for good." Okay, I really, really didn't want to kill anyone. What I wanted to do was to get Heath out of there, and then find Stevie Rae and have her explain to me how fledglings who were supposed to have died could be walking around with bad attitudes, glowing eyes, and smelling like mold and dust.

From the edge of my vision I saw a movement. I turned in time to see one of the creatures launch herself at Heath. I lifted my arms and flung the fire at her as if I were throwing a ball. As she screamed and went up in flames I recognized her and had to fight hard not to be sick. It was Elizabeth No Last Name—the nice girl who had died last month. Now her burning body writhed on the floor, reeking of spoiled meat and decay, which was all that was left of her lifeless shell.

"Wind and rain! I call you," I cried, and as the air around me began to swirl and fill with the scent of spring rain, I got a flash of

Damien and Erin sitting cross-legged beside Shaunee. Their eyes were closed in concentration and they were holding votives the color of their elements. I pointed my fiery finger at Elizabeth's smoldering body and it was washed in a sudden flush of rain, then a cool breeze took the green-tinged smoke, lifting it above our heads, and carried its stench down the tunnel and out into the night.

I faced the creatures again. "That's what I'll do to any of you who try to stop us." I motioned for Heath to walk in front of me, and I followed him, backing away from the creatures.

They followed us. I couldn't always see them as we rewound our way through the dark tunnel, but I could hear their shuffling feet and muffled snarls. It was about then that I began to feel the exhaustion. It was like I was a cell phone that hadn't been charged in a while, and someone was talking on me too long. I let the fire that outlined by arms go out except for a flickering flame that I cupped in my right hand. No way Heath could see to walk out of here without that, and I was still backing behind him, keeping an eye out for attacking creatures. After I passed two offshoot tunnel branches I called for Heath to stop.

"We should hurry, Zo. I know you have this power thing going on, but there are a lot of them—more than what were back there. I don't know how many you can handle." He touched my face. "Not to be mean or anything, but you look like shit."

I felt like poo, too, but I didn't want to mention it. "I have an idea." We'd just come around a curve where the tunnel had narrowed until I could touch either side of it by spreading out my arms. I walked back to the narrowest part of the curve. Heath started to follow me, but I told him, "Stand over there," and pointed farther down the tunnel the way we were heading. He frowned, but did as I told him.

I turned my back to Heath and concentrated. Lifting my arms,

I thought of newly plowed fields and pretty Oklahoma meadows filled with uncut winter hay. I thought about the earth and how I was standing within it . . . surrounded by it . . .

"Earth! I call to you!" As I lifted my arms a vision of Stevie Rae flashed across my closed eyelids. She wasn't as she used to be—sweet-faced and concentrating hard over a glowing green candle. She was curled up in the corner of a dark tunnel. Her face was gaunt and white and her eyes glowed scarlet. But her face wasn't an emotionless parody of herself or a cruel mask. She was weeping openly, her expression filled with despair. *It's a start,* I thought. Then, with a swift, powerful motion I lowered my arms while I commanded, "Close!" In front and above me, pieces of dirt and rock began to fall from the ceiling. At first it was just a trickle of pebbles, but soon there was a mini-avalanche going on that quickly drowned out the pissed-off growls and hisses of the trapped creatures.

A wave of weakness crashed over me and I staggered back.

"I got ya, Zo." Heath's strong arms were around me and I let myself rest against him for a moment. Several of his cuts had broken loose during our escape, and the ripe scent of his blood tickled against my senses.

"They're not really trapped, you know," I said softly, trying to keep my mind off how much I wanted to lick the line of blood that was trickling down his cheek. "We passed a couple other tunnels. I'm sure they'll be able to find their way out eventually."

"It's okay, Zo." Heath kept his arms wrapped around me, but he pulled back enough so that he could look into my eyes. "I know what you need. I can feel it. If you feed from me you won't be so weak." He smiled, and his blue eyes darkened. "It's okay," he repeated. "I want you to."

"Heath, you've been through way too much. Who knows how much blood you've already lost? My drinking more of it isn't a good idea." I was saying no, but my voice trembled with desire.

"Are you kidding? A big, studly football jock like me? I got plenty of blood to spare," Heath teased. Then his expression turned serious. "For you, I have anything to spare." While he looked into my eyes, he wiped one of his fingers down the damp red slash on his cheek and the rubbed the blood on his bottom lip. Then he bent and kissed me.

I tasted the dark sweetness of his blood and it dissolved in my mouth to send a surge of fiery pleasure and energy through my body. Heath pulled his lips from mine and guided me to the cut on his cheek. When my tongue snaked out and touched it, he moaned and pressed my hips closer to his. I closed my eyes and began to lick—

"Kill me!" Stevie Rae's broken voice shattered the spell of Heath's blood.

CHAPTER THIRTY

My face flamed with embarrassment as I pushed myself out of Heath's arms, wiping my mouth and breathing hard. Stevie Rae was standing down the tunnel just a few yards from us. Tears still rained down her cheeks and her face was twisted in despair.

"Kill me," she repeated on a sob.

"No." I shook my head and took a step toward her, but she backed away from me, putting up her hand as if she wanted to hold me off. I stopped and gulped some deep breaths, trying to get myself under control. "Come back to the House of Night with me. We'll figure out how this happened. It'll be okay, Stevie Rae, I promise. All that matters is that you're alive."

Stevie Rae had started shaking her head as I'd begun talking. "I'm not really alive, and I can't go back there."

"Of course you're alive. You're walking and talking."

"I'm not me anymore. I did die, and part of me—the best part of me—is still dead, just like it is for the rest of them." She gestured back at the cave-in.

"You're not like they are," I said firmly.

"I'm more like them than I am like you." Her gaze shifted from me to Heath, who was standing quietly beside me. "You wouldn't believe the awful things that go through my mind. I could kill him without a second thought. I would have already if his blood hadn't been changed by the Imprint with you."

"Maybe it wasn't just that, Stevie Rae. Maybe you didn't kill him because you really didn't want to," I said.

Her eyes found mine again. "No. I wanted to kill him. I still do."

"The rest of them killed Brad and Chris," Heath said. "And that was my fault."

"Heath, now's not the time—" I started, but he cut me off.

"No, you need to hear this, Zoey. Those things grabbed Brad and Chris because they were hanging around the House of Night, and that's my fault because I'd told them how hot you are." He gave me an apologetic look. "Sorry, Zo." Then his expression hardened and he said, "You should kill her. You should kill them all. As long as they're alive people will be in danger."

"He's right," Stevie Rae said.

"And how will killing you and the rest of them solve this? Won't more of you happen?" I made my mind up and closed the space between Stevie Rae and me. She looked like she wanted to take off, but my words stopped her. "How did this happen? What made you like this?"

Her face contorted with anguish. "I don't know how. I only know who."

"Then *who* did this?"

She opened her mouth to answer me and then, with a movement so fast her body blurred, she was suddenly cowering against the side of the tunnel.

"She's coming!"

"What? Who?" I crouched beside her.

"Get out of here! Fast. There's probably still time for you to get away." Then Stevie Rae reached out and took my hand in hers. Her flesh was cold, but her grip was strong. "She'll kill you if she sees you—you and him. You know too much. She may kill you anyway, but it'll be harder for her to do if you get back to the House of Night."

"Who are you talking about, Stevie Rae?"

"Neferet."

The name blasted through me and even as I shook my head in denial I felt the truth of it deep within me. "Neferet did this to you, to all of you?"

"Yes. Now get out of here, Zoey!"

I could feel her terror and I knew she was right. If Heath and I didn't leave, we would die.

"I'm not giving up on you, Stevie Rae. Use your element. You still have a connection with the earth, I can feel it. So use your element to stay strong. I'll come back for you, and somehow we'll figure this out—we'll make this okay. I promise." Then I hugged her hard, and after only a little hesitation, she hugged me back.

"Let's go, Heath." I grabbed his hand so I could guide him quickly down the darkness of the tunnel. The light in my palm had gone out when I'd called earth to me, and no way was I going to take a chance on relighting it. It might guide *her* to us. As we ran down the tunnel I heard Stevie Rae's whispered "Please don't forget me . . ." follow us.

Heath and I ran. The surge of energy his blood had given me didn't last long, and by the time we came to the metal ladder that led up to the grate in the basement, I wanted to collapse and sleep for days. Heath was all for rushing up the ladder and into the basement, but I made him wait. Breathing heavily, I leaned against the side of the tunnel and fished my cell phone out of my pants pocket, along with Detective Marx's card. I flipped open the phone and I swear my heart didn't beat until the bars started to light up green.

"Can ya hear me now?" Heath said, grinning at me.

"Sssh!" I told him, but smiled back. Then I punched in the detective's number.

"This is Marx," the deep voice answered on the second ring.

"Detective Marx, this is Zoey Redbird. I only have a second to talk, then I have to go. I've found Heath Luck. We're in the basement of the Tulsa Depot, and we need help."

"Hang tight. I'll be right there!"

A noise from above made me cut off the connection and switch the phone off. I pressed my finger to my lips when Heath started to speak. Heath put his arm around me, and we tried not to breathe. Then I heard the coo-coo of a pigeon and the fluttering of wings.

"I think it's just a bird," Heath whispered. "I'm going to go look."

I was too tired to argue with him, plus Marx was on his way and I was sick of the damp, nasty tunnel. "Be careful," I whispered back.

Heath nodded and squeezed my shoulder, then climbed up the ladder. Slowly and carefully he lifted the metal grate, sticking his head up and peering around. Pretty soon he reached down and motioned for me to climb up and take his hand. "It's just a pigeon. Come on."

Wearily, I climbed to him and let him pull me up into the basement. We sat in the corner by the grate for several long minutes, listening intently. Finally, I whispered, "Let's go outside and wait for Marx there." Heath had already started to shiver, but I remembered the blanket Aphrodite had made me bring. Plus, I'd rather take my chances with the weather than stay in the creepy basement.

"I hate it in here, too. It's like a damn tomb," Heath said softly between chattering teeth.

Hand in hand, we walked across the basement, passing

through the slatted grayish light that reflected down from the world above. We were at the iron door when I heard the distant wail of a police siren. The terrible tension in my body had just begun to relax when Neferet's voice came from the shadows.

"I should have known you would be here."

Heath's body jerked in surprise and my hand tightened in warning on his. As I turned to face her, I was centering myself and could feel the power of the elements beginning to shimmer in the air around me. I drew a deep breath and carefully blanked my mind.

"Oh, Neferet! I'm so glad to see you!" I squeezed Heath's hand one more time before I let go of him, trying to telegraph *play along with whatever I say* through touch. Then I ran, sobbing, into the High Priestess's arms. "How did you find me? Did Detective Marx call you?"

I could see indecision in her eyes as Neferet smoothly disentangled herself from my arms. "Detective Marx?"

"Yeah." I sniffed and wiped my nose on my sleeve, forcing myself to beam relief and trust to her. "That's him coming right now." The sound of the siren was very close, and I could hear that it had been joined by at least two other cars. "Thank you for finding me!" I gushed. "It was so terrible. I thought that crazy street person was going to kill both of us." I moved back to Heath's side and took his hand again. He was staring at Neferet, looking a lot like he was in shock. I realized that he was probably remembering pieces of the only other time he'd seen the High Priestess—the night the vampyre ghosts had almost killed him—and imagined his mind was too freaked out for Neferet to make much sense of what was going on inside his head. Good thing, too.

Then car doors were slamming and heavy feet were crunching through the snow.

"Zoey, Heath . . ." Neferet moved swiftly to us. She lifted her hands, which glowed with a weird, reddish light, suddenly reminding me of the undead things' eyes. Before I could run or scream or even take a breath, she grabbed our shoulders. I felt Heath go rigid as pain shot through my body. It blasted against my mind and my knees would have buckled had her hand not been like a vise, holding me up. *"You will remember nothing!"* The words echoed through my agony-filled mind, and then there was only darkness.

CHAPTER THIRTY-ONE

I was in a beautiful meadow that was in the middle of what looked like a dense forest. A warm, soft breeze was blowing the scent of lilacs to me. A stream ran through the meadow, its crystal water bubbled musically over smooth stones.

"Zoey? Can you hear me, Zoey?" An insistent male voice intruded on my dream.

I frowned and tried to ignore him. I didn't want to wake up, but my spirit stirred. I *needed* to wake up. I *needed* to remember. She needed me to remember.

But who was she?

"Zoey . . ." This time the voice was inside my dream and I could see my name painted against the blue of the spring sky. The voice was a woman's . . . familiar . . . magical . . . wondrous. "Zoey . . ."

I looked around the clearing and found the Goddess sitting on the other side of the stream, gracefully perched on a smooth Oklahoma sandstone rock with her bare feet playing in the water.

"Nyx!" I cried. "Am I dead?" My words shimmered around me.

The Goddess smiled. "Will you ask that of me each time I visit you, Zoey Redbird?"

"No, I'm, uh, sorry." My words were tinged pink, probably blushing like my cheeks.

"Don't be sorry, my daughter. You have done very well. I am

pleased with you. Now, it is time you awakened. And also I wish to remind you that the elements can restore as well as destroy."

I started to thank her, even though I didn't have a clue what she was talking about, but the shaking of my shoulder and a sudden blast of cold air interrupted me. I opened my eyes.

Snow swirled all around me. Detective Marx was bending over me, shaking my shoulder. Through the weird fog in my mind I found one word. "Heath?" I croaked.

Marx jerked his chin to his right and I tilted my head to see Heath's still body being loaded into an ambulance.

"Is he . . ." I couldn't finish.

"He's fine, just banged up. He's lost a lot of blood and they've already given him something for the pain."

"Banged up?" I was struggling to make sense of everything. "What happened to Heath?"

"Multiple lacerations, just like those other two kids. Good thing you found him and called me before he bled to death." He squeezed my shoulder. A paramedic tried to move Marx from my side, but he said, "I'll handle her. She just needs to get back to the House of Night and she'll be fine."

I saw the paramedic give me a look that clearly said *freak,* but Detective Marx's strong hands were helping me sit up and his tall body blocked my view of the muttering EMT.

"Can you walk to my car?" Marx asked.

I nodded. My body was feeling better, but my mind was still all mushy. Marx's "car" was really a huge, all-weather truck with giant wheels and a roll bar. He helped me up into the front seat, which was warm and comfortable, but before he closed the door I suddenly remembered something else, even though the effort made my head feel like it was going to split open. "Persephone! Is she okay?"

Marx looked confused for just a second, then he smiled. "The mare?"

I nodded.

"She's just fine. An officer is walking her to the police stables downtown until the roads are clear enough to get a trailer back to the House of Night." His grin widened. "Guess you're braver than the Tulsa police force. None of them volunteered to ride her back."

I rested my head against the seat as he threw the truck into four-wheel drive and navigated slowly through the drifts of snow away from the depot. There must have been ten cop cars, along with a fire truck and two ambulances parked with lights flashing red and blue and white against the empty, snow-curtained night.

"What happened here tonight, Zoey?"

I thought back, and had to squint my eyes against the sudden pain in my head. "I don't remember," I managed to say through the pounding in my temples. I could feel his sharp gaze on me. I met the detective's eyes and remembered him telling me about his twin sister, the vamp who still loved him. He'd said I could trust him, and I believed him. "Something's wrong," I admitted. "My memory is messed up."

"Okay," he said slowly. "Start with the last thing you can easily remember."

"I was grooming Persephone and all of a sudden I knew where Heath was, and that he was going to die if I didn't go get him."

"You two have Imprinted?" My surprise must have been easy to read, because he smiled and continued. "My sister and I talk, and I've been curious about vamp stuff, especially right after she first Changed." He shrugged as if it was no big deal for a human to know all sorts of vampyre info. "We're twins, so we're used to sharing everything. A change of species just didn't make that much difference to us." He glanced sideways at me again. "You have Imprinted, haven't you?"

"Yeah, Heath and I have Imprinted. That's how I knew where

he was." I left out the stuff about Aphrodite. No way did I feel up to explaining the whole her-visions-are-real-but-Neferet-has-been . . .

"Ah!" This time I gasped aloud at the agony inside my head.

"Deep, calming breaths," Marx said, shooting me worried looks whenever he could take his eyes from the treacherous road. "I said whatever was *easy* for you to remember."

"No, it's okay. I'm okay. I want to do this."

He still looked worried, but continued with his questioning. "All right, you knew Heath was in trouble, and you knew where he was. So, why didn't you just call me and tell me to go to the depot?"

I tried to remember and pain shot through my head, but along with the pain came anger. Something had happened to my mind. *Someone* had messed with my mind. And that really pissed me off. I rubbed my temples and gritted my teeth against the pain.

"Maybe we should stop for a while."

"No! Just let me think," I gasped. I could remember the stables and Aphrodite. I could remember that Heath needed me, and the wild, snowy ride on Persephone to the depot basement. But when I tried to remember past the basement the agony that speared through my head became too much for me.

"Zoey!" Detective Marx's concern penetrated through my pain.

"Something has messed with my mind." I wiped tears I hadn't realized I'd shed from my face.

"Pieces of your memory are gone."

It didn't sound like a question, but I nodded anyway.

He was silent for a while. It seemed he was concentrating on the deserted, snow-covered road, but I thought I knew better, and his next words told me I was right.

"My sister"—he smiled and glanced at me—"her name is Anne, warned me once that if I ever pissed off a High Priestess I would be in serious trouble because they had ways of erasing things, and what she meant by things was people and memories." He glanced from the road to me again, and this time his smile was gone. "So, I guess the question is: what have you done to piss off a High Priestess?"

"I don't know. I . . ." My voice trailed off as I thought about what he'd said. I didn't try to remember what had happened that night. Instead, I let my memory drift lazily backward . . . to Aphrodite and the fact that Nyx was still blessing her with visions, even though Neferet had spread the word that her visions were false . . . to the small, almost imperceptible sense of wrongness that had grown like a fungus around Neferet, until it culminated Sunday night in her undermining the decisions I'd made for the Dark Daughters . . . to the nasty scene I'd witnessed between Neferet and . . . and . . . I braced myself against the heat that was starting to throb through my head and, along with a flash of piercing pain, remembered the creature Elliott had become feeding from the High Priestess's blood.

"Stop the truck!" I yelled.

"We're almost at the school, Zoey."

"Now! I'm going to be sick."

We slid to the side of the empty road. I opened the door and dropped to the snowy street, staggered to the ditch, and puked up my guts into a snowbank. Detective Marx was beside me, pulling back my hair and sounding very dadlike as he told me to breathe and everything would be okay. I gulped air and finally stopped heaving. He handed me a handkerchief, one of those old-fashioned linen ones that was folded neatly into a clean square.

"Thanks." I tried to hand it back to him after wiping my face and blowing my nose, but he smiled and said, "Keep it."

I stood there, just gulping air and letting the throbbing in my head go away as I stared across a field of untouched snow to some distant oaks that grew along a massive stone and brick wall. And with a start of surprise, I realized where we were.

"It's the east wall of the school," I said.

"Yeah, I thought I'd take you the back way—give you more time to collect yourself, and maybe restore some of that memory."

Restore . . . What was it about that word? Tentatively, I thought hard, trying to remember while I braced myself against the pain I was sure would come. But it didn't, and into my memory came the vision of a beautiful meadow, and the wise words of my Goddess . . . *the elements can restore as well as destroy.*

And then I understood what I had to do.

"Detective Marx, I need a minute here, okay?"

"Alone?" he asked.

I nodded.

"I'll be in the truck, watching you. If you need me, call."

I smiled my thanks, but before he'd turned to go back to the truck I was walking toward the oaks. I didn't need to be under them—to actually be in the school grounds, but being near them helped me center myself. When I was close enough to see how their branches entwined like old friends, I stopped and closed my eyes.

"Wind, I call you to me and this time I ask that you blow clean any dark taint that has touched my mind." I felt a gust of cold, like I was being battered by my own personal hurricane, but it wasn't pressing against my body. It was filling my mind. I kept my eyes tightly closed and blocked out the throbbing ache that had returned to my temples. "Fire, I call you to me and ask that you burn from my mind any darkness that has touched it." Heat filled my head, only it wasn't like the hot spear that I'd felt earlier. Instead it was a nice warmth, like a heating pad on a pulled muscle. "Water, I call you to me and ask that you wash from my mind the darkness that has touched it." Coolness flooded through the warmth, soothing what had been overheated and bringing incredible relief. "Earth, I call you to me and ask that your nurturing strength take from my mind the darkness that has touched it." From the bottoms of my feet, where I was connected firmly to the earth, it was as if a faucet had opened and I imagined putrid darkness running down and out of my body to be consumed by the strength and goodness of the earth. "And, spirit, I ask that you heal what darkness has destroyed in my mind, and restore my memory!" Something snapped within me and a white-hot familiar sensation shot down my back, dropping me heavily to my knees.

"Zoey! Zoey! My God, are you okay?"

Once again Detective Marx's strong hands were shaking my shoulders and he was helping me to my feet. This time my eyes opened easily and I smiled into his kind face.

"I'm more than okay. I remember everything."

CHAPTER THIRTY-TWO

"You're sure this is how it has to be?" Detective Marx asked for what seemed like the zillionth time.

"Yep." I nodded wearily. "It has to be like this." I was so damn tired I thought I could fall asleep right there in the cop's ginormic monster truck. But I knew I couldn't. The night wasn't over yet. My job wasn't over yet.

The detective sighed, and I smiled at him.

"You're just gonna have to trust me," I said, sounding a lot like he had earlier that day.

"I don't like it," he said.

"I know, and I'm sorry. But I've told you everything I can."

"That some homeless kook is responsible for Heath and the other two boys?" He shook his head. "Feels wrong to me."

"Are you sure you're not a little bit psychic?" I smiled tiredly at him.

"If I was, I'd be able to figure out *what* feels wrong." He shook his head again. "Explain this—what happened to your memory?"

I'd already thought about my answer for this one. "It was the trauma of tonight. It made me block what happened. And then my affinity for the five elements helped me to overcome the block and remember."

"That's why you had all that pain?"

I shrugged my shoulders. "I guess so. It's gone now anyway."

"Look, Zoey, I'm pretty sure that there's more going on here than what you're telling me. I want you to know that you really can trust me," he said.

"I know that." I believed him, but I also knew that there were some secrets I couldn't share. Not with this really nice detective. Not with anyone.

"You don't have to deal with whatever it is on your own. I can help you. You're just a kid—just a teenager." He sounded totally exasperated.

I met his eyes steadily. "No, I'm a fledgling who is leader of the Dark Daughters and a High Priestess in training. Believe me, that's a lot more than *just a teenager*. I've given you my oath, and you know from your sister that my oath binds me. I promise I've told you everything I can, and if any more kids disappear, I believe I can find them for you." What I didn't say was that I wasn't one hundred percent sure how I was going to do that, but the promise felt right, and so I knew Nyx would help me keep it. Not that that would be easy. But I couldn't betray Stevie Rae's presence, which meant no one could know about the creatures, or at least not until Stevie Rae was safe.

Marx sighed again, and I could see that he was muttering to himself as he stomped around to help me down from his truck. But just before he opened the door to the main school building Marx (annoyingly) ruffled my hair and said, "All right, we'll do this your way. Of course, it's not like I have a choice."

He was right. He didn't have any choice.

I walked into the building before him and was instantly engulfed in the warmth of its familiar scents of incense and oil, and the soothing gaslights that flickered like eager, welcoming friends.

Speaking of . . .

"Zoey!" I heard the Twins squeal together, and then I was being smushed in the middle of them as they hugged me and cried and yelled at me for worrying them and talked nonstop about being able to feel it when I tapped into their elements. Damien was not far behind them. Then I was in Erik's strong arms as he hugged me and whispered how scared he'd been for me and how glad he was I was okay. I allowed myself to rest in his arms and return his hug. Later, I'd figure out what to do about Heath and him. Right now I was too tired, and anyway, I needed to save my strength to deal with—

"Zoey, you gave us quite a scare."

I stepped out of Erik's arms and turned to face Neferet.

"I'm sorry. I really didn't mean to upset everyone," I said, and it was the truth. I hadn't wanted to worry or upset or scare anyone.

"Well, I suppose there's no harm done, darling. We're all just so glad you're safely home." She smiled at me with that wonderful mom smile of hers that seemed so full of love and light and goodness, and even though I knew what that smile hid, I felt my heart squeeze and wished desperately that I was wrong, that Neferet was as wonderful as I used to believe.

Darkness does not always equate to evil, just as light does not always bring good. The Goddess's words echoed through my mind, giving me strength.

"Well, Zoey is definitely our hero," Detective Marx said. "If she hadn't been tuned into that boy, she could have never called us to that depot in time to save him."

"Yes, well, that's a little problem she and I will have to discuss later." She gave me a stern look, but her tone told everyone there that I wasn't really in much trouble.

If only they knew.

"Detective, did you catch the person who has been taking the boys?" Neferet continued.

"No, he escaped before we arrived, but there's plenty of

evidence that someone has been living in the depot, actually it looked like he was using it as some kind of headquarters. I think it'll be easy to find proof that the other two boys were killed there by someone who was trying to make it look like vampyres had taken the teenagers. And now, even though Heath doesn't remember much of anything because of the trauma, Zoey has given us a good description of the man to go by. It's just a matter of time before we catch him."

Was I the only one who saw surprise flash through Neferet's eyes?

"That's wonderful!" Neferet said.

"Yeah." I met the High Priestess's eyes. "I've told Detective Marx a lot. My memory's really good."

"I'm proud of you, Zoeybird!" Neferet came to me and put her arms around me, hugging me close. So close that only I heard her whisper into my ear, *"If you speak against me I will make sure no human or fledgling or vampyre will believe you."*

I didn't pull away from her. I didn't react in any way. But when she let me go, I made my final move—the one I'd planned since the white-hot familiar sensation had seared the skin on my back.

"Neferet, would you please look at my back?"

My friends had been chattering among themselves, clearly giddy with the relief they'd felt since I'd called them while Detective Marx and I talked outside the school and asked them to meet me inside the main building, and to make sure Neferet was there, too. Now my weird request, which I'd been sure to ask loud and clear, shut them up. Actually, everyone in the room, including Detective Marx, was looking at me like they wondered if I'd perhaps hit my head sometime during my adventures and some of my brains had leaked out.

"It's important," I said, and grinned at Neferet as if I were hiding a present just for her under the back of my shirt.

"Zoey, I'm not sure what—" Neferet began, her tone carefully pitched between worry and embarrassment.

I gave an exaggerated sigh. "Jeesh, just look." And before anyone could stop me, I turned so that my back was facing them, and lifted the bottom of my sweatshirt (being careful to keep the front of me covered).

I hadn't really been worried that I might be wrong, but the gasps and exclamations of awe and happy surprise from my friends were a relief to hear.

"Z! Your Mark has spread." Erik laughed and tentatively touched the newly tattooed skin of my back.

"Wow, it's awesome," Shaunee breathed.

"Totally cool," Erin said.

"Spectacular," Damien said. "It's the same labyrinth pattern as your other Marks."

"Yeah, with the rune symbols spaced between the spirals," Erik said.

I think I was the only one who noticed that Neferet said nothing at all.

I smoothed the bottom of my shirt back down. I was seriously looking forward to getting to a mirror so that I could see what I'd only been able to feel.

"Congratulations, Zoey. I imagine this means that you continue to be special to your Goddess," Detective Marx said.

I smiled at him. "Thanks. Thanks for everything tonight."

Our eyes met and he winked. Then he turned to Neferet. "I'd better be going, ma'am. There's a lot of work left to be done tonight. Plus, I imagine Zoey is eager to get to bed. Good night, everyone." He touched his hat, smiled at me again, and left.

"I am really tired." I looked at Neferet. "If it's okay, I'd like to go to bed."

"Yes, darling," she said smoothly. "That would be just fine."

"And also I'd like to stop by Nyx's Temple on the way to the dorm, if that's okay with you," I said.

"You do have quite a bit for which you should thank Nyx. Stopping by her temple is a good idea."

"We'll go with you, Z," Shaunee said.

"Yeah, Nyx was with all of us tonight," Erin said.

Damien and Erik made sounds of agreement, but I didn't look at any of my friends. I kept eye contact with Neferet and said, "I will thank Nyx, but there's really another reason I'm going to her temple." I didn't wait for her to question me, but continued earnestly, "I'm going to light an earth candle for Stevie Rae. I promised her I wouldn't forget her."

My friends were murmuring soft words of agreement, but I kept my attention focused on Neferet as I slowly and deliberately walked over to her.

"Good night, Neferet," I said and this time I hugged her, and as I pulled her close to me I whispered, *"Humans and fledglings and vampyres don't need to believe me about you because Nyx does. This is not over between us."*

I stepped out of Neferet's arms and turned my back on her. Together, my friends and I went outside and crossed the short distance to Nyx's Temple. It had finally stopped snowing, and the moon was peeking between wisps of clouds that looked like silken scarves. I stopped at the beautiful marble statue of the Goddess that stood before her temple.

"Here," I said firmly.

"Z?" Erik said questioningly.

"I want to put Stevie Rae's candle out here, at Nyx's feet."

"I'll get it for you," Erik said. He squeezed my hand and then hurried into Nyx's Temple.

"You're right," Shaunee said.

"Yeah, Stevie Rae would like it lit out here," Erin said.

"It's closer to the earth," Damien said.

"And so it's closer to Stevie Rae," I said softly.

Erik returned and handed me the green votive and a long, ritualistic lighter. Following my instincts, I lit the candle and placed it snugly at Nyx's feet.

"I'm remembering you, Stevie Rae. Just like I promised," I said.

"So am I," said Damien.

"Me, too," said Shaunee.

"Ditto," said Erin.

"I'm remembering, too," said Erik.

The scent of a grassy meadow suddenly swirled around Nyx's statue, making my friends smile through their tears. Before we walked away I closed my eyes and whispered a prayer that was a promise I felt deep in my soul.

I'll go back for you, Stevie Rae.

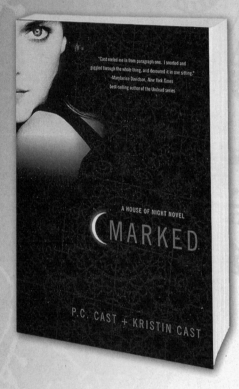
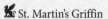